FiNALEonline.de

FiNALEonline ist die digitale Ergänzung zu deinem Abiturband. Hier findest du eine Vielzahl an Angeboten, die dich bei deiner Prüfungsvorbereitung zusätzlich unterstützen.

Das Plus für deine Vorbereitung:

- Original-Prüfungsaufgaben mit Lösungen (bitte Code von Seite 2 eingeben!)
- EXTRA-Training Rechtschreibung
  So kannst du einem möglichen Punktabzug bei deinen Abi-Klausuren vorbeugen.
- Videos zur mündlichen Prüfung
- Tipps zur stressfreien Prüfungsvorbereitung
- Abi-Checklisten mit allen prüfungsrelevanten Themen

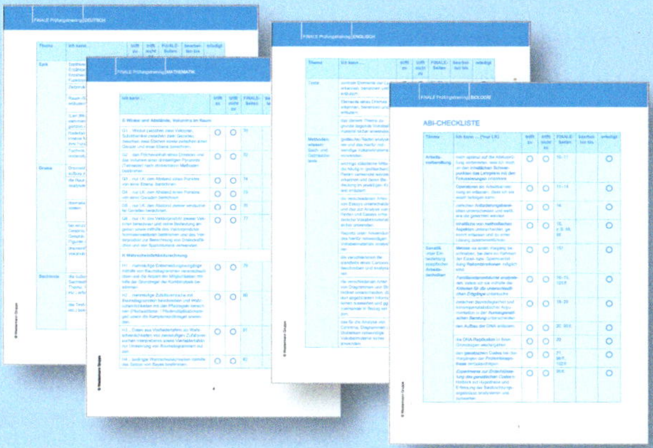

Abi-Checklisten

Sie helfen dir, den Überblick über den Prüfungsstoff zu behalten.

FiNALEonline.de

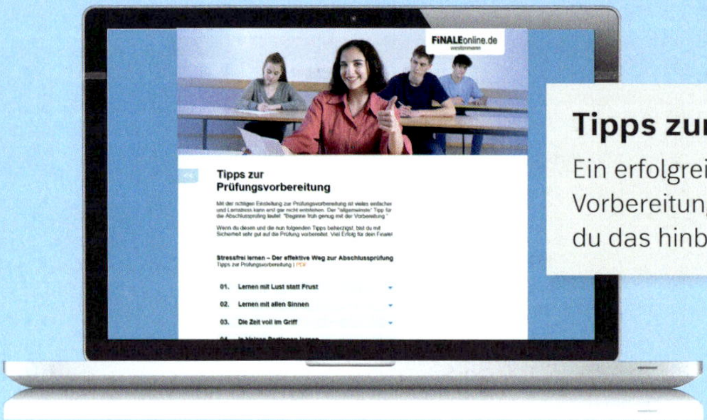

Tipps zur Prüfungsvorbereitung

Ein erfolgreiches Abitur erfordert eine gezielte Vorbereitung ohne unnötigen Lernstress. Wie du das hinbekommst, erfährst du hier!

Videos zur mündlichen Prüfung

Nur wenige Abiturienten wissen genau, wie sie abläuft, die „Mündliche“. Die Videos geben dir Einblick in den Ablauf der Prüfung und Tipps für die richtige Vorbereitung.

Die Kombination aus FiNALE-Buch und FiNALEonline bietet dir die optimale Vorbereitung für deine Prüfung und begleitet dich sicher zu einem erfolgreichen Abitur 2023!

www.finaleonline.de

westermann

FiNALE Prüfungstraining

Nordrhein-Westfalen

Abitur 2023

Englisch

Thomas Lehnen
Miriam Schulz
Claudia Schwarz-Brownbill

FiNALEonline.de

Liebe Schülerin, lieber Schüler,

sobald die Original-Prüfungsaufgaben zur Veröffentlichung freigegeben sind, können sie unter **www.finaleonline.de** zusammen mit ausführlichen Lösungen kostenlos heruntergeladen werden. Gib dazu einfach diesen Code ein:

EN8H3Y2

Einfach mal reinschauen: www.finaleonline.de

westermann GRUPPE

Bildnachweis:
|Peter Wirtz Fotografie, Dormagen: Titel.

Druck A[1]/Jahr 2022
Alle Drucke der Serie A sind im Unterricht parallel verwendbar.

Redaktion: Federlese GbR – Christina & Boris Kühne, Grevenbroich
Kontakt: finale@westermanngruppe.de
Layout: LIO Design GmbH, Braunschweig
Umschlaggestaltung: Gingco.Net, Braunschweig
Umschlagfoto: Peter Wirtz, Dormagen
Druck und Bindung: Westermann Druck GmbH, Georg-Westermann-Allee 66, 38104 Braunschweig

ISBN 978-3-7426-**2317-1**

Inhaltsverzeichnis

Arbeiten mit FiNALE

FiNALE Prüfungstraining Englisch möchte Ihnen eine praxisnahe Hilfe zur Vorbereitung auf die Abiturprüfung sein. Im Praxis-Teil finden sich zu allen geforderten Themenbereichen authentische Aufgaben, die dem aktuell geltenden neuen Format entsprechen. Daneben finden Sie die Original-Prüfungsaufgaben 2021. Unter unseren Beispielaufgaben sind sowohl Beispiele für Grundkurse als auch für Leistungskurse. Im Abitur unterscheidet sich die Aufgabe für Leistungskurse von denen für Grundkurse einerseits durch den Textumfang, andererseits durch den Schwierigkeitsgrad der Texte, der sich in der Regel aus der Komplexität der Syntax und des Wortschatzes ergibt. Beide Kriterien spielen für Übungstexte keine große Rolle. Auch als Grundkursschülerin oder -schüler sind Sie durch den Englischunterricht mit längeren und komplexeren Texten vertraut. Als Leistungskursschülerin oder -schüler können Sie eine Textanalyse auch an kürzeren, einfacheren Texten üben. Die inhaltlichen Vorgaben sind für beide Kursarten weitgehend gleich.

Je eine Aufgabe zu einem literarischen Text und einem Sach- und Gebrauchstext ergänzt um eine Sprachmittlungs-Aufgabe zu einem deutschen Text wird kleinschrittig erarbeitet und schließt mit einer Musterlösung. Dies soll für Sie eine exemplarische Hilfe sein auf dem Weg von den Ausgangstexten über das Textverständnis, die Methodik der Textanalyse, die Evaluation und die Sprachmittlung hin zur Gliederung und sprachlichen Darstellung der Zieltexte. Den weiteren Aufgabenbeispielen folgen Bewertungskriterien ganz in der Form, wie Ihre Lehrerinnen und Lehrer sie zur Korrektur der Abiturarbeiten an die Hand bekommen. Sie dienen Ihnen zur Selbstkontrolle in Ihrem fortschreitenden Prüfungstraining. Zu Ihrer Orientierung haben wir auch entsprechende Punkte vergeben. „Gummipunkte“, also Punkte für ein „weiteres aufgabenbezogenes Kriterium“, wie es sie im Abitur gibt, erschienen uns für die Beispielaufgaben jedoch wenig sinnvoll.

Geschrieben wurde dieses Buch im Jahr 2022, damit es frühzeitig zur Vorbereitung auf das Abitur 2023 beitragen kann. Die zu diesem Zeitpunkt aktuellen Abituraufgaben 2021 werden jeweils mit einer Musterlösung angeboten. Originallösungen unterliegen weiterhin der Geheimhaltung und können nicht veröffentlicht werden. Dennoch versuchen wir, unsere Musterlösung auf der Grundlage unserer Korrekturarbeit der Abiturarbeiten 2021 zu erstellen. Sie greifen die tatsächlich gegebenen Probleme und Fehlerschwerpunkte der Abiturientinnen und Abiturienten auf.

Der eindringliche Wunsch unserer Abiturienten nach einer kompakten inhaltlichen Übersicht über die verbindlich vorgegebenen Themen des Zentralabiturs hat uns bewogen, diese relevanten Inhalte im Kapitel „Basiswissen” zusammenzustellen. Natürlich kann dieses weder den Englischunterricht der Qualifikationsphase noch dessen Vor- und Nachbereitung ersetzen. Es hilft Ihnen jedoch, das im Unterricht erworbene Wissen zu strukturieren und in seinen Grundzügen abzurufen. Um den Umgang mit dem thematischen Vokabular zu vertiefen, ist dieser Teil in englischer Sprache geschrieben und wird durch Glossare zum thematischen Vokabular ergänzt.

Die sprachliche Leistung spielt in der Fremdsprache trotz aller inhaltlich-thematischer Kompetenz immer noch die herausragende Rolle. Während man in der Abiturklausur für den Inhalt maximal 60 Punkte erreichen kann, erhält man für eine perfekte sprachliche Leistung 90 Punkte. Ein sicherer Umgang mit den Strukturen und Wörtern der englischen Sprache ist also unabdingbar. Deshalb haben wir in FiNALE ein Kapitel zur sprachlichen Leistung aufgenommen, in dem es vor allem um kommunikative Textgestaltung und Ausdrucksvermögen geht, die im Zentralabitur – wie die sprachliche Richtigkeit – mit jeweils 30 Punkten bewertet werden.

Wir wünschen Ihnen viel Erfolg!

Informationen und Tipps zur Prüfung

Inhalte des Faches Englisch in der gymnasialen Oberstufe

Gelegentlich beklagen sich Schülerinnen und Schüler und auch Eltern über die Anforderungen und Inhalte des Englischunterrichts, insbesondere der Klausuren und der schriftlichen Abiturprüfung. Textanalyse und kreative Textproduktion erscheinen ihnen nicht als Fertigkeiten, die man im Leben braucht. Auf Unverständnis trifft gelegentlich auch die Bewertung – hat man doch gerade mit einem Australier gechattet, der sich anerkennend zu den Englischkenntnissen äußerte, oder im Urlaub einen Engländer getroffen, mit dem man sich prima bei einer Cola unterhalten konnte. Die Fähigkeit, sich mit anderen unterhalten zu können, ist also offensichtlich nicht der alleinige Aspekt, der in der Oberstufe und im Abitur bewertet wird.
Natürlich ist es primäres Ziel des Englischunterrichts, **kommunikative Kompetenz** zu vermitteln, also Schülerinnen und Schüler in die Lage zu versetzen, im englischsprachigen Ausland oder auch mit dem Englischen als *lingua franca* angemessen zu kommunizieren. Sieht man sich den Kernlehrplan für die Sekundarstufe I an, so wird man schnell erkennen, dass selbst die geforderten Kompetenzen für das Ende der Sekundarstufe I weit über die Kommunikation in Alltagssituationen hinausgehen. Zur Vorbereitung der Schülerinnen und Schüler auf ein Studium an der Hochschule, auf einen beruflichen Weg in Großunternehmen oder international tätigen mittelständischen Unternehmen orientiert sich der Kernlehrplan Englisch am Leitziel der interkulturellen Handlungsfähigkeit. Deshalb behandelt der Englischunterricht soziokulturell und global bedeutsame Themen, die in Texten und Medien dargestellt werden.

In diesem Zusammenhang spricht der Kernlehrplan von verschiedenen **Kompetenzbereichen:**
- funktionale kommunikative Kompetenz
- interkulturelle kommunikative Kompetenz
- Text- und Medienkompetenz
- Sprachlernkompetenz
- Sprachbewusstheit

Funktional kommunikative Kompetenzen sind Leseverstehen, Schreiben, Hör-/Hörsehverstehen, Sprechen und Sprachmittlung. Außerdem zählt man die Verfügbarkeit sprachlicher Mittel dazu, d. h. Wortschatz, Grammatik, Rechtschreibung und Aussprache.
Interkulturelle kommunikative Kompetenz ist das Zusammenspiel von Wissen, Einstellung und Bewusstheit. Vor dem Hintergrund ihrer eigenen Kultur sollen Schülerinnen und Schüler in der Lage sein, sowohl Empathie als auch kritische Distanz gegenüber kulturellen Besonderheiten zu entwickeln.
Für den Erwerb von **Text- und Medienkompetenz** vermittelt der Englischunterricht eine Fülle von Teilkompetenzen. Der Begriff Text umfasst hier – wie immer – Sachtexte

sowie literarische Texte, Filme, Bilder, Diagramme, Statistiken, Grafiken etc. Das Kapitel „Methoden der Textarbeit" wird sich eingehend damit befassen.

Für den **Umgang mit Texten** in der Q1 und der Q2 gibt der Kernlehrplan folgendes vor:

Sach- und Gebrauchstexte
Texte der privaten und öffentlichen Kommunikation:
Brief, Kommentar, Leitartikel, politische Rede, Leserbrief, Werbeanzeige
Texte in wissenschaftsorientierter Dimension:
Lexikonauszug, ein längerer Sachbuchauszug
Texte in berufsorientierter Dimension:
Stellenanzeige, PR-Material, Exposé, Protokoll

literarische Texte
lyrische Texte:
zeitgenössisches Gedicht, Gedicht in historischer Dimension
narrative Texte:
zeitgenössischer Roman, *short story*
dramatische Texte:
Auszüge aus einem oder aus verschiedenen Shakespeare-Dramen, ein zeitgenössisches Drama, Auszüge aus einem Drehbuch

diskontinuierlicher Texte
Text-Bild-Kombinationen:
Bild, Cartoon
Grafiken:
Tabelle, Karte, Diagramm

medial vermittelte Texte
auditive Formate:
radio feature / podcast, Auszüge aus einem Hörbuch
audiovisuelle Formate:
Spielfilm, *documentary/feature, news*
digitale Texte:
blog / video blog, Beiträge in Internetforen

Sprachlernkompetenz beinhaltet das selbstständige Gestalten des Lernens durch das Entwickeln von Strategien, aber auch durch den sicheren Umgang mit Hilfsmitteln, z. B. mit dem Wörterbuch.

Sprachbewusstheit beinhaltet Einsichten zum Beispiel in Varianten des Sprachgebrauchs, in verschiedene Register und Stilebenen, in Beziehungen zwischen Sprache und Kultur, aber auch die Bewusstheit von sprachlicher Manipulation.

Obligatorische Themen und Inhalte für das Zentralabitur

Das Ministerium gibt auf der Grundlage der Kernlehrpläne Vorgaben für eine Schwerpunktsetzung im Hinblick auf das Zentralabitur. Konkret gelten für das Abitur 2023 die folgenden Fokussierungen zu der im Kernlehrplan festgelegten Obligatorik. (Die vollständige Übersicht ist zu finden auf der Website des Ministeriums: https://www.standard sicherung.schulministerium.nrw.de/cms/zentralabitur-gost/faecher/fach.php?fach=3

Inhaltliche Schwerpunkte

Amerikanischer Traum – Visionen und Lebenswirklichkeiten in den USA
- American myths and realities: freedom and equality

Das Vereinigte Königreich im 21. Jahrhundert – Selbstverständnis zwischen Tradition und Moderne
- Tradition and change in politics and society:
  - the UK in the European context
  - multicultural society (Leistungskurs)

Postkolonialismus – Lebenswirklichkeiten in einem weiteren anglophonen Kulturraum
- Voices from the African Continent: Focus on Nigeria

Chancen und Risiken der Globalisierung
- Studying and working in a globalised world
- Voices from the African Continent: focus on Nigeria
- Ecological challenges and sustainable lifestyles (Grundkurs)
- Globalisation and global challenges: economic, ecological and political issues (Leistungskurs)

Medien in ihrer Bedeutung für den Einzelnen und die Gesellschaft
- The impact of Shakespearean drama on young audiences today:
  - study of film scenes (Grundkurs)
  - study of extracts and film scenes (tragedy or comedy) (Leistungskurs)
- Visions of the future:
  - utopia and dystopia
  - ethical issues of scientific and technological progress (Leistungskurs)

Fortschritt und Ethik in der modernen Gesellschaft (Leistungskurs)
- Visions of the future:
  - utopia and dystopia
  - ethical issues of scientific and technological progress
  - Globalisation and global challenges: economic, ecological and political issues

Lebensentwürfe, Studium, Ausbildung, Beruf international – Englisch als *lingua franca*
- Studying and working in a globalised world

Zieltextformate

In der dritten Teilaufgabe des Klausurteils A haben die Schülerinnen und Schüler die Wahl zwischen einer Stellungnahme und einer kreativen Aufgabe. Dazu wird Vertrautheit mit folgenden Textformaten vorausgesetzt:
- *letter/email (formal letter, letter to the editor, personal letter)*
- *speech script (talk, public/formal speech, debate statement)*
- *newspaper/internet article (report, comment)*
- im Leistungskurs zusätzlich: *(written) interview*
- Ausgestaltung, Fortführung oder Ergänzung eines literarischen Ausgangstextes (narrative Texte, zusätzlich im Leistungskurs: dramatische Texte, Filmskripte)

Die Fachkonferenzen jeder einzelnen Schule gestalten ihre Unterrichtssequenzen auf der Grundlage der geforderten Inhalte und der vom Lehrplan geforderten Obligatorik.

Grundsätze der Abiturprüfung

Aufgabenarten

Aus der Oberstufe sind Ihnen verschiedene Klausurvarianten bekannt. Von den fünf Kompetenzen Leseverstehen, Schreiben, Sprechen, Hör-/Hörsehverstehen und Sprachmittlung werden immer drei geprüft. So kennen Sie etwa die Textanalyse mit zusätzlicher Sprachmittlungsaufgabe oder die Filmanalyse mit zusätzlichem Multiple-Choice-Test zum Leseverstehen oder gar drei verschiedene Einzelaufgaben zu Leseverstehen, Schreiben und Sprachmittlung.

Für das Abitur 2023 ist vom Ministerium nur eine Aufgabenart vorgesehen, nämlich Schreiben und Leseverstehen in Klausurteil A, Sprachmittlung in Klausurteil B. Sie haben die Wahl zwischen zwei Aufgabenvorschlägen, die Ihnen im Klausurteil A entweder einen literarischen Text oder einen Sach- und Gebrauchstext vorlegen. Der Text kann in beiden Fällen durch eine Grafik, einen Cartoon o. Ä. ergänzt werden. Klausurteil B ist in beiden Fällen ein deutschsprachiger Sachtext.

Die Aufgabe des **Klausurteils A** besteht aus einem Text mit den Ihnen bekannten drei Teilaufgaben *(comprehension – analysis – evaluation/re-creation of text)*. In der dritten Teilaufgabe *(evaluation/re-creation of text)* wird Ihnen eine Wahlmöglichkeit zwischen einer kreativen Aufgabe und einer Stellungnahme gegeben. Die Übungsklausuren im Kapitel „Beispiele für Prüfungsaufgaben“ bieten beide Aufgabentypen, meist geben sie eine Wahlmöglichkeit.

Die Sprachmittlung, **Klausurteil B,** kann auch die erste Teilaufgabe der Klausur sein. Dann kann sich die Stellungnahme in Klausurteil A zusätzlich auf die deutsche Textvorlage beziehen.

Der englische Text hat im Leistungskurs einen Umfang von maximal 1000 Wörtern, im Grundkurs maximal 800 Wörtern. Der deutsche Text umfasst in beiden Kursarten zwischen 450 und 650 Wörter. Als Ausgangstexte eignen sich nur authentische Texte, d. h. sie dürfen nicht adaptiert oder stark gekürzt sein.

Anforderungsbereiche

Die Teilaufgaben der Prüfungsklausuren entsprechen den folgenden Anforderungsbereichen, die Sie bereits aus der Qualifikationsphase kennen.

Anforderungsbereich I: *comprehension/orientation/context*
- Wiedergabe der zentralen Aussagen eines Textes (meist Inhaltsangabe)
- Einordnung des Textes in einen Kontext unter Verwendung von Hintergrundwissen
- Einleitung eines komplexen Textes

Anforderungsbereich II: *analysis*
- Anwendung von Fachmethoden: textanalytische Verfahren, Einsatz von Lesetechniken
- gezielte Anwendung von Kenntnissen und Wissen – z. B. soziokulturelles oder metasprachliches Wissen (= Wissen über Sprache)
- exakte Arbeit am sprachlichen Detail, Belegen und Zitieren, problemlösende Argumentation

Anforderungsbereich III: *evaluation*
für die analytisch-interpretierende Aufgabenstellung:
- Bewertung der Problemlösung, Einordnen der Ergebnisse in einen größeren Zusammenhang
- persönliche Stellungnahme, eigene Meinung (erst hier und nicht etwa in AFB I oder II

Anforderungsbereich III: *evaluation/re-creation of text*
für die anwendungs-/produktionsorientierte Aufgabenstellung:
- Umsetzung, Bewertung, Reflexion der Problematik des Ausgangstextes bzw. der Analyse im Aufgabenbereich II in Form einer kreativen Aufgabe: Perspektivwechsel (Sicht einer anderen Figur)
- Füllen von Leerstellen (Weitererzählen, neues Ende)
- Textsortenwechsel (Brief an Protagonisten, Leserbrief, Brief an *agony aunt,* Tagebucheintrag, Dialog etc.)

Die einzelnen Anforderungsbereiche sollen nicht in drei voneinander unabhängigen Texten behandelt werden. Der Zieltext ist ein geschlossener, kohärenter Text, der sich als Essay in seinen drei Teilen etwa in eine Hinführung zum Thema, einen Hauptteil und eine Schlussbetrachtung gliedert. Eine kreative Teilaufgabe wird sich naheliegenderweise nicht in den geschlossenen Zieltext eingliedern, da sie in der Regel ein völlig anderes Textformat hat.

TIPP

Wichtig! Sie sind aus Ihren Oberstufenklausuren gewohnt, Stellungnahmen und kreative Texte mit engem Bezug zum Ausgangstext zu erstellen. Im Abitur wird es auch Aufgaben mit nur thematischem Bezug oder gar themenübergreifendem Bezug geben. Beispiele dazu finden Sie in den Abituraufgaben der Jahre 2021 und 2022 und auch in unseren Beispielaufgaben zum American Dream und zum Brexit.
Treffen Sie im Abitur Ihre Aufgabenauswahl also auch mit besonderem Blick auf den Anforderungsbereich III!

Operatoren

Für die Formulierung der Aufgaben gibt es klare Vorgaben. Verben für die Arbeitsanweisungen (= Operatoren) müssen in ihrer exakten Bedeutung verstanden werden. Eine ungefähre Ahnung, was gefordert ist, reicht keinesfalls aus.
Die folgende Operatorenübersicht ist der Website des Ministeriums entnommen. Die mittlere Spalte definiert die genaue Wortbedeutung des Verbs, die dritte Spalte gibt jeweils ein Beispiel für eine Aufgabenstellung.
Beachten Sie, dass die Operatoren im Anforderungsbereich I vor allem deutlich machen, welcher Umfang der inhaltlichen Wiedergabe von Ihnen verlangt wird. „Outline", „summarise" oder „write a summary" verlangen eine knappe Wiedergabe des Textes oder auch nur einer relevanten Textpassage. „Describe" und „point out" hingegen erwarten eine ausführliche Beschreibung bzw. Erläuterung des im Text dargestellten Sachverhalts. Letzteres kommt vor allem infrage, wenn der Ausgangstext sehr komplex ist, wie z. B. eine Erörterung, oder sehr dicht, wie beispielsweise ein Gedicht. Ihr Textverständnis weisen Sie dann nicht durch eine knappe Zusammenfassung, sondern durch eine Beschreibung oder Erläuterung in Ihren eigenen Worten nach.

TIPP

Achten Sie darauf, dass Sie, auch wenn Sie zu einer Skizzierung *(outline)* oder Zusammenfassung *(summary)* des Inhalts aufgefordert werden, stets die wesentlichen Inhaltspunkte benennen. Eine abstraktere, allgemeiner gehaltene Zusammenfassung kann durchaus eleganter sein, wird aber durch den Punktekatalog der Bewertungskriterien möglicherweise nicht erfasst.

Die Übersicht enthält Operatoren, die für das im Abitur vorgesehene Klausurformat Schreiben mit integriertem Leseverstehen in Klausurteil A und Sprachmittlung in Klausurteil B infrage kommen.
Weitere Operatoren für weitere Kompetenzbereiche sind auf der Website des Ministeriums zu finden (https://www.standardsicherung.schulministerium.nrw.de/cms/zentralabitur-gost/faecher/fach.php?fach=3).
Die Operatoren können unterschiedlichen Anforderungsbereichen zugeordnet werden.

Klausurteil A: Schreiben, Leseverstehen integriert

Operator	Erläuterung	Illustrierendes Aufgabenbeispiel	AFB
analyse	describe and explain in detail	Analyse the opposing views on class held by the two protagonists. Examine the author's use of language.	II
assess	express a well-founded opinion on the nature or quality of sb./sth.	Assess the importance of standards in education.	III
evaluate	express a well-founded opinion on the nature or quality of sb./sth.	Evaluate the author's view of the present impact of the American Dream ...	III
examine	describe and explain in detail	Examine the opposing views on social class held by the two protagonists.	II
give/write a characterisation of	provide a thorough analysis of a character	Characterise / Write a characterisation of the principal figures in the play.	II
comment (on)	state one's opinion clearly and support one's view with evidence or reasons	Comment on the writer's view of gender roles.	III
compare	show similarities and differences	Compare the attitude of the two characters towards war.	II
describe	give a detailed account of what sb./sth. is like	Describe the way the playwright creates an atmosphere of suspense.	I II
discuss	give arguments or reasons for and against, especially to come to a well-founded conclusion	Discuss the message of the cartoon, referring to work done on the British monarchy.	III
explain	make sth. clear by giving reasons for and details/aspects of sth.	Explain the protagonist's obsession with money.	II

illustrate	use examples to explain or make clear	Illustrate the way in which, according to the author, school life in Britain differs from that in Germany.	II
interpret	explain the meaning, purpose or message of sth.	Interpret the sonnet, focusing on the way structure and imagery are used to express the speaker's insight into the nature of time.	II
outline	give the main features, structure or general principles of sth.	Outline the author's views on love, marriage and divorce.	I
point out	find and explain certain aspects	Point out the author's main ideas on …	I
state	present the main aspects of sth. briefly and clearly	State the author's key reasons for taking a gap year.	I
summarise, sum up	give a concise account of the main points or ideas of a text, issue or topic	Summarise / Sum up the information about green energy given in the text.	I
write (+ text type)	produce a text with specific features	Write the ending of the story / a letter to the editor / a dialogue, etc. Write an interior monologue that reflects the character's view of the situation and her/his feelings.	III

Klausurteil B: Sprachmittlung isoliert

Die Aufgabenstellung für die Sprachmittlung enthält einen situativen Kontext mit Hinweisen zu Adressat/-in und Zieltextformat.

Operator	Erläuterung	Illustrierendes Aufgabenbeispiel
explain	make sth. clear taking into account culture-related differences if necessary	Based on the text on environmental policy, explain the principle of waste separation in Germany in an email to your British friend.
outline	give a concise account of the main points or ideas of a text, clarifying culture-related aspects if necessary	Outline Mr. Liu's career in Germany in an article for your international school project's website on "Successful Immigrants".
present	give a concise account of the main points or ideas of a text, clarifying culture-related aspects if necessary	For an international school project in the EU, present the relevant information on the image of migrants in German media in a formal email to your partner school in Spain.

summarise, sum up	give a concise account of the main points or ideas of a text, clarifying culture-related aspects if necessary	Sum up Manuel's views on working and living as a gap year student in India for your blog. Where necessary, add information which might help to avoid possible misunderstandings.
write (+ text type)	produce a text with specific features	Using the information in the German text write an article in English for your project website in which you inform your Polish partners how to get a sports scholarship at a German university.

Quelle: https://www.standardsicherung.schulministerium.nrw.de/cms/zentralabitur-gost/faecher/getfile.php?file=3828 (Zugriff: 01.04.2022)

Bewertung

Für die Bewertung wird den Lehrerinnen und Lehrern ein Raster mit Bewertungskriterien an die Hand gegeben, sowohl für die sprachliche als auch für die inhaltliche Leistung. Es können bei einer Abiturklausur insgesamt 150 Punkte erreicht werden, davon 90 für die Darstellungsleistung (Sprache) und 60 für den Inhalt. Dabei ist die Verteilung der Punkte auf die verschiedenen Anforderungsbereiche immer gleich.

Klausurteil A (Schreiben/Leseverstehen) Anforderungsbereich I : Anforderungsbereich II: Anforderungsbereich III:	 12 Punkte 16 Punkte 14 Punkte
Klausurteil B (Sprachmittlung):	18 Punkte
Gesamtpunkte Inhalt:	**60 Punkte**

Grundsätze für die Bewertung (Notenfindung)

Für die Zuordnung der Notenstufen zu den Punktzahlen ist folgende Tabelle zu verwenden:

Note	Punkte	Erreichte Punktzahl
sehr gut plus	15	150 – 143
sehr gut	14	142 – 135
sehr gut minus	13	134 – 128
gut plus	12	127 – 120
gut	11	119 – 113
gut minus	10	112 – 105
befriedigend plus	9	104 – 98
befriedigend	8	97 – 90
befriedigend minus	7	89 – 83
ausreichend plus	6	82 – 75
ausreichend	5	74 – 68
ausreichend minus	4	67 – 60
mangelhaft plus	3	59 – 50
mangelhaft	2	49 – 41
mangelhaft minus	1	40 – 30
ungenügend	0	29 – 0

TIPP zum Punktesammeln

Die Wertigkeit des Anforderungsbereiches III darf man nicht unterschätzen. Mit 14 Punkten ist er fast so gewichtig wie Anforderungsbereich II. Halten Sie sich mit der Analyse nicht so lange auf, dass Ihnen für eine Stellungnahme nur noch wenige Minuten bleiben. Das würde Sie viele Punkte kosten.

Überdies: Wenn Ihre Stärken nicht in der Textanalyse liegen, Sie aber aus anderen Fächern wie Erdkunde oder Biologie so viel Sachkenntnis haben, dass Sie qualitativ hochwertig zu Sachthemen Position beziehen können, dann setzen Sie dort Ihren persönlichen Schwerpunkt!

Die mündliche Abiturprüfung im Fach Englisch

Während einige von Ihnen Englisch als schriftliches Abiturfach gewählt haben, werden andere sich für Englisch als 4. Abiturfach entschieden haben und damit eine mündliche Abiturprüfung ablegen.
Auch für den Fall, dass Sie Englisch als schriftliches Abiturfach gewählt haben, könnte es trotzdem sein, dass Sie an einer mündlichen Nachprüfung teilnehmen müssen, nämlich wenn Sie Ihre Prüfungen nicht bestanden haben. In bestimmten Fällen besteht auch die Möglichkeit, die Abiturnote durch die Teilnahme an einer freiwilligen mündlichen Nachprüfung zu verbessern.
Ganz egal, welcher Fall für Sie von Bedeutung ist: Die Vorbereitung und der Ablauf der mündlichen Prüfung im Fach Englisch ist immer gleich.

Die mündliche Prüfung im Fach Englisch dauert insgesamt **mindestens 20,** aber **höchstens 30 Minuten** und ist in zwei Prüfungsteile aufgeteilt, deren Dauer ungefähr gleich lang ist.
Vor Beginn der Prüfung haben Sie **30 Minuten Zeit,** das Ihnen von Ihrem Fachlehrer oder Ihrer Fachlehrerin für den ersten Prüfungsteil vorgelegte **Material vorzubereiten.** Als Hilfsmittel stehen Ihnen hier ein **ein- und zweisprachiges Wörterbuch** und **gegebenenfalls ein herkunftssprachliches Wörterbuch** zur Verfügung. Die Notizen, die Sie hier anfertigen, dürfen Sie mit in die Prüfung nehmen und als Grundlage für Ihren Vortrag nutzen.

Anders als im schriftlichen Abitur können Sie hier **nicht** zwischen verschiedenen Materialien auswählen.
Das Material, das Ihnen von Ihrem Fachlehrer oder Ihrer Fachlehrerin vorgelegt wird, stellt einen **Bezug zu den Themenfeldern der Qualifikationsphase** her. Zur häuslichen Vorbereitung verweisen wir hier auf die Kapitel zum Basiswissen auf den Seiten 19 bis 77.

Im **ersten Prüfungsteil** sollen Sie – auf Basis des Ihnen zur Vorbereitung vorgelegten Materials – einen **zusammenhängenden und weitgehend freien Vortrag** halten, selbstständig eine **nachvollziehbare Argumentation** entwickeln und **eine Einordnung in den entsprechenden Themenkomplex** vornehmen.
Grundsätzlich ist der erste Prüfungsteil nichts anderes als eine „mündliche Version" einer Klausur. Daher empfehlen wir Ihnen, die in diesem Buch enthaltenen Klausuren zur Vorbereitung auf die mündliche Prüfung durchzuarbeiten.

Im Grunde bestehen zwei Möglichkeiten, wie das von Ihnen vorzubereitende **Material** aussehen kann.
Es können Ihnen ein oder mehrere Texte beziehungsweise ein längeres Zitat mit einem Wortumfang von **ca. 200 bis 300 Wörtern** vorgelegt werden. Bei den Texten kann es sich um **literarische Texte** oder um **Sach- und Gebrauchstexte** handeln.

Ihr Fachlehrer oder Ihre Fachlehrerin kann Ihnen aber auch eine oder mehrere visuelle **Darstellungen** (Diagramm, Grafik, Cartoon, Statistik, Bild) vorlegen, die er/sie gegebenenfalls um einen Text ergänzt.

Im **zweiten Prüfungsteil** wird Ihnen kein weiteres Material vorgelegt. Gegenstand dieses Prüfungsteils sind ein weiterer bzw. mehrere weitere **Themenkomplexe zu den Themenfeldern der Qualifikationsphase**.
Hier sollen Sie zeigen, dass Sie **größere Zusammenhänge erkennen und herstellen** können.

Da neben Ihrer inhaltlichen Leistung auch Ihre sprachliche Leistung bewertet wird, sei an dieser Stelle nochmals auf die Listen mit nützlichen Wörtern und Wendungen im Buch (ab S. 211) verwiesen.
Beachten Sie auch die Strategien zur Wortschatzarbeit und zur Vermeidung „gängiger" Fehler.
Achten Sie in beiden Prüfungsteilen darauf, dass Ihre Ausführungen für die Prüfungskommission verständlich und nachvollziehbar sind.
Bemühen Sie sich darum, im ersten Prüfungsteil Ihre Gedanken und Anmerkungen möglichst strukturiert und frei vorzutragen.
Nutzen Sie die Vorbereitungszeit dazu, Ihre Notizen zu strukturieren. Selbstverständlich dürfen und sollen Sie auf diese zurückgreifen, aber lesen Sie keinesfalls alles von Ihrem Notizzettel ab.

Basiswissen

American Myths and Realities – Freedom and Equality

Concepts of the American Dream

The USA

The USA was – and still is – a country of unlimited opportunities, where people can work their way "from rags to riches". It has attracted millions of both legal and illegal immigrants over the centuries, who hoped to find a better life without the kind of persecution or obstacles they had to face in their home countries.

> **Keyword**
> **The American Dream:** There is no single definition of what the American Dream actually is, as it varies for each and every American.
> The term was first used by James Truslow Adams, an American historian, in his book *The Epic of America,* in 1931: "[The] American Dream [is] the dream of a land in which life should be better and richer and fuller for every man, with opportunity for each according to his ability or achievement."

In the following pages we are going to take a look at some of the key concepts generally associated with the American Dream, many of which are often touched upon in political speeches.
Please note that these key concepts often overlap and are closely related.

Freedom

The first thing many immigrants saw when they came to New York City by ship during the 19th and the first half of the 20th century was the Statue of Liberty, which is located on Liberty Island.

The Statue of Liberty

- given to the USA as a gift from France in 1886, to celebrate the first 100 years of American independence from Britain
- a robed woman, holding a lit torch in her right and a tablet in her left hand, showing the date of the Declaration of Independence (4 July 1776)
- underneath her right foot the remains of broken shackles can be seen
- one of the most famous American icons, symbolising enlightenment, independence, liberty and freedom
- the theme of Emma Lazarus's famous poem "The New Colossus" (1883), which can be seen on a bronze plaque inside the statue
- located in Upper New York Bay, just like Ellis Island

Ellis Island

- the place where most immigrants first set foot on American soil
- an island of hopes but also an island of tears for a number of immigrants, as some of them were detained there for legal or medical reasons or even sent back
- the gateway to a new – better – life for the majority of immigrants
- a federal immigration station from 1892 to 1954

The Puritans

The Puritans' beliefs and values had a lasting impact on New England society:
- towards the end of the 16th century, some English Protestants felt that Protestantism in England was not much different from Catholicism
- decided to leave England, seeking their luck elsewhere
- first settled in Holland (1608), but moved back to England
- wished to remain English subjects but free to worship God the way they wanted to
- intention: to purify the Church of England, not to leave it
- September 1620: a group of 102 people left England, sailed on a ship called the *Mayflower*, arrived in America 65 days later, in a bay they called Plymouth Bay

The New Canaan

In the Bible, Canaan was the land God promised to the Israelites. God ordered Moses to lead the people from captivity in Egypt to Canaan – "a land of milk and honey". America sees itself in this tradition. The idea of America as the "New Canaan", the land of milk and honey, is closely linked to the idea of "manifest destiny".

Manifest Destiny / The frontier

Manifest Destiny

The term "Manifest Destiny" was coined by the American journalist John L. O'Sullivan in 1839:
- stands for the belief that America is the one nation ordered by God to expand across the North American continent
- "The Great Nation of Futurity" by John L. O'Sullivan: "[America is] the nation of progress, of individual freedom, of universal enfranchisement"; the American people have been chosen "to establish on earth the moral dignity and salvation of man – the immutable truth and beneficence of God"[1].
- America as the country that is superior to all other countries
- stresses virtue of the American people, as they are the ones to establish moral rules and values across the globe

American patriotism is deeply rooted in the concept of "Manifest Destiny", while the idea of "Manifest Destiny" is closely linked to the perception of the frontier and its continuing permutations.

[1] "The Great Nation of Futurity," *The United States Democratic Review*, Volume 6, Issue 23, pp. 426–430.

The frontier

- the expansion of the American nation from coast to coast, pushing the borderline between civilisation and wilderness further and further back
- Pacific coast was reached in the 2nd half of the 19th century
- after this mission new challenges – new frontiers – were needed, e.g. space exploration (like the moon landing in 1969), scientific and technological progress

Life, liberty and the pursuit of happiness

Declaration of Independence

- written in 1776 by Thomas Jefferson
- all American citizens are created equal: "We hold these truths to be self-evident, that all men are created equal, that they are endowed by their Creator with certain unalienable Rights, that among these are Life, Liberty and the pursuit of Happiness."
- possibility for every American (at first, women were excluded from this definition) to lead their life the way they want to, making their own personal dreams come true
- stresses the rights of the individual, while at the same time taking the rights of others into consideration
- 1776: the thirteen colonies declared their independence from England and were therefore at war with England
- Declaration of Independence questioned the rights of the British king, George III, in that it stated that everyone was created equal (a revolutionary idea at the time)
- The new American government was to be radically different from that of the British monarchy, as pointed out in the American Constitution.

American Constitution

- written in 1787
- new ideas of a democratic state stated in the preamble of the Constitution: "We the People of the United States, in Order to form a more perfect Union[2], establish Justice, ensure domestic Tranquility, provide for the common defense, promote the general Welfare, and secure the Blessings of Liberty to ourselves and our Posterity, do ordain and establish this Constitution for the United States of America."

Bill of Rights

- first ten amendments to the American Constitution
- written because some delegates feared that the new American government would threaten everyone's ability to achieve personal freedom and the pursuit of happiness
- First Congress of the United States originally proposed twelve amendments in 1789, ten of which were added to the constitution as a preamble
- amendments known as the Bill of Rights
- guarantee America's citizens certain inalienable rights, e.g. freedom of religion, freedom of speech and the press as well as the right to own and carry weapons

[2] Barack Obama took up the idea of "a more perfect union" in a speech he delivered on 28 May 2008, in which he elaborated on the issues of race and inequality in the USA.

The American Dream today

Keywords
Multicultural society: a society where various ethnic groups and their cultural heritage are accepted in their own right
Salad bowl: the various ethnicities living in the United States adding their own traditions, cultural values, etc. to the American people; the various heritages do not merge into one but stay distinct ("unity in diversity")
Melting pot: ethnic groups do not retain their cultural heritage but amalgamate into one new nation; term first appeared in an essay by Jean de Crèvecœur entitled "Letters from an American Farmer" (1782)
The term "salad bowl" is now considered to be more politically correct.

- The American Dream itself has come to be seen more critically.
- A considerable number of critics regard the American Dream as an illusion, as not everyone has access to the possibilities usually associated with it.
- Examples of American nightmares are the Vietnam War, 11 September 2001 and the financial crisis starting in 2008.

During his election campaign, current US president Joe Biden declared that he would reform the US immigration system and reverse the restrictions implemented by former US president Donald Trump. The number of prospective new immigrants would be increased and those immigrants living in the United States illegally should be pardoned and thereby been given the chance to become legal US citizens. In addition, restrictions would be lifted so that more refugees could be admitted to the USA. The number of green cards issued would be raised to match the increasing demand.
Instead of pursuing Trump's vision of building a wall on the border to Mexico to stop illegal immigration from South American countries, Biden plans to make border screening more effective.
On his first day in office, President Biden sent a bill to Congress to put his plans for a fair, human and reformed immigration system into action.
Unaccompanied minors are allowed to enter the USA while it is decided whether they are allowed to stay or will be sent back to their home country. This has led to false rumours that the US borders are open to migrants and an increased rise in the numbers of unaccompanied migrant children. Sadly, the number of these underage immigrants is still fairly high. Biden has urged families not to send their children unaccompanied on this dangerous journey to the USA.

The Present Economic Situation in the US

The question whether the American Dream is still alive today is one which cannot be answered with either "yes" or "no", as the concept of the American Dream is not static. It depends on several aspects, e. g. a person's individual definition of and belief in the concept of the American Dream and the point of view one takes.
With regard to the present economic situation in the US, it is often said that the American Dream has been shattered for many people. The financial crisis that began in 2008 made the aim of achieving financial security a distant prospect for many.
In the following you will find a brief overview of why the quest for financial security has become difficult over the last few years.
For many people, owning a house is the goal of a lifetime. This is also true for US citizens, and for many years getting a loan necessary to build or buy a house was not difficult, even for people without a steady or with a low income. This resulted in people taking bigger loans than they could actually afford. They hoped that in the worst case of not being able to pay back the loan, they could still sell their houses, thereby making a profit. In most cases paying back the loan was not a problem as long as the mortgage rates were low.
When the base rate *(Leitzins)* increased, many house owners had difficulties paying back their loans. A huge number of houses suddenly had to be sold, which lowered prices, as there was also a decline in demand. In some cases that actually meant that the price for which a house could be sold was lower than the house owner's loan. So instead of making a profit, selling a house often meant incurring a loss.
In the meantime, the banks had started to speculate with their customers' loans. Loans of good, average and bad credit rating were combined into so-called "Mortgage Backed Securities" (MBS). By combining loans of different credit rankings, banks hoped to limit the risk if someone failed to pay back a loan. These MBS were then sold to other banks worldwide, which meant profit for the seller. This practice went well for several years, but when more and more house owners could not pay back their loans, their banks started to lose large sums of money.
On 15 September 2008, one of America's biggest banks, Lehman Brothers, crashed. This marked the beginning of a series of bank crashes. Unemployment increased, and as many Americans had less money to spend, this led to a drop in consumption as well. The burst of the housing bubble did not remain an American problem for long. It soon affected the economy of other countries, among them Germany, the Benelux countries and Iceland. Government bailouts for banks and economic stimulus plans were decided and put into action. Nevertheless, many countries were hit by recession.

In 2022, the US economy was in parts still recovering from the economic crisis of 2008, but unemployment dropped from 10 % in October 2009 to just 3.8 % in February 2020.[3] During the COVID-19 crisis, the unemplyoment rate rose as high as 14.7 %, but has stabilised since and appears to be declining steadily again.

[3] http://data.bls.gov/timeseries/LNS14000000 (accessed on 1 April 2022)

For both major parties in the US, economic growth and an increase in the number of jobs are top issues, although their approaches are quite different.
On 3 November 2020, Joseph "Joe" Robinette Biden Jr., the Democratic Party candidate, won the US presidential election against Donald Trump. During both of Barack Obama's terms in office as US president, Joe Biden served as Vice-President of the USA. Prior to his finally successful run for the presidency, Biden had announced his candidacy in 1988 and 2009, but on both occasions he withdrew from the race for presidency.
Born on 20 November 1942, Biden grew up in Pennsylvania and Delaware. He worked as a lawyer until he was sworn in as a senator for the state of Delaware at the age of 29. He kept this position until his election as Vice-President to Barack Obama in 2009. Kamala Harris was elected with Biden as the first female Vice-President of the USA. She is also the first African American and first Asian American to hold this office.
Among Biden's election pledges were fighting COVID-19, dealing with the climate crisis, making healthcare affordable for everyone and renewing the country's immigration system. Rejoining the Paris Climate Agreement, which the USA had left under Donald Trump, was a first step to acknowledging the urgent global challenge of the climate crisis.
Given the relatively narrow margin of Biden's victory in the presidential election, Donald Trump, together with his supporters and many members of the Republican Party, did not readily accept the outcome. Trump continued to use the social micro-blogging platform Twitter to spread his theory of fraudulent elections and a "stolen" victory. Several of his tweets questioned the legitimacy of the election. Many were also regarded as a glorification of violence. As a consequence, Twitter permanently suspended Donald Trump's account. In the build-up to the 2024 presidential elections, Trump's election lie is still spread by a large portion of the Republican party.
The tension in the USA that erupted in the wake of Trump's constant accusations of electoral fraud led to a large number Trump supporters violently storming the Capitol in Washington, D.C. on 6 January 2021 – a mere two weeks before Biden's inauguration. Trump had summoned his supporters to march to Washington to protest against the "stolen" election and Joe Biden's congressional certification. The angry mob that stormed the Capitol wreaked havoc. Photographs and videos taken during the raid showed that some of the protesters were heavily armed and aggressive.
Media coverage of this incident went around the globe and caused horror, shock, disgust and disbelief in governments and citizens worldwide. American and international politicians alike criticised Trump for not condemning but rather inciting, the violence. In the aftermath of the riots, there were attempts to press legal charges against Trump for the role he played in this incident. On 7 January 2021, Donald Trump – again on Twitter – promised a smooth transition of power.
Trump himself did not attend Joe Biden's inauguration ceremony, thereby breaking with a 152-year-long tradition. Instead, outgoing Vice-President Mike Pence paid his respects to Joe Biden and new Vice-President Kamala Harris.

During his election campaign President Joe Biden frequently declared the dangers of climate change to be one of the most pressing current global challenges. He kept his promise to rejoin the Paris Climate Agreement by releasing the following statement on

20 January 2021, only a few hours after being sworn in as President: "I, Joseph R. Biden Jr., President of the United States of America, having seen and considered the Paris Agreement, done at Paris on 12 December 2015, do hereby accept the said Agreement and every article and clause thereof on behalf of the United States of America"[4]. Accordingly, Biden's "Build Back Better Plan" includes initiatives to reduce the effects of climate change.

Glossary – Freedom and Justice

assimilation	Assimilation; Angleichung an Bestehendes
base rate	Leitzins
civil disobedience	bürgerlicher Ungehorsam
Civil Rights Movement	die Bürgerrechtsbewegung
credit rating	Beurteilung der Kreditwürdigkeit, Bonitätsbeurteilung
cultural heritage	Kulturerbe; kulturelles Erbe
Declaration of Independence	Unabhängigkeitserklärung
discrimination; deprivation	Diskriminierung; Mangel/Entzug
drop in consumption	Konsumrückgang
"E pluribus unum"	lat.: „aus vielen Eines"; ursprünglich bezogen auf die verschiedenen Staaten der USA; heute vielmehr bezogen auf die vielen ethnischen Gruppen, aus denen sich die Bevölkerung der USA zusammensetzt
economic stimulus plan	Konjunkturprogramm
entrepreneur	Unternehmer
equality; equal opportunities	Gleichheit; gleiche Chancen
fame	Ruhm
freedom; ~ of speech; ~ of the press; religious ~	Freiheit; Redefreiheit; Pressefreiheit; Religionsfreiheit
frontier	Grenze (zwischen Zivilisation und Wildnis)
gold rush	Goldrausch
government bailouts	Rettungsaktion durch die Regierung
identity	Identität
Immigration Act	Einwanderungsgesetz

[4] White House Briefing Room, https://www.whitehouse.gov/briefing-room/statements-releases/2021/01/20/paris-climate-agreement/ (accessed on 1 April 2022). Biden's act of rejoining the Paris Climate Agreement was internationally received with praise and relief.

"In God we trust"	„Wir vertrauen auf Gott"; offizieller Wahlspruch der USA
inauguration; inaugural speech	Amtseinführung; Amtsantrittsrede
liberation	Befreiung
loan	Darlehen
melting pot vs. salad bowl	„Schmelztiegel" vs. „Salatschüssel" (unterschiedliche Konzepte, die die Vielfalt unterschiedlicher Kulturen in den USA charakterisieren)
mortgage	Hypothek
multiculturalism	Multikulturalität
naturalisation	Einbürgerung
pioneer; pioneer spirit	Pionier/-in; Pioniergeist
Promised Land; the land of milk and honey; God's own country; the New Canaan	das gelobte Land
recession	Rezession
refugee; refugee camp	Flüchtling; Flüchtlingslager
segregation; desegregation	Rassentrennung; Aufhebung der Rassentrennung
success	Erfolg
supply and demand	Angebot und Nachfrage
housing bubble	Immobilienblase
the pursuit of happiness	das Streben nach Glück
to achieve financial security	finanzielle Sicherheit erlangen
to attain self-fulfillment	sich selbst verwirklichen
to be persecuted; religious/political persecution	verfolgt werden; religiöse/politische Verfolgung
from rags to riches; from dishwasher to millionaire	vom Tellerwäscher zum Millionär
to immigrate; immigrant; immigration; an influx of immigrants	einwandern; Einwandernde/-r; Einwanderung; Zustrom von Einwandernden
to incur a loss	(einen) Verlust machen
to pledge allegiance to the flag	den Fahneneid leisten
to prosper	Erfolg haben; in Wohlstand leben
to settle; settler; settlement	besiedeln; Siedler/-in; Siedlung
unalienable/inalienable rights	unveräußerliche Rechte

Tradition and Change in Politics and Society – The UK in the European Context

The Political System of the UK

> **Keyword**
> **British constitution:** not set out in a single document
> The British constitution is based on conventions that are universally accepted but which have never been formally defined. It also rests upon numerous acts and resolutions of Parliament, as each individual act of Parliament contributes to the constitution. Thus, it is adaptable to changing political conditions.

Separation of Powers

The following three branches represent the powers and areas of responsibility:
Legislature: Parliament
Executive:
- government departments responsible for national administration
- local authorities
- public corporations responsible for particular nationalised industries (controlled by Government; most of these have now been privatised)

Judiciary: the Courts

There are **two kinds of law:**
- common law: historic body of conventions ('it has always been like that')
- statute law: parliamentary and EU legislation

Parliament

Functions of Parliament
- pass laws
- scrutinise government policy and administration
- debate the major issues of the day

Elements of Parliament
Queen – House of Lords – House of Commons
- agreement of all three elements required to pass legislation
- Parliament directly responsible to the electorate; no written constitution
- Act of Parliament cannot be disputed by the law courts

The House of Lords (House of Peers, Upper House, Second Chamber)
The House of Lords consists of hereditary peers, who inherit their peerage, and life peers, whose peerages are granted to them personally for their lifetime.
The political power of the peers has been gradually reduced over the years, and they have recognised the supremacy of the elected chamber, the House of Commons.

The House of Commons (Lower House)
646 members are directly elected by voters in their constituencies.
The House of Commons is the actual legislative body of the United Kingdom.

The Queen

The Queen has no overt power but is formally part of the government system.
The Queen is the
- head of State,
- symbol of national unity,
- head of the executive,
- head of the judiciary,
- commander-in-chief of the armed forces,
- "supreme governor" of the Church of England.

Important functions
The Queen
- appoints the Prime Minister by inviting the leader of the majority in the House of Commons to form a government,
- summons and dissolves Parliament,
- gives Royal Assent to legislation (as a matter of course),
- formally appoints ministers, judges, officers, diplomats, bishops,
- can pardon people,
- confers peerages (see above) and knighthoods,
- represents the country at home and abroad.

Political parties

The Conservative Party (Tories)
rightwing party, associated with
- nationalism
- law and order
- private enterprise
- minimal interference of the state in the economy

The Labour Party
traditional party of the "working class", formerly associated with
- state control and planning
- nationalisation of key industries
- welfare
- affiliation to the trade unions

However, with Tony Blair the party now known as New Labour changed direction away from socialist ideals towards an acceptance of the free market economy, opening itself to voters from the middle classes.

Her Majesty's Government

Important members of the present cabinet (April 2022)

Prime Minister	Boris Johnson
Chancellor of the Exchequer	Rishi Sunak
Secretary of State for the Home Department	Priti Patel
Secretary of State for Foreign, Commonwealth and Development Affairs	Elizabeth Truss
Secretary of State for Defence	Ben Wallace

Devolution

Devolution is the granting of powers to the parliaments of Scotland, Wales and Northern Ireland. At the end of the 1990s, the National Assembly of Wales and the Scottish Parliament were inaugurated, with competence to rule on issues like agriculture, fisheries and forestry, education, health and tourism, whereas Westminster (the UK government) retained power in fields such as foreign affairs, defence, taxation, fiscal policy and labour market policy. Because of the Troubles, devolution in Northern Ireland was only implemented in 2007. In the 2014 referendum on full independence held in Scotland, there was a narrow majority for the country to remain in the UK.
After the Brexit decision the Scottish Parliament decided to ask the British Government to be allowed to hold a second referendum on independence in order to give Scotland the chance to stay in the EU.

Society

Class

The British are very class-conscious. Class distinctions are recognisable in speech, habits, style, tastes and values. The Office of National Statistics produced a detailed socio-economic classification in 2020[1]. Although many top-ranking people may earn a lot of money, the classification is not based on income alone but on the differences mentioned above. In the last three decades class differences have become less obvious. The country has become more of a meritocracy, i. e. a society where achievement counts most. But traditional everyday terms are still used to refer to social classes: *upper class, upper-middle class, lower-middle class, working class.*

Ethnicity

Britain has become a multinational society in the last half century (see chapter “Multicultural society”, p. 33)

[1] https://www.ons.gov.uk/methodology/classificationsandstandards/standardoccupationalclassificationsoc/soc2020/soc2020volume3thenationalstatisticssocioeconomicclassificationnssecrebasedonthesoc2020#classes-and-collapses (accessed on 1 April 2022)

Britain and Europe

A European context has been relevant to the UK since the 1950s.
Before: Britain as imperial power with military alliances
In 1957, France, West Germany, Belgium, Italy, Luxembourg and the Netherlands signed the Treaty of Rome, which was the foundation of the European Economic Community (EEC), the predecessor the European Union. Economic cooperation between European nations, especially in the coal and steel industry, was believed to prevent war.
When the United Kingdom applied for membership in the EEC in 1963, France's President Charles de Gaulle vetoed its application because he thought Britain was leaning towards America rather than Europe.

Britain and the EU

Traditionally, Britain has preferred to stay out of Europe. The terms "Europe" and "the Continent" have always referred to the European mainland.
Britain had been a member of the EU since 1973 (then the EC). Britain never joined the monetary union (i. e. they did not have the euro) and never signed the Schengen Agreement, which permits travelling between 25 European countries.
On 23 June 2016, a referendum about Britain's membership in the EU was held (cf. p. 31). There is a continuing debate on Brexit in Britain between those in favour of the EU and the "Eurosceptics", who are usually to be found among the supporters of the nationalist right and the Conservative party but also among Labour Party members. Anti-European propaganda is to be found particularly in tabloid papers like the *Sun* or the *Daily Mail*.

Main arguments of the Eurosceptics

According to Eurosceptics, the EU is
- expensive to run,
- dominated by wealthy countries at the expense of the less affluent members,
- too powerful and undemocratic
- trying to impose regulation in policy areas that should be the responsibility of national governments (e. g. health, education, law, tax, etc.),
- corrupt and money-wasting,
- a security risk with its open borders,
- host to millions of immigrants, some of them hostile and violent.

Arguments in favour of the European Union

- has created the world's largest international trade market
- choice to live and work anywhere in the EU
- formerly poor countries have prospered in the EU; poor regions receive special grants
- cooperation on crime (Europol)
- many laws to ensure better environmental, consumer and health standards
- free medical aid for tourists
- easier and cheaper travel
- improved human rights legislation

Brexit

Keyword
Brexit: shorthand way of saying the UK is leaving the EU – merging the words **Brit**ain and **exit**

Cause: referendum on 23 June 2016 → „Leave“ campaign won by 52 % to 48 %.
The referendum turnout was 71.8 %, with more than 30 million people voting.

UK Breakdown

England voted for Brexit by 53.4 % to 46.6 %
Wales voted for Brexit by 52.5 % to 47.5 %.
Scotland and Northern Ireland both backed staying in the EU.
Scotland backed Remain by 62 % to 38 %.
Northern Ireland voted Remain by 55.8 % to 44.2 %.

After the referendum

Prime Minister David Cameron, who was against Brexit, resigned.
Britain was supposed to leave the EU on 29 March 2019, but the departure date had to be postponed. There were lengthy negotiations after the referendum. Basically, they concerned the ‘deal’, the conditions under which the UK would leave the EU. The outcome of these negotiations was the “Withdrawal Agreement”, which covered several key points, the most controversial of which dealt with the border between the Republic of Ireland and Northern Ireland. This border, which is invisible today, would become an external border of the EU. Hardening this border was an unpopular idea for many. Although the Withdrawal Agreement was approved by the EU and UK negotiators, it was never approved by the British Parliament. Prime Minister Theresa May’s deal was rejected three times by Parliament. Therefore, she resigned.

In July 2019, Boris Johnson became Prime Minister and promised to take Britain out of the EU by 31 October, with or without a deal, but this deadline was again extended to 31 January 2020.
Johnson persuaded enough opposition MPs to agree to an early general election. His Conservative Party won an 80-seat majority, which in turn voted for his Withdrawal Agreement (“Get Brexit done.”). The most important changes to the deal agreed by Theresa May with the EU concerned the Irish border after Brexit.
The new agreement replaced the controversial Irish backstop plan in Theresa May’s deal. It established a customs border between Northern Ireland (which is part of the UK) and the Republic of Ireland (which is part of the EU), but in practice there are no border checks. The actual checks are between Great Britain and the island of Ireland, with goods being checked at “points of entry” into Northern Ireland.
On 31 January 2020, Britain left the EU. There was a transition period until 31 December 2020. During this transition period, everything stayed as it was. In the meantime, there were to be negotiations on the future relationship between the UK and the EU regarding

all details. The Corona crisis hit Britain in spring 2020, which further hindered progress of the negotiations with the EU.
Finally, Britain and the EU reached a deal just in time on 24 December: The deal contained new rules for how the UK and EU will live, work and trade together. Important issues were workers' rights, social and environmental regulations, travel, fishing and financial services. The UK now follows its own trade policy and hopes to negotiate deals with other countries, particularly with the US, Australia and New Zealand.
Most importantly, there is no longer freedom of movement between the UK and the EU. For longer stays, people now need visas.
Many of the EU's rules stay in effect in Northern Ireland in order to avoid a hard border with the Republic of Ireland. Checks are carried out on goods leaving Northern Ireland for Great Britain. At the time FiNALE 2023 is being written, the agreement on the Irish border is in question. Pro-British Unionists in Northern Ireland fear alienation from the UK. The UK has demanded renegotiation of the agreement, which the EU rejects.
For up-to-date information you should check e. g. bbc.com, guardian.com or TLDR News on YouTube, especially shortly before your English exam, in order to deal with a possible task on Britain leaving the EU and its consequences.

Consequences of Brexit

Free movement between the UK and EU has ended. Europeans living in the UK must have permits from the UK government allowing them to remain.
New border rules have led to a significant disruption of trade and delays on the border. Travellers between the EU and the UK must have passports ready to show.
The UK must pay a "divorce bill" of approximately 34 billion pounds by 2064. This is to fulfil any remaining financial commitments made while a member of the EU.
The economy has slowed, and many businesses have moved their headquarters to the EU. Employers are having a hard time finding employees. One reason is that EU workers left the UK and immigration rules are stricter. This hits low-skilled and medium-skilled occupations most. Shortage of lorry drivers has led to supply shortages.
The UK must negotiate new trade agreements with countries outside of the EU, which had more than 45 trade agreements with over 70 countries.

Consequences for EU

Brexit has weakened forces in the EU that favour integration and multiculturalism. Members of right-wing, anti-immigration, anti-EU parties in France and Germany are becoming stronger. However, the majority of EU citizens still strongly support the union.

Scotland

Scotland's First Minister, Nicola Sturgeon, said it is "democratically unacceptable" that Scotland has to leave the EU when it voted overwhelmingly to remain. There might be a second independence referendum for the country (cf. Devolution, p. 29).

Northern Ireland

The Republic of Ireland is part of the EU. Northern Ireland voted to remain. Some politicians see this as a reason for a vote on reunification. We will have to wait and see how this issue develops (see above).

Multicultural Society

Keyword
Imperial Act (1914): Inhabitants of the colonies were given British citizenship.

- Between the 1960s and 1980s, many Indians, Pakistanis and Bangladeshis immigrated to Britain. They now form the largest immigrant communities.
- Many of them settled in the Midlands or in towns in Lancashire, Yorkshire and Strathclyde, where they worked in the textile industry.

Britain today

- Britain consists of three countries (England, Scotland, Wales). Together with Northern Ireland it forms the United Kingdom. 12.4 % of the population in the UK were born abroad (2013).[2]
- **Ethnic diversity** enriches Britain, not only when it comes to music, fashion and food.
- Many embrace the possibilities and advantages of ethnic diversity (such as the former Foreign Secretary Robin Cook, who said that Chicken Tikka Masala "is now a true British national dish"[3]).
- Others fear that "Britishness" will eventually be lost; they interpret multiculturalism as meaning that various cultures coexist peacefully but without having a common basis of shared values.
- **Second generation immigrants,** i. e. children born to parents who immigrated to Britain prior to (or shortly after) their children's birth, face a variety of problems:
  - They often experience a clash of cultures. Outside their parents' home they adopt a western lifestyle, similar to that of their friends and classmates. At home, however, they live according to values, beliefs and traditions typical of their parents' home countries, which many of these children and teenagers have never visited. Quite often they do not speak their parents' language any more either. For some, the transition between these two different lifestyles is not easy.
  - They have difficulties when it comes to living up to the expectations of their parents, friends, teachers, etc.
  - They often face discrimination.

2 http://visual.ons.gov.uk/uk-perspectives-a-recent-history-of-international-migration (accessed on 1 April 2022)
3 "Robin Cook's *Chicken Tikka Masala Speech*", *The Guardian*, 19 April 2001, https://www.guardian.co.uk/world/2001/apr/19/race.britishidentity (accessed on 1 April 2022)

Glossary – Tradition and Change

act/law; bill the law	Gesetz; Gesetzesentwurf das Gesetz
agreement	Abkommen
asylum seekers	Asylsuchende
to blend in	sich einfügen / integrieren
citizenship	Nationalität, Staatsangehörigkeit
clash between/of two cultures	das Aufeinanderprallen zweier Kulturen
citizen	Bürger/-in
conservative Conservative Party a conservative	konservativ die Conservative Party ein/-e Konservative/-r
constitution	Verfassung
delegate	Delegierte/-r
democracy	Demokratie
to discriminate against someone	jemanden benachteiligen/diskriminieren
to elect to be elected election electorate election period election campaign	wählen gewählt werden Wahl Wählerschaft Wahlperiode Wahlkampf
ethnic minorities ethnicity	ethnische Minderheiten Ethnizität/Volkszugehörigkeit
executive	die Exekutive
federal	Bundes-...
government govern	Regierung regieren
to hold racist attitudes	eine rassistische Einstellung haben
House	Kammer des Parlaments
imperialism; imperialistic	Imperialismus; imperialistisch
indefinite leave to remain	unbeschränkte Aufenthaltserlaubnis
judiciary	die Judikative
labour	Arbeit
Labour Party	die Labour Party
legislature legislative	die Legislative gesetzgebend
loss of identity	Identitätsverlust

minister prime minister (the Prime Minister) ministry	Minister Premierminister Ministerium
Member of Parliament (MP)	Abgeordnete/-r
mutual understanding and respect	gegenseitiges Verständnis und Respekt
office to hold office Home Office; Foreign Office	Amt/Ministerium ein Amt innehaben Innenministerium; Außenministerium
open-minded; narrow-minded	aufgeschlossen; engstirnig
outsider	Außenseiter/-in
parliament	Parlament
party	Partei
policy economic policy foreign policy	politisches Ziel / Maßnahmen Wirtschaftspolitik Außenpolitik
pluralistic society	eine pluralistische Gesellschaft
politics political politician	Politik politisch Politiker/-in
poll polling station	Abstimmung/Umfrage/Wahl Wahllokal
racial equality	Gleichwertigkeit verschiedener Rassen
to receive / to be granted citizenship	die Staatsbürgerschaft erhalten
referendum	Volksbefragung, Volksentscheid
representative	(Volks-)Vertreter/-in
secretary foreign secretary	Minister/-in Außenminister/-in
the people	das Volk
to support	unterstützen
vote to vote voter	Stimme abstimmen/wählen Wähler/-in
wing right/left wing	Flügel rechter/linker Flügel (einer Partei)

Voices from the African Continent: Focus on Nigeria

From Empire to Commonwealth

Keywords

Postcolonialism: This term, first used in the middle of the 20th century, refers to the time after the British had left the colonies, i. e. after their formal rule over the colonies had come to an end.
Political independence did not necessarily lead to economic independence. The withdrawal of the British regularly revealed imperialism's harmful legacy, often resulting in problems for the former colonies. Postcolonial nations therefore often struggle to set up a functioning government which guarantees the people the freedom they dream of.

The Commonwealth: a group of 52 states; many former British colonies joined at the end of the decolonisation process; aims at racial equality and national sovereignty; Queen is the head of the Commonwealth

- At the **beginning of the 17th century**, Britain started to expand its empire across the globe.
- In most cases, the British colonisers ruled with brutal force, seizing land at will, ending rebellion in bloodshed, causing widespread famine as well as implementing slavery and exterminating whole ethnic groups.

- **After the Second World War**, the British Empire changed rapidly.
- Most British colonies had become independent by 1970, but a large number of them stayed closely connected with their former coloniser by joining the Commonwealth.

- While the British ruled the colonies, they regarded their culture, values, traditions and language as superior to those of the colonised.
- Now, after independence, the colonised faced the difficult task of recreating their own identity, bridging the gap between their country's native traditions and values and British ones.
- As people from member countries of the Commonwealth were allowed to immigrate to Britain, lots of people did so in the second half of the 20th century. First they were welcomed, as workers were needed after the Second World War, but in the 1970s, when more and more workers faced unemployment because of the economic crisis, immigration came to be seen more critically.

- Much **postcolonial writing** – both from former the colonies and in Britain – deals with the issue of being caught between two cultures or of trying to find one's identity.

Postcolonialism in an Anglophone Culture: Nigeria

Keywords

The Transatlantic Slave Trade: As part of the trade triangle between Europe, Africa and America, enslaved Africans were transported by Western European slave traders to the Americas, where they had to work on tobacco, coffee, sugar, cotton and cocoa plantations. The transatlantic slave trade started in the late 15th / early 16th century, with the Portuguese being the first nation to engage in it. They were soon followed by other European nations, in particular the British, Spanish, Dutch and French. The trade lasted until the 19th century, when most European countries prohibited slave trade and ended slavery.

Protectorate: (from Latin "protegere" = "protect") a country protected and ruled by another country, often one with superior military power (in Nigeria's case, the British)

Republic: a country in which the power is held by representatives elected by the people

Military rule: a government by an authoritarian body, controlled by the military instead of being elected by the people

Nigerian history

A short overview of British rule in Nigeria and the country's way to independence

- late 15th century: Nigeria starts to be affected by the transatlantic slave trade led by the Portuguese, from whom the Christian religion is initially adopted.
- 18th century: British replace Portuguese as the driving force of the slave trade.
- 1851: Lagos is invaded by British forces and formally annexed in 1865.
- 1901: Nigeria becomes a British protectorate.
- 1914: British protectorates of Northern and Southern Nigeria are joined.
- 1 October 1960: Nigeria succeeds in gaining independence from Britain.
- 1963: Nigeria becomes a republic but remains a member of the Commonwealth.
- 1966: The Nigerian Republic surrenders to military rule.
- 1967: A separatist movement leads to the "Republic of Biafra", and the three-year Nigerian Civil War breaks out, in which over 1 million people lose their lives.
- 1979: Nigeria becomes a single republic again, but the military seize power again in 1983.
- 1993: Plans to establish a third republic are dissolved by the Nigerian dictator, General Sani Abacha. After his death in 1998, a fourth republic is established in 1999, after almost three decades of military rule. President Obasanjo rules until 2007, from 2004 under emergency legislation.
- In 2007, Umaru Yar'Adua is elected president but dies after a long illness in 2010. Goodluck Ebele Jonathan, who had already been acting president, succeeds him.
- In 2015, Jonathan loses in the elections against Muhammadu Buhari, who is also the current president.
- Obasanjo, Jonathan and Buhari were all military generals at one time in their career.

Nigeria today[1]

- **General information:** The country's official name is "Federal Republic of Nigeria"; it is located on the western coast of Africa. The capital is Abuja, the largest and most important city is Lagos. Due to its booming economy and large population it is often referred to as the "Giant of Africa". The country's geography is diverse, with climates ranging from arid to humid/equatorial.
- **Culture:** With its many languages spoken by various ethnic groups, Nigeria has a very rich and diverse national culture. Nigeria is also known for its English language literature. Among the most famous Nigerian writers are Chinua Achebe *(Things Fall Apart)* and the winner of the Nobel Prize for Literature, Wole Soyinka. Since the 1990s, the Nigerian film industry, also dubbed "Nollywood", has become important for the whole of Africa.
- **Society:** Nigeria is considered to be the seventh most populous country in the world and the most populous one in Africa, with the world's third highest youth population after India and China. Primary education, free and compulsory, begins at age six and lasts for six years. Secondary education is free and compulsory for three years. There are 400 universities in Nigeria. The population is half urban, half rural. Over 500 languages are spoken by the more than 250 ethnic groups living in Nigeria. English serves as the official language. In addition to English, Hausa, Yoruba, Igbo, Fula and English Creole are widely spoken. Many of the languages exist in written form. Just over 53 % of the population are Muslim (mainly in the north); about 46 % are Christians of various denominations.
- The Nigerian **legal and judicial system** contains three codes of law: customary law, Nigerian statute law (following English law) and Sharia (Islamic law).
- **Economy and the environment**: Nigeria is regarded as an emerging global power, due to its oil and natural gas industry, especially in the south of the country. The GDP in 2020 was 432.3 billion USD, i. e. 2,083 per capita.

Challenges

- Nigeria's rapidly growing population causes several problems, e. g. poverty and the inability to provide enough food for everyone without relying on food imports.
- 43 % of the population are under 15, another 27 % are under 30 (2018). The youth literacy rate of the age group 15–24 is 75 %. However, unemployment poses a major challenge.
- inequality between men and women
- battling various forms of crime, e. g. organised crime (especially drug trafficking), child labour and female genital mutilation
- Religious tension between the two major faiths is rising, especially in the "middle belt" of the country. Religious fundamentalism can be noticed in both Muslim and Christian communities, a major cause being the uneven distribution of natural resources and hence wealth.

[1] Statistical information based on: https://www.bpb.de/internationales/weltweit/innerstaatliche-konflikte/176466/nigeria; https://www.britannica.com/place/Nigeria; https://data.unicef.org/country/nga/; http://data.un.org/en/iso/ng.html (all accessed on 1 April 2022)

- Inside the growing Nigerian cities, waste management is a problem and the fact that waste is often simply dumped outside the cities results in the pollution of both waterways and groundwater. Oil spills also threaten the environment.
- Terrorism is another major problem: the Islamic terrorist group Boko Haram is responsible for numerous attacks and the abduction of school children.
- In recent years, the Biafran hostilities between the two major ethnic groups in the south of the country, the Igbo and Yoruba has resurfaced. The conflict first came to a head in the Biafran Civil War (1967–1970) when the Igbo population of south-east Nigeria attempted to form a republic (Biafra) of their own. It remains unsolved, without any prospect of a positive outcome.

Glossary – Voices from the African Continent: Focus on Nigeria

civil war	Bürgerkrieg
corruption	Korruption
to adapt to sth.	sich an etwas anpassen
to be oppressed by someone	von jemandem unterdrückt werden
citizenship	Nationalität, Staatsangehörigkeit
clash between/of two cultures	das Aufeinanderprallen zweier Kulturen
colonialism; coloniser; colonised	Kolonialismus; die/der Besiedelnde; kolonisiert
to discriminate against someone	jemanden benachteiligen/diskriminieren
empire	das Imperium
ethnic minorities	ethnische Minderheiten
ethnicity	Ethnizität, Volkszugehörigkeit
to be excluded (from)	(von) etw. ausgeschlossen sein
to hold racist attitudes	eine rassistische Haltung/Einstellung haben
hostile	feindlich, feindselig, ablehnend
imperialism; imperialistic	Imperialismus; imperialistisch
indigenous	Einheimische/-r eines Landes
loss of identity	Identitätsverlust
hegemony	Vorherrschaft
famine	Hungersnot
infant mortality	Kindersterblichkeit
to bribe someone	jmd. bestechen
to regain independence	Unabhängigkeit wiedererlangen
independence-minded	nach Unabhängigkeit strebend
to decolonise	in die Unabhängigkeit entlassen
to thrive and prosper	wachsen und gedeihen

Globalisation and Global Challenges

Keyword

Globalisation: a worldwide movement, involving the integration of financial, economic and communications systems; often seen as an unstoppable process, affecting people all around the globe, no matter whether they live in industrialised or developing countries, in big cities or rural villages; transfer of goods, capital and services, as well as communications, made easier; not everyone profits from the development; smaller economies may suffer

The world is said to be getting smaller, i. e. it has become a "global village". The term was coined by Marshall McLuhan, a Canadian philosopher and media specialist.

It is not easy to say when globalisation actually started:
- Did it start with the discovery of America?
- Does it go even further back in time?
- Is it a phenomenon of the modern era?

Everyone can experience the results of globalisation, e. g. when
- travelling,
- keeping in touch with friends or business partners in distant countries with the help of new means of communication or
- buying goods which come from far away.

Globalisation is not always regarded as a positive process:
- Some people fear that individual cultures will finally blend into a single global culture, thereby losing all their characteristic features.
- Globalisation has failed the thousands of people in developing countries still suffering from malnutrition or dying of curable diseases.
- Others work under cruel working conditions, producing goods which will be shipped to and sold in industrialised countries at a low price.
- One of the latest financial crises, starting in the USA in 2008, shows that such catastrophes will ultimately affect other countries as well, as businesses are linked and global trade is the rule.
- Due to increased mobility, diseases like H1N1 ("Swine Flu") or the coronavirus can easily spread all around the globe, developing into a pandemic.
- The refugee crisis in Europe (peaking in 2015) can partly be seen as connected to globalisation: People from all over the world want to participate in growing economic wealth. Many of those from poor countries want to find a better future and leave their homes – just like people have always done over the centuries (e. g. emigration to America in the last two centuries). At the same time, civil and other wars as well as climate change force people to emigrate. As more and more countries close their borders, problems in many regions are growing. Among these problems are huge refugee camps and people drowning and starving during dangerous journeys (cf. also p. 49).

- Terrorism has become an ongoing global threat, which has led to a growing feeling of insecurity in many societies. In some countries (e.g. Israel) terrorist attacks have been permanent aspect of everyday life for six or seven decades. In most Western, as well as Middle Eastern countries, what we know as Islamist terrorism (Al-Qaeda, the "Islamic State") began with the "9/11" attacks on the World Trade Center in New York and the Pentagon in Washington on 11 September 2001. This led to the controversial „War on Terror" on the part of the USA and its allies. Since then, the world has seen a large number of terrorist attacks connected with Islamist ideology (e.g. in France, England, Nigeria and Germany) or with the ideology of white supremacy (e.g. in Christchurch in New Zealand or Utøya in Norway).

Aspects of Globalisation

Progress

- The development of planes, fast ships and trains made quick transportation of goods from one country to another possible.
- New means of communication, especially the internet, have made the collaboration of business partners much easier.
- Multinational companies have branches all over the world, and cost-effectiveness is a decisive factor when new production sites are set up.

Economic challenges

As today's customers wish to buy products at the best cost/performance ratio, the global market has become very **competitive,** with the following (and related) consequences:

- While global players consider efficiency, speed, flexibility and profits as most important, employees are increasingly unable to defend their rights.
- More and more jobs are being outsourced or off-shored to cut down production costs, thereby severely damaging local labour markets.
- When jobs are outsourced to low-wage countries, the workers often work in so-called **"sweatshops"** for long hours at a stretch, earning only minimum wages and under working conditions that are often inhumane. Safety measures in sweatshops are by no means comparable to western standards. Sadly, the lack of efficient safety measures often results in catastrophes. On 24 April 2013, a building housing several garment factories near Bangladesh's capital Dhaka collapsed, resulting in the death of more than 1,000 workers. Despite the fact that factory owners had previously been warned about deep cracks which appeared in the building's structure and had been ordered to evacuate the building, workers were sent in to work. Two weeks after the tragedy, a fire broke out in another clothing factory, killing several people.
- Critics like the Canadian journalist Naomi Klein accuse multinational companies of exploiting the poor and indirectly supporting child labour for their own profit.
- Workers often assemble products which they will never be able to afford or do not know how to use, e.g. computers.

- People in developing countries often live in poor conditions, without a decent education or access to new means of communication. Therefore they cannot reap the benefits of globalisation.
- Advocates of sweatshops claim that these factories provide work for the poor, enabling them to provide for their families. They also say that critics of sweatshops argue from a western point of view without considering the actual situation of people in developing countries. In order to reduce the number of sweatshops, fair trade is becoming increasingly important. Its aim is to ensure that workers and small-scale producers in poor countries are paid a fair price for their work and products.
- Despite these attempts, a growing number of experts and laypeople alike fear that the gap between the rich and the poor is widening.
- The close links and collaboration between companies all across the globe is both a blessing and a curse.

Ecological challenges and sustainable lifestyles

Environmental pollution is growing rapidly. The following factors in particular create global problems:
- Particularly in developed nations, rampant consumerism is still increasing **energy consumption and waste gases** from factories.
- Over the last decades the number of **vehicles** on the roads has steadily increased. Cars are no longer found only in industrialised countries. The number of people travelling by **plane** is also greater than ever, due to the fact that plane tickets have become affordable for a larger number of people. Short-haul **flights** have become particularly popular.
- **food miles:** Whereas some years ago many people bought fruit and vegetables locally and ate seasonal products, they now want to eat strawberries and cherries in December. Hence more goods are air-freighted. Ecologically conscious customers ask themselves whether it is better to buy local products than food (even fair trade) which has been flown across continents. The non-sustainable production of meat and dairy foods is another critical factor in global warming.
- **Greenhouse gases** such as carbon dioxide (CO_2) and methane cause chemical damage to the atmosphere (e. g. ozone hole) as well as global warming.

Global warming and its consequences

- As Al Gore explains in his film *An Inconvenient Truth,* greenhouse gases form a layer around the earth trapping heat and thereby causing the temperature on the ground to rise ("global warming").
- There are many consequences of climate change. Principally, extreme weather phenomena increase in strength and intensity, resulting in, for example, floods, heavy rainfall in some regions and drought in others as well as melting polar ice caps.
- Biodiversity is likewise threatened, as many plants, flowers and animals die out. Desertification (see below) is an increasingly frequent phenomenon today: Due to

overgrazing[1], over-extraction of groundwater, unwise use of water resources, e.g. diverting rivers for industrial use or human consumption, deforestation ("slash-and-burn farming") and rising soil salinity (amount of salt in the ground), vast areas of land in relatively dry areas deteriorate and become useless (desertification).

Attempts to reduce global warming

- Environmental sustainability is on the agenda of many governments and has been an important topic at various summits to date. Significant results are nonetheless still rare.
- The **Kyoto Protocol** from 2005 aimed to reduce the emission of greenhouse gases by an annual 5.2% by the year 2012, taking 1990 levels as a basis for most countries.
- **Paris UN Climate Change Conference (2015):** A global agreement on the reduction of climate change (Paris Agreement) has been reached and adopted by 195 countries. Among the decisions made was the resolution to limit the long-term increase of global average temperature to well below 2°C above pre-industrial levels. The agreement went into effect on 4 November 2016, as enough countries ratified it. The USA withdrew their consent to the agreement under President Trump.
- On his first day in office, President Biden fulfilled a promise he made during his election campaign and returned to the Paris Climate Agreement.
- **Glasgow UN Climate Change Conference (2021):** In the face of urgently needed action, COP 26 failed to implement significant policies. Participants agreed on reducing coal mining, phasing out cars that run on fossil fuels (a resolution Germany was notably absent from) and halting deforestation. These pledges, however, remain first tentative steps. More significantly perhaps, there was strong disagreement on how developed nations should offer financial compensation for their long-standing contributions to climate change.

Fridays for Future

- In August 2018, Greta Thunberg, a then 16-year-old Swedish student, started protesting outside the Swedish parliament in Stockholm in order to raise awareness of the dangers of climate change.
- According to Thunberg, politicians are not taking enough action against climate change, which is putting our planet's future at risk. Thunberg's solitary school strikes soon caught the attention of the media in countries all over the world.
- Up to May 2019, an estimated 1.4 million teenagers and young adults worldwide followed her example by going on strike from school every Friday and protesting against climate change. This movement, known as "Fridays for Future", was seriously hampered by the COVID-19 pandemic.
- Greta Thunberg has delivered several public speeches in which she has put pressure on politicians and world leaders to combat climate change more swiftly and resolutely. She spoke at various important global meetings, e.g. the United Nations Climate

[1] One speaks of "overgrazing" if the number of cattle on a piece of land is too high to be sustainable (in the long term).

Change Conference in Katowice, Poland in December 2018 and at the 2019 UN Climate Action Summit, to which she arrived by boat.
- The speed of the reaction and the immense sums of money provided by governments during the COVID-19 crisis seem to prove Fridays for Future's point: Immediate global action is possible, but the governments all over the world do not seem to regard an effective fight against global warming as a top priority.

Conflict between economic and ecological aspects of globalisation

- Companies face global competition: cost-effectiveness and profits seem more important than ecological issues.
- Some governments are hesitant to set up strict laws to protect the environment, as this might drive away multinational companies that offer employment.
- As environmental pollution does not stop at borders, international cooperation is crucial – and will become even more so in future.

Sustainable lifestyles

- There is a growing awareness among consumers that due to various global challenges our current lifestyles have to change to more sustainable ones. Some of these changes can be put into action by each individual himself/herself, others have to be initiated and carried out by governments, e. g. reforming urban life by planning cities according to citizens' needs.
- Some of the changes everyone can implement individually are:
  - Eating fewer animal products:
    Large amounts of water are needed to produce animal-based food, while the animals' manure pollutes the groundwater. The more meat we eat, the more industrial factory farming is booming. Prices for meat are relatively low compared to the prices for other groceries. Ethical questions also have to be considered when it comes to the consumption of animal-based food. In addition, working conditions in meat factories are often questionable, with workers barely making minimum wage and working overtime.
  - Buying regional products:
    Supporting local shops and producers instead of merely resorting to online shopping reduces the ecological cost of transportation. Additionally, buying fruit and vegetables when they are in season makes it more likely that these are not sourced in from distant countries. In addition, food waste can be reduced by only buying the groceries one needs instead of buying in bulk and running the risk of food going bad.
    Using public means of transport, car sharing, bikes, etc. to get from A to B is a quick way to fight CO_2 production.
  - Producing less waste:
    This sound fairly straightforward but can make a huge difference. It really is that simple: The less waste one produces, the less of it can cause environmental pollution.

- Buying less but better:
  If one buys less or buys products second-hand, one actively helps to minimise electronic and textile waste. In many cases, defective items can be repaired. In case of clothing, the idea of a “capsule wardrobe”, where a person possesses a limited number of good-quality key items that can be mixed and matched with one another, becomes more and more popular. Studies have shown that lots of pieces of clothing in our wardrobes are never or seldomly worn. Why not swap unwanted but wearable pieces of clothing with other people? Or why not consider buying second-hand? Gadgets which one only temporarily needs, e. g., electric power drills or other tools, can also rented or shared with others.

There are many more things each one of us can change about our lifestyles to transform them from a consumption-orientated to a more sustainable one. Basically, all these changes aim at reducing one’s carbon footprint. Of course, not everything works for everyone, but even minor changes make a difference.

Corona – a virus that changed the world

- COVID-19 (Coronavirus disease 2019) is a highly infectious disease with symptoms usually similar to those of the common flu, e.g. fever, cough and shortness of breath. In more severe cases, it impacts on a wide variety of organs, including the heart and lungs, possibly resulting in chronic health issues or even death. People with a weakened immune system as well as older persons run a higher risk of experiencing severe symptoms, in worst cases multi-organ failure, but most cases only exhibit light symptoms.
- Due to intense and efficient research, several vaccines against COVID-19 were developed, but the availability in different countries varies, as does the vaccination strategy. Most countries, e.g. Germany, prioritised certain population groups regarded as vulnerable before vaccinating other sections of the population.
- The number of people having received at least one vaccination against COVID-19 is growing rapidly. The WHO (World Health Organisation) reports that, as of 15 March 2022, a total of 11 billion vaccine doses had been administered.
- COVID-19 was first identified in Wuhan, China in December 2019. It is thought to have been transmitted from animals to humans at a seafood and animal market. On 31 December 2019, Chinese authorities informed the WHO of the outbreak of a new form of pneumonia. Since then it has spread across the world.
- On 12 January 2020, the WHO named this previously unknown form of the coronavirus disease COVID-19, and on 20 March 2020, it was officially declared a pandemic.
- As of 15 March 2022, almost 460 million cases and over 6 million deaths had been reported.

How countries and governments attempt to tackle the virus

- Governments all across the globe are encouraging the public to take up basic protective measures for the sake of both themselves and others, e.g. frequently washing

one's hands, avoid touching one's face, practise respiratory hygiene, social distancing, wearing face masks.
- In some countries wearing a mask or covering your mouth and nose with a scarf or piece of cloth is obligatory while out in public. Shops and service providers with in-person contact are required to limit the number of people inside and/or to ascertain that all customers are fully vaccinated or recently recovered from an infection. Getting tested and/or providing negative test results in writing several times a week is mandatory for German teachers and students (March 2022).
- In order to "flatten the curve", i.e. restrict the number of new infections so that health services can still cope, many countries have imposed restrictions at some point during the pandemic: closing schools, kindergartens, restaurants and shops not necessary to fulfil basic needs, restricting or banning visitors from hospitals and nursing homes and imposing travel restrictions, e. g. closing borders or imposing quarantine on people crossing national borders. People wishing to enter Germany temporarily faced a test obligation and were only allowed to enter the country if they could provide proof of a negative test result no older than 48 hours.
- Businesses were required to allow their employees to work from home to limit personal contacts. Events that attract large crowds, such as concerts, theatre performances and festivals were often cancelled.
- Hospitals and clinics in some countries have faced difficulties meeting the increasing demand for intensive care due to COVID-19.

Consequences of these governmental measures

- Economic: Closing shops put severe strain on shop owners and employees. Many governments, including that of Germany, have installed programmes that offered some financial compensation. It was feared that many companies would not survive the restrictions during the pandemic.
- Personal: The number of people working from home has increased drastically due to changes in the organisation of the workplace and as a result of schools and kindergartens closing frequently. Many parents struggle to balance childcare and work. Governments encouraged families not to visit grandparents and family members at risk or even forbade visits, which can lead to isolation and loneliness. Digital media have therefore played an important role in keeping in touch with one another while being physically apart.
- Neighbourly help has become more important, e. g. doing grocery shopping for those at risk and checking regularly on those affected by the virus.
- After over two years of living with and fighting COVID-19, many countries are lifting some of the restrictions as milder mutations of the virus and an increasing number of fully vaccinated citizens lead to less severe infections.
- On 24 February 2022, the UK released the "Living with Covid-19" plan. It focuses on everyone's personal responsibility to keep the virus in check. While legal restrictions were lifted, UK citizens are still encouraged to become fully vaccinated and to act sensibly to avoid spreading the virus.

The UN and the EU

The UN

- 24 October 1945: A group of 51 countries founded the United Nations (UN) as a replacement/successor for the League of Nations.
- The UN headquarters is located in New York City and the current Secretary General is António Guterres.
- The UN has 193 member states (April 2022).
- It defends human rights and fundamental freedoms.

Five of six **main organs** of the UN (General Assembly, Security Council, Economic and Social Council, Trusteeship Council and Secretariat) are located in New York City, while the International Court of Justice is in The Hague in the Netherlands.
There are **various programmes** and funds affiliated to the UN. Two of the best known are UNICEF (United Nations Children's Fund) and the UNHCR (Office of the United Nations High Commissioner for Refugees). The latter deals with the needs of refugees and displaced persons in post-conflict countries, e. g. Djibouti.

Aims of the UN

- to preserve international peace and security
- to promote friendly relations between member countries
- to support international cooperation with regard to economic, social and cultural as well as humanitarian issues
- Apart from **peacekeeping** and **peacemaking** operations, **peacebuilding** has become more and more important.
- The UN and its affiliated organisations work to equip national groups with the necessary skills in conflict management and to ensure that lasting peace can be established.
- Currently (April 2022), the UN is involved in twelve peacekeeping operations, e. g. in Cyprus, Mali and the Democratic Republic of the Congo.
- **Humanitarian aid** is also of major importance, e. g. providing relief for people affected by either man-made or natural disasters and helping refugees and displaced persons.
- Other main concerns of the UN are **international law and development**, e. g. sustainable development, agriculture, international trade.

The EU

- Currently 27 states belong to the European Union (EU). The newest members are Bulgaria and Romania, which both joined the EU on 1 January 2007, and Croatia, which became a member on 1 July 2013.
- After the Second World War there was a desire for a united Europe in order to prevent extreme forms of nationalism. The European Coal and Steel Community, the European Economic Community (EEC) and the European Atomic Energy Community (Euratom) were merged into the European Community (EC) in 1967.

- The EU as we know it came into existence in 1993, when the Maastricht Treaty – which, among other things, initiated the euro as common currency – was ratified. The individual member states came to be regarded as a single global player.
- At present the EU faces the challenge of maintaining its unity – and indeed remaining a union at all – in the face of the refugee crisis, to which EU countries have very differing attitudes. The current Russian invasion of Ukraine will likely also put the unity within the EU to the test.
- In 2020, the United Kingdom left the EU ("Brexit", cf. p. 31).
- On 24 February 2022, the Russian army invaded Ukraine. This aggression is condemned by the EU and other countries worldwide. EU countries agreed on swift political, financial and humanitarian support for Ukraine and imposed severe sanctions on Russia.

Aims of the EU

- to promote prosperity and social progress with European citizenship for its peoples while still keeping their diversity alive
- to promote friendly relations between member countries
- to guarantee freedom and justice for the European peoples
- to internationally represent the member states with a single voice, tackling the various challenges of globalisation as well as respecting human rights

When it comes to defence, the individual member countries are sovereign. However, there is military cooperation in peacekeeping missions.
The three main groups which make up the EU are the **Council of Ministers,** the **European Parliament** and the **European Commission.**
Although the EU has no capital, the official seat of the European Commission, the Council of the European Union and the second seat of the European Parliament are located in Brussels, Belgium.

International peacekeeping

International peacekeeping is one of the aims of the UN:
- Once peace has been established in a country or region, peacekeepers are sent to the country or region in question to oversee the peace process.
- This can be done by supervising elections, providing reconstruction aid and managing the withdrawal of combatants.
- Very often, UN peacekeepers are soldiers, but they can also be police officers or other civilian personnel.
- The UN Security Council authorises peacekeeping missions, which are then carried out by the international community.
- Many of these missions are organised and led by the UN, even though the UN itself has no army. While the troops acting as peacekeepers are under the control of the UN, they still belong to the armed forces of their country of origin. The UN itself is controlled by the Security Council and the UN Secretariat. This reduces the risk that one peacekeeping party only follows its own interests.

- Regional organisations (e.g. NATO) can be authorised by the UN to lead peacekeeping missions. These regional organisations can also organise peacekeeping missions of their own.

Migration – a global challenge

- Migration has been a worldwide phenomenon since the beginning of human history.
- People have had a number of reasons for leaving their places of origin: poverty and the dream of a better life elsewhere, climatic reasons, wars and civil unrest or religious persecution, to name only the most important.[2]
- One has to distinguish between migrants and refugees:
- **Migrants** leave their countries of origin for a limited period of time or permanently, usually for economic reasons. They might have job offers in a different country or they might have heard of good opportunities. Examples of this are emigration from European countries to the USA in the 19th century, immigrants from Poland to the Ruhr district (also during the 19th century), migrant workers inside Europe today, for example to help on farms, as carers for elderly people or to work in hospitals, and people from Africa trying to find better living conditions in Europe.
- **Refugees** usually flee their homes in order to escape persecution or wars. Unlike migrants, refugees are forced to leave their home countries. Examples of this at present are the Ukrainians fleeing the Russian invasion and Syrian or Afghan people fleeing to Europe. An important example from the past are the Jews from Germany and other countries, who had to flee from the Nazis.
- The International Migration Report of the UN from 2022 states that migration has increased worldwide, with most migrants going to Europe, Asia and North America. The countries with the most immigrants are the USA, Germany and Saudi Arabia. According to the UN, as of 2022, there were about 281 million people living in countries other than the ones they were born in.
- The UNHCR (United Nations refugee agency) states in its statistical report covering trends and developments up to the end of 2021 that the world is now witnessing the highest levels of displacement on record. 82.4 million people around the world have been forced to leave their homes. Among them are nearly 26.4 million refugees, over half of whom are under the age of 18. 48 million are internal refugees, i.e. they flee from one part of the country to another (e.g. Nigeria). There are 4.1 million asylum seekers worldwide. However, 73 % of refugees stay in neighbouring countries: Syrian refugees mainly flee to Turkey, Jordan and other countries close by. More than half the refugees worldwide at present come from Syria, Afghanistan and South Sudan.
- In 2020, Turkey hosted the largest refugee population worldwide, with 3.6 million refugees and asylum seekers, followed by Colombia (1.8 million), Lebanon (1.6 million), Pakistan (1.4 million) and Uganda (1.4 million). Most refugees come from Syria (6.6 million), Venezuela (3.7 million), Afghanistan (2.7 million), South Sudan (2.2 million)

[2] Information based on:
https://www.un.org/en/development/desa/population/migration/publications/migrationreport/docs/MigrationReport2019_Highlights.pdf; https://www.unhcr.org/figures-at-a-glance.html; https://refugeesmigrants.un.org/refugees-compact; https://www.refugeesinternational.org/reports-overview (all websites accessed on 1 April 2022)

and Myanmar (1.1 million). Over 4 million people have fled the Ukraine in the current war (April 2022).
- There are also millions of stateless people who have been denied nationality and access to basic rights such as education, healthcare, employment and freedom of movement.
- About 1 percent of the world's population have fled their homes.
- Nearly 1 person is forcibly displaced every two seconds as a result of conflict or persecution.
- The fact that most refugees seek help in neighbouring, not always wealthy countries can cause major problems there: The population of these countries has to share access to education, healthcare and jobs with the refugees. Compared to rich nations like Germany, countries like Jordan or the Lebanon find it far more difficult to cope with the situation. Colombia is another example of these conflicts, as it only just beginning to overcome the effects of a civil war. Recently it has also been the destination of over 1 million refugees from Venezuela.
- On the other hand, migration always also means enrichment: The destination country will, with time, integrate the new arrivals. Their culture, beliefs and customs will become part of the country, thus leading to a more diverse culture in general.
- Many migrants and refugees wish to return to their home countries if the situation allows them to. Seasonal migrants, for example, usually leave their families behind and return when their work has finished for the year, and refugees often want to return to their old home after the end of a war. Others would like to stay in their new home and build a new life there.

Glossary – Globalisation

Americanisation	Amerikanisierung
anti-globalist	Globalisierungsgegner/-in
backwardness	Rückständigkeit
company philosophy	Geschäfts-/Firmenphilosophie
competition to be competitive	Konkurrenz(kampf)/Wettbewerb konkurrenzfähig sein
corporate identity	Firmenimage
crop diseases	Krankheiten von Pflanzen/Saatgut
debt relief	Schuldenerlass, Entschuldung
desertification	die Desertifikation/Wüstenbildung, das Vordringen der Wüste
developing countries	Entwicklungsländer
development aid	Entwicklungshilfe
driving forces of globalisation	die Antriebskräfte der Globalisierung
drought	Dürre, Dürreperioden

earth's atmosphere	die Erdatmosphäre
economic growth	Wirtschaftswachstum
economic prosperity	ökonomischer Wohlstand
emerging markets	Schwellenländer
environmental commitment	Umwelteinsatz
environmental damage	Umweltzerstörung
environmentally friendly	umweltfreundlich
expansion of capitalism	Ausbreitung des Kapitalismus
fair trade	fairer Handel
floods	Hochwasser, Überschwemmungen
global interconnection	globale Querverbindungen
global marketplace	globaler Marktplatz
global player	Weltfirma
global super power	globale Supermacht
global warming	Erderwärmung
greenhouse gases	Treibhausgase
human rights	Menschenrechte
human-generated greenhouse gases	durch Menschen produzierte Treibhausgase
to increase profit margins	die Gewinnspanne erhöhen
Industrial Age	das Industriezeitalter
industrial nations	Industrieländer/-nationen
interdependence of economy and ecology	gegenseitige Abhängigkeit/Verflechtung von Ökonomie und Ökologie
international stock markets	internationale Börsenmärkte
investment climate	Investitionsbedingungen
labour laws	Arbeitsgesetze
labour market	Arbeitsmarkt
long-range goals	langfristige Ziele
low-wage countries	Niedriglohnländer
mass communication; mass media	Massenkommunikation; Massenmedien
mass tourism	Massentourismus
melting of glaciers	das Schmelzen von Gletschern
micro-credits	Kleinkredite
NGO (non-governmental organisation)	Nichtregierungsorganisation
outsourcing	Produktionsverlagerung
political turmoil	politischer Aufruhr, politische Turbulenzen

pollution	Verschmutzung
population overshoot, overpopulation, excess of population	Überbevölkerung
poverty	Armut
reduce greenhouse gas emissions	den Ausstoß von Treibhausgasen reduzieren
reduce the cost of production	die Produktionskosten senken
rise in global temperature	weltweiter Temperaturanstieg
robotised production	computergesteuerte Produktion/Fertigung
short-haul flights	Kurzstreckenflüge
surface transport	Bodentransport
supremacy	Vormachtsstellung, Überlegenheit
sustainability	Nachhaltigkeit, Zukunftsfähigkeit
sweatshop	ausbeuterischer Betrieb
trade	Handel
trademark policy	Markenpolitik
undernutrition; malnutrition	Unterernährung; Mangelernährung
unemployment	Arbeitslosigkeit
working conditions	Arbeitsbedingungen

The Impact of Shakespearean Drama on Young Audiences Today

The Elizabethan Age

Keyword
The Elizabethan Age: named after Queen Elizabeth I, born 1533, crowned 1558, died 1603 (reign of 45 years)

Politics and economics

- England emerged as a world power
- international trade → rise of capitalism
- strongest naval force (defeat of Spanish Armada in 1588)
- internal problems: constant clash between Catholics and Protestants; firm establishment of Protestant Church with Elizabeth as head of the Church of England

Exploration of the New World

- Sir Francis Drake
- Sir Walter Raleigh

Culture

Keyword
The Golden Age: term used for the Renaissance in Britain at the time of Elizabeth I
- freedom of spirit → imagination
- Greek and Roman thought
- domestic study of the Bible, widely read and heard
- opened new worlds of history and poetry, stimulated English culture
- cultural flowering: theatre, music, poetry, art, architecture
- Writers: William Shakespeare, Christopher Marlowe, Edmund Spenser
- Architect: Inigo Jones (introduced Italianate architecture to England)
- Composers: Thomas Tallis, William Byrd

The era was dominated by contrast: life for ordinary people could be hard, but economic growth also meant better conditions for many.
negative aspects:
- harsh criminal laws (e.g. whipping and hanging for minor offences)
- illiteracy
- short life-expectancy
- no rights for women

positive aspects:
- public provision for the poor (possible because of economic growth)
- few beggars

The Elizabethan World Picture

The Great Chain of Being

- vertical chain, hierarchically ordered → universal order
- every single speck of creation a link in the chain → almost infinite chain
- place in the chain determined by the relative proportion of spirit and matter
- the more spirit the higher the place in the chain

Hierarchy of the chain

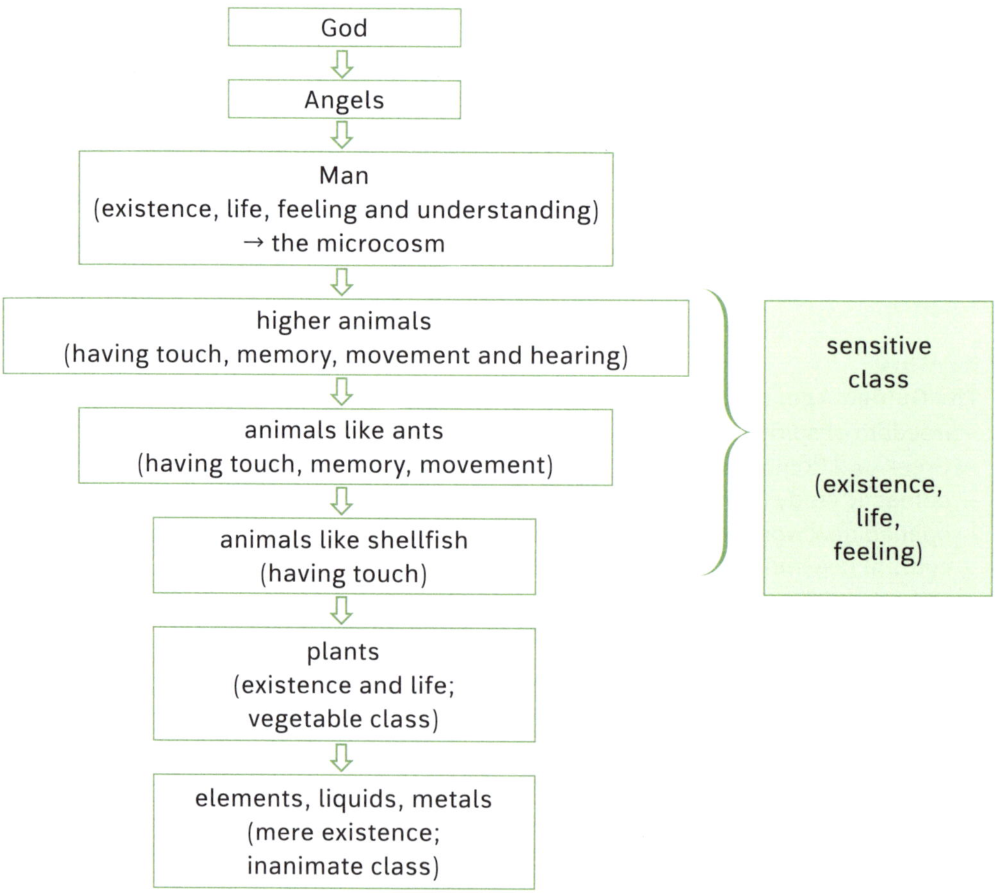

The hierarchical order also applies within the classes:
- Water is nobler than earth.
- Gold is nobler than silver.
- The oak is nobler than the bramble.
- The lion is nobler than the dog.

The corresponding planes

Different segments of the chain are reflected in other segments. This means there is universal interdependence, i. e. correspondences.

Corresponding planes

divine and angelic	universe or macrocosm	commonwealth or body politic
man or microcosm	lower creation	

The planes were connected by an immense net of correspondences.

> **Keyword**
> **Correspondences:** Since the planes were interconnected with each other, order and disorder in one plane had the same repercussions in the other planes as well. For instance, the sun governs the other planets as the father rules his children. Elizabethan literature abounds with examples of this idea: for example, King Lear's madness is mirrored in the thunderstorm he walks in, and on the night Macbeth murders the king, horses are seen eating one another.

Examples of correspondences

macrocosm/microcosm	storms and earthquakes in the macrocosm ↔ passions of human beings
macrocosm / body politic	hierarchy of sun/moon/rainbow ↔ hierarchy of king/princes/governors
body politic / microcosm	debates of king and council ↔ commotions in a person's mind

Elizabethan thinking in terms of correspondences led to the abundance of images in Elizabethan literature.

Elements and humours

Since the human being was seen as a microcosm (literally, a "little world"), it reflected the structure of the world as a whole, the macrocosm. The world was composed of four "elements" (earth, water, air, fire), the qualities of which were founded on the notions of hot and cold, dry and moist.
Correspondingly, the human body was composed of four substances called "humours" with characteristics corresponding to the four elements. Imbalance or "disorder" among the humours, i. e. when they did not exist in proper proportion to each other, caused illness.

element	humour	common quality
earth	melancholy	cold and dry
water	phlegm	cold and moist
air	blood	hot and moist
fire	choler	hot and dry

Elizabethan Drama

Important playwrights: William Shakespeare, Christopher Marlowe *(Dr. Faustus)*, Ben Jonson *(The Alchemist)*, later: John Webster *(The Duchess of Malfi)*.
Before the age of Elizabethan drama, plays were usually based on biblical stories and other religious themes. Elizabethan drama instead focussed on secular issues.

Elizabethan Theatre

Theatres in Elizabethan London were venues of mass entertainment.

Theatres

- were situated outside the city
- offered performances every day
- presented plays, dances and music
- were also used for bear baiting, cruel killing of bears
- were attended by people from all social ranks.

- All performances were presented during the day.
- There was no lighting or special sound effects.
- Women's roles were played by men.
- The audience could smoke, eat and drink.

→ Imagination depended totally on the language used in the play.

Common complaints about the theatre
- disorderly
- corrupts youth
- leads to evil and immoral ("ungodly") character and behaviour
- stage stories are morally uncontrolled and primitive, not religiously inspiring
- leads to lewdness
- keep people away from work and prayer
- attracts criminals

Types of Elizabethan plays

Histories

- glorified England's "heroic past", e. g. in Christopher Marlowe's *Edward II* and Shakespeare's *Henry IV, Henry V*
- served as vehicle for nationalistic pride and as propaganda for the monarch
- dramas like *Julius Caesar*, *Antony and Cleopatra* and *Macbeth* not considered histories because they do not deal with English history

Tragedies

- end in a catastrophe (death of the protagonist(s))
- catastrophe is a result of a character's flaw (Macbeth's ambition, Othello's jealousy)
- tragic hero still arouses sympathy and interest in his fate

Comedies

- happy ending
- often bawdy
- the audience went there for a good laugh
- sexual allusion and undertones very frequent even in tragedy: comic passages with strong sexual allusions often serve as comic relief (porter in *Macbeth,* Mercutio in *Romeo and Juliet)*

Romances

Shakespeare's late comedies (e. g. *The Winter's Tale, The Tempest)* are generally classified as romances. They are distinguished from comedies by certain elements:
- redemption, forgiveness, reuniting of long-lost family members
- magic
- pastoral setting (beautiful nature, virgin island)

Elizabethan Poetry
Sonnets

Keyword
Sonnet form: originally from Italy, 14th century
Sonnets were made popular by Francesco Petrarca (engl.: Petrarch).
The fashion of sonnet writing spread to France and England.

Important Elizabethan sonnet writers:
- Thomas Wyatt (introduced sonnets to England, translations from Petrarch)
- Sir Philipp Sidney
- Edmund Spenser
- John Donne
- William Shakespeare

The Italian (Petrarchan) sonnet

	rhyme scheme	
octave/octet	a	quatrain
	b	
	b	
	a	
	a	quatrain
	b	
	b	
	a	
turn		turn
sestet	c	tercet
	d	
	e	
	c	tercet
	d	
	e	

Characteristics of the sonnet
- addressed to a beloved
- 14 lines
- clearly defined rhyme scheme (the most common seen above)
- divided into an octet and a sestet
- turn after the octave

The turn after the octave is a shift of thought or feeling, often indicated by "but" or "yet". Variations of rhyme scheme within the conventional structure are justified by the function they serve.

The English (Shakespearean) sonnet

	rhyme scheme	
octave/octet	a b a b	quatrain
	c d c d	quatrain
turn		
sestet	e f e f	quatrain
		turn
	g g	couplet

The turn in the English sonnet occurs after the third quatrain. Ideally there should be "three turns of the screw" in the three quatrains, before the point is driven home in the couplet. The couplet therefore offers a conclusion or a summary. However, one should still be aware that there can be the traditional turn after the octave.

Shakespeare's sonnets

- Shakespeare wrote 154 sonnets.
- Sonnets 1 to 126 are addressed to a young man.
- Sonnets 127 to 154 are addressed to a "dark lady".

Main themes: love, beauty, transience, old age, death

The **basic metre** is iambic pentameter, but Shakespeare does not use it slavishly. Metre is used functionally, e. g.
- regular metre: harmony, peace, tranquillity, balance, stability, etc.
- irregular metre: disharmony, confusion, parody

Shakespeare's Language

Prose

ordinary speech, no metric pattern

Visual clues
- Printed lines extend from the left to the right margin.
- Lines do not start with a capital letter (unless following a full stop).

Function of prose
- often used by characters of low status (murderers, servants, craftsmen, etc.) but not as a dogmatic rule
- low comedy (especially dirty jokes) often written in prose
- suggests a realistic tone
- used for bantering, e.g. Beatrice and Benedick in *Much Ado About Nothing*
- sometimes indicates madness (Lady Macbeth, Lear)

Verse

Rhymes

- usually occur as rhymed couplets (aa bb cc)
- rhyme pair in iambic pentameter called "heroic couplet"

Function of rhymes
They often serve the same function as in a sonnet: concluding a scene, hammering the point home ("capping couplet").

Rhymes are used for:
- highly lyrical passages,
- choruses, prologues, epilogues,
- romantic passages which are slightly exaggerated,
- supernatural beings (e. g. witches, fairies).

Blank verse

- an **unrhymed iambic pentameter**
- the standard verse in Shakespeare's plays

Blank verse resembles prose in that the final words of the lines do not rhyme in any regular pattern.
Unlike in prose, there is a recognisable metre: most (not necessarily all) lines are in iambic pentameter, i. e. they consist of ten syllables alternating unstressed and stressed syllables: da**dum** da**dum** da**dum** da**dum** da**dum**.

Example:
Give **me** your **han**d bef**ore** this **ho**ly **fri**ar.
I **am** your **hus**band **if** you l**ike** of **me**.
(from: *Much Ado About Nothing*, Act V, Scene 4)

Visual clues
- Printed lines do not extend from the left to the right margin.
- Lines start with capital letters.

Function of blank verse
Unlike rhyme, which sounds artificial, blank verse comes close to the natural speaking rhythms of English. Yet it makes it sound more elevated, less ordinary.

Other types of metre

Dimeter
*A **drum** a **drum***
*Mac**beth** doth **come.** (Macbeth,* Act I, Scene 3)
→ echoing the drum

Tetrameter
***Dou**ble, **dou**ble **toil** and **trou**ble,*
***Fire** **burn** and **caul**dron **bub**ble. (Macbeth,* Act IV, Scene 1)

***Fair** is **foul** and **foul** is **fair.** (Macbeth,* Act I, Scene 1)

The tetrameter here is used for spells (i. e. the witches' incantations in *Macbeth*).

Shakespeare's relevance to modern audiences

Pros	Cons
timeless themes: – love – hate – rejection – jealousy – envy – greed – ambition – revenge – equivocation – appearance and reality etc.	outdated world picture
authentic characters, human and understandable modern adaptations in all literary genres: – opera – musical – drama – novel – film – poetry – pop song – Hollywood blockbusters	outdated attitudes and values regarding: – gender roles – loyalty – generations – science – religion – superstition – social hierarchies etc.
aesthetically pleasing language great influence on: – idioms – proverbs – quotations – titles – allusions	outdated language partly incomprehensible imagery, allusions and jokes

Glossary – Shakespeare and the Elizabethan Age

actor actress (not in Elizabethan times)	Schauspieler Schauspielerin
aside	beiseite gesprochener Text, der die Gedanken des Charakters offenbart
blank verse	Blankvers
play drama tragedy comedy history romance	Schauspiel/Theaterstück Drama Tragödie Komödie Historiendrama Romanze
Elizabethan age/era	elisabethanisches Zeitalter
enter exit/exeunt	tritt/treten auf (Regieanweisung) geht/gehen ab (Regieanweisung)
fatal flaw	verhängnisvolle Schwäche (des Tragödienhelden)
groundlings	im elisabethanischen Theater: Zuschauende, die im Bereich direkt um die Bühne stehen
hero heroine	Held Heldin
Jacobean	aus der Zeit James I. (1603–1625)
Master of the Revels	für Theater zuständiger Beamter
medieval the Middle Ages	mittelalterlich Mittelalter
performance to perform	Vorstellung vorführen
playhouse	Theater
playing company / troupe (The Lord Chamberlain's Men, The Admiral's Men)	Theatertruppe (berühmte Truppen der Shakespeare-Zeit)
playwright dramatist	Bühnenautor
Renaissance	Renaissance
scenery	Kulisse
soliloquy	Selbstgespräch
stage; stage props	Bühne; Requisiten
wit	Geist, Witz

Visions of the Future

Utopia and Dystopia

Keywords

Utopian literature: a fictional text dealing with an ideal (future) society

Dystopian literature: a fictional text dealing with a future society in which human freedom is severely limited. A dystopia often criticises our present-day society by exposing trends and tendencies towards totalitarian control.

Extrapolation: here: fictitious description of elements of a future society on the basis of present day phenomena and developments. The writer criticises his or her own society by demonstrating what certain trends may lead to or what point society has already reached.

School classics – background knowledge

The three novels presented here are so well known in and outside of English-speaking countries that you may encounter references to any one of these works in numerous texts. They will be presented here in the order of their first publication.

Aldous Huxley: *Brave New World*

written in 1931; set in the distant future (26th century)

Generally known elements

- total control of society by in-vitro fertilisation, artificial breeding of humans, "cloning" of work force and conditioning
- society strictly divided into Alpha, Beta, Gamma, Delta and Epsilon people with Alphas constituting the ruling class and Epsilons constituting a slave-like work force
- natural reproduction outlawed, sex as pure entertainment, monogamy regarded as unnatural and immoral
- people kept happy by means of a drug called "soma"
- religion replaced by a strong belief in technology and science

Extrapolation of developments of 20th century society in *Brave New World*

- ardent belief in science, technology and progress
- misuse of science
- political and economic control and manipulation
- mass production and mass consumption
- decline of religious and moral values
- decline of educational standards
- drugs

- mass entertainment
- sensationalism

George Orwell: *Nineteen Eighty-Four*

written in 1948; set in the relatively near future

Generally known elements

- **Big Brother:** constant surveillance, "Big Brother is watching you" (origin of the name of the popular, present-day TV show)
- **Newspeak:** invention of a new, simplified form of the English language to manipulate thought; complex (i. e. critical) thinking cannot be put into words anymore
  Examples:
  - words like *goodthink, oldthink, crimethink:* simplify expressions of thought, make them imprecise, one-dimensional, eventually devoid of meaning
  - euphemisms like *Miniluv, Minipax, Minitrue:* sound positive, conceal their true meaning (Ministry of Love = police; Ministry of Peace = organises the military; Ministry of Truth = produces and spreads propaganda)
- **rewriting of history:** books and newspapers are manipulated

Extrapolation of elements of 20th century society in *Nineteen Eighty-Four*

precursors in Nazi Germany and Soviet Uniun under Stalin:
- intrusion in people's privacy, spying on people
- propaganda, misuse of mass media
- psychological torture

21st century relevance

- electronic surveillance and digital tracking
- fake news
- nationalism
- censorship

Ray Bradbury: *Fahrenheit 451*

written in 1953; set in 2049

Generally known elements

- **451 degrees Fahrenheit:** the temperature at which paper starts to burn
- society marked by entertainment, speed, restlessness and superficiality: extremely fast driving; multi-screen television with very shallow programmes, usually set at high volume; constant exposure to sound and advertising (individually by the wearing of ear-plugs or collectively by loudspeaker announcements)
- critical thought impeded as books are forbidden
- the firemen's job: to burn books

Extrapolation of elements of 20th century society in *Fahrenheit 451*

- burning of books (Nazi Germany)
- atomic bomb (Hiroshima)
- rise of television and audio media, effect on reading
- acceleration in all areas of life: transport, communications, work, production, consumption
- dominance of entertainment
- decline of education

Science Fiction

Science fiction is a genre of fiction dealing with imaginary content set in the future, with particular focus on science and technology.
As opposed to fantasy, its imaginary elements are largely possible within scientifically postulated laws of nature.
The settings for science fiction are often contrary to known reality, but most science fiction relies on potential scientific explanations or solutions to various fictional elements. There is no magic involved.

Elements of science fiction

- a setting in the future
- a setting in outer space (e. g. spaceflight), in other worlds or in remote regions of the earth (underground, bottom of the sea)
- characters that include aliens, mutants, androids or other types of artificial intelligence (AI)
- technology that is futuristic (e. g. ray guns, teleportation machines, humanoid computers, space ships, artificial planets, independent AI)
- scientific principles that are new and have overcome known laws of nature, for example time travel, wormholes or faster-than-light travel
- new and different societies, especially post-apocalyptic worlds
- paranormal abilities such as mind control, telepathy and telekinesis

There is considerable overlap between utopia/dystopia and science fiction. However, one may say that science fiction is a lot more concerned with futuristic science and technology, which is central to the story, whereas utopian/dystopian narratives rather put their focus on social aspects. The element of extrapolation therefore plays a greater role in dystopian films and novels.
As an example, the films *Star Wars* or *Alien* do not essentially extrapolate from today's society. The novels *Fahrenheit 451* and *Brave New World* or productions such as *Gattaca* and *Black Mirror* do so extensively.

Classic science fiction narratives

These classics are so well known in and outside of English-speaking countries that you may encounter references to any one of these works in numerous texts.

Mary Shelley, *Frankenstein; or, The Modern Prometheus* (1818)

Dr Frankenstein brings to life a creature made of dead body parts and is then repulsed by what he has done. The creature becomes lonely and violent after being rejected by its creator and turns against him.
As one of the most easily recognised icons of fantastic fiction, Frankenstein's creature has inspired innumerable works of art, from films to mangas and computer games. "Frankenstein's monster" has become synonymous with things, in particular an invention, that become destructive to its inventor.

H. G. Wells, *The Time Machine* (1895)

In this novel the nameless Time Traveller visits a future in which the human race has evolved into two separate species: the childlike Eloi, leading relatively carefree and happy lives, and the brutal Morlocks, who provide for the Eloi's wealth but also eat them. The Time Traveller is forced to retrieve his machine from the Morlocks before he can return home.
Wells's story has popularised the concept of time travel, using a machine that allows an operator to travel to whatever period of history they want. It has inspired countless science fiction stories, the most popular probably being the Hollywood production *Back to the Future*. The term "time machine", coined by Wells, is now universally used.

H. G. Wells, *The War of the Worlds* (1898)

The War of the Worlds tells the story of a Martian invasion, apparently to harvest humans. As mankind's weapons turn out to be useless against the Martians, the aliens are eventually killed by earthly bacteria.
The story has become particularly famous because of its adaptation in the 1938 radio broadcast by Orson Welles, which allegedly led to widespread panic among listeners who thought the invasion was real. Significantly, the novel also gave birth to the fictional theme of the Martians and their potential invasion.

20th and 21st century science fiction novels and films are so abundant that there is no use listing any of them here. For your final exam, make sure you are familiar with the texts you studied.

Glossary – Utopia and Dystopia

anti-individualist	anti-individualistisch
anti-utopian	anti-utopisch
authoritarian	autoritär
brainwashing to brainwash so.	Gehirnwäsche jmd. einer Gehirnwäsche unterziehen
to dissent dissenter	abweichende Meinung haben Andersdenkender
dystopia	Anti-Utopie, Dystopie
extrapolation	Fortführung, Ableitung
fiction fictitious fictional	Dichtung, erzählende Literatur fiktiv, erfunden erdichtet
future futuristic	Zukunft, zukünftig futuristisch
hierarchy	Hierarchie
imaginary	erfunden
individualist	Individualist, individualistisch
indoctrination	Indoktrinierung
oppression	Unterdrückung
restriction	Einschränkung
surveillance	Überwachung
totalitarian	totalitär
utopia	Utopie

Ethical Issues of Scientific and Technological Progress

Science

Keyword
Genetics: field of study examining the way living organisms inherit certain qualities from their ancestors via DNA. These qualities are called traits. Traits are e.g. a person's eye-colour or height.

- Genetic information is carried by a molecule called DNA, which is copied and passed on across generations.
- DNA is widely known as the "double helix" and looks like a twisted ladder. It is made up of nucleotides, which are the rungs of the ladder. There are four types of nucleotides (adenine, cytosine, guanine and thymine; A, C, G and T). The sequence of the nucleotides determines the genetic code of an organism.
- Genes are segments of DNA which provide information used to encode proteins. They are like sentences spelled out by means of the "letters" of the nucleotide alphabet.
- The complete set of genes in a particular organism is known as a genome.
- Genes are copied each time a cell divides into two new cells. It is through a similar process that a child inherits genes from its parents, when a copy from the mother is mixed with a copy from the father.

Genetic engineering

Altering strings of DNA in a cell can produce a new trait. For example, crop plants can be given a gene from an Arctic fish, so they produce an antifreeze protein in their leaves. This may prevent frost damage. Other crops can be given genes including a natural insecticide, which will protect the plant.
People with genetic disorders can be treated by means of gene therapy. The idea is to replace a malfunctioning gene with one that functions properly.

Important steps in genetic engineering

- 1953: discovery of double helix by Watson and Crick, Cambridge, UK
- 1973: first insertion of foreign DNA into an organism
- 1978: production of human protein insulin
- 1980s: beginning of work with human genes
- 1986: open-air experimentation with genetically modified plants
- 1992: first commercial cultivation of genetically modified plants
- 1996: cloning of mammals (sheep "Dolly")
- 2003: sequencing of the human genome
- 2009: first transgenic primates
- 2013: use of cloning to create human embryonic stem cells

- 2016: cultivation of crops that are modified on a large scale by means of "genetic scissors" is permitted in the US
- 2018: babies modified by means of "genetic scissors" have been allegedly born in China

Applications of GMOs (genetically modified organisms)
- biological and medical research
- production of pharmaceutical drugs
- experimental medicine (e. g. gene therapy)
- agriculture (e. g. golden rice)
- The **widest application** exists for crops resistant to herbicides or for crops producing pesticides from within.
- In 2019, 190.4 million hectares of biotech crops were planted by up to 17 million farmers in 29 countries.[1]

Transgenic microbes

Bacteria were the first organisms to be modified in the laboratory. These organisms are now used for several purposes and are particularly important in producing human proteins for use in medicine.
Genetically modified bacteria are used
- to produce insulin to treat diabetes,
- to produce clotting factors to treat haemophilia,
- to produce human growth hormone to treat various forms of dwarfism,
- to facilitate crop growth in some soils or prevent crop pests.

Transgenic animals

Transgenic animals are used
- as experimental models to test genes whose function is unknown,
- for the production of human hormones such as insulin.

Transgenic mice are used to study diseases and test treatments. Mice can be grown with the same genetic disorders that occur in human beings.
first genetically modified pet: the GloFish, a patented brand of genetically modified, fluorescent zebra fish with bright red, green and orange fluorescent colours

Transgenic plants

Transgenic plants have been engineered to
- resist pests, herbicides or harsh environmental conditions,
- improve product shelf life,
- increase their nutritional value,
- produce bigger yields, thus making farmland more efficient.

"Terminator" Technology: GM plants do not yield seeds. This means that farmers have to buy new seeds every time.

[1] https://isaaa.org/resources/publications/pocketk/16/default.asp (accessed on 1 April 2022)

Designer babies (Reprogenetics)

The colloquial term "designer baby" refers to a baby whose genetic makeup has been artificially selected to ensure the presence or absence of certain characteristics, especially with regard to the sex of the child.

Cloning

Cloning is the creation of an organism that is an exact genetic copy of another. This means that every single bit of DNA is the same between the two.
Dolly (5 July 1996 – 14 February 2003): A female sheep (ewe) was the first mammal to be cloned from an adult body cell. She lived until the age of six, when she developed severe diseases.

Ethics

Biotechnology in agriculture

Pros	Cons
higher productivity	genes can end up in unexpected places
more efficient land use	genes can mutate with harmful effect
more ecological farming (no ploughing, no fertilising, no insecticides, no pesticides)	"sleeper" genes could be accidentally switched on, active genes could become "silent"
solution to problem of famine in the world	loss of farmers' control over material; "terminator" technology prevents sustainable farming → dependence on big corporations
higher quality of food	transfer of allergenic genes
longer shelf life	GM products in the food chain
rehabilitation of damaged land	transfer of antibiotic resistance
	interaction with wild and native plant populations: negative impact on birds, insects and soil

Reprogenetics

Pros (once it is safe)	Cons
parents have a right to choose	technology is not safe yet
moral obligation to give children the best life possible	bioethical codes condemn experiments with human beings
will lead to improvement of the whole species	"super humans" may look down on normal people

	"imperfect" human beings would be discriminated against
	rich people would be at an advantage
	the human gene pool may be damaged
	"New Eugenics": people are designed to suit the needs of society
	people may be thought of as products
	human beings should not play God

Sex selection

Pros (once it is safe)	**Cons**
parents have a right to choose	preferences in patriarchal cultures lead to demographic imbalance
in some cultures male offspring are important to provide support for old age	members of the unwanted sex may be discriminated against
theory that having sisters (as opposed to brothers) enhances adults' quality of life	the child may not be loved if sth. goes wrong and it is not of the desired sex
	parents fulfil their own wishes, disregarding the rights of the child
	human beings should not be allowed to play God

Human cloning

Pros	**Cons**
medical reasons: resource of bone marrow or replaceable organs	cloning is inherently evil, an intrusion into human life
infertile couples may have children	a person who wants to clone himself/herself is self-centred
	cloning in order to produce superior beings is discriminatory (eugenics)
	using human beings as a resource for "spare parts" is unethical
	reproduction by means of cloning might have long-term consequences for human relationships
	children may be thought of as products
	Hinduism: What about the person's karma?
	dictators may become immortal

Glossary – Ethical Issues

achievement of scientists	Errungenschaft/Leistung der Wissenschaftler/-innen
artificial insemination	künstliche Befruchtung
development	Entwicklung
DNA (deoxyribonucleic acid)	DNS (Desokyribonukleinsäure)
double helix	Doppelhelix
error rate	Fehlerrate
genetic disorders	genetische Funktionsstörung
genetic engineering	Gentechnik, Genmanipulation
genetic fingerprint	genetischer Fingerabdruck
genetic make-up, genetic constitution	Erbgut
genetic modification (GM)	genetische Veränderung
heredity, inheritance	Vererbung
to inherit	erben
insecticide	Insektizid
in-vitro fertilisation	In-vitro-Befruchtung
laboratory	Labor
to modify modification	modifizieren, verändern Modifizierung
molecule	Molekül
to mutate mutation	mutieren Mutation
non-polluting	umweltverträglich
organ donor	Organspender/-in
to pass on	vererben
pesticide	Unkrautvernichtungsmittel, Pestizid
progress (no article, no plural)	Fortschritt
reproductive cloning	Klonen von Menschen
research (into)	Forschung (über)
research facility	Forschungseinrichtung
resistance	Resistenz
stem cell	Stammzelle
technology	Technologie, Technik
test-tube baby	Retortenbaby
therapeutic cloning	therapeutisches Klonen
transgenic	transgen (genetisch verändert)

Studying and Working in a Globalised World

With the world constantly becoming smaller due to globalisation, it has become much easier to spend some time in a foreign country for educational reasons, both during one's time at school and/or as part of university studies or vocational training.

Benefits for Oneself

- getting a personal insight into other cultures
- improving one's foreign language skills
- experiencing different educational systems
- contributing to one's personal development, e. g. to become more independent, self-confident, adaptable to different situations
- making new friends
- improving one's career opportunities
- broadening one's horizon on various levels

Studying and working abroad also has benefits for employers. Employees who have studied abroad are said to possess key job skills, e. g. cultural empathy, excellent foreign language skills, self-organisation, adaptability, open-mindedness and flexibility. Some employers therefore consider it an essential aspect of a prospective employee's CV (résumé) to have spent some time abroad, very often in an English-speaking country.

Volunteerism and Voluntourism

In the last couple of years, **volunteerism** has become more popular. It means that a person volunteers to use his/her time and skills to contribute to a community without receiving any payment. An increasing number of people combine being a volunteer with spending some time abroad. There are various ways in which one can contribute to a community, e. g. humanitarian aid or teaching at a local school in a rural village.
Volunteerism should not be confused with **voluntourism,** which can generally be defined as a combination of volunteering and sightseeing.
Voluntourism is a neologism based on the words "volunteer" and "tourism" and has been criticised as counterfeiting the original idea of volunteering.
Some of the arguments critics put forward against voluntourism are that it is not truly beneficial for communities, since "voluntourists" only spend a relatively short time in the communities in question and therefore often do not immerse themselves enough in their culture to truly contribute. In addition, voluntourists are said to enjoy all the benefits of an ordinary tourist, e. g. staying in hotels far above the living standards of the community they are helping, and are thus often unprepared for their placement. Whereas in the past charities and NGOs were mostly in charge of matching volunteers with the right projects, some major travel agencies now also specialise in offering placements for "voluntourists" against payment.

English as a *Lingua Franca*

English is a *lingua franca,* which means that it is a language spoken by such a vast number of people all over the world that it enables speakers of different first languages to successfully communicate with each other.
These non-native speakers of English have a huge impact on the English language, e.g. when it comes to grammar or pronunciation, for when non-native speakers of English communicate with each other, it is their main intention to communicate a message. As a consequence, grammatical constructions regarded as incorrect by native speakers of English are accepted by both speakers and do not impede the flow of their conversation.
Code mixing and code switching also occur. It means that a speaker uses words, syntax, etc. from his mother tongue as well as English words in the same sentence. In contrast to that, the term code switching is used to refer to a speaker who switches between the vocabulary, syntax, etc. of his or her mother tongue and English, often in the same sentence.
Nowadays English language skills are not considered a special feature but are taken for granted in many areas of life.

The Changing World of Work

Past generations often spent their entire working life with one employer, retiring from the same company with which they started. But, due to globalisation, the world of work has changed rapidly over the last half century. Advances in information technology have made it possible for a company's employees in different countries to work on the same project and to exchange information on the spot. Due to new technological and economic developments, new types of jobs have been created which were unheard of only half a century ago.
Still, finding one's dream job has not become easier, and employees are often expected to show a high level of flexibility and adaptability. Changing jobs and places of residence frequently is not uncommon, as there is high competition in certain jobs.
Nor do the realities of the job market always match one's expectations and wishes. Despite the fact that there is employment growth in the United Kingdom, Germany and the USA, not everyone profits from it. The number of jobs for people with no or low work skills is decreasing and the gap between the rich and the poor is widening all over the world.

Minimum Wage and Living Wage

21 countries of the European Union as well as the USA, have a statutory minimum wage. In 2015, Germany introduced a minimum wage, calculated either on the basis of an hourly rate or as a monthly payment. The minimum wage varies in different fields of work. Being paid a minimum wage means that an employee receives the lowest wage his/her employer is legally allowed to pay. Some of the arguments put forward in favour of the minimum wage are that it prevents people from being exploited by employers, forcing them to rely on social benefits in order to make ends meet.

In the UK some companies and institutions voluntarily pay their employees a "living wage" instead of the legal minimum wage. While a "minimum wage" is calculated in accordance with the development of the job market, a "living wage" is an hourly rate calculated on the basis of the cost of living index (e. g. accommodation, travel, food and drink, costs for heating, water and electricity), which in the UK is adjusted annually. In 2021, the voluntarily paid living wage in the UK was £9.90 an hour, with the exception of London where it is £11.05 an hour, due to higher costs of living. In the same year the compulsory "national living wage" for people aged 23 or older was £8.91 per hour – significantly lower than the living wage calculated by the Living Wage Foundation.

Living Wage Foundation

On its website, the London-based Living Wage Foundation says that it developed from a citizens' movement in 2001, when the charity "Citizens UK" brought parents together to exchange views on the ups and downs of family life: "It emerged that too many parents were working two jobs just to make ends meet and so had no time to spend with their children. They worked hard but couldn't earn enough to afford a decent standard of living."[1] The Living Wage Foundation is supported by the UK's political parties, and both Houses of Parliament are among those who pay their employees a living wage.

In January 2017, Finland launched a social experiment in which the Finnish government granted 2,000 unemployed people an unconditional basic income (UBI) of €560 for 24 months, without urging them to look for employment or to accept job offers. Those who took a job during this period still received UBI.
The intention behind this social experiment was to find out whether UBI motivates unemployed people to find jobs or enter job training. UBI provides a "safety net" so that they will not feel too much financial pressure.
It is not easy to say whether this experiment has been a success or not. The number of unemployed participants in the experiment did not decrease as much as had been hoped, but those who participated said that they felt more contented for the duration of the experiment.

1 https://www.livingwage.org.uk/sites/default/files/Recommendations%20for%20Living%20Wage%20Leadership_1.pdf (accessed on 1 April 2022)

Glossary – Studying and Working in a Globalised World

adaptability	Anpassungsfähigkeit
apprenticeship, vocational training	Berufsausbildung, Lehre
charity	Wohlfahrtsorganisation
community service	ehrenamtliche Tätigkeit
compulsory education/schooling	Schulpflicht
CV (curriculum vitae) (BE) / résumé (AE)	Lebenslauf
exchange student	Austauschschüler/-in Austauschstudent/-in
flexibility	Flexibilität
gap year	etwa einjährige Auszeit vor/nach Ausbildung/Studium, oftmals zum Sammeln von Wissen oder Arbeitserfahrung
job advertisement/offer	Stellenanzeige/-angebot
job interview	Bewerbungsgespräch
key qualifications	Schlüsselqulifikationen
minimum wage	Mindestlohn
open-mindedness	Aufgeschlossenheit
placement/internship	Praktikum
scholarship	Stipendium
school exchange	Schüleraustausch
social commitment	soziales Engagement
social skills	soziale Kompetenz
study abroad	Auslandsstudium
to apply for (a job)	sich (für eine Stelle) bewerben
to broaden one's horizon	seinen Horizont erweitern
to carve out a career	Karriere machen
to donate/give sth. to charity	etw. an eine Wohltätigkeitsorganisation spenden/weiterleiten
to gain experience	Erfahrungen sammeln
to get an insight into foreign cultures	einen Einblick in fremde Kulturen erhalten
to speak from one's own experience	aus eigener Erfahrung sprechen
volunteer	Freiwillige/-r

Methoden der Textarbeit

Literarische Texte

Narration

Keyword
Narrative texts: Narrative texts can have many forms, among them short story, novel, fairytale, satire, parable, legend, etc.
Most relevant for your final exam are the short story and the novel.

When asked to analyse a narrative text, you will have to focus on particular elements that are characteristic of short stories or novels.

Elements of narration
Plot

INFO Elements of a complete plot

exposition → rising action → climax/turning point → falling action → ending

A **plot** need not necessarily be complete (e. g. open ending).

The **sequence** need not necessarily be in chronological order.
There may be foreshadowing or flashbacks or there may be reverse narration (*umgestelltes Erzählen*).
In particular, an excerpt from a longer text, which is the most common sort of text in the final exam, may not contain all the elements of plot.

Certain **key events** within the action of a story will raise the tension; they will create suspense, rising to a climax or turning point. After that there will be falling tension or relief.

INFO Tension curve

rising tension → climax or turning point → falling tension or relief

Theme

The **theme** of a story is always abstract. Themes are e. g. love, poverty, racism, childhood, etc.
The **subject matter** of a story is the concrete realisation of a theme.

Example:
Two stories may have the same theme: racism. The subject matter of the one may be the murder of an African-American, while the other may be dealing with the bullying of a black schoolgirl.

Characters

When asked to characterise a figure from a narrative text, you will have to be aware of different aspects. There are key questions that can guide you.

Direct characterisation
- What does the narrator say about the character?
- What do other characters say about the character?
- What does the character say about himself/herself?
- How objective is what they say? Be aware of words with negative or positive connotations.

Indirect characterisation
- How does the character act?
- What does the character say?
- What kind of language does he/she use?

It might help to fill in a table with the following headings:

Character's outward appearance	Character's language	Character's actions	What the character says	Other characters' statements (or actions)
…	…	…	…	…

Narrator / Point of view

INFO Narrator

The narrator is usually either a first-person or a third-person narrator.
The first-person narrator is NOT the author!

limited point of view	unlimited/omniscient point of view
first-person narrator	third-person narrator (neutral omniscience, God-like know-ledge about all facts)
third-person narrator (one character's point of view)	third-person narrator (several characters' points of view)

The narrator always works like a camera operator, taking a point-of-view shot through a character's eyes or looking at the characters from the outside.

Example:
In Alan Sillitoe's novel *Saturday Night and Sunday Morning* (1975), the reader is presented with an episode in a pub (cf. p. 10). When the narrator says, "Brenda and two other women sitting at Arthur's table saw him push back his chair and stand up with a clatter", he takes Brenda's and the women's point of view. Arthur is clearly seen from outside, not by a neutral narrator but through the women's eyes: The women sitting at Arthur's table saw him push back his chair, NOT "Arthur pushed back his chair".
→ limited point of view A

A few lines later the point of view changes: "He felt electric light bulbs shining and burn ing into the back of his head".
The narrator takes Arthur's point of view, knows what Arthur feels.
→ limited point of view B

If the point of view switches multiple times between various different characters, this usually indicates an unlimited/omniscient point of view.

Mode of presentation

Panoramic presentation (telling) vs. scenic presentation (showing)
There are two modes of presentation to be found in narratives: the **panoramic** and the **scenic** mode.

The **panoramic** mode is employed when the narrator summarises several events, whereas **scenic** mode is used when the narrator describes scenes in great detail.

Interior monologue is a particular kind of scenic presentation, in which the thoughts and feelings passing through a character's mind are depicted. In **reported thought** the thoughts are presented as reported speech.

This is closely connected with the concepts of *narrated time* and *narrating* (or *acting) time:*

narrated time longer than narrating time	usually summary of events
narrated time identical with narrating time	e. g. direct speech
narrated time shorter than narrating time	e. g. stream of consciousness, interior monologue, detailed description of a scene, comparable to slow motion in film

INFO Function of mode of presentation and point of view

A neutral, omniscient narrator, who observes the action and the characters from above and who uses a panoramic mode of presentation, is more detached and thus creates a distance between the reader and the action. On the other hand, a narrator who takes a character's point of view creates immediacy and directly involves the reader in what happens.

Setting

The place and time where the action is set is called the setting. It is especially important for *atmosphere* and *symbolism*.

Atmosphere

Atmosphere is created by means of setting, objects, colours, light and darkness but also by reference to a character's mood or the use of language.

Example:
In Kate Chopin's short story "Desirée's Baby" a "yellow stuccoed house" is described with a roof that comes down "steep and black like a cowl" (cowl: *Mönchskutte*). It is surrounded by "big, solemn oaks", the "thick-leaved, far-reaching branches" shadowing "it like a pall" (pall: *Leichentuch*).

colour	black, dirty yellow
light/darkness	shadow of the oaks
language: similes, "like a pall", "like a cowl"	→ connotations of death, darkness, mystery

The atmosphere created here is gloomy, sombre, sinister, threatening and eerie.

Symbolism

Symbols are part of the setting of the narrative.

INFO Established symbols

These are conventional symbols which have long been used and have a certain, traditional significance which everybody knows. Examples of established symbols: rose, cross, the colour white.

INFO Created symbols

Something becomes symbolic within a certain context, because it is closely connected to an event, a situation or a character.

Example:
In the novel *Angela's Ashes* (1996), Angela, the family's mother, vomits over the side of the ship when they leave New York harbour for Ireland and the wind from the Atlantic blows it all over the family (cf. p. 53).
In the course of the novel, the reader will learn how unfortunate the family's decision to leave America will turn out to be and how disastrous the wind from the Atlantic will be for the family. Thus, this passage from the first chapter of the book is symbolic.

INFO Symbols and metaphors

Symbols are NOT metaphors!
Symbols are really there, are part of the story. Metaphors or similes are figures of speech.

Examples:
She was a rose, so beautiful. → metaphor
She was like a rose, so beautiful. → simile/comparison
They fell in love when they first met in her father's rose garden. → symbol

Language and style

In order to determine the style of a text it is necessary to examine aspects such as register, diction (choice of words), tone and also sentence structure.

Register is the level of language used in a particular situation. It may be formal, neutral, informal or vulgar. There may be a lot of slang words, even taboo words, or technical terms or jargon.

The **tone** may be ironic, sarcastic, sad, humorous, serious, playful, angry, etc., depending on the emotional attitude it expresses. This has an effect on the choice of words, level of speech, rhythm, sentence length, etc.

Stylistic devices will be considered at length in the chapters on poetry and non-fictional texts (pp. 86 f., 93 f.).

Poetry

Poetry focuses on the **aesthetic function** of language.
Poetry appeals to the senses. It is usually to be enjoyed for its beauty, its cleverness, its wit or its impact. This is achieved by
- the sound of words,
- the rhythm of the words and phrases,
- the choice of words,
- the structure of the sentences,
- the composition of the poem,
- the visual arrangement of words and lines, and
- the means of imagery.

In your final exams, however, you will be asked not so much to enjoy the poem but to examine its meaning and the effect of the language the speaker uses.

How to proceed

Questions to be asked
- Who is the speaker of the poem?
- Where is the speaker?
- Does the speaker address somebody?
- Does the speaker contemplate something?
- Does the speaker describe something or somebody?
- Does the speaker tell a story?
- Does the speaker explain something?
- Does the speaker argue against or in favour of something?
- What is the speaker's attitude? What is he/she saying?
- How is the poem composed? Is it structured by rhyme scheme, by division into stanzas or by some other device?
- Is there a correspondence between the structure of the poem and the structure of the speaker's thoughts?
- What is the significance of the title?
- What words does the speaker use? What do they mean?
- What is the structure of the sentences? Simple? Complex?
- What poetic devices does the speaker use?
- And what is the effect of all this? What is the experience of reading the poem?

In order to understand and describe poetry you need to be familiar with its most important elements.

Elements of poetry

INFO Speaker and author

The speaker of the poem is NOT the author. Poems may be autobiographical, but you must still refer to the "speaker of the poem".

Poems are composed of **stanzas** and **lines**.
Stanzas may have a certain **rhyme scheme.**

Rhyme

Types of rhyme schemes

rhyme pair	a a b b
alternate rhyme	a b a b
embracing rhyme	a b b a

Types of rhymes

masculine rhyme (stress on final syllable)	kiss/this
feminine rhyme (stress on penultimate syllable)	dreary/weary
true rhyme	kiss/this, dreary/weary
slant rhyme assonance (same vowel) consonance (same consonant)	 comb/coat hope/heap

Metre

Lines may also be marked by a certain rhythm. The smallest unit that determines rhythm is the foot, consisting of at least one stressed and one or two unstressed syllables. The pattern of stressed and unstressed syllables is called **metre.**

A sequence of stressed and unstressed syllables is nothing artificial. It is the natural rhythm of the English language. It is the poet's skill to choose words in a way that this pattern will constitute a regular metre.

Types of feet

foot	**stresses**		**example**
iamb/iambic	– /	(da-**dum**)	compare
trochee/trochaic	/ –	(**dum**-da)	lovely
spondee/spondaic	/ /	(**dum dum**)	drop dead
anapest/anapestic	– – /	(da-da-**dum**)	lemonade
dactyl/dactylic	/ – –	(**dum**-da-da)	whispering

The number of feet or stressed syllables in a line determines its metre. The most common types are shown here:

number of feet	**metre**	**example**
1	monometer	"And **find** / What **wind**" (John Donne, "Song", ll. 7 – 8)
2	dimeter	"Why **dost** thou **thus**" (John Donne, "The Sun Rising", l. 2)
3	trimeter	"**Go**, Soul, the **bo**dy's **guest** / U**pon** a **thank**less **er**rant;" (Sir Walter Raleigh, "The Lie", ll. 1 f.)
4	tetrameter	"**Bu**sy old **fool**, un**ru**ly **sun**" (John Donne, "The Sun Rising", l. 1)
5	pentameter	"If **mu**sic **be** the **food** of **love**, play **on**" (William Shakespeare, *Twelfth Night*, I.i)
6	hexameter	"And **in** your **dread**ful **verse** in**grav'd** the **pro**phe**cies**" (Michael Drayton, "Poly-Olbion", l. 33)

INFO Most important metre in English poetry

Iambic pentameter:
"But **thy** e**ter**nal **sum**mer **shall** not **fade**" (William Shakespeare, Sonnet 18).

Lines

end-stop lines	The meaning requires a pause at the end of the line.	"Shall I compare thee to a summer's day**?**" (William Shakespeare, Sonnet 18)
run-on lines (enjambement)	The meaning requires no pause between the lines.	"When yellow leaves, or none, or few, do **hang** **Upon** those boughs which shake against the cold" (William Shakespeare, Sonnet 73)
caesura	The meaning requires a pause in mid-line.	"Let me not to the marriage of true minds Admit **impediments; love** is not love" (William Shakespeare, Sonnet 116)

Imagery

A writer or speaker using language beyond its dictionary meaning makes use of **imagery.** All figurative use of language is imagery. Imagery appeals to all the senses, it is meant to stimulate the reader's or listener's imagination.

INFO Watch out!

The word *imagery* is an abstract noun. There is no plural. You can only talk about single *images*.

Types of imagery

metaphor	A metaphor compares two basically dissimilar things without using the words 'like' or 'as'. Some characteristics of the one are thus transferred to the other in order to illustrate its qualities. "All the world is a stage." (William Shakespeare, *As You Like It*, II.viii)
simile/ comparison	Like a metaphor, a simile draws a comparison, but it explicitly uses the words 'like' or 'as' to do so. "my luve is like a red, red rose" (Robert Burns, "A Red, Red Rose", l. 1)
personification	This is a kind of metaphor in which animals, plants, inanimate objects or abstract ideas are represented as if they were humans or possessed human qualities: "Busy old fool, unruly sun, / Why dost thou thus, / Through windows, and through curtains call on us?" (John Donne, "The Sun Rising", ll. 1–3)
symbol	see examples in previous chapter, p. 82

Other poetic devices

stylistic device	definition	example
alliteration	repetition of a sound (usually a consonant) at the beginning of adjacent words	"From forth the fatal loins of these two foes" (William Shakespeare, *Romeo and Juliet,* Prologue)
onomatopoeia (adj.: onomato-poeic)	the use of words which imitate the sound they refer to	"the stuttering rifles' rapid rattle" (Wilfred Owen, "Anthem for Doomed Youth", l. 3)
anaphora	repetition of one or more words at the beginning of ad-jacent sentences or lines	"In every cry of every man In every infant's cry of fear In every voice, in every ban" (William Blake, "London", ll. 5–7)
chiasm	reversal of order of the words in the two parts of a sentence	"Fair is foul, and foul is fair" (William Shakespeare, *Macbeth*, I.i)
oxymoron	a combination of contradicto-ry words and meanings	"O heavy lightness, serious vanity, Misshapen chaos of well-seeming forms" (William Shakespeare, *Romeo and Juliet*, I.i)

Drama

When asked to analyse a dramatic text, you will have to focus on particular elements that are characteristic of plays or film scripts.

Elements of drama

Plot

The action is presented to the audience on a stage or on a screen directly. There is no narrator. Yet one can identify the same elements of plot as are found in narration.

INFO Elements of a dramatic plot

exposition → rising action → climax/crisis → falling action → dénouement/catastrophe

In tragedy, the opponents of the hero gain the upper hand in the falling action, which ends in the catastrophe.

Comedy has a happy ending, in which conflicts are resolved (dénouement).

Stage directions

The dramatic text consist of **two kinds of text:** the more important kind of text is **spoken by the characters** (i.e. dialogues, monologues, soliloquys and asides).
The **stage directions** are the second kind of text. They give instructions concerning the stage design, about sounds to be heard, visual effects, the characters' actions and also the way some of the dialogue has to be spoken.
The following visual and acoustic elements will have to be considered in your analysis of stage directions. They will help to characterise, to create a specific atmosphere or they will function as symbols (cf. p. 82).

concerning the actors		**concerning the stage**	
visual	**acoustic**	**visual**	**acoustic**
size facial expression gestures costumes	voice intonation language of the play non-verbal noises	scenery stage design lighting properties/props *(Requisiten)*	music noise sound

Characters

The characters are not mediated via a narrator but are presented through action, interaction and dialogue and, of course, their outward appearance on stage (see above). There are **flat** characters, types that act in a predictable way, and **round**, lifelike characters that are fully developed and usually go through some form of inner development over the course of the play.

Language/Dialogue/Communication

Analysing the language of a play you have to keep in mind that it works on two levels:

1. the inner system of communication, i.e. the communication among the characters
2. the outer system of communication between the playwright and the audience

outer system of communication

playwright

inner system of communication

characters

audience

Dramatic irony
Dramatic irony is an important effect that is created by these two levels of communication. It arises when there is a sharp contrast between what the audience knows and what a character knows or utters. Dramatic irony often serves to great comic effect as well. Shakespeare, for example, puts it to great effect in his comedies when he introduces cases of mistaken identity.
Examples:
In Shakespeare's tragedy Macbeth, *King Duncan praises the peaceful atmosphere at Macbeth's castle, whereas the audience knows that Macbeth is planning to murder Duncan.*
In Shakespeare's comedy Twelfth Night, *Viola, disguised as a man, is asked by the Duke, whom she has fallen in love with, to woo Olivia for him.*

Aside
In an aside an actor speaks to the audience in order to provide information on his thoughts and feelings or intentions. The other characters on stage supposedly do not hear what she/he says.

TIPP
As many of Shakespeare's plays are written in verse, you may approach their language in the same way as poetry.

Glossary – Vocabulary for Analysing Literary Texts

the narrator tells of / shows / relates / reveals
the narrator takes xy's point of view
the narrator is omniscient
the story is told in the first/third person
the story is told from the first-person-singular point of view
the narrator uses / employs / makes use of
this metaphor shows / stands for / suggests
the narrator speaks in an ironic/satirical/detached/matter-of-fact/serious tone
the story deals with / treats of / concentrates on / focuses on
the ... atmosphere is created by
tension/suspense is created / built up
the poem is written/composed
the poem is read/spoken/recited
a recital of a poem

the poem is by Shakespeare
it is a song by Genesis
the speaker of the poem / the lyrical "I" / the poetic persona
the poem consists of / is composed of / is arranged in stanzas
the comedy ridicules/mocks/satirises
the exposition sets the action in motion
the action moves towards and culminates in a turning point
the play/film has a simple/complex/tight plot
it has a happy/unhappy ending
there are main/major/minor characters
the protagonist is in conflict with an opponent
the antagonist fights the protagonist
the spectator/audience follows the play
the play is performed/produced/staged
scenery is shifted
actors perform/play/enact
an actor enters / makes an entrance
an actor exits / makes his exit

Sach- und Gebrauchstexte

Argumentative Texts: How to Deal with (Political) Speeches

Keyword

(Political) speeches: aim at convincing *(überzeugen)* the audience of the speaker's position, winning them over to his/her side. Very often, the speaker tries to persuade (überreden) the listener by appealing to his/her feelings. In some cases, the orator may even attempt to manipulate *(manipulieren)* his audience.
You should always keep in mind that the speaker wants to present his/her opinion / conviction / point of view as positively as possible.

When asked to analyse a political speech, you will have to focus on the topic as well as characteristic features.

How to proceed

Reading the text

1. Read the (political) speech (or, more likely, an extract from it) as a whole, trying to identify the main topic (reading for gist).
2. Re-read the (political) speech or extract several times, paying close attention to certain characteristic features of such speeches. Mark words or phrases in the text and take notes (intensive reading).

Pay special attention to

- key words and phrases
- references to historical events
- use of symbols, key words, slogans
- references to famous people
- references to works of literature
- stylistic devices (see below)

Questions to be asked

When it comes to analysing a (political) speech, you should always ask yourself the following questions:

- What is the main topic of the speech?
- What is its political, historical and social context?
- What do I know about the speaker (biography, political orientation)?

Elements of a (political) speech

Structure

(Political) speeches can usually be divided into **introduction**, **main part** and **conclusion**. These parts serve different purposes:

INFO Introduction to a speech

In the introduction the orator announces the topic/purpose of the speech and explains why it is of major importance. He/she also wants to attract the audience's attention so that they will follow the speech closely and accept his/her opinion.

There are several ways to make listeners interested:
- The speaker can open by telling the audience **something about their personal history/recent experiences**, thereby underlining the fact that the topic of the speech is of personal importance to them. By relating a **little story** to the audience, the speaker will also appear more human and less flawless.
- Another common way of starting a speech is to **open it with a question** that refers to the main topic and which will be answered later in the speech. By asking the audience a question, the speaker actively involves them, indirectly asking them to think more deeply about an issue.
- A speaker may also **present visuals to the audience**, e.g. pictures, concrete objects or a short extract from a film. This also helps to attract the audience's attention: listeners will become curious about how the object or visual is related to the content of the speech.

INFO Main part of a speech

In the main part of the speech the orator needs to keep the audience interested and to make sure that they can follow the train of thought.

Again, there are several ways to do this. The following techniques are particularly effective:
- **using short and simple sentences**, developing the argumentation step by step and ensuring that the audience can follow,
- quoting reliable sources/experts, referring to statistics and **providing the audience with facts and necessary background information**, which shows that the speaker is well-informed and has researched the subject ,
- **pointing out problems** but also providing solutions for them, thus showing that the speaker is competent, and
- **including personal experiences** and vivid, specific events, again aiming for a personal relationship to the audience, **often using personal pronouns like "we", "us", "our".**

Towards the end of a speech the speaker might
- take up a question posed at the beginning of the speech,
- appeal once more to both the audience's heads and hearts,
- ask for support, giving the listeners the feeling that their support is important, and
- develop a vision for the future.

Argumentative comments use the same stylistic means as political speeches.

Language and style

There are certain stylistic devices, which are often used in (political) speeches. They aim at making the speech more lively and interesting.

Important stylistic devices

analogy	A resemblance is established between things which are dissimilar.
simile	This is a direct comparison using the words "like" or "as", e.g. *He fought like a lion in the battle.*
metaphor	This is an indirect comparison without using the words "like" or "as", e.g. *He was a lion in battle.*
alliteration	A consonantal sound of two or more adjacent words is repeated, e.g. *We will win; "We must understand that ties of trade bind nations in closest intimacy"* (Warren G. Harding: Inaugural address, 4 March 1921).
repetition	Repeating certain words or phrases puts emphasis on the meaning of the words and phrases in question, e.g. *"The answer to the slavery question was already embedded within our Constitution – a Constitution that had at its very core the ideal of equal citizenship under the law; a Constitution that promised its people liberty, and justice "* (Barack Obama: *A More Perfect Union)*.
parallelism	Two or more parts of a sentence (or two or more sentences) have the same (or similar) syntactical structure. Like repetition, parallelism puts stress on the parts of the sentence in question, intensifying the force of the statement and encouraging the audience to think about its meaning, e.g. *"Let us be our sister's keeper. Let us find that common stake we all have in one another, and let our politics reflect that spirit as well."* (Barack Obama: *A More Perfect Union)*
antithesis	Two ideas are opposed to one another, using a parallel syntactical structure to reach the desired effect, i.e. establishing a contrast, e.g. *"It's a story that hasn't made me the most conventional candidate. But it is a story that has seared into my genetic makeup the idea that this nation is more than the sum of its parts – that out of many, we are truly one."* (Barack Obama: *A More Perfect Union)*

rhetorical question	A rhetorical question is one to which no answer is expected; instead, the listener is asked to think about the question and its relevance, e. g. *How long should this suffering continue?*
irony	Words or phrases are used to mean something different, often the opposite of their literal meaning. This is often done for rhetorical or humorous effect.

Glossary – Vocabulary for Analysing Speeches

By telling the listeners something about his personal history he attempts to establish a personal relationship with his audience.	Er bemüht sich, eine persönliche Beziehung zu seinen Zuhörern aufzubauen, indem er seinem Publikum etwas über seine persönliche Geschichte erzählt.
She attempts to win her listeners over to her side.	Sie versucht, das Publikum auf ihre Seite zu ziehen.
He draws a comparison between ... and ...	Er zieht einen Vergleich zwischen ... und ...
He puts emphasis on the meaning of his words by using a parallelism/repetition in line X.	Durch den in Zeile X verwendeten Parallelismus / die in Zeile X verwendete Wiederholung verleiht er seinen Worten Nachdruck.
He refers to well-known historical events such as ...	Er bezieht sich auf allgemein bekannte historische Ereignisse wie z. B. ...
He wants to call/draw the audience's attention to the fact that ...	Er möchte die Aufmerksamkeit des Publikums auf die Tatsache lenken, dass ...
His frequent use of rhetorical questions is intended to show that ...	Sein häufiger Gebrauch rhetorischer Fragen soll verdeutlichen, dass ...
His metaphorical use of language is intended to make his speech more lively and interesting.	Sein metaphorischer Sprachgebrauch soll seine Rede interessanter und lebendiger machen.
In lline X he directly criticises his political opponents.	In Zeile X kritisiert er offen seine politischen Gegner.
The frequent use of personal pronouns such as "we", "us" and "our" gives the audience the impression that he does not regard himself as superior to them but as one of them.	Der häufige Gebrauch der Personalpronomen „wir", „uns" und „unser" soll dem Publikum das Gefühl geben, dass er sich als einer von ihnen und nicht als eine höher gestellte Person sieht.
The speaker appeals to the audience's emotions by ...	Der Redner / Die Rednerin spricht die Gefühle des Publikums an, indem er/sie ...
The speaker begins by ...	Der Redner / Die Rednerin beginnt mit ...

The speaker makes frequent use of metaphors/similes/symbols/examples to point out / to underline that ...	Der Redner / Die Rednerin macht regen Gebrauch von Metaphern/Vergleichen/Symbolen/Beispielen, um herauszustellen / zu unterstreichen, dass ...
The speaker tries to convince his audience of his point of view by ...	Der Redner / Die Rednerin versucht sein/ihr Publikum von seinem/ihrem Standpunkt zu überzeugen, indem er/sie ...
The speaker aims to convince/persuade/manipulate the audience.	Es ist das Anliegen des Redners / der Rednerin, das Publikum zu überzeugen/überreden/manipulieren.

Expository Texts: How to Deal with Essays

Keyword

Essay: There are various kinds:

a) essays which reflect the author's opinion on a certain topic **(comment)**

b) essays in which the author weighs the pros and cons of a particular subject (**argumentative essay**)

c) essays in which a topic is presented in a clear and logical way and which do not contain the author's opinion (**expository essay**)

How to proceed

First you have to find out which kind of essay you are asked to analyse.

TIPP Argumentative comments

Argumentative comments use the same stylistic means as political speeches.

For details on how to analyse **comments** you can refer to the section on **political speeches** above.
Here we will focus on the **argumentative essay.**

Structure

- In the **introduction** the author expresses the main idea of the essay. Instead of giving a personal opinion, she/he might choose to provide the reader with some background information, or start with a question which will serve as a guideline and be answered in the course of the essay.
- For the **main part** of the essay, the author can decide on a dialectical or an enumerative approach.
- In an **enumerative approach** the author will enumerate all the aspects of the subject in a neutral way. A **dialectical approach** can either present all the arguments in favour of a position before focusing on the counterarguments (or vice versa), or it can present the pros and cons alternately. The latter is usually considered more skilful.

- Each **new aspect** is usually presented in a new paragraph. The various **arguments** can be backed with examples from real life, established facts, an expert opinion or other reliable sources. These pieces of evidence are very important, as they enable the author to make his/her argument convincing and thus to persuade the reader.
- In the **conclusion** the author sums up the arguments, frequently also restating his/her own opinion and giving an outlook on the future.

Glossary – Vocabulary for Analysing Essays

The author discusses the pros and cons of …	Der Verfasser / Die Verfasserin diskutiert die Vor- und Nachteile von …
The author gives his/her personal opinion on the problem of …	Der Verfasser / Die Verfasserin äußert seine/ihre eigene Meinung zum Thema …
He/She believes / is convinced / presumes that …	Er/Sie glaubt / ist überzeugt davon / nimmt an, dass …
She/He wants to persuade the reader …	Sie/Er möchte die Lesenden überreden …
One can easily follow his train of thought.	Man kann seinen Gedankengang leicht nachvollziehen.
At the end of her essay she draws / comes to the conclusion …	Am Ende ihres Berichts kommt sie zu dem Schluss …
His/Her arguments are (not) convincing/ well-chosen.	Seine/Ihre Argumente sind (nicht) überzeugend / gut gewählt.
The main topic of the essay is …	Das Thema des Berichts ist …
The tone of this essay is humorous/neutral/ironic/serious.	Der Ton des Berichts ist humorvoll/neutral/ironisch/ernst.
The author uses real examples to convince her/his readers.	Die Verfasserin / Der Verfasser verwendet reale Beispiele, um ihre/seine Leserschaft zu überzeugen.
The author's choice of words shows/underlines that he/she is for/against …	Die Wortwahl des Verfassers / der Verfasserin zeigt/unterstreicht, dass er/sie für/gegen … ist.
In the introductory paragraph of her/his essay, he/she asks a rhetorical question which serves as a thread for the whole text.	Im einleitenden Abschnitt seines/ihres Berichts stellt er/sie den Lesenden eine rhetorische Frage, die sich wie ein roter Faden durch den Text zieht.
The author uses adjectives with a positive/negative connotation to support his/her point of view.	Der Verfasser / Die Verfasserin verwendet Adjektive mit einer positiven/ negativen Konnotation, um seinen/ihren Standpunkt zu verdeutlichen.
Her attempt to persuade the readers backfires / works very well.	Ihr Versuch, die Lesenden zu überreden, misslingt/gelingt.

Narrative Texts: How to Deal with Reports

Keyword
Report: This is a special kind of newspaper article.
It provides answers to the five "W" questions *(Who? What? Where? When? Why?)*, as well as the *How* question. Its aim is to inform its readers and NOT to manipulate or influence them.
A report deals with current events and only contains facts.

Sometimes students have problems when it comes to differentiating between a *report* and an *article*, which might also deal with current events but which is usually a mixture of both fact and opinion.
The style of an **article** is usually more personal and its main aim is to entertain the reader. This is ensured by using many adverbs and adjectives to make the article lively and by addressing its readers directly, often by asking them a hypothetical question, e. g. *How would you feel if you discovered that someone had stolen your brand-new car?*
The main characteristics of a **report** are outlined below.

Elements of a report

Structure

- To arouse the reader's curiosity, reports have **headlines** containing basic information without providing too much detail.
- The basic information is generally provided in the first paragraph, which serves as an **introduction.**
- The **main body** of a report consists of different paragraphs, which contain one piece of information each.
- The last paragraph serves as a kind of **conclusion.**

Language and style

- A report is written in a factual style and neither reflects the author's personal opinion nor contains any kind of speculation.
- Individual paragraphs are relatively short and consist of short sentences, which aim to ensure that the reader understands the information presented.
- Experts – or people who have first-hand experience of the topic in question – are often quoted, but no authorial comment is given about what they say.

Glossary – Vocabulary for Analysing Reports

The report [title] written by [author] deals with / is about / relates / describes ...	Der Bericht [Titel] von [Verfasser] beschäftigt sich mit / handelt von / berichtet von / beschreibt ...
The theme(s) of the report is (are) ...	Das Thema / Die Themen des Berichts ist/sind ...
In the introduction the reader learns about / gets to know ...	In der Einleitung erfährt der Leser / die Leserin ...
The report can be divided into ... paragraphs.	Der Bericht kann in ... Absätze gegliedert werden.
The report consists of ... paragraphs.	Der Bericht besteht aus ... Absätzen.
It is the author's aim to inform the reader about ...	Es ist das Anliegen des Autors / der Autorin, den Leser / die Leserin über ... zu informieren.
The 2nd/3rd paragraph contains information on ...	Der 2./3. Absatz enthält Informationen über ...
The author quotes an eye-witness/expert who says that ...	Der Autor / Die Autorin zitiert einen Augenzeugen/Experten, der sagt, dass ...
The author describes how ...	Der Verfasser / Die Verfasserin beschreibt, wie ...
The author does not give his/her personal opinion on the subject/problem/question but merely relates facts.	Der Verfasser / Die Verfasserin äußert nicht seine/ihre eigene Meinung zum Sachverhalt / Problem / zu der Frage, sondern gibt Fakten wieder.
The factual style of writing shows that it is the author's aim to inform the reader and not to entertain him/her.	Der sachliche Sprachgebrauch verdeutlicht, dass es das Anliegen des Autors / der Autorin ist, die Lesenden zu informieren und nicht, sie zu unterhalten.

How to Deal with Cartoons, Diagrams and Statistics

Keywords:
Cartoons are visual images aimed at criticising, ridiculing or commenting on current events or ideas.
Diagrams and statistics: intend to present information by comparing different items and their relations to each other. Diagram types include pie charts, bar charts, tables and line graphs.
In written exams cartoons, diagrams and statistics will always be accompanied by a text.

Dealing with cartoons

Taking a closer look: What is shown?
Describe all the important elements of the cartoon in detail and point out the relation between them:
- start with the foreground and end with the background; of course, you can also proceed from top to bottom or from left to right, but make sure that your reader can easily follow your train of thought,
- indicate the key features of each object or character, including captions and speech bubbles.

Analysing the message: What is the cartoonist's intention?
Explain what the artist wants to express by
- examining the use of colours if the cartoon comes in colours,
- focusing on the relation of the objects and characters presented in the cartoon (e.g. size, situation and role within the cartoon),
- interpreting the meaning of the caption or speech bubble (if the cartoon has these features).

In written exams cartoons will not have to be analysed alone but always in combination with a text. Therefore, one should always pay close attention to the respective task.
It might also be necessary to consider the political, historical or social context and to refer to one's background knowledge.
Here it is also important to look at the task once more (What is the connection between cartoon and text?).

Evaluating the cartoon: Does the cartoonist get his/her message across? Is the cartoon effective?
After having described and analysed the cartoon, you should evaluate whether it is effective or not. You are free to give your own opinion, but do not forget to give reasons for it.

Dealing with Diagrams and Statistics

Taking a closer look:
What is the diagram about? / What are the statistics about?
First state what kind of diagram (table, pie chart ...) you are describing and what it is about.
Diagrams or statistics usually come with a heading, which includes necessary information about what is being described, referred to or compared, as well as the source the information is taken from. Do not forget to mention this.

Analysing the diagram/statistics:
What can be concluded from the diagram/statistics?
Describe the relation between the different items (e.g. in bar charts and pie charts) and/or the development shown (e.g. in line graphs).
Then it is time to draw your conclusions from what is shown. In written exams you should also point out the connections between the diagram/statistics and the text.

Glossary – Vocabulary for Analysing Cartoons, Diagrams and Statistics

pie chart	Tortendiagramm
bar chart	Säulendiagramm
table	Tabelle
line graph	Kurvendiagramm
per cent / percentage	Prozent / prozentualer Anteil
The cartoon / pie chart shows / depicts / presents / is about ...	Der Cartoon / Das Tortendiagramm stellt ... dar / zeigt ... auf / handelt von ...
The cartoon/diagram is taken from ...	Der Cartoon / Das Diagramm stammt von/aus ...
The artist mainly uses light/bright/dark colours to achieve the desired effect.	Der/Die Künstler/-in verwendet überwiegend helle/strahlende/dunkle Farben, um den gewünschten Effekt zu erzielen.
The cartoonist wants the spectator to ...	Der/Die Karikaturist/-in möchte, dass der/die Betrachtende ...
The artist intends to ...	Der/Die Künstler/-in beabsichtigt ...
The message of the cartoon is that ...	Die Botschaft des Cartoons ist, dass ...
In the foreground/background of the cartoon one can see ...	Im Vorder-/Hintergrund des Cartoons kann man ... sehen.
In the top left-hand corner / in the bottom right-hand corner ... is shown.	In der linken oberen / der rechten unteren Ecke wird ... gezeigt/dargestellt.
The bar chart compares the development of ... and ...	Das Säulendiagramm vergleicht die Entwicklung von ... und ...

The pie chart is divided into ... slices, each slice representing ...	Das Tortendiagramm ist in ... Stücke aufgeteilt, von denen jedes ... darstellt.
Looking at the size of the different slices of the pie chart / at the height of the different bars of the bar chart, one can conclude that ...	Wenn man die Größe der verschiedenen Stücke des Tortendiagramms / die Höhe der verschiedenen Balken des Balkendiagramms betrachtet, kann man erkennen / darauf schließen, dass ...
The bar chart describes the relation between ... and ...	Das Säulendiagramm beschreibt die Beziehung zwischen ... und ...
The line graph shows the population development in ... from (month/year) to (month/year).	Das Kurvendiagramm stellt die Bevölkerungsentwicklung in ... von (Monat/Jahr) bis (Monat/Jahr) dar.
Over the period of time covered by the line graph, the population of ... increased/decreased from ... to ... / the number of inhabitants remained constant.	In dem Zeitraum, der durch das Kurvendiagramm abgedeckt wird, hat sich die Bevölkerung in ... von ... auf ... vergrößert/ verrringert / ist die Zahl der Einwohner/-innen in ... gleich geblieben.
The horizontal axis of the line chart shows ..., while the vertical axis represents ...	Die horizontale Achse (x-Achse) des Kurvendiagramms zeigt ..., während die vertikale Achse (y-Achse) ... abbildet.
The number of ... in ... is compared in the pie chart / bar chart.	Das Tortendiagramm/Balkendiagramm vergleicht die Anzahl von ... in ...
All figures are given in per cent.	Alle Zahlen werden in Prozent angegeben.

Sprachmittlung

Im Klausurteil B, der Aufgabe zur Sprachmittlung, werden Sie dazu angehalten, die wesentlichen Inhalte von authentischen deutschen Texten sinngemäß und zusammenfassend in englischer Sprache wiederzugeben. Dabei ist es wichtig, dass Sie darauf achten, Ihren Text zielgruppengerecht und situationsangemessen zu verfassen.

Eine Sprachmittlungsaufgabe gibt immer eine fiktive Situation vor, die eine Mittlung des deutschen Ausgangstextes verlangt. Im Gegensatz zu einer Übersetzung, die die wörtliche Übertragung eines Textes in die andere Sprache mitsamt aller möglicherweise vorhandenen Untertöne, Bildhaftigkeit, Ironie etc. erfordert, geht es bei der Sprachmittlung nur um die sinngemäße Übertragung in die Fremdsprache.

Je nach Aufgabenstellung geht es entweder um eine Zusammenfassung des Textes, häufiger jedoch um das „Herauspicken" relevanter Informationen. Die Methodik für die inhaltliche Bearbeitung der Aufgabe gleicht also der Methodik für die Erstellung von Inhaltsangaben.

Beim Schreiben des englischen Textes berücksichtigt man die verschiedenen Aspekte der Sprachmittlung, wie sie hier in einer Übersicht dargestellt werden:[1]

sinngemäß	– keine wortwörtliche Übersetzung – keine Übernahme von Stilmitteln oder Ton – ggf. implizierte Inhalte – nur die Inhalte des Textes, kein eigenes Wissen
situationsangemessen	– angemessener Stil – Beachtung der vorgegebenen Textform
zielgruppengerecht	– passendes Register (Freund? Professor? Gastmutter?) – Erläuterung von sprachlichen und kulturellen Eigenheiten[1]
zusammenfassend	– wesentliche Inhalte – ggf. wesentliche Details – nicht detailliert – nicht kommentiert (d. h. keine eigene Meinung)

TIPP zum Punktesammeln

Beachten Sie – wie immer – genau die Aufgabenstellung! Anders als bei der kreativen Teilaufgabe in Klausurteil A müssen Sie möglicherweise nicht den kompletten Zieltext erstellen, sondern nur den Teil, den die Sprachmittlung ausmacht. So kann die Aufgabenstellung z. B. lauten: "Write the part of your email that is based on ..." oder "Write the part of your article that deals with ...".

[1] Viele Eigennamen oder Konnotationen werden sich dem fremdsprachlichen Adressaten nicht erschließen. Sie bedürfen daher einer Erklärung oder Umschreibung (z. B. *Rosenmontag, Abigag, BILD-Zeitung).*

Zieltextformate

In der anwendungs-/produktionsorientierten Teilaufgabe *re-creation of text* des Klausurteils A werden die in diesem Kapitel behandelten Textformate vorausgesetzt:
- *letter/email, letter to the editor*
- *speech script: talk, public/formal speech, debate statement*
- *newspaper/internet article*
- nur im Leistungskurs: (written) interview
- Ausgestaltung, Fortführung oder Ergänzung eines literarischen Ausgangstextes: narrative Texte; zusätzlich im Leistungskurs: dramatische Texte, *film script*

In Klausurteil B (Sprachmittlung) wird Vertrautheit mit den folgenden Zieltextformaten vorausgesetzt:
- *letter/email*
- *newspaper/internet article*

Letter/Email

Formal Letter (förmlicher Brief)

Äußere Form

Adresse:
- eigene Adresse: anders als in Deutschland oben rechts, üblicherweise ohne Namen
- Empfänger: darunter auf der linken Seite

Datum:
unter der Anschrift entweder rechts oder links, Monat als Wort

persönlich bekannter Empfänger:
Anrede:
Dear Mr/Mrs/Miss/Ms/Dr/Professor/...
(*Ms* ist die neutrale Form, um *Mrs* bzw. *Miss* zu umgehen)

Schlussformel:
Yours sincerely / Kind regards

unbekannter Empfänger:
Anrede:
Dear Sir / Dear Madam,
Dear Sir or Madam,

Schlussformel:
Yours faithfully

Unterschrift:
- persönliche Unterschrift
- darunter Name in Druckschrift

Inhaltliche Gliederung

Einleitung:
Bezug und Zweck des Briefes

Hauptteil:
relevante Informationen, klar und logisch dargelegt, keine Schnörkel und Abschweifungen

Ende:
Erwartung an den Empfänger, üblicherweise als Bitte oder Aufforderung

Sprache

förmlich, **keine** *informal language,* d. h. **vermeiden** Sie
- *short forms* wie *it's, would've, can't*
- Interjektionen und Füllwörter wie *well, alright, okay, I see, you know*
- *question tags (isn't it, don't you, etc.)*

Benutzen Sie Wendungen wie
- *With reference to your letter of May 13th ...*
- *Thank you for your letter of ...*

- *I am writing to apply / to enquire about / to inform you / to lodge a complaint regarding ...*
- *I should be delighted if ...*
- *I would be very glad if ...*
- *It would be very convenient if ...*
- *Please find enclosed ...* (In der Anlage finden Sie ...)

- *I should very much appreciate it if ...*
- *Please note that ...*

- *Thank you very much in advance.*

Die Regeln für die äußere Form gelten für eine E-Mail nicht. Die Form wird ja im Browser oder Client vorgegeben. Sprachlich gelten dieselben Regeln.

Letter to the Editor (Leserbrief)

Ein Leserbrief ist eher ein Zeitungsartikel als ein förmlicher Brief.
Zur sprachlichen und inhaltlichen Gestaltung siehe *Comment* (S. 109).

Äußere Form

Anrede:
Sir, oder *Madam,* – kein *Dear* (gilt nicht bei einer Schülerzeitung)

Unterschrift:
Name, Stadt, ggf. Land/US-Staat

Personal Letter (persönlicher Brief)

Äußere Form

Adresse und Datum:
- eigene Adresse: anders als in Deutschland oben rechts, üblicherweise ohne Namen
- Datum darunter

Anrede:
Dear ...

Schlussformel:
Yours (nicht: *your) / Best wishes / All the best / (Lots of) Love* (nicht: *in love) / Your friend ...*

Unterschrift:
Vorname

Inhaltliche Gliederung

Einleitung:
Bezug zum Ausgangstext, Grund des Schreibens

Hauptteil:
z. B. Erzählung, Erklärung, Erläuterung, relevante Informationen

Ende:
z. B. Fragen, Vorschläge, Ausblick

Sprache

- freundlicher Ton
- *informal language,* d. h.:
  - *short forms* wie *it's, would've, can't*
  - Interjektionen und Füllwörter wie *well, alright, okay, I see, you know*

  - *question tags (isn't it, don't you* etc.*)*
  - weitgehend einfache Satzgefüge
- Alltagsvokabular, thematisches Vokabular

Speech Script (Rede)

Denkbar – und in den vergangenen Jahren im Abitur als kreative Teilaufgabe vorgekommen – sind verschiedene Formen der Rede wie *talk* (Vortrag), *public/formal speech* (öffentliche/formelle Rede) oder *statement* (Erklärung).

Talk (Vortrag)

Einleitung:
- Begrüßung der Zuhörerschaft
- ggf. Vorstellung der eigenen Person
- Anknüpfung an den Ausgangstext
- Zusammenfassung von Inhalt und Zielen des Vortrags
- ggf. vorgesehene Gliederung

Hauptteil:
richtet sich nach dem Zweck des Vortrages:
- etwas mitteilen
- Interesse für ein Thema wecken
- für Publikation, Produkt, Dienstleistung werben
- einen Standpunkt verteidigen
- Zuhörer überzeugen
- Diskussion anregen

Strukturieren Sie ihren Hauptteil inhaltlich stringent! Ein inhaltlicher Aspekt folgt dem anderen, Argumente und Beispiele unterstreichen die einzelnen Aspekte.

Ende:
- Zusammenfassung
- Appell
- Ausblick
- Dank an die Zuhörer

Public/Formal Speech

Die öffentliche Rede ist meist politischer Art und dient der Überzeugung der Zuhörerschaft.

Einleitung:
weniger sachlich als der Vortrag, d. h.:
- keine Zusammenfassung von Inhalt und Zielen
- keine Vorstellung der Gliederung
- keine persönliche Vorstellung

Begrüßung der Zuhörer
- Anknüpfung an den Ausgangstext
- provokative oder plakative Hinführung zum Thema
- Problemstellung (und evtl. Lösung in Aussicht stellen)

Hauptteil:
- klare Argumentation
- Kausalketten beachten
- Belege durch logische Argumente, Beispiele, Expertenmeinungen, Verweis auf Autoritäten (Regierung, Kirche, Wissenschaft)

Ende:
- Zusammenfassung
- Appell

Statement

Ein Statement wird gewöhnlich im Vorfeld einer Debatte abgegeben, um die Fronten zu klären. Ziel eines Statements ist es, einen Standpunkt zu verteidigen oder gar die Zuhörenden zu überzeugen. So wird es den objektiven Ton eines Vortrages mit den Zielen der öffentlichen Rede verbinden.

Anrede:
Unbedingt der vorgebenen Situation anpassen, z. B.
- *Dear Students / Dear Listeners / Dear Members of ... (talk)*
- *Fellow Citizens / Friends / Dear Citizens of ... (public speech)*
- *Ladies and Gentlemen*
- bei Anwesenheit hochrangiger Personen oder auch nur Gastgeberinnen/Gastgebern: *Mr President / Your Majesty / Prime Minister / Mr Chairman / Mr Jones*

Hinführung:
- plakative Aussagesätze
- weitgehend einfache Satzgefüge
- Fragen

public speech:
- rhetorische Fragen
- Anspielungen
- Ironie

Hauptteil:
talk/statement:
- klare, weitgehend einfache Aussagesätze
- sachlicher, objektiver Stil

public speech:
emphatische Mittel: Parallelismen, Aufzählungen, Wiederholungen
(s. „Methoden der Textarbeit", S. 93)

Ende:
appellative Strukturen:
- *We must / We have to / We should ...*
- *It is imperative that ...*
- *Let us ...*

TIPP zum Punktesammeln

Überfrachten Sie Ihre Rede nicht mit Metaphern und emphatischen Mitteln! Das kann albern wirken.

Dank:
- *Thank you.*
- *Thank you for your attention.*

Newspaper Article / Internet Article

Report

Ein *report* ist ein Bericht beziehungsweise ein objektiver, sachlicher Artikel, dem eine Begebenheit oder eine Geschichte zugrunde liegt. Damit handelt es sich um einen narrativen Text. Sie können einen *report* in einer kreativen Aufgabe erwarten, wann immer eine Geschichte zu erzählen ist, insbesondere dann, wenn der Ausgangstext gerade kein Zeitungsartikel ist.
Dramen oder Gedichte bieten häufig Stoff als Grundlage für einen Bericht.

Beachten Sie die Merkmale eines Berichtes, wie sie im Kapitel „Methoden der Textarbeit" zusammengefasst werden (S. 97 f.).

Comment

Ein *comment* ist die Textform, die Sie besonders häufig als Sachtextvorlage Ihrer Analyseaufgabe finden. Als kreative Aufgabe sind verschiedene *comments* vorstellbar:
- ein Artikel aus Ihrer persönlichen Sicht
- ein Artikel aus der persönlichen Sicht einer Figur des Ausgangstextes
- ein Artikel aus der persönlichen Sicht des lyrischen Ichs eines lyrischen Ausgangstextes
- ein Artikel aus der persönlichen Sicht einer Figur aus Werken, die Sie im Unterricht behandelt haben

Sollten Sie die Aufgabe mit engem Bezug zum Ausgangstext gewählt haben, so stellen Sie sicher, dass Sie Ihre Erkenntnisse aus den Teilaufgaben 1 und 2 heranziehen, um die Aufgabe optimal zu lösen! Der Schlüssel zu Ihrer persönlichen Stellungnahme, aber auch zur fiktiven Person einer Verfasserin bzw. eines Verfassers und deren/dessen persönlicher Meinung liegt genau darin.

Sprache und Aufbau

Beachten Sie die Merkmale eines Essays, wie sie im Kapitel „Methoden der Textarbeit" (s. S. 95 f.) zusammengefasst werden! Für den Sprachgebrauch orientieren Sie sich an der Rhetorik der öffentlichen Rede (s. S. 91–95)!

(Written) Interview (nur LK)

Auch im Interview geht es um eine persönliche Stellungnahme, allerdings nicht um Ihre persönliche Meinung, sondern um die eines fiktiven Gesprächspartners.

> **Achtung, häufiger Fehler:**
> Schreiben Sie nur in Dialogform! Schreiben Sie keinen Erzähltext, in dem wörtliche Rede nur anteilig enthalten ist!

Struktur

Beginn:
- Aufnahme der situativen Vorgabe der Aufgabenstellung
- Begrüßung, Vorstellung
- Anknüpfung an den Ausgangstext
- Hinführung zum Thema, ggf. Vorstellung des Anliegens

Hauptteil:
- Frage/Antwort in sinnvoller Verknüpfung
- Argumente und Beispiele

Schluss:
- Abrundung, z. B.:
  - Zusammenfassung
  - Witz
  - Ausblick
  - Dank
  - Verabschiedung

Sprache
- freundlicher Ton
- *informal language*, d.h.:
  - *short forms* wie *isn't, I'm, should've*
  - Interjektionen und Füllwörter wie *well, alright, okay, I see, you know*
  - *question tags (isn't it, don't you* etc.*)*
  - weitgehend einfache Satzgefüge
- Alltagsvokabular, thematisches Vokabular

- rhetorische Mittel: Wiederholungen, Aufzählungen, Anaphern, aber keine ausgefeilten Stilfiguren
- Grußformel: *Good morning/afternoon/evening Mr/Mrs Jones / Sir / Ma'am*
- Schlussformel: z. B. *Thank you for your time, goodbye ..., Thank you very much for the interview. Goodbye ...*

Literarische Texte

Narrative Texte

Im Abitur werden Ihnen narrative Ausgangstexte meist als Roman- oder Kurzgeschichtenauszug begegnen. Folgende Varianten einer kreativen Aufgabenstellung sind denkbar:

- Lücken füllen (d. h. Begebenheiten, die im Ausgangstext nur erwähnt werden oder die der/die Lesende nur aus dem Handlungsverlauf erschließen kann, sollen kreativ ausgestaltet werden),
- ein Ende oder eine Fortsetzung schreiben,
- ein alternatives Ende schreiben,
- Perspektivwechsel.

Übernehmen Sie – falls die Aufgabenstellung es nicht ausdrücklich anders verlangt – die Erzählperspektive des Ausgangstextes!
Beachten Sie, dass Figuren sich weiterhin so verhalten, wie es ihrem Charakter entspricht, auch in ihrer Sprache!

> Schreiben Sie keine neue Story mit einem vollständigen *plot* und einem neuen Höhepunkt. Es geht nicht um die Erfindung einer spannenden oder besonders originellen Handlung, sondern um eine logisch-konsequente Ausgestaltung des Ausgangstextes.

Sprache

Übernehmen Sie, soweit es geht, den Stil des Ausgangstextes.

Übernehmen Sie das Tempus des Ausgangstextes. In der Regel werden narrative Texte im *past tense* erzählt. Beachten Sie die Tempora der Vergangenheit.

<u>Beispiel:</u>
*The ground **was** wet because it **had been raining** all morning and although the rain **had stopped** and the sun **was shining** now, it **would be** difficult to find the track. On dry ground it **would have been** easy.*

was wet – Erzähltempus
it had been raining – vorzeitig; andauernd bis hin zum Erzählzeitpunkt; Betonung der Dauer/Kontinuität einer Situation
had stopped – vorzeitig; Situation zum Erzählzeitpunkt abgeschlossen; Betonung der Beendigung / des Effekts einer Situation
was shining – gerade ablaufende Hintergrundhandlung
it would be difficult – Zukunft aus der Sicht der Vergangenheit
it would have been easy – reine Hypothese in der Vergangenheit

Wechsel der Textform

Sollte die Aufgabenstellung eine vollständige Erzählung z. B. auf der Grundlage eines Gedichtes oder eines Zeitungsartikels verlangen, so achten Sie auf einen plausiblen inhaltlichen Bezug. Für die Ausgestaltung Ihrer Erzählung beachten Sie die Erzählelemente, wie sie im Kapitel „Methoden der Textarbeit“ (S. 78–83) vorgestellt werden.

Dramatische Texte (Schauspiel/Film)

Folgende Varianten einer kreativen Aufgabenstellung sind denkbar:
Bei einem dramatischen Ausgangstext:
- Lücken füllen (d. h. Begebenheiten, die im Ausgangstext nur erwähnt werden, sollen kreativ ausgestaltet werden)
- ein Ende oder eine Fortsetzung schreiben
- ein alternatives Ende schreiben

Bei anderen Ausgangstexten (z. B. Erzählung, Zeitungsartikel, Gedicht):
- Wechsel der Textform

Beachten Sie, dass Figuren sich so verhalten, wie es ihrem Charakter entspricht, auch in ihrer Sprache.

Sprache

Dialogtext:
- gesprochene Sprache, d. h.
  - *short forms* wie *isn't, I'm, should've*
  - Interjektionen und Füllwörter wie *well, alright, okay, I see, you know*
  - *question tags (isn't it, don't you* etc.*)*
  - weitgehend einfache Satzgefüge
- Alltagsvokabular, thematisches Vokabular

stage directions:
- in Klammern
- stichpunktartig
- *present tense*

Achtung, häufiger Fehler!
Erzählen Sie keine Geschichte mit wörtlicher Rede! Schreiben Sie ein Bühnenstück mit Dialogen und Regieanweisungen!

Beispiele für Prüfungsaufgaben zu den Fokusthemen

Die Beispielaufgaben sind vom Umfang und vom Schwierigkeitsgrad her teilweise für Leistungskurse, teilweise für Grundkurse konzipiert. Für Grundkurse gilt eine maximale Wortzahl von 800 Wörtern, für Leistungskurse von 1000 Wörtern. Der deutsche Text für die Sprachmittlungsaufgabe umfasst in beiden Kursen zwischen 450 und 650 Wörtern. Für ein Prüfungstraining spielt die Zuordnung keine entscheidende Rolle.

Um den verschiedenen Vorgaben für die beiden Kursarten gerecht zu werden, wurden überwiegend Texte ausgewählt, die den Vorgaben beider Kursarten entsprechen (Ausnahme: Shakespeare).

Aufgaben mit Bearbeitungsschritten und Beispiellösungen

Themenfeld *Voices from the African Continent: Focus on Nigeria*

Aufgabenbeispiel Abitur Englisch Leistungskurs
Aufgabenart gemäß KLP: 1.1: Schreiben mit Leseverstehen integriert und Sprachmittlung isoliert
Thematischer Bezug gemäß KLP (Soziokulturelles Orientierungswissen): Postkolonialismus – Lebenswirklichkeiten in einem weiteren anglophonen Kulturraum: *Voices from the African Continent: Focus on Nigeria*
Auszüge aus einem englischsprachigen literarischen Text (437 W. und 411 W.) (Klausurteil A, Texte 1 und 2) Auszug aus einem deutschsprachigen Sach- und Gebrauchstext (534 W.) (Klausurteil B, Text 3)
Quellenangaben: Text 1 und 2: Chimamanda Ngozi Adichie, *Americanah,* London 2013, pp. 3–4, pp. 385–386 Text 3: Lorenz Maroldt, „Image der deutschen Hauptstadt. Warum finden alle Berlin so toll – außer den Berlinern?“, *Der Tagesspiegel,* 22.04.2018, https://www.tagesspiegel.de/berlin/image-der-deutschen-hauptstadt-warum-finden-alle-berlin-so-toll-ausser-den-berlinern/21200348.html (Zugriff: 01.04.2022, gekürzt)

Aufgabe

Klausurteil A: Leseverstehen/Schreiben (Text 1) 1. Describe Princeton and Lagos as presented in the excerpts. *(Comprehension)*

2. Examine the way the narrator presents Princeton and Lagos respectively. Consider the narrative point of view, atmosphere, characters and the language used. *(Analysis)*

3.1 Comment on the narrator's presentation of Lagos and Ranyinudo. Assess to what extent it represents Nigeria's as well as Africa's social, cultural and economic situation. *(Evaluation: Comment)*

3.2 Ifemelu and Ranyinudo apparently often talk about the situation in Nigeria as compared to the Western world (ll. 100–105). Write a dialogue between them considering aspects hinted at in the texts as well as aspects discussed in class. *(Evaluation: Recreation of text)*

Klausurteil B: Sprachmittlung (Text 3)

4. During an exchange visit at an English school, you are doing an e-zine project in class on views people hold on various metropolises in the world. Your class comes across many English articles on Berlin. You are asked to write a short article for the e-zine on what an insider's view on Berlin is like. Write your article based on Maroldt's article. *(Mediation)*

Text 1 Americanah *Chimamanda Ngozi Adichie*

(excerpt from chapter 1)

Princeton, in the summer, smelled of nothing, and although Ifemelu liked the tranquil greenness of the many trees, the clean streets and stately homes, the delicately overpriced shops and the quiet, abiding air of earned grace, it was this, the lack of a smell that most appealed to her, perhaps because the other American cities she knew well had all smelled distinctly. Philadelphia had the musty scent of history. New Haven smelled of neglect. Baltimore smelled of brine, and Brooklyn of sun-warmed garbage. But Princeton had no smell. She liked taking deep breaths here. She liked watching the locals who drove with pointed courtesy and parked their latest model cars outside the organic grocery store on Nassau Street or outside the sushi restaurants or outside the ice cream shop that had fifty different flavours including red pepper or outside the post office where effusive staff bounded out to greet them at the entrance. She liked the campus, grave with knowledge, the Gothic buildings with their vine-laced walls, and the way everything transformed, in the half-light of night, into a ghostly scene. She liked, most of all, that in this place of affluent ease, she could pretend to be someone else, someone specially admitted into a hallowed American club, someone adorned with certainty.

But she did not like that she had to go to Trenton to braid her hair. It was unreasonable to expect a braiding salon in Princeton – the few black locals she had seen here so light-skinned and lank-haired she could not imagine them wearing braids – and yet as she waited at Princeton Junction station for the train, on an afternoon ablaze with heat, she wondered why there was no place where she could braid her hair. The chocolate bar in her handbag had melted. A few other people were waiting on the platform, all of them white and lean, in short, flimsy clothes. The man standing closest to her was eating an ice cream cone; she had always found it a little irresponsible, the eating of ice cream cones by grown-up American men, especially the eating of ice cream cones by grown-up American men in public. He turned to her and said. "About time," when the train finally creaked in with the familiarity strangers adopt with each other after sharing in the disappointment of a public service. She smiled at him. The greying hair on the back of his head was swept forward, a comical arrangement to disguise his bald spot. He had to be an academic, but not in the humanities or he would be more self-conscious. A firm science like chemistry, maybe.

[...]

Text 2 Americanah *Chimamanda Ngozi Adichie*

(excerpt from chapter 44)

[...]

At first, Lagos assaulted her; the sun-dazed haste, the yellow buses full of squashed limbs, the sweating hawkers racing after cars, the advertisements on hulking billboards (others scrawled on walls – PLUMBER CALL 080177777) and the heaps of rubbish that rose on the roadsides like a taunt. Commerce thrummed too defiantly. And the air was dense with exaggeration, conversations full of overprotestations. One morning, a man's body lay on Awolowo Road. Another morning, The Island flooded and cars became gasping boats. Here, she felt, anything could happen, a ripe tomato could burst out of solid stone. And so she had the dizzying sensation of falling, falling into the new person she had become, falling into the strange familiar. Had it always been like this or had it changed so much in her absence? When she left home, only the wealthy had mobile phones, all the numbers started with 090, and girls wanted to date 090 men. Now her hair braider had a mobile phone, the plantain seller tending a blackened grill had a mobile phone. She had grown up knowing all the bus stops and the side streets, understanding the cryptic codes of conductors and the body language of street hawkers. Now, she struggled to grasp the unspoken. When had shopkeepers become so rude? Had buildings in Lagos always had this patina of decay? And when did it become a city of people quick to beg and too enamoured of free things?

"Americanah!" Ranyinudo teased her often. "You are looking at things with American eyes. But the problem is that you are not even a real Americanah. At least if you had an American accent we would tolerate your complaining!"

Ranyinudo picked her up from the airport, standing by the Arrivals exit in a billowy bridesmaid's dress, her blusher too red on her cheeks like bruises, the green satin flowers in her hair now askew. Ifemelu was struck by how arresting, how attractive, she was. No longer a ropy mass of gangly arms and gangly legs, but now a big, firm, curvy woman, exulting in her weight and height, and it made her imposing, a presence that drew the eyes.

"Ranyi!" Ifemelu said. "I know my coming back is a big deal but I didn't know it was big enough for a ball gown."

"Idiot. I came straight from the wedding. I didn't want to risk the traffic of going home first to change."

They hugged, holding each other close. Ranyinudo smelled of a floral perfume and exhaust fumes and sweat; she smelled of Nigeria.

[...]

Annotations

Princeton – elite university in the US

plantain – kind of banana

Americanah – *Nigerian:* emigrant to America

Text 3 Image der deutschen Hauptstadt. Warum finden alle Berlin so toll – außer den Berlinern? *Lorenz Maroldt*

Exzellent organisiert, erschwinglich, cool: Eine neue Begeisterung für die deutsche Hauptstadt wächst in der Welt. In Berlin dagegen überwiegt der Ärger über alltägliche Mängel. Wie passt das zusammen?

Kaum zu fassen, was da gerade so alles über Berlin geschrieben wird, vor allem in Großbritannien und den USA. Das soll unsere Stadt sein? Wir zwängen uns in übervolle Busse, quälen uns durch den Schienenersatzverkehr, lernen auf dem Bahnsteig wartend immer neue Arten von Betriebsstörungen bei der S-Bahn kennen – und lesen in der Londoner „Times": „Excellent public transport." What?

Wir erleben stark steigende Mieten und Wohnungspreise, spüren den Druck von Immobilienspekulanten, fürchten, uns die eigene Stadt nicht mehr leisten zu können – und bekommen gesagt: „Berlin is very affordable". Really?

Wir wissen nicht, wohin mit den Kindern, stehen vor gesperrten Spielplätzen, hören, dass stadtweit 500 davon demoliert sind – und lesen sprachlos in der „New York Times": „Berlin is a playground paradise." Wir stolpern über wild abgestellten Sperrmüll, lesen von Rattenalarm in heruntergekommenen Häusern, erkennen unter Tonnen von Tüten, Pappen und Flaschen nach den Wochenenden unsere Parks nicht mehr – und lassen uns von New Yorks Ex-Bürgermeister Rudy Giuliani sagen: „Berlin ist eine sehr saubere Stadt."

Die Stadt ist nicht die aus den Netflix-Serien

Haben wir, die ewigen Nörgler, eine Wahrnehmungsstörung? Finden wir nicht heraus aus unserer folkloristischen Meckerattitüde? Oder übersehen die Gäste bei ihren Stippvisiten, berauscht von was auch immer, was hier wirklich läuft – oder vielmehr: was nicht? Verwechseln sie gar die echte Stadt mit der, die in Serien von Sky, Netflix und Amazon in mehr als hundert Ländern der Welt gezeigt wird? Allein die Zahl der in Berlin lebenden US-Amerikaner ist in den vergangenen zwei Jahren um 9,6 Prozent gestiegen. 46.600 sind es jetzt, dazu kommen noch die Botschaftsangehörigen.

Auch der Blick von außen aufs große Ganze verblüfft. Im „Economist" erscheint unter dem Titel „Cool Germany" eine Hymne auf unser Land, das doch eigentlich erschöpft ist: von der Pflege-, Diesel- und Flüchtlingskrise, der quälenden

Regierungsbildung, vom Aufmarsch der Rechtspopulisten, der außenpolitischen Orientierungslosigkeit. Aber auf dem Titel der „Times“ steht, zu einem Bild der Hauptstadt Berlin: „A Titan of Europe“.

Schließen wir mal aus, dass es eine virtuelle Parallelwelt gibt, die Berlins Stadtmarketingprofis bei Bedarf präsentieren. Woran liegt es dann, dass andere so begeistert sind von diesem Ort, Ordnung loben, wo wir Chaos sehen, Modernität erkennen, wo wir mit der Verwaltung nur analog in Kontakt treten können? Dass sie unsere Internationalität so anziehend finden, aber wir einen polyglotten belgischen Theaterintendanten nicht mal ein Jahr lang ertragen können?

[...]

In Berlin erleben wir das weitgehend klassenlose Zusammenleben zwar als spannend, aber auch als Anstrengung. Wir sind stolz auf unsere Toleranz, aber die ist stressfrei kaum zu haben. Andererseits stimmt ja auch: Wenn hier alles nur so schrecklich wäre, wie wir uns oft gegenseitig in geselliger Runde versichern, wären wir längst woanders. Die Kunst, das Theater, die Musik, Bars und Restaurants, Markthallen, die Food-Szene, relaxen an den Ufern der Spree und den zwei großen Seen – so ertragen wir das Bürgeramt, die Verkehrslenkung. Und wer an das Londoner U-Bahnnetz gewöhnt ist, wo das Schild „No Service on Victoria Line“ zur Ausstattung gehört, oder die maroden, unzuverlässigen New Yorker Züge kennt, empfindet das Angebot der BVG schon eher nachvollziehbar als „excellent“, relativ gesehen.

[...]

Bearbeitungsschritte und Musterlösungen

Klausurteil A: Leseverstehen/Schreiben
Anforderungsbereich I (Teilaufgabe 1)

1. Describe the places and people presented in the excerpts. *(Comprehension)*

Der Operator „describe“ verlangt eine gewisse Ausführlichkeit, anders als „outline“ oder „sum up“. Eine solche Aufgabe bietet sich an, wenn die Textvorlage selbst sehr deskriptiv ist oder wenn es keine wirkliche Handlung gibt. Wenn Sie einen Blick auf die zweite Teilaufgabe werfen, so sehen Sie, dass auch die Analyse sich mit der Beschreibung der beiden Städte befasst. Beachten Sie die Trennschärfe zwischen den beiden Aufgabenstellungen! Charaktere und sprachliche Besonderheiten, Bildhaftigkeit und Erzähltechnik gehören erst in die zweite Teilaufgabe. Princeton und Lagos werden im engeren Sinne jeweils nur im ersten Textabschnitt beschrieben. Der Mann auf dem Bahnsteig in Princeton und Ranyinudo in Lagos tragen dann als Charaktere zu der Darstellung der jeweiligen Stadt bei. Dieses sollte in Teilaufgabe 2 Erwähnung finden.

Das Isolieren von Schlüsselwörtern ist eine unabdingbare Methode, profundes Textverständnis zu erlangen. Dies geschieht normalerweise durch Markierungen und Notizen im Text. Hier werden wir sie auflisten. Danach sollten sie in einen Sinnzusammenhang gebracht werden.

paragraph	keywords	→
Text 1, paragraph 1 (note: p. 3, i. e. beginning of the novel)	"Princeton" (l. 1)	place, location
	"had no smell" (l. 13)	sensation
	"tranquil greenness" (l. 3) "many trees" (l. 3) "clean streets" (l. 4) "stately homes" (l. 4) "delicately overpriced shops" (ll. 4 f.)	visual appearance
	"locals" / "pointed courtesy" (ll. 15 f.)	people's behavior
	"latest-model cars" (l. 16) "organic grocery store" (l. 17) "sushi restaurants" (l. 18) "ice cream shop" (l. 19)	visual appearance
	"effusive staff bounded out to greet them" (ll. 21 f.)	people's behaviour
	"campus" (l. 23) "Gothic buildings" (l. 24) "[no] braiding salon" (l. 34)	visual appearance
Text 2, paragraph 1	"Lagos" (l. 64)	place, location
	"sun-dazed haste" (ll. 64 f.) "sweating hawkers" (l. 66) "heaps of rubbish" (l. 70) "air dense with exaggeration, conversations full of over-protestations" (ll. 72–74)	sensation
	"buses full of squashed limbs" (ll. 65 f.) "sweating hawkers" (l. 66) "heaps of rubbish" (l. 70) "advertisements on hulking billboards, (others scrawled on walls [...])" (ll. 67 f.)	visual appearance
	"a man's body " (l. 74) "flooded" (l. 76)	visual appearance
	"shopkeepers become so rude" (l. 95)	behaviour
	"patina of decay" (ll. 96 f.)	visual appearance
	"quick to beg" (l. 98)	behaviour

Vor dem Verfassen des Textes rufen Sie sich die Prinzipien der Inhaltsangabe ins Gedächtnis:

Gliederung des Textes / Textverständnis:

- Text in Sinnabschnitte unterteilen – meist helfen bereits Absätze des Textes

Schreiben:
- eigene Formulierungen
- einleitender Satz
- Antwort auf die geforderten W-Fragen (hier: Wo, Was und Wer)

Bei Ihrer Sammlung von Schlüsselwörtern sollten Sie prüfen, ob Inhaltsaspekte sich wiederholen (siehe Spalte 3). Ihren eigenen Text sollten Sie dann nicht anhand der Textchronologie, sondern anhand der Inhaltsaspekte strukturieren.

TIPP zum Punktesammeln

Reduzieren Sie Ihre Inhaltsangabe auf das Wesentliche (keine Ausschmückung durch besondere Adjektive, keine kleinen Details, keine Zitate, keine Metaphorik). Lassen Sie aber auch keine Merkmale, die die beiden Städte ausmachen, weg! Beschreiben Sie nur die Städte, nicht die Charaktere!
Verweisen Sie nicht auf Abschnitte oder Zeilen im Ausgangstext! Zitieren Sie nicht! Nehmen Sie keine Wertung vor!
Grundtempus ist das *simple present.*

Hier eine mögliche Umsetzung:
Chimamanda Ngozi Adichie's novel "Americanah", which was published in 2013, begins with a description of Princeton as perceived by Ifemelu, apparently the main character of the novel. Unlike other American cities, Princeton has no smell, which is the most appealing feature to Ifemelu. It is presented as very green and clean, with stately houses and expensive shops, fancy restaurants, ice-cream parlors and an extravagant post office but no braiding salon. The campus is marked by its Gothic buildings.
In a later chapter of the novel, Lagos, Nigeria, is described, also as perceived by Ifemelu, who is evidently from Lagos and comes back after her stay in America. Lagos is hot and moist, people are sweating, and buses are overcrowded. There are large advertising billboards and informal adverts simply scribbled on walls. The roadside is full of rubbish, buildings seem to be decaying. Hawkers try to sell their merchandise to drivers, and everybody has a mobile phone. Shopkeepers seem unfriendly, and there are a lot of beggars. One day there is a dead body in the street, another day the city is flooded.

Anforderungsbereich II (Teilaufgabe 2)

2. Examine the way the narrator presents Princeton and Lagos respectively. Consider the narrative point of view, atmosphere, characters and the language used. *(Analysis)*

Prinzipiell geht es im Anforderungsbereich II immer um Struktur und/oder Sprache des Textes oder um die Analyse von Erzählelementen wie *character* oder *point of view,* nicht mehr um Inhalt, wenngleich dieses Prinzip leider nicht immer gewahrt wird.

Die Aufgabenstellung spezifiziert ausdrücklich *point of view, atmosphere, characters* und *language* (d. h. *choice of words, imagery* und *stylistic devices).* Sie sollten dies somit sehr genau nehmen und diese Anweisung als Checkliste benutzen. Mit einer Analyse der Textstruktur sollte man sich also auch nicht aufhalten.
Passagen, in denen die Erzählperspektive *(point of view)* eine besondere Wirkung erzielt, sind ebenso im Text zu markieren wie die für die Atmosphäre relevanten Beschreibungen des *settings* und der Charaktere sowie Besonderheiten der Sprachverwendung.
Im Zieltext muss dann nicht zwingend jeder einzelne Beleg zitiert werden; Verweise auf die entsprechenden Zeilen sollten jedoch in jedem Fall erfolgen. Wir werden im Folgenden die zu unterstreichenden Elemente benennen.

quotation	**narrative technique/ element of narration/**	**aspect of language**	**function/ effect**
Text 1			
"tranquil greenness" (l. 3) "many trees" (l. 3) "clean streets" (l. 4)	setting, atmosphere	choice of words: "tranquil", "green", "clean", "stately", "delicately", "pointed, "courtesy"	positive connotation: pleasant, lovely
"stately homes" (l. 4), "delicately overpriced shops" (ll. 4 f.), "locals" / "pointed courtesy" (ll. 15 f.), "latest-model cars" (l. 16), "organic grocery store" (l. 17), "sushi restaurants" (l. 19), "ice cream shop [...] fifty different flavours" (ll. 19 f.), "effusive staff bounded out to greet them" (ll. 21 f.), "[no] braiding salon" (l. 34) "grave with knowledge", (ll. 23 f.), "affluent ease“ (l. 28)	setting, atmosphere		people's lifestyle: luxurious, cosmopolitan, ecological → high class, bourgeois, academic, wealthy, quiet, white-dominated, traditional
"the lack of a smell, that most appealed to her" (ll. 6 f.)	point of view		character's thoughts
"she knew well" (ll. 8 f.)			character's experiences
"She liked [...] She liked [...] She liked" (ll. 13–27)		anaphora	emphasis

"she could pretend" (ll. 28 f.)			character's thoughts
"hallowed American club" (l. 30)		choice of words/ imagery	exclusiveness of Princeton University
"But she did not like" (l. 32)		antithesis	emphasis
"It was unreasonable to expect" (ll. 33 f.)			character's reasoning
"She could not imagine" (ll. 36 f.), "she wondered" (l. 40)			character's thinking
"she had always found" (ll. 46 f.)			character's thoughts
"He had to be" (l. 58)		reported thought	
"short, flimsy clothes" (ll. 44 f.), "greying hair [...] swept forward, a comical arrangement" (ll. 55–57), "academic" (l. 58)	character		fitting in with the setting
Text 2			
Beschreibung des setting, *wie für Teilaufgabe 1 unterstrichen*	setting, atmosphere	choice of words: "assault", "sun-dazed", "squashed", "sweating", "hulking", "exaggeration", "dense", "heaps", "over-protestation"	atmosphere of being exposed to too much of everything: climate, population; activity: lively, diverse, overwhelming, threatening
"Lagos assaulted her" (l. 64)	point of view	personification	threat
"she felt" (l. 77)			character's feeling
"cars became gasping boats" (ll. 76 f.), "a ripe tomato could burst out of solid stone" (ll. 78 f.)	setting/ atmosphere	personification/ imagery	Lagos as dynamic, unpredictable, amazing
"she had the dizzying sensation of falling" (ll. 79 f.)	point of view		

"Had it always been ...?" (ll. 82–84)		reported thought	insight
"When had ...?" (l. 94)			
"And when did ...?" (l. 97)			
"was struck" (l. 111)	point of view		character's perception
"billowy [...] dress" (ll. 107 f.), "blusher too red [...] like bruises" (ll.108 f.), "big, firm, curvy" (ll. 113 f.), "exulting [...] imposing" (ll. 114 f.)	character	choice of words imagery	fitting in with Lagos
"Ranyinudo smelled of ... she smelled of" (ll. 124 f.)	point of view		character's sensation

Es ergibt meist wenig Sinn, die Texte rein chronologisch zu beschreiben. Dies braucht viel zu viel wertvolle Arbeitszeit und Energie und führt zu Wiederholungen sowie einem unübersichtlichen und viel zu umfangreichen Zieltext. Viel eleganter ist es, den Zieltext inhaltlich anhand der vorgegebenen Formelemente und sprachlichen Mittel zu strukturieren und nicht Zeile für Zeile des Ausgangstextes zu behandeln. Jeder Ihrer Sinnabschnitte erhält dann aussagekräftige Zitate und ergänzende Textverweise. Wichtig sind Aussagen zur Funktion der Elemente, selbst wenn diese in der Aufgabenstellung nicht ausdrücklich genannt wird. Es reicht z. B. nicht, eine Metapher zu finden und zu benennen, man muss sie auch erläutern.
Die Aufgabenstellung verlangt die Untersuchung der Romanelemente *point of view, atmosphere* und *character*. Es bietet sich an, diese Elemente auch nacheinander zu untersuchen und dabei die Sprachverwendung im Blick zu behalten.

Da die Vorgaben einen zusammenhängenden Zieltext fordern, sollte man Teil II elegant an Teilaufgabe 1 anbinden. Ein erneuter Einleitungssatz wäre genauso unglücklich wie eine Formulierung wie „Now I am going to analyse ..." gefolgt von einer Paraphrase der Aufgabenstellung. Es wäre ein regelrechter Bruch, keine kohärente Anbindung. Eine solche Formulierung strukturiert allenfalls einen mündlichen Vortrag, nicht jedoch einen Aufsatz. Meist ist gar keine Überleitung nötig. Wichtig ist nur Textkohärenz.

Hier eine mögliche Umsetzung:
The atmosphere created in the narrator's description of Princeton contrasts starkly with the atmosphere of Lagos. Princeton, home to one of America's elite universities, appears as an extremely pleasant place with its many trees and clean streets. Positively connotated words like "tranquil", "green" and "clean" (ll. 3 f.) suggest a pleasant, even graceful town. It is a wealthy environment with an atmosphere marked by people's upper-class lifestyle as it is revealed in "stately homes", "delicately overpriced shops", "latest model cars" and "fifty different flavors" in the "ice cream shop" (ll. 4 f., 15–20).

People live an upper-class, academic lifestyle of "affluent ease" (l. 28), buying ecologically in "organic grocery store[s]" (l. 17) and feeling cosmopolitan by eating in "sushi restaurants" (l. 18). The lack of a braiding salon shows that Princeton society is almost exclusively white. Princeton University is referred to as a "hallowed American club", "grave with knowledge" with its "Gothic buildings" and "vine-laced walls" (ll. 23–30), which again expresses the exclusiveness and venerability of this place, even at night, when it becomes a "ghostly scene" (ll. 27).

All this is presented to the reader from Ifemelu's point of view. We participate in her perception right from the beginning, when we are told that "Princeton [...] smelled of nothing" (ll. 1 f.). We are also told how much she likes the appearance of the place. The anaphorical repetition of "She liked" supports this as much as the antithetical phrase "But she did not like" (ll. 13–27, 32). The reader also gets an insight into her thinking and reasoning throughout the passage: "she could pretend to be" (ll. 28 f.), "It was unreasonable to expect" (ll. 33 f.), "she could not imagine" (ll. 36 f.), "she wondered" (l. 40) and "she had always found" (ll. 46 f.).

The characters on the platform fit in with the setting and support the atmosphere. "[S] hort, flimsy clothes" (ll. 44 f.) and ice cream suggest pleasant temperatures, and especially the man described by Ifemelu fits in with the academic environment. With the "comical arrangement" of his "greying hair" (ll. 55–57), he has the typical appearance of a university scientist. Again, this is observed from Ifemelu's point of view: she "had always found it a little irresponsible" to eat ice cream in public (ll. 46–51). She supposes he is an academic, expressed by the narrator by means of reported thought ("He had to be", l. 58).

Like Ifemelu's fondness for Princeton, her bewilderment when she returns to Lagos is expressed by the narrator's taking the third-person, limited point of view: She feels "assaulted" by Lagos (l. 64). Unlike Princeton, the atmosphere created here is unpleasant, threatening, overwhelming. There is too much of everything, which is expressed in the first three sentences. The atmosphere is hectic, people are in "haste", and hawkers are "racing after cars" (ll. 66 f.). The yellow buses, which are as characteristic of the traffic of Lagos as the yellow cabs are of New York, are full of "squashed limbs", an amorphous mass of body parts rather than people. The signs of commerce like billboards, writing on the walls, and heaps of rubbish overwhelm the observer. This idea of 'too much' is also expressed in lines 64 to 79: The noises of commerce defying poverty, the noise of conversations and exaggeration in general. Adjectives like "sun-dazed" (ll. 64 f.), "squashed", "sweating" (l. 66), "hulking" (ll. 67 f.) and "dense" (l. 72) give the impression that breathing is hard in Lagos. Even the cars, which metaphorically turn into boats when part of Lagos is flooded, are personified as "gasping" (ll. 76 f.). With the image "a ripe tomato could burst out of solid stone" (ll. 78 f.) the narrator expresses how dynamic, unpredictable, amazing and even uncanny Lagos can be.

As said above, the reader perceives this through Ifemelu's thoughts and feelings. We are told she "felt anything could happen" (ll. 77 f.). She is immersed into the familiar but strange culture she is coming back to. She has a "dizzying sensation of falling" (ll. 79 f.), with the word "falling" repeated twice (l. 81), which suggests suddenness and speed but also duration. Her thinking is again expressed by reported thought when she ponders

the changes that have occurred since she left, the mobile phones, communication, the people's behavior and the condition of the buildings in Lagos (cf. l. 84–99).
The character of Ranyinudo fits in with this appearance of and atmosphere in Lagos and supports it. Her appearance, too, seems to be exaggerated in a "billowy" dress and her cheeks "too red", with her blusher compared to bruises (ll. 107–109). Ifemelu perceives her as a "big, firm, curvy woman, exulting in her weight and height". With Ifemelu, the reader perceives her intense smell when they hug, which – to Ifemelu – is the smell of Nigeria (cf. ll. 125 f.).

Anforderungsbereich III (Teilaufgabe 3.1)

3.1 Comment on the way Lagos and Ranyinudo are presented. Assess to what extent it represents Nigeria's as well as Africa's social, cultural and economic situation. *(Evaluation: Comment)*

Der Operator „comment" verlangt eine persönliche Stellungnahme zum Ausgangstext, in diesem Fall nur zu Text 2. Im Unterricht erworbene Kenntnisse sind hier hilfreich. Ihre Sammlungen zu den Anforderungsbereichen I und II geben hinreichend Anlass zur Betrachtung der soziokulturellen Situation Nigerias bzw. Afrikas. Sie können am Anfang der Stellungnahme ganz knapp darauf Bezug nehmen. Wiederholen Sie aber ja nicht konkret alles, was Sie bereits geschrieben haben! Im Hinblick auf die Anforderungen des Anforderungsbereichs III geht es hier um Verallgemeinerung. Gegebenenfalls könnten Sie diese Aspekte durch weitere Aspekte, die Sie aus dem Unterricht kennen, erweitern. Ein eleganter Bezug kann auch zum letzten Satz des Textauszuges hergestellt werden, der in der Beispiellösung ja auch am Ende von Teilaufgabe II erwähnt wird.

aspects mentioned in the texts	**generally true of Nigeria**
"Lagos assaulted her"	general impact of African megacity
"sun-dazed haze"	climate
"exaggeration, conversations, over-protestations", "yellow buses full of squashed limbs", "sweating hawkers" "shopkeepers [...] rude", "mobile phone"	people, growing population, noise, young population, modern, affinity to modern media, class differences
"a man's body", "flooding", "patina of decay", "quick to beg"	problems: crime, infrastructure, poverty, gap between rich and poor
"advertisements on hulking billboards", "others scrawled on the wall", "heaps of rubbish", "mobile phone"	economic situation, commerce, environ-mental awareness, lifestyle
"Ranyinudo [...] clothes [...] smell	exuberance
"Ifemelu [...] Americanah	problems of migration

Die Stellungnahme schließt sich ebenso nahtlos an die Analyse an, wie diese sich an die Inhaltsangabe anschließt. Wichtig ist, dass ein Bezug hergestellt wird zum bisherigen Zieltext. Da die Formulierung der Aufgabenstellung so nicht im Text erscheint, darf auf sie nicht z. B. mit Pronomen Bezug genommen werden. Ganz schlecht ist auch der sofortige Einstieg mit „I think" oder „In my opinion", denn auch die eigene Meinung erfordert eine Hinführung.

Hier eine mögliche Umsetzung:
Bearing the "smell of Nigeria", Ranyinudo is indeed a representative not only of Nigeria but of Africa, at least sub-Saharan Africa. She completely fulfills the cliché of the full-figured black lady, clothed in a colorful traditional dress and talking with a big smile and bright white teeth, giving the cliché of exuberance a lot of truth.
More than just a cliché is the appearance of Lagos and its people. The passage reveals the socio-economic problems of African megacities. It hints at class differences, the large gap between rich and poor, the poor infrastructure, which is vulnerable to natural disaster, and the decay of large parts of the inner cities.
Like any African megacity, Lagos assaults the visitor as the urban nightmare that it is: the buzzing, bustling, fast-paced life of overpopulated African cities trying to come to terms with capitalist achievements and aspirations. Business, trading and advertising play an important part. Making money has become people's main concern and has infected them with selfishness and greed, some even having lost their dignity. Huge billboards and hand-scribbled adverts on the wall witness the predominant role of commerce. Nigeria is Africa's biggest economy. Lagos attracts millions of people who want to get their slice of the cake. Many of them only get a very small slice or none, as few get the lion's share. Nigeria has more millionaires and billionaires than any other African country, while half of the population lives in extreme poverty.
Crime is a serious problem of African cities. The body that is mentioned in the text hints at this omnipresence of crime but also at the negligence of the authorities, the police even, which is also mirrored by the piles of trash in the streets. Indeed, there are enormous sanitary problems in African cities not only concerning rubbish but also sewage, water shortage and poor drainage. This last problem, too, is hinted at in the text when the narrator refers to flooding.
Ifemelu, as a so-called "Americanah", a Nigerian emigrant to America, represents the millions of Africans who try to find a better life abroad. Apparently, Ifemelu, who has got as far as Princeton University, has succeeded. She is only teased about her accent, which does not seem to be properly American. Very often, however, Africans coming back to their home countries are despised as failures, as losers, people who got nowhere – an attitude that makes the problem of migration even bigger.
Nigeria's (and Africa's) population is young; 40 % in sub-Saharan Africa are younger than 15. Therefore, people are up-to-date, using modern media extensively. As in many countries, mobile phones have become an indispensable accessory used in all walks of life. Unfortunately, the text does not hint at many more positive features of Africa, apart from the presentation of Ranyinudo as a likeable person. It may slightly hint at tradition and fashion, which both play an important role in Nigeria and even Africa. Thus, the text does not do much against the negative view of African cities most of us may hold.

Anforderungsbereich III (Teilaufgabe 3.2)

3.2 Ifemelu and Ranyinudo apparently often talk about the situation in Nigeria as compared to the Western world (ll. 100–105). Write a dialogue between them considering aspects hinted at in the texts as well as aspects discussed in class. *(Evaluation: Recreation of text)*

Für die kreative Aufgabe ist zu beachten:

Perspektivwechsel
- Wie ist die zusätzliche Sicht der Dinge aus der Perspektive Ranyinudos?
- Was für eine Art Sprache benutzt sie?

Inhaltliche Anknüpfung an Teilaufgaben 1 und 2 durch einleitenden Satz.
Inhaltlicher Bezug zu Teilaufgaben 1 und 2, z. B. durch:
- Vergleich (Ähnlichkeiten/Unterschiede)
- Kritik
- Wertung
- Gegendarstellung

Eine textkohärente Anknüpfung an Teilaufgabe 2 ist in diesem Fall nicht möglich, denn die Textform ist eine völlig andere.

Hier eine mögliche Umsetzung:
Ifemelu: Ranyinudo, I don't know what has become of Nigeria, what has become of Lagos. As if it was not hot enough in Africa, people have to squeeze into these little yellow buses; they can hardly breathe there. And the hawkers are really getting on my nerves, they harass me.
Ranyinudo: You're looking at all this with American eyes. You are not even a real Americanah, because you haven't got the accent.
Ifemelu: Oh, come on, I may not have the accent, but I really got used to living in the States and to the American way of life. This hassle and this noise is something I can't get used to.
Ranyinudo: Hey, you can't compare Lagos to your beloved Princeton. Princeton is a rich university town, people living there are privileged anyway.
Ifemelu: Yes, you're right. Princeton isn't the place that compares with Lagos, but look at New York City. I've been to New York many times. It's just around the corner from Princeton. New York is as big as Lagos. But it's organised a lot better, a lot less chaotic.
Ranyinudo: Is it?
Ifemelu: I'm sure there must be the same number of people but half the amount of noise. It's clean – at least Manhattan is –, there are no piles of rubbish and people don't throw litter on the streets. Sure, there's a lot of crime, but you don't see dead bodies lying around for days. And the sewage system works. There's never any flooding.
Ranyinudo: Yes, I see your point. There's a lot which is not perfect in this country. But what do you expect? Lagos has become so popular among all kinds of people that they

literally flock here. Lagos's infrastructure was not built for this. The city is trying hard to cope with it and to improve – for example – public transport. The sewage system and the waste management are important tasks that we have to tackle. And you know, corruption has always been a problem, and it hasn't changed that much. Petty corruption has declined somewhat thanks to measures taken by the government, but big corruption is still increasing. The bigger the project, the greater the opportunity to divert cash. So a lot of money doesn't get where it's supposed to go.
Ifemelu: Yes, but what about the people? They've changed so much. Everybody seems to have a mobile phone.
Ranyinudo: Yes, but isn't this a phenomenon that we see all over the world? Don't tell me it's not like this in the States. And if it isn't, look at Europe. Texting is what young people do all the time. And Nigeria is extremely young. There aren't so many old people like in Europe or America. And of course, that's why it's a lot more lively.
Ifemelu: But all this commerce everywhere. Everybody seems so greedy, everyone is chasing after money, and shopkeepers are so unfriendly.
Ranyinudo: What do you expect? People have learned the lesson of democracy; people have learned the lesson of free enterprise and competition. This is based on your American Dream – a Nigerian Dream, Ifemelu. Look at the things that Nigeria has to offer: our cultural diversity, our youth, our talents, our resilience and happiness. We still cherish our traditions and we still fear God. Isn't this something to be proud of?
Ifemelu: Yes, maybe you're right.

Klausurteil B: Sprachmittlung
(Teilaufgabe 4)

4. During an exchange visit at an English school, you are doing an e-zine project in class on views people hold on various metropolises in the world. Your class comes across many English articles on Berlin. You are asked to write a short article for the e-zine on what an insider's view on Berlin is like. Write your article based on Maroldt's article.

Vergegenwärtigen Sie sich die Prinzipien der Sprachmittlung, wie wir sie auf Seite 101 dargestellt haben. Für den vorliegenden Text beachten wir konkret:

Zieltext: *Talk* (vgl. Zieltextformate, S. 106)
Für eine knappe, sachliche Wiedergabe gehen Sie wie bei einer Zusammenfassung vor. Der Text ist bereits vorstrukturiert, sodass Sie nur noch die einzelnen Aspekte zusammenfassen müssen:

- die positive Sicht auf die Stadt in der angloamerikanischen Presse hinsichtlich
  - ÖPNV,
  - Lebenshaltungskosten,
  - Kinderfreundlichkeit und
  - Sauberkeit;

- die Reflexion, ob die Wahrnehmung der Berliner/-innen oder jene der Besucher/-innen gestört ist:
  - Berliner/-innen als notorische Meckerer,
  - Reisende, die die wahren Zustände übersehen,
  - Beeinflussung durch Netflix etc.;
- der ebenso verblüffend positive Blick auf Deutschland als *cool Germany* und *Titan of Europe,* ungeachtet der derzeitigen Krisen:
  - Pflegenotstand,
  - Flüchtlingskrise,
  - Dieselskandal,
  - Rechtsextremismus,
  - Regierungsbildung,
  - außenpolitische Orientierungslosigkeit;
- die Erklärung, die die Klagen der Einheimischen relativiert: Unzulänglichkeiten bei Infrastruktur und Verwaltung werden wettgemacht durch
  - Kunst, Theater, Musik,
  - Gastronomie,
  - Flair,
  - Entspannung an Fluss und Seen,
  - einen Vergleich des Berliner ÖPNV mit den U-Bahnen in New York und London.

Zielgruppenorientiertung
In Ihrer fiktiven Situation als Teilnehmer/-in an einem Kurs in einer englischen Schule müssen Sie dafür sorgen, dass Ihr Kurzvortrag zielgruppengerecht gestaltet wird. Wörter wie „Schienenersatzverkehr" oder „Betriebsstörungen", die wir unweigerlich mit nervigem Bus- und Bahnfahren assoziieren, müssen angemessen umschrieben werden beziehungsweise am besten in einer verallgemeinerten Beschreibung aufgehen. Das gleiche gilt für „ewige Nörgler", „Wahrnehmungsstörung" und „folkloristische Meckerattitüde". Einer kurzen Erklärung bedürfen die politischen Anspielungen, weil eine bloße Übersetzung den fiktiven britischen Mitschülern nichts sagen würde. Einer Erklärung bedarf wohl nicht das Wort „Food-Szene". Auch in London spricht man von der *food scene,* wenn von trendigen Restaurants oder *street food markets* die Rede ist. Ganz schlecht ist eine Übernahme eines Wortes in Anführungsstrichen (z. B. „BVG"). Anführungsstriche helfen des Deutschen unkundigen Menschen gar nicht beim Verständnis.

Hier eine mögliche Umsetzung:
I found an article on the internet which deals with views on Berlin. It's astonishing how positive the view on Berlin is in the British and American press.
It says "Excellent transport" in "The Times", whereas Berliners feel that buses are crammed and many trains do not run for all kinds of reasons. It says that "Berlin is very affordable", whereas Berliners feel that due to rising rents and property prices, they can't afford to live in their own city anymore. The "New York Times" writes that Berlin is a "playground paradise", whereas Berliners experience more and more closed-down and vandalised playgrounds, and the former mayor of New York, Rudy Giuliani, calls

Berlin a clean city, whereas Berliners hear of houses full of rats and see their streets and parks full of rubbish.
So, whose perception is skewed? Do Berliners notoriously complain about everything, or are the visitors so impressed by whatever aspect that they don't see the downsides? Or is the image influenced by the way Berlin is presented by series on Netflix, Sky or Amazon? Even Germany as a whole is presented as "cool Germany" or the "Titan of Europe" despite a catastrophic shortage of hospital staff, despite the arrival of many refugees from the Middle East and fierce controversy on their acceptance, despite a worldwide scandal on manipulated Diesel cars, despite a renaissance of the extreme right and a government which doesn't seem fit to rule.
Yet, it's true, Berlin cannot be that terrible. Otherwise, people would have left. What makes up for administrative failure and insufficient infrastructure is the large variety of theatre, art and music events, pubs and restaurants, market halls and the food scene as well as the river and the lakes, where people can relax. Even the public transport system is not too bad, if you compare it to London or New York.

Themenfeld *Tradition and Change in Politics and Society – The UK in the European Context*

Aufgabenbeispiel Abitur Englisch Leistungskurs
Aufgabenart gemäß KLP: 1.1: Schreiben mit Leseverstehen integriert und Sprachmittlung isoliert
Thematischer Bezug gemäß KLP (Soziokulturelles Orientierungswissen): Das Vereinigte Königreich im 21. Jahrhundert – Selbstverständnis zwischen Tradition und Wandel *Tradition and change in politics and society – The UK in the European context*
Auszug aus einem englischsprachigen Sachtext (741 W.) (Klausurteil A, Text 1) Auszug aus einem deutschsprachigen Sachtext (497 W.) (Klausurteil B, Text 2)
Quellenangaben: Text 1: Owen Jones, „Brexitland: So much for the fractured nation – I haven't found it", *The Guardian,* 20.04.2017, https://www.theguardian.com/commentisfree/2017/apr/20/brexitland-fractured-nation-politicians-unite-labour (Zugriff: 01.04.2022, gekürzt); Copyright Guardian News & Media Ltd 2022 Text 2: Tanja Dückers, „Von Geburt an Multikulturalist", *ZEIT online*, 06.02.2015, http://www.zeit.de/gesellschaft/zeitgeschehen/2015-02/europa-identitaet-migration-einwanderung/komplettansicht (Zugriff: 01.04.2022, gekürzt)

Aufgabe

Klausurteil A: Leseverstehen/Schreiben (Text 1)

1. Point out people's motivations and conflicts when voting in the referendum, according to Jones's article. *(Comprehension)*

2. Examine Owen Jones's language and argumentative strategies when dealing with "fractured" British society. Consider the way he composes his text as well as his use of language and imagery. *(Analysis)*

3. Choose one of the following tasks:

3.1 Considering the personal backgrounds and statements of the people interviewed, evaluate the usefulness of the Brexit referendum as well as referendums in general in a modern democracy. (Evaluation: Comment)

3.2 You are asked to take part in a debate on the role of supranational bodies in the globalised world at your partner school in Britain. Write your initial statement about the role of the EU with regard to ecological challenges as well as working and studying. *(Evaluation: Recreation of text)*

Klausurteil B: Sprachmittlung (Text 2)

4. At your British host school, notions like "freedom", "independence" and "identity" used by Brexiteers are irritating you. You strongly agree with the view on European identity Tanja Dückers puts forward in *ZEIT online*. Write a short article for the school magazine based on Tanja Dückers's article. *(Mediation)*

Text 1 Brexitland: So much for the fractured nation – I haven't found it (excerpt) *Owen Jones*

[...]

We'll hear a lot about Britain being a bitterly divided nation as we head into a general election. And it would be delusional to deny the referendum has created rifts. But having spent the last few months travelling between English communities that plumped for Brexit, I didn't find much evidence of ordinary voters brimming with venom for each other. People who voted leave didn't regard remainers as effete metropolitan elitist saboteurs; remainers didn't see leavers as knuckle-dragging bigoted Neanderthals. The appetite to turn neighbour against neighbour over the referendum – and to transform the aftermath into a full-blown culture war – certainly exists in certain media and political circles. My suspicion is that people are growing pretty weary of it. I found that most are too decent and busy to hate each other.

Take Laura and Dan: they are a couple in the South Yorkshire town of Doncaster in their early 20s who have just moved in together. Laura is a hairstylist who voted to remain: she thinks "people voted to leave because of immigrants" and bemoans the loss of her freedom of movement. Her partner Dan, who repairs domestic appliances, did indeed vote to leave because of "refugees". I press him, and he actually means Romanians, rather than refugees – and he notes there was an expectation of "instant change", not least over the promise of extra cash for the NHS.

But he said something that summed up how so many people I met seem to feel. "It's not that I particularly needed it or wanted it to happen. We were asked to vote so I voted, and that was the answer I came up with, with the information I had." Politicos live in a world where breathlessly scanning through Twitter for crumbs of gossip is one of the first and last rituals of the day. It is not a world most live in. Politics provokes little passion among most people, even if individual issues do. As I left them, remainer Laura and leaver Dan kissed and got on with their lives.

Or take 55-year-old Lynne, a communications manager for an IT company in Fareham, Hampshire. Her husband voted remain; she voted leave, but, like so many on both sides of the divide, was conflicted about her vote. We are not as polarised as the binary choice of "remain" or "leave", she says. As it happens, she was motivated to vote leave because she felt there was a democratic deficit, yet she believes the post-referendum rhetoric on immigration "is a disaster", and thinks "it'll be a great pity if it damages positive migration and immigration policies".

In Stockport, Greater Manchester, it's easy to find different democratic choices but little sign of bitter division. Karen, 43, is a proud, working-class Stopfordian who couldn't get a council house. She's on a weekly shop in Tesco when we speak. She was a passionate remainer, and worries about how the NHS will cope if foreign doctors and nurses leave. "Where will that leave us then?" she asks.

It's an anxiety about the future that she shares with many who voted to leave. It is difficult to divorce the pessimism that 64-year-old Tony, for instance, feels about his hometown and his democratic decision. "It's going downhill fast," he says, pointing at the empty shops in a town centre that is undoubtedly struggling to thrive. A mother and daughter I met in its Merseyway shopping centre voted for remain, but they also feel the sense of abandonment that many leavers have felt for a long time.

Do small towns such as Stockport get a bit forgotten? "Definitely!" was their immediate response. But, again, with all the people I have spoken to, there's no bitterness, no hatred, no contempt for the other side. We were asked a question, is the general gist, and we answered it.

From Doncaster and Sheffield in the north of England, down to Barking and Dagenham in London and South Thanet in Kent, I found an abundance of reasons why millions voted to leave. Low pay, a sense of decline, feeling abandoned or ignored, a housing crisis, immigration, a perceived democratic deficit, wanting to give the establishment a kicking. For some, their choice was based on a passionate inner belief; for others, their vote was made with a shrug of the shoulders.

[...]

Annotations

effete – affected and incapable of effective action; **knuckle-dragging** – i. e. dragging their knuckles over the ground; **NHS** – National Health Service; system providing free medical treatment in Britain; **politico** – person strongly involved in politics

Text 2 „Von Geburt an Multikulturalist“ *Tanja Dückers*

[...]

Was Europa derzeit fehlt, ist ein neuer Identitätsbegriff. Bislang haben wir unsere europäische Identität in erster Linie über Abgrenzung konstruiert: Wir sind nicht wie die Amerikaner, die Russen oder die Afrikaner. Statt sich zu einer Identität zu bekennen, haben sich Europäer nur gegen andere Nationen, Kulturen und zum Teil auch pauschal gegen nicht-christliche Religionen gerichtet.

Erinnern wir uns nur an die peinliche Leitkultur-Debatte. Sie hat es Migranten nicht leicht gemacht, sich diesem merkwürdigen, sich ständig selbst spiegelnden Goethe-und-Dieter-Bohlen-Land in der Mitte Europas zugehörig zu fühlen. Dabei wurden Trennlinien zwischen Christen und Muslimen gezogen, ungeachtet der Tatsache, dass in Deutschland mittlerweile fast die Hälfte der Menschen keiner der beiden großen christlichen Kirchen angehört. In Berlin leben mehr Muslime als Katholiken.

Viele Menschen beklagen zwar, dass die Binnenkräfte, die Europa zusammenhalten, vor allem ökonomischer Natur seien. Sie haben aber, nach ihrem Identitätsverständnis von Europa befragt, selber wenig zu bieten. Dass die Europäer sich schwer damit tun, eine europäische Identität festzulegen, ist verständlich. Zu viele Einflüsse haben historisch den Kontinent geprägt.

Der Kontinent war zwar schon immer geprägt von regem Handel und Austausch – aber auch von vielen Kriegen. Es gibt keine Region in der Welt, in der so viele von der Fläche her kleine Länder eng beieinanderliegen und keine, deren Geographie so kleinteilig und ineinandergreifend ist. Europa müsste sich jetzt auf seinen Platz in der Welt als Drehkreuz zwischen Ost und West berufen.

Denn Europa kann sich eigentlich nur als regen Marktplatz der Welt, als Vielvölkerstaat mit zahllosen kulturellen, linguistischen und ökonomischen Verbindungen zur außereuropäischen Welt verstehen. Der Europäer ist, wenn er diese Offenheit zulässt, qua Geburt ein Multikulturalist. Es war der kürzlich verstorbene deutsche Soziologe Ulrich Beck, der als einer der ersten den Europäer als Kosmopolit gedacht hat. Doch für Beck bedeutete Europa nicht das Ende der alten Nationalstaaten. Das neue Europa könne vielmehr das alte in sich bergen und zugleich sanft verändern.

Das eine – die transnationale Identität – schließt nämlich das andere – die Herkunftsidentität – nicht aus. Mit dieser Einsicht können wir die große Angst vor einem transnationalen Identitätsbegriff besiegen, die in vielen Regionen Europas geschürt wird, erst recht vor einem, der außereuropäische Fremde miteinschließt. Die Angst ist verständlich, denn es scheint zunächst schwer vorstellbar, dass die Erweiterung eines Identitätsbegriffs nicht gleichzeitig einem Verlust an anderer Stelle gleichkommt.

Berlinerin, Atheistin, Europäerin

Unsere Aufgabe ist es deshalb, einen facettenreichen, multidimensionalen Identitätsbegriff zu etablieren. Einer Identität, die sich gleichwertig aus einem nahen Herkunftsbereich („Berlinerin“) speist, einer soziokulturellen und religiösen Zugehörigkeit („atheistische Schriftstellerin“) und einem geographisch weitergefassten Bereich („Zugehörigkeit zu einem sich als heterogenes Staatengebilde verstehenden Europa“). Was bislang eher als exkludierend empfunden wurde, könnte in Zukunft integrierend verstanden werden. Wenn europäische Bürger sagen: Ich stamme aus einem Kontinent, in dem ich nicht nur jeden Tag Deutsch höre, nicht nur Nachbarn mit meiner Hautfarbe habe. Zu meiner Identität gehört es dazu, mehrere Sprachen zu sprechen und viele Sprachen ein wenig zu verstehen.

Ich lebe in einem Kontinent, der sich dem keineswegs toten, sondern von 500 Millionen Menschen täglich gelebten Multikulturalismus verschrieben hat.

Bearbeitungsschritte und Musterlösungen

Klausurteil A: Leseverstehen/Schreiben
Anforderungsbereich I (Teilaufgabe 1)

1. Point out people's motivations and conflicts when voting in the referendum, according to Jones's article. *(Comprehension)*

Was den Text angeht, so verlangt der Operator „point out" eine zusammenfassende Darstellung der Ausführungen und Argumente des Autors. Die entsprechenden Schlüsselbegriffe werden im Text unterstrichen oder mit Textmarker farbig markiert. Hier werden wir auflisten, was im Ausgangstext markiert sein sollte:

passage	key phrases
ll. 1–21	"bitterly divided" – "didn't find much evidence" "exists in certain media"
ll. 22–49	Laura: "remain", "bemoans the loss of her freedom of movement" Dan: "leave", "refugees"/"Romanians", "extra cash for the NHS", "asked to vote, so I voted"
ll. 50–63	Lynn: "leave", "democratic deficit", "pity if it damages positive [...] immigration policies"
ll. 64–86	Karen: "couldn't get a council house", "passionate remainer", "worries about [...] foreign doctors and nurses leav[ing]", "anxiety [...] she shares with many who voted to leave" Tony: "leave", "downhill fast", "mother and daughter [...] voted for remain", "also feel sense of abandonment"
ll. 87 – end	"no bitterness, no hatred, no contempt" "asked a question, [...] answered" "abundance of reasons why [...] leave": "a sense of decline, feeling abandoned or ignored, a housing crisis, immigration, a perceived democratic deficit, wanting to give the establishment a kicking" "passionate inner belief" vs. "shrug of the shoulders"

Nachdem diese Vorarbeiten abgeschlossen sind, geht es nun darum, Ihre Notizen und Markierungen in einen zusammenhängenden Text zu bringen. Es bietet sich an, die einleitende Aussage Jones's als *topic sentence* voranzustellen, dann seine Beispiele und Argumente anzuführen und mit seinem Fazit abzuschließen.
Beginnen Sie mit einem Einleitungssatz, der sich auf die jeweilige Textvorlage bezieht (s. S. 208), und vergegenwärtigen Sie sich die Grundsätze für das Verfassen von Zusammenfassungen.

TIPP zum Punktesammeln

Vermeiden Sie Wendungen wie „in the first paragraph", „from line x to line y", „then the author says". Dies sind Wendungen, die eine Strukturanalyse charakterisieren; sie gehören nicht in eine Zusammenfassung.

Hier eine mögliche Umsetzung:
The text "Brexitland: So much for the fractured nation – I haven't found it" by Owen Jones, which was published in "The Guardian" on 17 April 2017, deals with the alleged bitter divide of the British nation after the Brexit referendum. Jones claims that this image exists in certain media but that it is not true for ordinary voters.
Laura, a hairstylist from Doncaster, for instance, voted remain, whereas her partner, who is an electrician, voted to leave. While Laura's motivation was free movement, her partner's vote was directed against EU immigrants and also motivated by the promise of extra money for the NHS. But their votes did not divide them, as they do not attribute great importance to political issues.
Another example is Lynne, a communications manager from Hampshire, who voted leave and whose husband voted to remain. Yet she is conflicted about her vote. Her motivation was the EU's democratic deficit, but she seriously worries about the new aggressive rhetoric on immigration.
Karen from Greater Manchester voted remain, but she also shares her worries with many people who voted to leave, namely for the future of the NHS without staff from the EU or the declining infrastructure of their hometown. This sense of abandonment is something leavers have felt for a long time, but which remainers feel too. Reasons to vote to leave were low wages, the declining infrastructure, a feeling of being ignored, housing costs, immigration, the feeling of not having a say in Brussels or simply protest. Some believed in their decision passionately, others just voted without giving it much thought. Yet, there is no bitterness, no hatred and no contempt for the other side. People say they were asked a question and they simply answered it.

Anforderungsbereich II (Teilaufgabe 2)

2. Examine Owen Jones's language and argumentative strategies when dealing with "fractured" British society. Consider the way he composes his text as well as his use of language and imagery. *(Analysis)*

Die Aufgabe verlangt eine Analyse der Textstruktur und eine Analyse der Stilmittel. Diese Analysen sollten Sie getrennt voneinander angehen.
Die Struktur des Textes zeigt sich schon in den Notizen zum Inhalt. Untersuchen Sie die einzelnen Sinnabschnitte auf ihre Funktion für den Aufbau des Textes und notieren Sie sie auf der Textvorlage.
Hier stellen wir dies wieder als Tabelle dar.

argumentative structure	**key phrases**
introduction: claim ll. 1–21	"bitterly divided": "didn't find much evidence" "exists in certain media"
evidence/example ll. 22–49	Laura: "remain", "bemoans the loss of her freedom of movement" Dan: "leave", "refugees"/"Romanians", ...
evidence/example ll. 50–63	Lynn: "leave", "democratic deficit", "pity if it damages positive [...] immigration policies"
evidence/example ll. 64–86	Karen: "couldn't get a council house", "passionate remainer", ... Tony: "leave", "downhill fast", ...
conclusion ll. 87 – end	"no bitterness, no hatred, no contempt", ...

Innerhalb dieser Struktur bedient sich der Autor verschiedener Strategien, seine Leserschaft zu überzeugen. Ohne dass wir die Textpassagen hier einzeln aufführen müssen, werden Sie leicht erkennen, wie nicht nur beispielhaft Menschen aus der britischen Bevölkerung angeführt werden, sondern sie auch zitiert werden, was dem Text Glaubhaftigkeit verleiht. Überdies werden immer stets *leavers* und *remainers* einander gegenübergestellt – ein Kontrast, den wir auch in den Stilmitteln wiederfinden.
Es handelt sich hier um einen persuasiven Text – einen Text, der den Leser überzeugen möchte. Ein solcher Text bedient sich neben seiner Argumente auch der Stilmittel, wie sie im Kapitel zur Analyse einer Rede dargestellt sind. Wenn Ihnen diese nicht sofort ins Auge fallen, suchen Sie gezielt nach den Ihnen bekannten Stilmitteln (Checkliste im Kopf) und markieren Sie sie im Text (vgl. S. 93 f.).

Im Einzelnen finden wir in diesem Text:

lines	**words/phrases**	**stylistic devices**
title	"fractured nation"	imagery
l. 3	"bitterly divided nation"	choice of words
l. 6	"rifts"	imagery
ll. 9 f.	"brimming with venom"	imagery
l. 12	"effete metropolitan elitist saboteurs"	choice of words / imagery

ll. 13 f.	"as knuckle-dragging bigoted Neanderthals"	choice of words / imagery
ll. 14 f.	"The appetite to turn neighbour against neighbour"	choice of words
l. 16	"aftermath"	choice of words
l. 17	"full-blown culture war"	choice of words
l. 21	"decent and busy"	choice of words
l. 41	"Politicos"	choice of words
l. 42	"breathlessly scanning"	choice of words / exaggeration
l. 43	"crumbs of gossip"	imagery
l. 44	"first and last rituals of the day"	choice of words
ll. 90 f.	"no bitterness, no hatred, no contempt"	enumeration/parallelism
ll. 98 ff.	"Low pay, a sense of decline, feeling abandoned or ignored, a housing crisis, immigration, a perceived democratic deficit, wanting to give the establishment a kicking"	enumeration
ll. 102 ff.	"For some [...] for others"	antithesis

Nennenswerte Stilmittel fallen zwischen Zeilen 45 und 89 nicht auf. Das ist dann eben so. Suchen Sie nicht krampfhaft etwas, was Sie dann selbst nicht glauben! Der Text wurde ja nicht für die Schule geschrieben.
Wenn Sie nun Ihren Text verfassen, ordnen Sie die Resultate wieder, anstatt textchronologisch vorzugehen. Auffällig sind die Wortwahl und die Metaphorik, aber auch emphatische Strukturen fallen ins Auge. Sinnvollerweise beginnt man mit dem vorherrschenden Stilmittel.
Bei der Umwandlung Ihrer Notizen in einen zusammenhängenden Text, müssen Sie darauf achten, nicht den Inhalt, sondern die Funktion sowohl der einzelnen Abschnitte als auch der rhetorischen Mittel wiederzugeben. Mit dem Inhalt haben sie sich hinreichend in Teilaufgabe 1 befasst. Inhaltliches wir hier auf ein Mindestmaß reduziert. Bitte paraphrasieren Sie nicht endlos den Ausgangstext!
Überdies wird verlangt, dass Ihre Klausur aus einem zusammenhängenden Gesamttext besteht. Fangen Sie also nicht mit einem neuen Einleitungssatz an, sondern schließen Sie nahtlos an Teilaufgabe 1 an. Bitte schreiben Sie nicht: *„Now I am going to examine Owen Jones's language ..." – do it, don't talk about it!*

TIPP zum Punktesammeln

Im Anforderungsbereich II ist Ihr Thema nicht Brexit. Ihr Thema ist Sprache – es geht um Wörter, Ausdrücke und Sätze. Eine Formulierung wie „The author says that" führt daher in die falsche Richtung.
Denken Sie auch daran, dass eine Analyse Belege in Form von Verweisen oder Zitaten verlangt!

Hier eine mögliche Umsetzung:

Jones tries to prove his evaluation of people's attitudes by giving his text a classic structure. He introduces his article by referring to the alleged divide and hatred between leavers and remainers (ll. 2–18). In order to disclaim this allegation, he gives various examples. From lines 22 to 49, he illustrates his point with a married couple who voted for opposite sides without any damage to their relationship. His next example (ll. 50–63) shows that voting to leave does not always follow clear-cut political views but can be rather conflicted. A further example (ll. 64–86) reveals how people's worries about their daily lives are very much the same on both sides. Thus, Jones concludes (ll. 87 – end) that a lot of people did not give particular weight to the referendum.

The people referred to by Jones do not only serve as examples of one or the other side. Quoting their opinions in direct speech makes them witnesses, experts on the topic, thus giving the text credibility. Jones contrasts leavers and remainers in each example, in each case coming to the conclusion that there is no hostility. In the case of Laura and Dan (ll. 48–50), he confirms this by stating that "remainer Laura and leaver Dan kissed and got on with their lives".

As early as in the title and again in line 6, Jones uses geological metaphors to illustrate the alleged division of Britain. He speaks of "a fractured nation" and "rifts" that divide the country. The word "bitterly" (l. 3) underlines this division, suggesting hardship, sorrow, grimness, disappointment and hatred at the same time. This hatred is then illustrated with the metaphor "brimming with venom" (ll. 9 f.), which conjures the image of venomous snakes or a witch's cauldron.

People with contrasting attitudes are referred to as "effete metropolitan elitist saboteurs" (ll. 11 f.) or described with the metaphor "knuckle-dragging bigoted Neanderthals" (ll. 13 f.). Thus, people in favour of the EU are allegedly and stereotypically regarded as Londoners, who profit from comfortable professional life in the big city, do not know what hard work is and are unpatriotic or even traitors as they destroy traditional political structures. On the other hand, leavers are regarded as retarded, as having regressed to some pre-homo sapiens state and thus having lost their minds (ll. 13 f.).

Words and expressions from the semantic field of war and aggression ("turn neighbour against neighbour", "aftermath", "full-blown cultural war", ll. 14–17) underline this opposition. As the author rejects this view, he also uses the positively connotated words "decent" and "busy" (l. 21), which in turn instead allude to the typical British characteristics of reserve and politeness, of avoiding confrontation and wanting to keep harmony. In the end, what is left of the harsh contrast of leavers and remainers is simply an unspectacular, antithetical sentence saying "For some, their choice was based on a

passionate inner belief; for others, their vote was made with a shrug of the shoulders" (ll. 102–105).
According to Jones, it is the politicians and politically strongly involved people that may be too agitated by the results of the referendum. He therefore ridicules them and their activity with the word "[p]oliticos" (l. 41), who "breathlessly" scan the media for "crumbs of gossip" (ll. 42 f.) with almost religious zeal ("first and last rituals", l. 44) – words and images that contrast them sharply with "decent" (l. 21) people and makes them appear almost insane and obsessed.
The last part of Jones's text is rather marked by emphatic structures than by a particular choice of words. He hammers his thesis home by using enumeration and parallelism in line 90 f.: "no bitterness, no hatred, no contempt". He also lists reasons why people voted leave (ll. 98 ff.), i. e. the factors that make people unhappy and disappointed in today's Britain in order to emphasise what is wrong with the nation and what one should be aware of shortly before a general election (l. 3 f.).

Anforderungsbereich III (Teilaufgabe 3.1)

3.1 Considering the personal backgrounds and statements of the people interviewed, evaluate the usefulness of the Brexit referendum as well as referendums in general in a modern democracy. *(Evaluation: Comment)*

Im Anforderungsbereich III wird von Ihnen eine Stellungnahme verlangt. Nachdem Sie sich intensiv mit der Textvorlage befasst haben, sollten Sie in der Lage sein, sich eine eigene Meinung zu bilden. Wichtig ist,
- dass Sie Ihre Stellungnahme auf den Ausgangstext bzw. die Ausgangstexte beziehen,
- dass Sie ihre eigenen Behauptungen mit Argumenten und Beispielen untermauern und
- dass Sie zu einer dezidierten persönlichen Stellungnahme gelangen, einer persönlichen Meinung, die sich aus Ihren Ausführungen ergibt.

Markieren Sie im Text diejenigen Elemente, die Sie für Ihre Stellungnahme heranziehen möchten. Sammeln und ordnen Sie Ihre Gedanken auf Ihrem Konzeptblatt. Wählen Sie dazu eine Mindmap oder auch eine Liste.

people involved	**personal backgrounds and statements** (should be highlighted in the text)	**comment**
Laura	"hairstylist", "people voted to leave because of immigrants", "bemoans the loss of her freedom of movement"	education: ability to understand consequences of vote? freedom of movement relevant?

Dan	"repairs domestic appliances", "did indeed vote to leave because of 'refugees' [...] he actually means Romanians, rather than refugees", "expectation of 'instant change', not least over the promise of extra cash for the NHS" "We were asked to vote so I voted, and that was the answer I came up with, with the information I had"	education: does not see the difference between Romanians and refugees, i.e. between the right of free movement and the refugee policy of the EU
Lynn	"communications manager for an IT company", "conflicted about her vote", "We are not as polarised as the binary choice of 'remain' or 'leave'"	complexity of political and economic issues, more multifaceted than yes or no
Karen	"a proud, working-class Stopfordian", "remainer", "anxiety about the future that she shares with many who voted to leave"	no simple solutions, causes of social and economic problems not necessarily linked to EU membership
Tony	"pessimism", "It's going downhill fast"	as above

TIPP zum Punktesammeln

Beginnen Sie Ihre Stellungnahme nicht mit „In my opinion", „I think" etc.! Beziehen sie sich auf den Ausgangstext! Beziehen Sie sich vor allem nicht mit einem „this" oder „it" auf die Aufgabenstellung der Teilaufgabe! Ihre Gesamtaufgabe ist ein zusammenhängender Zieltext, der ohne Kenntnis der Formulierung der Teilaufgaben verständlich sein muss. Beenden Sie Ihre Stellungnahme mit Ihrem persönlichen Fazit!

Hier eine mögliche Umsetzung:

The examples and statements of ordinary British citizens brightly illustrate the usefulness – or rather uselessness – of a referendum on British membership in the EU and of referendums in general. In the film "Brexit – The Uncivil War", Benedict Cumberbatch's Dominic Cummings says that referendums are "the worst way to decide anything" and calls it "a really dumb idea". Looking at what the citizens interviewed by Jones say, it becomes clear that this fictional Cummings is right in what he says, be it authentic or not. Lynn is a hairdresser, who cannot be expected to fully understand the consequences of a political decision as fundamental as the membership of the European Union. She says she'll miss her freedom of movement, which shows she is not really informed. She does not seem to have planned to move to Spain with her husband in order to work there, and her travelling as a tourist in Europe will not be restricted by Brexit. Like her, Dan, a repairman, does not seem to give much thought to academic matters and does not see the difference between those that seek asylum and EU migrants. He too was deceived by the campaign's lie about funding for the NHS. Yet, he voted "with the information [he] had" (l. 41).

A complex political decision cannot be made on the basis of two opposed views. The conflicting votes of the people interviewed in Hampshire and Greater Manchester undeniably reveal that there are no clear-cut boundaries along which people could have voted for one or the other option. This will be the case in any referendum on far-reaching issues. The example of the made-up promise of "extra cash for the NHS" shows how much a referendum is decided by populist strategies. The leave campaign were able to claim whatever they wanted without taking responsibility for it afterwards. Remain, as backed by the government, was held accountable for everything they said. Thus, the leave campaign was able to get away with fearmongering on Turkey's joining the EU, with lies on the actual costs of EU membership and the false promise of extra funding of the NHS. Considering how emotionally loaded many political questions are – just think of penal law or immigration policy –, populist manipulation is generally to be expected in any referendum.

It has also been proved that people in Britain were manipulated by being microtargeted with advertising on social media. This may seem normal in today's digital world, but, again, it is definitely easier to manipulate voters into giving a simple yes or no vote than into voting for a party programme, which also involves traditional affinity or social identity.

Turnout is another issue. The referendum turnout was a little over 70 percent. About 17 million people voted leave. The electorate was 46.5 million with a total population of 65 million people. Referring to those 17 million voters as "the people" is highly questionable to me. Polls on binary issues will always have results like this. They cannot represent the people's will. We are faced with the same pitfall as in the first-past-the-post system in parliamentary or presidential elections.

Lastly, a yes-or-no decision can also be easily influenced just by the wording of the question. A good example is the outcome of a poll in Germany in which people opted for the continuous use of daylight saving time. The German word "Sommerzeit" ('summertime') sounds so pleasant that people voted for it. Another poll avoiding this word had contrary results.

In short, I totally agree with what the Dominic Cummings character says in the film „Brexit“: A referendum is the dumbest idea to decide anything. Political decisions have to be made in parliament in accordance with the required procedures.

Anforderungsbereich III (Teilaufgabe 3.2)

3.2 You are asked to take part in a debate on the role of supranational bodies in the globalised world at your partner school in Britain. Write your initial statement about the role of the EU with regard to ecological challenges as well as working and studying. *(Evaluation: Recreation of text)*

Dieses Aufgabenformat ist neu seit 2021 (vgl. S. 12). Das Format ist Ihnen aus Ihren Klausuren nicht bekannt, weil wir in Nordrhein-Westfalen eine enge Anbindung an den Ausgangstext verlangen. Im Abitur wird eine der beiden Teilaufgaben 3 nur thematisch an den Ausgangstext angebunden sein. Zudem ist diese Aufgabe dann themenübergreifend. Deshalb werden Sie eine solch offene Aufgabe in Ihren Oberstufenklausuren, die ja Kursthemen abschließen, eher nicht finden.
Der Anspruch dieser Aufgaben, dass man sich nach stundenlanger Beschäftigung mit dem einen Thema nun auch noch einem weiteren Thema zuwendet, legt den Schluss nahe, diese Teilaufgabe zu vermeiden und in jedem Fall die andere zu wählen.
Es mag aber sicher gute Gründe geben, dieser Teilaufgabe eine Chance zu geben:
- Das jeweils andere Textformat (*comment* oder *recreation of text*) liegt Ihnen gar nicht.
- Die Thematik liegt Ihnen oder Sie haben das Thema sehr intensiv vorbereitet.
- Sie kennen sich mit der Thematik über die Inhalte eines anderen Faches bestens aus.
- Sie mögen sich zum Ausgangstext nicht äußern.

Zur Bearbeitung dieser Aufgabe lassen Sie nun Jones's Text beiseite und sammeln Ihre Gedanken zu den beiden Kursthemen „Ecological challenges and sustainable lifestyles" und „Studying and working in a globalised world" in einer Mindmap oder Liste.

ecological issues
- climate change – no frontiers
  - international regulations
  - international research
  - cooperation on technology and green energy
  - strong power against corporations
  - international prosecution
  - distribution of climate refugees

working and studying
- Erasmus programme, benefits
  - EU money
  - personality-/character-building
  - independence
  - language learning
  - meeting people and cultures
  - widen horizons
- freedom of movement
  - working for international companies
  - opening businesses in EU countries
  - Gen Z: flexibility (working from home / availability around the clock)

conclusion: national borders are an anachronism; words like freedom and independence in this context are simply buzzwords

Hier eine mögliche Umsetzung:
I was asked to take part in this debate and I agreed with pleasure because I am an ardent internationalist and I still can't really get over what Britain did in the referendum. In my statement, I will share a few thoughts on the role of the EU, focussing on two aspects which are very close to my heart. The first aspect is ecology, the second aspect is the issue of working and studying abroad.
As far as ecology is concerned, climate change is the most important issue of our times. It can't be targeted on a national basis. Climate and weather don't stop at national borders. It's a worldwide issue, it's true, but with the EU being one of the most powerful economies in the world, effective measures can be introduced on a European footing.
With the relevant institutions in place and working, it should be easy to take the appropriate steps in a minimal amount of time. And, of course, although it seems nothing has been done to improve the situation, we have to admit that steps in the right direction have been taken already. There are regulations on emissions and there are regulations on carbon dioxide reduction and, above all, there is awareness. There's no need to say that coordinated criminal prosecution of environmental offenders is likewise only possible if there's international law enforcement.
But it's not just the politicians and their regulations that have to target climate change. There is a network of international cooperation between all kinds of institutions, above all universities, so that the full impact of international expertise is ready to be used against this threat. Again, this being an international issue, international research should target climate change and indeed does so. Of course, close ties between different countries, like in the EU, immensely facilitate international cooperation and exchange.
Being an enormous economic power, the EU may also have a powerful stance when facing international corporations that don't comply with climate protection measures. One country alone can do little against global players. But even corporations that have learned the lesson themselves will be a lot more effective on a European basis when it comes to introducing new technologies like photovoltaics or green hydrogen or with respect to responsible production.
The consequences of climate change, which we are already experiencing, can also only be dealt with internationally. And again, with a supranational body already in place, it will be far easier to attend to those issues. One of the gravest consequences of climate change is and will be the number of climate refugees. The challenge of fair and equal distribution of refugees can only be addressed with international consent. Even though the EU has so far failed in this respect, the handling of refugees from Ukraine seems to show the potential of this supranational body.
The other issue I'd like to broach is studying and working. With the Erasmus programme the EU provides a scheme that facilitates studying abroad immensely. The benefits of this are obvious: With scholarships from the EU, students are able to learn about different cultures, master new languages, develop their personalities. They become independent, get fresh views, meet people and make friends with people from all over Europe, broaden their horizons. In this respect the EU is really the peace project that it was originally designed as.

The same is true for work. Without worrying about immigration and visa regulations or even restrictions, the principle of freedom of movement gives you the chance of working anywhere between Greece and Ireland or Portugal and Finland. You can work for international or national companies, you can open your own business, you can be as flexible as you want, working from home in different countries or even on your smartphone from anywhere. To Generation Z, national borders are really an anachronism. It's truly a shame that certain countries are rebuilding or seeking to rebuild borders.
Thank you for your attention.

Klausurteil B: Sprachmittlung (Text 2)

4. At your British host school, notions like "freedom", "independence" and "identity" used by Brexiteers are irritating you. You strongly agree with the view on European identity Tanja Dückers puts forward in *ZEIT online*. Write a short article for the school magazine based on Tanja Dückers's article. (Mediation)

Vergegenwärtigen Sie sich die Prinzipien der Sprachmittlung, wie wir sie auf Seite 101 dargestellt haben.
Für eine knappe, sachliche Wiedergabe gehen Sie wie bei einer Zusammenfassung vor.

Zielgruppenorientierung
In Ihrer fiktiven Situation als Gastschüler/-in an einer britischen Schule müssen Sie Ihren Artikel zielgruppengerecht gestalten. Häufig müssen Begriffe oder Eigennamen, die es im Englischen so nicht gibt, erläutert werden. In diesem Text sollte man sich überlegen, wie man mit der Erklärung der verschiedenen Identitäten umgeht. Die Erklärung der Autorin (Berlinerin, Atheistin, Schriftstellerin) zu übernehmen, wird in dem neuen Kontext merkwürdig erscheinen, denn Sie stellen die Autorin ja nicht explizit vor. Auch das Wort „Drehkreuz" in diesem übertragenen Sinne kann nicht einfach so wie im Deutschen benutzt werden. Insbesondere die Begriffe „Leitkultur" und „Goethe-und-Dieter-Bohlen-Land" könnten Probleme bereiten. In der Beispiellösung gehen sie einfach in der Zusammenfassung auf.

Hier eine mögliche Umsetzung:
<u>Our identity ought to be European</u>
Unlike Americans, Russians or Africans, we Europeans don't have a common notion of identity. Instead of acknowledging one common European identity, Europeans have always defined themselves against other nations, other cultures or non-Christian religions, even though in Germany, for instance, half of the population are not members of the Church and in Berlin there are more Muslims than Catholics.
People complain a lot about Europe being just an economic union, yet they find it hard to define a European identity. Of course, European history has always been ambivalent. There has always been internal as well as external trade but also many wars. There's no other region in the world where so many countries share a relatively small geographical area. Today, Europe should really see itself as a crossroads between East and West.

Europe's self-image should be that of an international marketplace, a multi-ethnic place with cultural, linguistic and economic ties with the rest of the world. A European is multicultural by birth. This doesn't mean that we have to give up our national identities. If we understand that transnational identity doesn't exclude national identity, we will overcome the fear that is being fuelled in many European countries and regions, especially if this notion includes non-European immigrants.
We have to establish a multidimensional notion of identity, which includes identity of origin, of sociocultural background and religion as much as being part of a wider geographical area. In my case this would mean being German from the Rhineland, a Catholic high-school student and multicultural European. To sum up, European identity should be multilingual, multiracial and multicultural.

Aufgaben mit Bewertungskriterien

Themenfeld *American Myths and Realities – Freedom and Equality*

Aufgabenbeispiel Abitur Englisch Leistungskurs
Aufgabenart gemäß KLP: 1.1: Schreiben mit Leseverstehen integriert und Sprachmittlung isoliert
Thematischer Bezug gemäß KLP (Soziokulturelles Orientierungswissen): – Amerikanischer Traum – Visionen und Lebenswirklichkeiten in den USA: *American myths and realities: freedom and equality* – Chancen und Risiken der Globalisierung: *Globalisation and global challenges: economic, ecological and political issues*
Auszug aus einem englischsprachiger Sachtext (987 W.) (Klausurteil A, Text 1) Auszug aus einem deutschsprachigen Sachtext (475 W.) (Klausurteil B, Text 2)
Quellenangaben: Text 1: Joseph R. Biden, Inaugural address, 20 January 2021, https://www.whitehouse.gov/briefing-room/speeches-remarks/2021/01/20/inaugural-address-by-president-joseph-r-biden-jr/ (Zugriff: 01.04.2022, gekürzt) Text 2: Donata Riedel, „Sozialer Aufstieg in Deutschland bleibt die Ausnahme – OECD fürchtet Vergeudung von Talent" © *Handelsblatt GmbH*. Alle Rechte vorbehalten. 15.06.2018, https://www.handelsblatt.com/politik/deutschland/studie-zur-chancengerechtigkeit-sozialer-aufstieg-in-deutschland-bleibt-die-ausnahme-oecd-fuerchtet-vergeudung-von-talent/22690454.html (Zugriff: 01.04.2022)

Aufgabe

Klausurteil A: Leseverstehen/Schreiben (Text 1)

1. Sum up what challenges America faces and what has to be done to meet them according to Biden. *(Comprehension)*

2. Analyse the rhetorical means and strategies that Biden uses to convince his listeners. *(Analysis)*

3. Choose one of the following tasks:

3.1 Comment on lines 1 f. ("This is America's day. This is democracy's day. A day of history and hope, of renewal and resolve.") against the background of the speech and your work in class about the US and the American Dream. *(Evaluation: Comment)*

3.2 The debating club of your American host school deals with the challenges America and the world are facing in the 21st century. You are asked to contribute to the debate on climate change from your European perspective. Write your initial statement to the debate. Refer to work done in class on ecological issues of globalisation. *(Evaluation: Recreation of text)*

Klausurteil B: Sprachmittlung (Text 2)

4. Your American friend asks you about social mobility in Germany in an email. Write an answer based on the article from *Handelsblatt*. *(Mediation)*

Text 1 Inaugural address, January 20th, 2021 (excerpt) *Joseph R. Biden*

[...]

This is America's day. This is democracy's day. A day of history and hope. Of renewal and resolve. Through a crucible for the ages America has been tested anew and America has risen to the challenge. Today, we celebrate the triumph not of a candidate, but of a cause, the cause of democracy. The will of the people has been heard and the will of the people has been heeded. We have learned again that democracy is precious. Democracy is fragile. And at this hour, my friends, democracy has prevailed.

So now, on this hallowed ground where just days ago violence sought to shake this Capitol's very foundation, we come together as one nation, under God, indivisible, to carry out the peaceful transfer of power as we have for more than two centuries. We look ahead in our uniquely American way – restless, bold, optimistic – and set our sights on the nation we know we can be and we must be.

I thank my predecessors of both parties for their presence here. I thank them from the bottom of my heart. You know the resilience of our Constitution and the strength of our nation. As does President Carter, who I spoke to last night but who cannot be with us today, but whom we salute for his lifetime of service.

I have just taken the sacred oath each of these patriots took – an oath first sworn by George Washington. But the American story depends not on any one of us, not on some of us, but on all of us. On "We the People" who seek a more perfect Union.

This is a great nation and we are a good people. Over the centuries through storm and strife, in peace and in war, we have come so far. But we still have far to go.

We will press forward with speed and urgency, for we have much to do in this winter of peril and possibility. Much to repair. Much to restore. Much to heal. Much to build. And much to gain.

Few periods in our nation's history have been more challenging or difficult than the one we're in now. A once-in-a-century virus silently stalks the country. It's taken as many lives in one year as America lost in all of World War II. Millions of jobs have been lost. Hundreds of thousands of businesses closed. A cry for racial justice some 400 years in the making moves us. The dream of justice for all will be deferred no longer. A cry for survival comes from the planet itself. A cry that can't be any more desperate or any more clear. And now, a rise in political extremism, white supremacy, domestic terrorism that we must confront and we will defeat.

To overcome these challenges – to restore the soul and to secure the future of America – requires more than words. It requires that most elusive of things in a democracy: Unity. Unity.

In another January in Washington, on New Year's Day 1863, Abraham Lincoln signed the Emancipation Proclamation. When he put pen to paper, the President said, "If my name ever goes down into history it will be for this act and my whole soul is in it."

My whole soul is in it. Today, on this January day, my whole soul is in this: Bringing America together. Uniting our people. And uniting our nation. I ask every American to join me in this cause. Uniting to fight the common foes we face: Anger, resentment, hatred. Extremism, lawlessness, violence. Disease, joblessness, hopelessness.

With unity we can do great things. Important things. We can right wrongs. We can put people to work in good jobs. We can teach our children in safe schools. We can overcome this deadly virus. We can reward work, rebuild the middle class, and make health care secure for all. We can deliver racial justice. We can make America, once again, the leading force for good in the world.

I know speaking of unity can sound to some like a foolish fantasy. I know the forces that divide us are deep and they are real. But I also know they are not new. Our history has been a constant struggle between the American ideal that we are all created equal and the harsh, ugly reality that racism, nativism, fear, and demonization have long torn us apart. The battle is perennial. Victory is never assured.

Through the Civil War, the Great Depression, World War, 9/11, through struggle, sacrifice, and setbacks, our "better angels" have always prevailed. In each of these moments, enough of us came together to carry all of us forward. And, we can do so now.

History, faith, and reason show the way, the way of unity. We can see each other not as adversaries but as neighbors. We can treat each other with dignity and respect. We can join forces, stop the shouting, and lower the temperature. For without unity, there is no peace, only bitterness and fury. No progress, only exhausting outrage. No nation, only a state of chaos.

This is our historic moment of crisis and challenge, and unity is the path forward. And, we must meet this moment as the United States of America. If we do that, I guarantee you, we will not fail. We have never, ever, ever failed in America when we have acted together.

And so today, at this time and in this place, let us start afresh. All of us. Let us listen to one another. Hear one another. See one another. Show respect to one another. Politics need not be a raging fire destroying everything in its path. Every disagreement doesn't have to be a cause for total war. And, we must reject a culture in which facts themselves are manipulated and even manufactured.

[...]

Annotations

inaugural address – first speech of the President on the day of his inauguration

we the people – first words of the US constitution

Text 2 Studie zur Chancengerechtigkeit: Sozialer Aufstieg in Deutschland bleibt die Ausnahme – OECD fürchtet Vergeudung von Talent *Donata Riedel*

Für Kinder aus Arbeiterfamilien ist der soziale Aufstieg in Deutschland besonders schwer – ähnlich wie in den USA. Das hat Folgen für die Wirtschaft.

Berlin. „Der soziale Aufzug ist kaputt", schreiben die Ökonomen der Industrieländer-Organisation OECD. In einer neuen Studie vergleichen sie die soziale Mobilität in 30 Industrie- und Schwellenländern.

Die ist schwer eingeschränkt. In Deutschland kann es sechs Generationen dauern, bis die Nachkommen einer einkommensschwachen Familie das Durchschnittseinkommen erreichen, heißt es in der Studie. In Dänemark seien es nur zwei Generationen, in den übrigen skandinavischen Ländern drei Generationen. Nur in Schwellenländern wie China und Indien brauchen Menschen aus einkommensschwachen Familien noch länger – nämlich sieben bis acht Generationen.

Vergleicht man Väter und Söhne in Deutschland, dann gelingt nur neun Prozent der Söhne von Vätern mit geringem Einkommen der Aufstieg in die höchste Verdienstgruppe. Ganz anders sieht es für Kinder von Vätern mit hohem Verdienst aus: Die Hälfte von ihnen wird später einmal gut verdienen.

Ebenso schlecht sieht es bei den Bildungschancen aus: 53 Prozent der Kinder von Eltern mit hohem Bildungsstatus schaffen einen Uni-Abschluss, aber nur jedes zehnte Kind von Hauptschulabsolventen.

Ein gewisser Trost mag sein, dass es in anderen europäischen Ländern nicht besser aussieht, etwa in Frankreich und Großbritannien. Die Skandinavier allerdings haben es geschafft, Chancengerechtigkeit weitgehend herzustellen.

Die OECD-Ökonomen glauben, dass in Deutschland das Bildungssystem eine entscheidende Rolle für die fehlende soziale Mobilität spielt: Noch immer gebe es zu wenig Kitas und Ganztagsschulen, die Kindern aus sozial schwachen Familien mehr Bildung bieten könnten.

Die frühe Trennung nach der Grundschule in Gymnasien und andere Schulen verbaue zudem vielen Schülern die Chance auf Abitur und Universität.

Die OECD fürchtet, dass Deutschland damit Chancen verspielt und Talent verschwendet. Dies drücke auf die Produktivität der Wirtschaft insgesamt. Auch die Chance auf möglichst viele innovative Unternehmensgründer verspiele Deutschland so.

Die Ökonomen haben zudem die Aufstiegschancen innerhalb einer Generation verglichen, also die Frage gestellt, wie gut es gelingt, aus einem Niedriglohnjob in höhere Einkommenssphären aufzusteigen.

Auch diese Einkommensmobilität ist in Deutschland begrenzt. 58 Prozent der Geringverdiener bleiben für immer arm. Viele Teilzeitbeschäftigte blieben unter ihren Möglichkeiten, vor allem Frauen. „Ein Arbeitsplatz allein ermöglicht oftmals keine großen Schritte auf der Einkommensleiter", heißt es in dem Bericht.

Wer allerdings erst einmal einen Job mit hohem Einkommen erreicht hat, wird ihn kaum je verlieren: 74 Prozent aus dieser Gruppe steigen nicht wieder ab. Dies erhöhe die Gefahr, dass sich Vermögen in Händen weniger konzentrieren.

Die Ökonomen empfehlen als Gegenmittel eine Erbschaftsteuer mit niedrigeren Freibeträgen und weniger Ausnahmen. Gleichzeitig sollten niedrigere Einkommen von Steuern und Sozialabgaben entlastet werden. Denn je höher das Nettoeinkommen, desto eher gelingt der Bildungsaufstieg der Kinder.

Die Zahlen der OECD sind allerdings mit gewisser Vorsicht zu betrachten. Sie sind relativ alt und stammen überwiegend aus dem Jahr 2014. Seither gibt es mehr Kitas und Ganztagsschulen. Dass die Zahl allerdings bei weitem nicht ausreicht, wissen in Deutschland alle Eltern kleiner Kinder.

Bewertungskriterien

In diesem Kapitel finden Sie die Aspekte aufgelistet, die bei einer gelungenen Lösung von Ihnen erwartet werden. Sie sind für jede Teilaufgabe getrennt in einer Tabelle zusammengefasst. In der Spalte daneben sehen Sie jeweils die maximal zu erreichende Punktzahl.

Klausurteil A: Schreiben/Leseverstehen
Anforderungsbereich I (Teilaufgabe 1)

Die Schülerin / Der Schüler	**max. Punkte**
benennt die Herausforderungen, denen sich die USA stellen müssen: – die Coronapandemie und ihre Folgen (Arbeitslosigkeit, Insolvenz), – die Klimakrise, – Rassismus, der sich seit Jahrhunderten fortsetzt, – Extremismus, Terrorismus und Glaube an weiße Vorherrschaft, – generell: Hass, Unmut, Kriminalität, Gewalt, Hoffnungslosigkeit.	8
führt aus, wie diese Krisen nur gemeinsam bekämpft werden können.	4
	12

Anforderungsbereich II (Teilaufgabe 2)

Die Schülerin / Der Schüler	**max. Punkte**
führt den Patriotismus in Bidens Rede aus, der sich manifestiert in z. B. – Schlüsselwörtern (*America, democracy, nation, unity strength, great* etc.), – historischen Bezügen (Washington, Lincoln, historische Ereignisse) und – religiöser Überhöhung: „hallowed ground“ (Z. 14), „under God“ (Z. 17), „sacred oath“(Z. 31) „better angels“ (Z. 103 f.).	4
erläutert den Gebrauch figurativer Sprache in ihrer jeweiligen Funktion, z. B. – die Metapher „a crucible for the ages“ (Z. 4 f.), – die Metonymie/Metapher „shake this Capitol's very foundation“ (Z. 15 f.), – die Metapher „storm“ (Z. 38), – die Metapher „winter of peril“ (Z. 43), – die Personifikation „cry for survival“ (Z. 55 f.), – die Personifikation „virus silently stalks“ (Z. 48 f.).	4

benennt die emphatischen Mittel in ihrer jeweiligen Funktion, z. B. – zahlreiche Wiederholungen, – Alliterationen und Aufzählungen (auch Fakten und Zahlen) zur besonderen Betonung der Missstände, – Kontraste (Antithese) zusammen mit Parallelismen bzw. Anaphern zur Betonung der Stärke und Größe Amerikas, der Größe der Herausforderungen und der Bedeutung der Einheit, – Anaphern und Aufzählungen zur Betonung der Größe der Aufgaben und der Entschlossenheit und Stärke Amerikas, die Situation zu verbessern, – Parallelismen und Wiederholungen zur Betonung einzelner Kernsätze, – kurze oder elliptische Sätze.	4
benennt die Zielgruppenorientierung durch – *collective „we“* (durchgehend), – „my friends“ (Z. 13), – „We the people“ (Z. 35 f.), – Appelle („Let us .. “, „We must ...“ Z. 125 ff.). – Zuhörer und Redner als zusammenstehende Amerikaner	4
	16

Anforderungsbereich III (Teilaufgabe 3.1)

Die Schülerin / Der Schüler	**max. Punkte**
knüpft an den Ausgangstext an, indem sie/er sich auf den Beginn der Rede bezieht.	2
erläutert die Grundsätze des Amerikanischen Traums, die sich aus der Unabhängigkeitserklärung und dem Pioniergeist und Nationalstolz ergeben (Glaube an Erfolg, Streben nach Glück, Anpacken von Schwierigkeiten, Freiheit und Gleichheit, Einigkeit)	6
beschreibt die derzeitige (von Biden beschriebene oder allgemein bekannte) Situation als dem Amerikanischen Traum widersprechend, z. B. – Ungleichheit und Privilegien Einzelner, – Rassismus, – Spaltung der Gesellschaft, – Unglück und Tod.	4
kommt zu einer dezidierten persönlichen Einschätzung.	2
	14

Anforderungsbereich III (Teilaufgabe 3.2)

Die Schülerin / Der Schüler	**max. Punkte**
formuliert eine Einleitung ihres/seines Statements, z. B. mit Hinweis auf die Flutkatastrophe in NRW und RLP 2021.	2
benennt die Ursachen der Klimakrise, insbesondere die Konzentration von Treibhausgasen, z. B. durch Verkehr, Industrie, Landwirtschaft, Rodungen.	4
benennt die Folgen der Klimakrise, z. B. Anstieg des Meeresspiegels, Extremwetter, Dürre, Kälte, Unbewohnbarkeit von ganzen Regionen, Massenmigration, Krieg um Land und Wasser.	4
benennt notwendige Maßnahmen, z. B. Verzicht auf fossile Energieträger, Einschränkung von Konsum und Produktion, Verzicht auf tierische Produkte, massive Systemveränderungen, weltweite Bildungsoffensive, Infragestellung des Bevölkerungswachstums, technologische Lösungen.	4
	14

Klausurteil B: Sprachmittlung (Teilaufgabe 4)

Die Schülerin / Der Schüler gibt die wesentlichen Inhalte im Sinne der Aufgabenstellung sinngemäß zusammenfassend und zielgruppengerecht wieder:	**max. Punkte**

– die OECD-Studie der sozialen Mobilität in 30 Ländern;
– das schlechte Bild Deutschlands im Vergleich zu anderen Ländern (innerhalb der Generationen und über Generationen hinweg);
– die diesbezüglichen Zahlen (einschränkender Hinweis auf ihr Alter);
– die Gründe, die im Bildungssystem zu finden seien:
  – zu wenig Betreuung,
  – zu frühe Differenzierung;
– die Folgen für die Wirtschaft:
  – Auswirkungen auf die Produktivität,
  – Vergeudung von Talenten,
  – Verspielen von Innovationspotential;
– Lösungsvorschläge:
  – Erbschaftssteuer,
  – Entlastung von Steuern und Abgaben auf niedrige Einkommen.
	18

Themenfeld *Globalisation and Global Challenges: Economic, Ecological and Political Issues*

Aufgabenbeispiel Abitur Englisch Leistungskurs
Aufgabenart gemäß KLP: 1.1: Schreiben mit Leseverstehen integriert und Sprachmittlung isoliert
Thematischer Bezug gemäß KLP (Soziokulturelles Orientierungswissen): Chancen und Risiken der Globalisierung *Globalisation and global challenges: economic, ecological and political issues*
Auszug aus einem englischsprachigen Drama (1000 W.) (Klausurteil A, Text 1) Auszug aus einem deutschsprachigen Sachtext (594 W.) (Klausurteil B, Text 2)
Quellenangaben: Text 1: Jordan Hall, „The Donation", C. Bilodeau und T. Petersen, *Lighting the Way. An Anthology of Short Plays About the Climate Crisis,* The Arctic Cycle, 2020, S. 169–176 Text 2: Jonas Klüter, „Folgen des Klimawandels – Wie Deutschland bis 2050 aussehen könnte", 21.07.2021, www.zdf.de/nachrichten/panorama/klimawandel-auswirkungen-wohnen-gesundheit-landwirtschaft-100.html (Zugriff: 01.04.2022, gekürzt)

Aufgabe

Klausurteil A: Leseverstehen/Schreiben (Text 1)

1. Sum up Tommy's arguments for his decision to make a "donation" and Jen's reaction towards it. *(Comprehension)*

2. Analyse the way the play develops and how it reveals the two characters' attitudes. In doing this, consider both Jen's and Tommy's behaviour and their communicative strategies. *(Analysis)*

3. Choose one of the following tasks:

3.1 Discuss the issue of climate change and assess the individual's role in it. *(Evaluation: Comment)*

3.2 Write an ending to the play taking the characters' attitudes into account. *(Evaluation: Recreation of text)*

Klausurteil B: Sprachmittlung (Text 2)

4. Your friend in Texas has written a disrespectful remark on Joe Biden and his environmental policies in his last email. Apparently, your friend is a climate sceptic. Although you do not really think he will want to read this, you tell him in an email what you read on the ZDF website about what we can expect. *(Mediation)*

Text 1 The Donation (excerpt) *Jordan Hall*

JEN sits at her desk. She's an overworked nonprofit kind of girl.

Jen: Alright. So if we lower the thermostat by another two degrees ...

TOMMY, a discharged soldier, a little drunk, starts hammering on JEN's office window.

Tommy: Anyone?

Jen: ... and get Alison to wear a goddamn sweater instead of using that bloody space heater ...

Tommy: Hello? Anyone?

Jen: That could save us another fifty kilos or so ...

Tommy: I can see you there ignoring me!

With a sigh, JEN opens the window. Just a crack.

Jen: We aren't open. If you're here for a canvassing job, there's another intake on Monday.

Tommy: I'm here to make a donation.

Jen: That's terrific. You can do that on the website.

Tommy: It's not that kind of donation.

Jen: Oh. No. We don't accept gifts-in-kind. We're a nonprofit so we don't have the infrastructure –

Tommy: I want to give you my life.

There's a beat. TOMMY pushes the window open the rest of the way and hops inside.

Jen: What?

Tommy: I want to donate my life.

Jen: Do – you mean you want to volunteer? God. If I had a nickel for every guilt-ridden drunk who rolls up wanting to save the world. Look. I'm just the office manager. There are pamphlets outside, you sign up and – you might not get to kayak in front of an oil rig right away, but –

Tommy: No – I mean, the kayaking sounds exhilarating. But I want to donate my life.

Jen: I'm missing something, aren't I?

Tommy: I thought if I came here the donation would be properly recorded. And you could advise me about the most carbon-neutral way to do it? Because I was thinking about pills – but then I might be sending the toxins into the groundwater? And there's always a gun – but that would mean supporting weapons manufacturing and I'm not really comfortable with that.

Jen: Are you – are you talking about killing yourself? Can I call somebody to help you? Like a friend? Or a therapist? Or a hotline?

Tommy: This isn't a suicide thing.

Jen: It kinda sounds like one.

Tommy: No. I know. I get it. But think of it like this. If we were in a foxhole, taking fire, and I could cover you to get to the Jeep – but laying down cover was gonna get me shot? If I did that – knowing I was gonna get shot – that's not suicide. Not really.

Jen: But you aren't talking about –

Tommy: Of course I am. I've seen the UN report. Droughts. Sea-level rise. Climate change casualties are at 400,000 per year, and it's gonna get higher. And in order to stop it, we need to hit net zero by 2050. That's how we get to the Jeep. I'm 25. Say I've got 50 years left, that's 900 tons of carbon. I can give that back to you. I can give you that much cover.

Jen: That's oddly noble – and – I can see you've thought about this – but neither I nor the organization I represent want you to do that. There are – there are better ways for you to help.

Tommy: Not really. Not that'll save us 900 tons.

Jen: Green living. Public transit. Vegetarian diet.

Tommy: 300 at best.

Jen: Well then, make a bigger difference. Protest, lobby for green candidates.

Tommy: Because that's been a roaring success for the last 50 years, hasn't it. Look. I'm not here to make you feel bad. You seem lovely. With your night school law books, here at 7 a.m. If you really don't want my life, I'll just nip over to Greenpeace –

Jen: No!

Tommy: It's really no trouble.

Jen: No. You should stay here. Stay here, and I'll make a cup of tea, and we'll talk.

Tommy: You're just going to keep trying to talk me out of it.

Jen: Well, I – Yes. Please. Have some tea. Things always seem better after a cup of tea. Give me that long. And if I can't talk you out of it, I'll let you go ... donate to Greenpeace.

Tommy: ... Alright.

Jen: Alright. Alright. Now you just stay ... Stay ...

Keeping her eyes on him at all times, she nips offstage for a second, and then dashes back on.

Jen: There. Kettle's on. So. So-so-so. How did you – how did you think of your – donation?

Tommy: Oh. Well. I was down at the pub. Nowhere else to be. And the news came on with the UN report and I looked at my beer – leaving this half-moon of wet on the bar – and I wondered how much carbon went into it? Into me. All the cold beers and steak pies and my Da's car. What had I done to be worth so much? What had I done at all? Except get discharged –

Jen: Discharged?

Tommy: That's not the important part. And anyway, it all comes back to this.

Jen: Comes back to this how?

Tommy: All of it. Army. Police. We say democracy. Human rights. But mostly we help old men say where the money goes. Or the oil. Or the mine. You know it because when it really is about democracy or human rights, they tell you to protect the pipeline, and not the people.

Jen: Is that what happened?

Tommy: I told you that doesn't matter. What matters is I can do this now. And it will save lives. 900 tons. That's five people in South America. Fifteen in India. Thirty-six in Maldives.

Jen: Or one here.

Tommy: Pretty much my point.

Jen: Well then, maybe I should do it too.

Tommy: Do what?

Jen: Donate my life.

Tommy: But – no. I don't want you to do that.

Jen: Oh. I see. It's fine for you, but not for me?

Tommy: Yes. I'm a grotesque waste of resources, and you're – you're –

Jen: What? I'm worth at least 600 tons. And what am I doing, really? Looking for improvements in heating technology and paperless office procedures? Going to law school at night so that in five years I can intern for a lawyer who supports Indigenous land claims or environmental class action suits? Band-Aid on a bullet hole. Your way is much better – all the good I'm ever going to do, all rolled up into one moment. And best of all, I don't have to stick around and find out the hard way if it doesn't work. Or – y'know – for the cleanup.

Annotations

discharged soldier – person that is no longer working for the military, in this case because of wrongdoing

canvassing – trying to convince people – usually strangers – to support a certain cause

nickel – 5-cent coin (US)

toxins – highly unhealthy substances

UN report – annual report by the United Nations on climate change

Indigenous – people who are native to a certain place (usually before the arrival of European colonists)

class action suit – a case brought to court by one person acting on behalf of a group of people

Band-Aid – a sticky plaster used to cover small wounds

Text 2 Folgen des Klimawandels – Wie Deutschland 2050 aussehen könnte (Auszug) *Jonas Klüter, dpa*

[...]

Die Hochwasserkatastrophe in Nordrhein-Westfalen und Rheinland-Pfalz hat neuen Druck im Kampf gegen den menschengemachten Klimawandel erzeugt. Kurz zuvor hatte das Potsdam-Institut für Klimafolgenforschung (PIK) im Auftrag der Deutschen Bahn eine Analyse zu klimatischen Veränderungen in der Bundesrepublik vorgelegt.

Demnach wird es hierzulande etwa bis 2060 deutlich mehr Hitzetage und weniger harte Winter geben. Innerhalb der EU ist man sich weitgehend einig, dass man bis zum Jahr 2050 klimaneutral sein will. Die Folgen des Klimawandels aufhalten wird man damit laut Experten nicht – höchstens abmildern. Wie es in Deutschland bis dahin aussehen könnte, zeigen Klimaforscher und andere Fachleute.

Hitze

Dass langanhaltende hohe Temperaturen mit dem menschengemachten Klimawandel verbunden sind, daran gibt es in der Fachwelt kaum Zweifel. Daniela Jacob, Meteorologin und Direktorin des German Institute for Climate Services (Gerics) in Hamburg, betont: „Um 2050 müssen wir damit rechnen, dass die Sommermonate deutlich heißer und trockener sind.“ [...] Etwa für den Oberrheingraben bei Karlsruhe lasse sich schon heute projizieren, dass sich dort bis zur Mitte des Jahrhunderts die Zahl der heißen Tage im Vergleich zum Zeitraum von 1970 bis 2000 etwa verdoppeln werde.

Gesundheit

Entgegen der Vorstellung von strahlendem Sonnenschein und Urlaubsatmosphäre kann „warmes Wetter" sehr schlecht für unsere Gesundheit sein. „Wenn die Temperatur auch nachts nicht unter 20 Grad fällt, bedeutet das, dass wir uns nicht richtig ausruhen können und weniger leistungsfähig sind." Daniela Jacob, Gerics-Direktorin

Andreas Marx vom Helmholtz-Zentrum für Umweltforschung in Leipzig geht davon aus, dass die Hitze das Gesundheitssystem zusätzlich belasten wird. So könne es etwa zu mehr Kreislauferkrankungen kommen.

Landwirtschaft

Anhaltende Hitze und langer, starker Regen wird Experten zufolge auch eine Umstellung für diejenigen bedeuten, die sehr auf das Wetter angewiesen sind. „In der Landwirtschaft müssen wir auf Sorten setzen, die mit diesen starken Temperatur- und Feuchtevariationen zurechtkommen." Daniela Jacob, Gerics-Direktorin

Ein Problem ist demnach auch, dass Wasser bis 2050 knapper wird. „Die Landwirtschaft muss sich so umstellen, dass sie die Böden nicht so oft bewässern muss", ergänzt Jacob.

Hochwasserschutz

Als Folge des menschengemachten Klimawandels werde Hochwasser mit Blick auf das Jahr 2050 vor allem in Gebieten in Nord- und Westeuropa zunehmend eine Bedrohung darstellen, sagt Ralf Merz. Der Hydrologe arbeitet am Standort Halle an der Saale des Helmholtz-Zentrums für Umweltforschung.

Diese Entwicklung hänge vor allem mit dem sogenannten Jetstream zusammen. Dieser treibt in der oberen Atmosphäre die Hoch- und Tiefdruckgebiete über Europa hinweg. Wegen des Klimawandels habe sich der Strom verändert, sodass Hoch- oder Tiefdruck-Systeme länger an einem Ort stehen bleiben.

„Und das ist auch jetzt wieder passiert bei dem Tiefdruckgebiet ‚Bernd'", so Merz. Demnach wäre früher ein solches Tief nach zwei Tagen weitergezogen, jetzt ist es an einem Ort stehengeblieben – mit verheerenden Folgen.

[...]

Wohnen

Wenn es draußen unerträglich warm ist, flüchten wir uns auch schon heute gerne in kalte Innenräume. Dass diese auch energieintensiv mit Klimaanlagen runtergekühlt würden, verschärfe das Problem des menschengemachten Klimawandels, sagt Jacob.

Wissenschaftler Marx, Mitglied der Helmholtz-Klima-Initiative, empfiehlt daher, Gebäudehüllen wesentlich besser zu dämmen, „dann hat das auch im Sommer den Effekt, dass Hitze nicht so schnell ins Haus kommt". Gerade deutsche Städte müssen seiner Einschätzung nach neu gedacht werden. „Wir brauchen in der Stadt grüne und blaue Infrastruktur, das heißt Parkanlagen und Gewässer." [...]

Dass mehr getan werden müsse, um den Anstieg des Klimawandels zu bremsen, betonen die Experten im Gespräch mit der Deutschen Presse-Agentur.

Nach Einschätzung des Hydrologen Merz ist der Klimawandel zwar fortgeschritten, „aber wir stehen hoffentlich immer noch vor dem Kipppunkt, an dem sich das Klima auf Dauer stark verändert. Das heißt, wir müssen jetzt die Entwicklung aufhalten, bevor es zu spät ist."

Bewertungskriterien

Klausurteil A: Leseverstehen/Schreiben
Anforderungsbereich I (Teilaufgabe 1)

Die Schülerin / Der Schüler	max. Punkte
führt Tommys Vorschlag an, wegen seiner persönlichen Ressourcenverschwendung sein Leben für den Klimaschutz zu geben.	2
führt Tommys Argumente an: – die Folgen der Klimakrise (Dürre und Anstieg des Meeresspiegels verbunden mit 400.000 Toten pro Jahr), – seine Rechnung, auf diese Weise 900 Tonnen CO_2 zu sparen, – seine Zurückweisung von Alternativen als zu ineffektiv, – seine Drohung bei Ablehnung zu Greenpeace zu gehen, – die Hinterfragung seines Fußabdrucks, – seine Kapitalismuskritik.	6
benennt Jens Positionen dazu: – die Alternative ökologisch zu leben, – die Alternative des politischen Aktivismus, – ihre Drohung, es Tommy gleichzutun.	4
	12

Anforderungsbereich II (Teilaufgabe 2)

Die Schülerin / Der Schüler	max. Punkte
beschreibt die Entwicklung des Dialoges: – die anfänglichen Missverständnisse, – Jens plötzliches Entsetzen über das Anliegen, – die sachliche Argumentation Tommys, – seine Analogie zum bewaffneten Kampf, – seine ironisch-spöttische Widerlegung der Argumente Jens, – seine Ausführungen zu seinem persönlichen CO_2-Fußabdruck, – Jens Entschluss, es ihm gleichzutun, – Tommys Zurückweisung des Entschlusses, – Jens Argumente.	6
beschreibt Jen als engagierte Klimaschützerin, die – sich in einer Organisation engagiert, – individuelle Beiträge zum Klimaschutz forciert (Thermostat, Pullover), – sich für papierlose Büroarbeit einsetzt, – nachhaltiges Leben und Essen befürwortet, – politischen Aktivismus im realistischen Rahmen befürwortet, – Anwältin für indigene Völker und Umwelt-Sammelklagen werden will,	6

– Tommy voller Empathie von seinem Vorhaben abbringen möchte, – schließlich den Nutzen ihres ökologischen Engagements infrage stellt.	
beschreibt Tommy als angetrunkenen Soldaten, der die individuelle Verantwortung für die Klimakrise in letzter Konsequenz akzeptiert, dies jedoch von Jen nicht erwartet.	4
	16

Anforderungsbereich III (Teilaufgabe 3.1)

Die Schülerin / Der Schüler	max. Punkte
knüpft an den Ausgangstext an, indem sie/er sich z. B. auf Tommys radikalen Ansatz bezieht.	2
benennt – Ursachen der Klimakrise, insbesondere die Konzentration von Treibhausgasen, z. B. durch Verkehr, Industrie, Landwirtschaft, Rodungen, und – Folgen der Klimakrise, z. B. Extremwetter, Dürre, Kälte, Unbewohnbarkeit von ganzen Regionen, Massenmigration, Krieg um Land und Wasser.	4
benennt zu treffende Maßnahmen, z. B. Verzicht auf fossile Energieträger, Einschränkung von Konsum und Produktion, Verzicht auf Fleisch, massive Systemveränderungen, weltweite Bildungsoffensive, Infragestellen des Bevölkerungswachstums, technologische Lösungen.	4
führt die Bedeutung individuellen Handelns aus, mit Blick auf Bewusstmachung, Vorbildfunktion und Glaubwürdigkeit, aber betont das Primat staatlichen und supranationalen Handelns.	4
	14

Anforderungsbereich III (Teilaufgabe 3.2)

Die Schülerin / Der Schüler	max. Punkte
knüpft plausibel an den Text an unter Berücksichtigung der herausgearbeiteten Merkmale der Charaktere.	2
führt den Text fort, z. B. mit einer kontroversen Auseinandersetzung über Jens Vorschlag, mit der Akzeptanz des Vorschlags und der gemeinsamen Planung oder mit dem vollständigen Rückzug Tommys.	8
gelangt zu einem plausiblen Ende.	4
	14

Klausurteil B: Sprachmittlung (Teilaufgabe 4)

Die Schülerin / Der Schüler gibt die wesentlichen Inhalte im Sinne der Aufgabenstellung sinngemäß zusammenfassend wieder:	max. Punkte

die Hochwasserkatastrophe 2021 als Folge des Klimawandels,	18
allg. Folge: mehr Hitze, weniger harte Winter,	
spezielle Folgen: – Hitze: heißer, trockener; Verdopplung der Tage, – Gesundheit: Schlafmangel, Kreislauferkrankungen, – Landwirtschaft: Wasserknappheit, – Wohnen: Klimaanlage als zusätzliche Klimabelastung.	

Themenfeld *Visions of the Future – Utopia and Dystopia*

Aufgabenbeispiel Abitur Englisch Leistungskurs
Aufgabenart gemäß KLP: 1.1: Schreiben mit Leseverstehen integriert und Sprachmittlung isoliert
Thematischer Bezug gemäß KLP (Soziokulturelles Orientierungswissen): Medien in ihrer Bedeutung für den Einzelnen und die Gesellschaft *Visions of the future – utopia and dystopia*
Englischsprachiger literarischer Text (235 W., Gedicht) (Klausurteil A, Text 1) Auszug aus einem deutschsprachigen Sach- und Gebrauchstext (576 W.) (Klausurteil B, Text 2)
Quellenangaben: Text 1: Roger Mc Gough, "The Lake", http://www.englishdaily626.com/poetry_corner.php?047 (Zugriff: 01.04.2022) Text 2: „Müll zu trennen reicht nicht" (FAZ.NET, 07.01.2018) von Christoph Schäfer, © Alle Rechte vorbehalten. Frankfurter Allgemeine Zeitung GmbH, Frankfurt. Zur Verfügung gestellt vom Frankfurter Allgemeine Archiv. http://www.faz.net/aktuell/wirtschaft/muell-zu-trennen-reicht-nicht-15376781.html (Zugriff: 01.04.2022)

Aufgabe

Klausurteil A: Leseverstehen/Schreiben (Text 1)

1. Describe the physical and biological state of the lake in detail. *(Comprehension)*

2. Examine the way the speaker presents people and their environment and the results of pollution. In doing this, consider the speaker's choice of words and the syntax and imagery of the poem. *(Analysis)*

3. Choose one of the following tasks:

3.1 Evaluate the criticism inherent in the poem. Give arguments and examples to support or refute the author's negative view of the way people treat the environment. *(Evaluation: Comment)*

3.2 Imagine you are an environmentalist in the town where the lake is situated. Write an article for the local newspaper, stating how bad the environmental situation has become. *(Evaluation: Recreation of text)*

Klausurteil B: Sprachmittlung (Text 2)

4. While you are visiting your partner school in Ireland, you read an article in the school magazine which praises German awareness of environmental issues. Having read Schäfer's article, you feel obliged to write an answer. Write your article for the school magazine on the basis of Schäfer's article in *Frankfurter Allgemeine.*

Text 1 The Lake *Roger McGough*

For years there have been no fish in the lake.
People hurrying through the park avoid it
like the plague. Birds steer clear
and the sedge of course has withered.
Trees lean away from it,
and at night it reflects, not the moon,
but the blackness of its own depths.
There are no fish in the lake.
But there is life there. There is life.

Underwater pigs glide between reefs of coral debris.
They love it here. They breed and multiply
in sties hollowed out of the mud
and lined with mattresses and bedsprings.
They live on dead fish and rotting things,
drowned pets, plastic and assorted excreta.
Rusty cans they like the best.
Holding them in webbed trotters
their teeth tear easily through the tin,
and poking in a snout, they noisily suck out
the putrid matter within.

There are no fish in the lake.
But there is life there. There is life.
For on certain evenings after dark
shoals of pigs surface

and look out at those houses near the park.
Where, in bathrooms,
children feed stale bread to plastic ducks,
and in attics,
toy yachts have long since run aground.
Where, in living-rooms,
anglers dangle their lines on patterned carpets,
and bemoan the fate of the ones that got away.
Down on the lake, piggy eyes glisten.
They have acquired a taste for flesh.
They are licking their lips. Listen ...

Annotations

sedge – kind of grass growing in water; G.: Schilf

debris – small pieces of rubbish

sty – very dirty building or room (compare *pigsty*: pen where pigs are kept)

trotter – pig's foot

putrid – rotten; stinking

shoal – large group of fish

Text 2 Müll zu trennen reicht nicht *Christoph Schäfer*

China will unseren Plastikabfall nicht mehr ins Land lassen. Das teure deutsche Entsorgungssystem wird noch teurer werden. Doch Jammern hilft nichts: Um unseren Abfall müssen wir uns schon selbst kümmern.

Plastikmüll hat im Meer nichts verloren. Wenn in den Abendnachrichten Bilder gezeigt werden, wie in entfernten Weltgegenden Tausende Folien, Flaschen und Tüten auf der Wasseroberfläche treiben, ist die Empörung zu Recht groß. Glücklicherweise sind die deutschen Badeseen sauber. Das bestätigt die Deutschen darin, Klimaschützer und Recyclingmeister zu sein. Fast alle haben drei bis vier Mülltonnen vor dem Haus, um den Abfall zu trennen. Eine braune für den Bioabfall, eine blaue fürs Papier, die schwarze für den Restmüll und die gelbe für Metall und Kunststoff. Darüber hinaus gibt es Wertstoffhöfe und diverse Sammelbehälter für Elektroschrott, Altkleider und Schuhe. Gefühlt ist alles wunderbar in Ordnung.

Leider will sich eine Meldung der vergangenen Woche nicht ins harmonische Bild einfügen: Demnach droht Deutschland im Müll zu versinken, weil China unseren Plastikabfall nicht mehr haben will. Moment mal, denkt man da. Wieso exportiert Deutschland überhaupt Plastikmüll ins ferne China? Wer genauer nachliest, erfährt ganz Erstaunliches: Von den sechs Millionen Tonnen Plastikmüll, die hierzulande jedes Jahr anfallen, geht etwa ein Viertel ins Ausland. Etwa die Hälfte des exportierten Mülls landet im Reich der Mitte. Die Menge ist gigantisch: Allein im vorvergangenen Jahr kaufte China rund 750 000 Tonnen Plastikmüll aus Deutschland. Das entspricht mehr als 80 000 randvollen Müllwagen.

Was mit dem deutschen Müll in China passiert ist, will keiner so genau wissen. In die offiziellen Statistiken jedenfalls fließt das nach China verschiffte Plastik als erfolgreich recycelt ein. Dabei arbeitet laut Experten sogar die Müllverbrennung in Deutschland ökologischer als die chinesische Kunststoffverwertung. Aber weg ist weg, aus den Augen aus dem Sinn.

Müll trennen alleine reicht nicht

Bedauerlicherweise entpuppt sich die Vorstellung von den mülltrennenden Umweltchampions auch mit Blick auf andere Werte als Lüge. Der typische Bundesbürger hat laut EU-Statistikamt im vorvergangenen Jahr exakt 37,4 Kilo Plastikverpackungen als Abfall hinterlassen. Das ist dreimal mehr als ein Bulgare verursacht, und sogar sechs Kilo mehr als der durchschnittliche EU-Bürger ansammelt. Bei der Wiederverwertung sieht es besser aus, aber längst nicht vorbildlich. Das Recycling von Altpapier, Altglas, Weißblech und Aluminium klappt gut, die Aufbereitung von Kunststoffverpackungen hingegen unzureichend. Noch immer wird in Deutschland die Hälfte der Plastikabfälle verbrannt oder landet im Ausland. Tschechien und Bulgarien hingegen erreichen Aufbereitungsquoten von 62 Prozent. Immerhin ist Besserung in Sicht. Ende dieses Jahres tritt das neue Müllgesetz in Kraft, das steigende Recyclingquoten verlangt.

Doch auch damit wird längst nicht alles gut. Der bisherige Ablasshandel (Ich trenne meinen Müll, also darf ich sorgenlos einkaufen) greift zu kurz. Hersteller wie Konsumenten müssen umdenken. Um nur ein paar Beispiele zu nennen: Muss es wirklich sein, dass in eine große Gummibärchentüte Dutzende kleine Tütchen kommen? Muss jede einzelne Gurke im Supermarkt in Plastik verpackt werden? Müssen so viele Kaffee „to go“ sein?

Auch an der Akzeptanz für wiederaufbereitete Materialien hapert es. Die Industrie ist nur in engen Grenzen bereit, bei der Qualität der Ausgangsstoffe Abstriche hinzunehmen. Die deutschen Verbraucher hingegen werden es definitiv akzeptieren müssen, dass die Preise für Plastikwaren etwas steigen. Das chinesische Importverbot für Müll wird dazu führen, dass Handel und Industrie mehr an den Grünen Punkt zahlen müssen. Das teure deutsche Entsorgungssystem wird noch teurer werden – und viele Produzenten werden die höheren Kosten durchreichen. Das ist trotzdem besser, als den alten Plastikmüll nach Fernost zu exportieren, wo er oft genug im Meer landet. Um unseren Abfall müssen wir uns schon selbst kümmern.

Bewertungskriterien

Klausurteil A: Leseverstehen/Schreiben
Anforderungsbereich I (Teilaufgabe 1)

Die Schülerin / Der Schüler	max. Punkte
beschreibt das dunkle Aussehen der Oberfläche des Sees, in der sich nicht einmal der Mond spiegelt.	2

führt an, dass keine Fische darin leben und das Riedgras verwelkt ist.	2
führt an, dass Tiere und Menschen gleichermaßen den See meiden.	2
beschreibt, was sich an Unrat in dem See befindet, z. B. – tote Haustiere, – Plastik, – Fäkalien, – alte Matratzen, – rostige Büchsen.	4
beschreibt die mutierten Monsterschweine, die den See bewohnen.	2
	12

Anforderungsbereich II (Teilaufgabe 2)

Die Schülerin / Der Schüler	**max. Punkte**
analysiert die Wortwahl des lyrischen Ich, die Ekel, Fäulnis, Tod und Bedrohung suggeriert *(plague, withered, blackness, debris, sties, dead, rotting, excreta* etc.).	4
analysiert syntaktische Merkmale des Gedichtes, insbesondere – die sich wiederholenden Zeilen 8/9 und 21/22 („There are no fish in the lake. / But there is life there. There is life.“), – die Wiederholung innerhalb der Zeilen, die Bedrohung suggeriert, – die Auslassung in der letzten Zeile („Listen ...“), die ebenfalls bedrohlich wirkt.	4
erläutert die Symbolik der sich neigenden Bäume zur Illustration der Widerwärtigkeit und die Symbolik der Schweine als – Indikator für den Verschmutzungsgrad (Schweinestall), – Mutanten und damit Resultat der Veränderung der Natur durch den Menschen, – Bedrohung, die eines Tages über den See hinaus spürbar wird und dem Menschen selbst gefährlich wird.	4
erläutert die Bedeutung des Verhaltens der Menschen sowie die Symbolik ihrer Gegenstände, die immer wieder Widernatürlichkeit, Unappetitlichkeit sowie Verfall suggerieren und somit den Verfall der Umwelt widerspiegeln, z. B. – altes Brot, – Plastikenten im Badezimmer (statt Enten in der Natur), – vergessene Spielzeugjachten (nutzlos, kaputt, als Pendant zum See), – Angeln auf dem Teppich (statt in der Natur).	4
	16

Anforderungsbereich III (Teilaufgabe 3.1)

Die Schülerin / Der Schüler	**max. Punkte**
nimmt einleitend Bezug auf die Intention des Gedichtes.	2
erläutert anhand von Beispielen den Zustand unserer Umwelt, der dem Gedicht Recht gibt oder führt an, dass allerdings auch viele Anstrengungen zum Schutz der Umwelt unternommen werden.	8
wägt die Punkte gegeneinander ab und kommt zu einer begründeten Schlussfolgerung.	4
	14

Anforderungsbereich III (Teilaufgabe 3.2)

Die Schülerin / Der Schüler	**max. Punkte**
wählt den Zustand des Sees als Aufhänger für seinen Artikel.	2
führt die Konsequenzen der Verschmutzung aus und/oder benennt und beschreibt weitere Bereiche, in denen Umweltschutz geboten ist.	6
benennt Lösungsvorschläge für das Problem des Sees und andere Probleme der Umweltverschmutzung.	4
appelliert an die Lesenden, zu einer Verbesserung beizutragen.	2
	14

Klausurteil B: Sprachmittlung (Teilaufgabe 4)

Die Schülerin / Der Schüler gibt die wesentlichen Inhalte im Sinne der Aufgabenstellung sinngemäß zusammenfassend wieder:	**max. Punkte**
der scheinbar vorbildliche Umgang mit Plastikmüll in Deutschland,	18
die Verschiffung ins Ausland,	
das hohe Aufkommen trotz Recycling,	
die Kritik an bestimmten Produkten *(coffee to go,* Gummibärchen),	
die mangelnde Akzeptanz recycelter Materialien,	
die steigenden Kosten.	

Themenfeld *The Impact of Shakespearean Drama on Young Audiences Today*

Aufgabenbeispiel Abitur Englisch Leistungskurs
Aufgabenart gemäß KLP: 1.1: Schreiben mit Leseverstehen integriert und Sprachmittlung isoliert
Thematischer Bezug gemäß KLP (Soziokulturelles Orientierungswissen): Literatur und Medien in ihrer Bedeutung für den Einzelnen und die Gesellschaft *The impact of Shakespearean drama on young audiences today: study of extracts and film scenes*
Auszug aus einem deutschsprachigen Sachtext (459 W.) (Klausurteil B, Text 1) Auszug aus einem englischsprachigen literarischen Text (365 W.) (Klausurteil A, Text 2)
Quellenangaben: Text 1: Frank Günther, „Sein oder Nichtsein?", *Frankfurter Neue Presse* 19.04.2014, online https://www.genios.de/presse-archiv/artikel/FNP/20140419/sein-oder-nicht-sein-mit-shakespeare/5127EE30653D66223000.html (Zugriff: 01.04.2022, gekürzt) Text 2: William Shakespeare, *The Taming of the Shrew,* Act V, Scene II

Aufgabe

Klausurteil A: Leseverstehen/Schreiben (Text 1)

1. At an international summer school, your group is doing an e-zine project on Shakespeare's relevance worldwide. Of course, you have the part on Germany. Write your e-zine article based on Günther's view on Shakespeare's still being up-to-date. *(Mediation)*

Klausurteil A: Leseverstehen/Schreiben

2. Point out the view of a wife's duty as it is presented by Katherina. *(Comprehension)*

3. Explain the comparisons used in this monologue as well as their function. In doing this, also refer to the Elizabethan world picture. *(Analysis)*

4. Choose one of the following tasks:

4.1 Evaluate Katherina's speech from today's point of view. *(Evaluation: Comment)*

4.2 After you have attended a performance of *The Taming of the Shrew,* write an article for an international online magazine with the title "The interest of young audiences in Shakespeare", in which you critically discuss the relevance of Shakespeare's plays for today's audiences. Refer to the excerpt from the play, Frank Günther's article and other texts you have studied. *(Evaluation: Recreation of text)*

Text 1 Sein oder Nichtsein? *Frank Günther*

Zum 450. Geburtstag des meistgespielten Theaterdichters der Welt fragt der Shakespeare-Experte in einem Gastbeitrag: Verstaubt oder nicht verstaubt?

Nun feiern wir also Shakespeares 450. Geburtstag. Es gibt nur wenige Autoren der Weltliteratur, bei denen man auf eine vergleichbare Wirkungsgeschichte zurückblicken kann; Dante könnte man nennen, und Cervantes, auch wenn sein „Don Quichote“ – trotz Windmühlen und Dulcinea – nicht Shakespeares breitgefächerte Wirkungsmacht erreichte. Shakespeare ist eine einzigartige literarische Ikone.

Wie es euch gefällt

Was sagt man über eine 400 Jahre alte Ikone? Über Shakespeare ist dieser Tage als bewunderndes Statement häufig zu lesen, er sei „auch heute noch aktuell“. Das sagt sich so leicht dahin. Unklar ist, was es bedeuten soll. Es ist nämlich ein seltsam vergiftetes Lob. Im „auch-heute-noch“ schwingt als Unterton ja mit, dass solche uralten Werke nach 400 Jahren eigentlich längst zum historischen Schutt gehören müssten. Aber nein, nicht bei Shakespeare – und dann folgt dieses Wörtchen „aktuell“. Shakespeare ist auch heute noch aktuell! Also wichtig, relevant, bedeutsam für unsere heutigen Probleme, für dich und mich, hier und jetzt. Noch aktuell. Also morgen vielleicht schon nicht mehr?

Es ist gut gemeint, aber etwas glitschig, dieses schlagzeilenhascherische Adjektiv „aktuell“. Wir gebrauchen es gewöhnlich im Kontext der „aktuellen Nachrichten“, des „aktuellen Straßenzustandsberichts“, der „aktuellen Herbstmode“, der „aktuellen Frühjahrsfarben“, der „aktuellen Looks“, der „aktuellen Trends“ – also für lauter entschieden flüchtige, nur für den konkreten Moment gültige Erscheinungen, zumeist in ranschmeißerischer Werbesprache formuliert. Was „aktuell“ ist, ist schnellebig; es trägt sein baldiges Ende schon in sich, denn das Wörtlein „aktuell“ signalisiert, dass es alsbald von noch „Aktuellerem“ abgelöst werden wird. Was heute aktuell ist, ist schon morgen von gestern.

Was ihr wollt

Shakespeare, der „auch heute noch aktuell“ sein soll, soll offenbar einen entscheidenden Beitrag zum heutigen Aktuellen leisten. Was aber sind unsere aktuellen Probleme zu Shakespeares Geburtstag? Die Euro-Krise. Die Griechenland-Krise. Die Energie-Krise. Die Ukraine-Krise. Die Migrationsproblematik. Der NSU-Skandal über Nazi-Umtriebe. Der NSA-Skandal über Geheimdienstumtriebe. Die Probleme mit Very Big Data. Die Frage der sozialen Gerechtigkeit. Die Quotenregelung für Frauen in Führungspositionen. Die EU-Regelung zu Energiesparbeschränkungen bei Staubsaugern und Kaffeemaschinen. Haben Shakespeares Werke uns dazu irgendetwas zu sagen? Nein, natürlich nicht. Die Rede vom „auch heute noch aktuellen“ Shakespeare entpuppt sich schnell als hilflose Hohlfloskel. Seinem Werk ist mit solchen wohlfeilen Etiketten wohl nicht beizukommen.

[...]

Unter der „Aktualität“ der Oberflächenzeitumstände, die von „verstaubten“ Verhältnissen erzählen mag, brodelt sehr lebendig das Eigentliche, das Shakespeares Glanz ausmacht: die niemals an ein Ende kommende, niemals auserzählbare existenzielle menschliche Werdens- und Wandlungsmöglichkeit. So kommt es, dass wir durch Shakespeares paradoxe Erzählkunst uns selbst auch hinter der verblichenen Aktualität vergangener Weltverhältnisse wiedererkennen können. In seinen zahllosen Gestalten, in ihren Leiden und Freuden, ihren Gemeinheiten und Bösartigkeiten, ihren Irrtümern und Selbsttäuschungen, ihren Egoismen und ihrer Fähigkeit zu Güte, Liebe und Mitleid erscheinen wir uns selbst, nah und vertraut.

Text 2 The Taming of the Shrew (Act V, Scene 2) *William Shakespeare*

Katherina, who is the woman to be tamed in this comedy, speaks this monologue in the final scene.

Katherina
Fie, fie! unknit that threatening unkind brow,
And dart not scornful glances from those eyes,
To wound thy lord, thy king, thy governor:
It blots thy beauty as frosts do bite the meads,
Confounds thy fame as whirlwinds shake fair buds,
And in no sense is meet or amiable.
A woman moved is like a fountain troubled,
Muddy, ill-seeming, thick, bereft of beauty;
And while it is so, none so dry or thirsty
Will deign to sip or touch one drop of it.
Thy husband is thy lord, thy life, thy keeper,
Thy head, thy sovereign; one that cares for thee,
And for thy maintenance commits his body
To painful labour both by sea and land,
To watch the night in storms, the day in cold,
Whilst thou liest warm at home, secure and safe;
And craves no other tribute at thy hands
But love, fair looks and true obedience;
Too little payment for so great a debt.
Such duty as the subject owes the prince
Even such a woman oweth to her husband;
And when she is froward, peevish, sullen, sour,
And not obedient to his honest will,
What is she but a foul contending rebel
And graceless traitor to her loving lord?
I am ashamed that women are so simple
To offer war where they should kneel for peace;
Or seek for rule, supremacy and sway,
When they are bound to serve, love and obey.
Why are our bodies soft and weak and smooth,

Unapt to toil and trouble in the world,
But that our soft conditions and our hearts
Should well agree with our external parts?
Come, come, you froward and unable worms!
My mind hath been as big as one of yours,
My heart as great, my reason haply more,
To bandy word for word and frown for frown;
But now I see our lances are but straws,
Our strength as weak, our weakness past compare,
That seeming to be most which we indeed least are.
Then vail your stomachs, for it is no boot,
And place your hands below your husband's foot:
In token of which duty, if he please,
My hand is ready; may it do him ease.

Annotations

unknit your brows ≠ knit your brows; **blot** – stain; **meads** – meadows; **confounds thy fame** – destroys your reputation; **meet** – appropriate; **moved** – bad-tempered; **bereft** – robbed; **deign** – consent, want; **froward** – hardheaded; **big** – arrogant; **haply** – perhaps; **bandy** – hit back and forth (as at tennis); **vail** – lower; **stomach** – pride, temper; **no boot** – no use

Bewertungskriterien

Klausurteil B: Sprachmittlung

Die Schülerin / Der Schüler gibt die wesentlichen Inhalte im Sinne der Aufgabenstellung sinngemäß zusammenfassend wieder.	**max. Punkte**
Sie/Er führt aus, dass Günther den Begriff „aktuell“ ablehnt, da er Schnelllebiges und Vergängliches wie Modetrend bezeichnet.	18
Sie/Er führt an, dass Shakespeare auch zu den aktuellen Problemen der Welt nichts Relevantes beitragen kann, z. B. zu internationalen Krisen, humanitären Belangen oder politischen Skandalen.	
Sie/Er führt an, dass es vielmehr Shakespeares Charaktere sind, in deren Facetten wir uns stets wiedererkennen, selbst vor dem Hintergrund vergangener Weltbilder.	

Klausurteil A: Leseverstehen/Schreiben
Anforderungsbereich I (Teilaufgabe 2)

Die Schülerin / Der Schüler	**max. Punkte**
führt aus, dass die Frau freundlich zu sein hat, denn nur das macht sie liebenswert und attraktiv.	4

führt aus, dass sie ihrem Mann Liebe zu erweisen, zu gefallen, zu dienen und zu gehorchen hat, als eher noch zu geringe Gegenleistung für seine Sorge und die Strapazen und Entbehrungen, die er für Sie auf sich nimmt.	4
führt aus, dass diese Rolle in den natürlichen körperlichen und charakterlichen Eigenschaften der Frau begründet liegt.	4
	12

Anforderungsbereich II (Teilaufgabe 3)

Die Schülerin / Der Schüler	**max. Punkte**
analysiert den zentralen Vergleich zwischen Ehe und Staatswesen, Untertan und König ("subject vs. lord", "sovereign", "prince"), und benennt weitere Vergleiche, die Hierarchie ausdrücken: "keeper", "head". Sie/Er erläutert, dass der Souverän Sorge für seine Untertanen trägt und sie zu Dienst und Loyalität verpflichtet sind. Sie/Er führt auf, dass insofern auch die Frau, die sich gegen den Ehemann auflehnt, gleichzusetzen ist mit der Verräterin oder dem Verräter, die/der sich gegen die Königin / den König auflehnt.	4
benennt weitere Vergleiche (Störung der Natur: "frost"/"meads", "whirlwinds"/"buds", "fountain"/"mud") und ihre Funktion: weibliches Missverhalten erscheint als Auflehnung gegen die gottgewollte Ordnung.	4
erkennt und benennt weitere Vergleiche, die Schwäche und Machtlosigkeit der Frau illustrieren: "unable worms", "lances are but straws".	4
erkennt die elisabethanische Sichtweise der korrespondierenden Beziehungen von – Mensch und Natur, – Mensch und Staatswesen sowie – Mikrokosmos und Makrokosmos.	4
	16

Anforderungsbereich III (Teilaufgabe 4.1)

Die Schülerin / Der Schüler	**max. Punkte**
erläutert die Ungleichheit der Geschlechter, wie Katherina sie propagiert.	2
äußert sich vor dem Hintergrund der modernen demokratischen, freiheitlichen, egalitären westlichen Weltanschauung kritisch zu diesem Frauenbild, z. B. mit Verweis auf: – Menschenrechte und Menschenwürde, – Frauenbewegung des 20. Jahrhunderts, – Veränderung der Familienstrukturen, – Veränderung in der Arbeitswelt.	5

weist hin auf immer noch bestehende Ungleichheit, z. B. – im Berufsleben, – in patriarchalischen Gesellschaftsformen, – in kriminellem Kontext (Gewalt gegen Frauen).	5
formuliert eine zusammenfassende, wertende persönliche Stellungnahme zur Rolle der Geschlechter.	2
	14

Anforderungsbereich III (Teilaufgabe 4.2)

Die Schülerin / Der Schüler	**max. Punkte**
nimmt einleitend Bezug auf die vorgegebene Situation und die Textpassage als Anlass ihres/seines Artikels.	1
äußert sich vor dem Hintergrund der modernen demokratischen, freiheitlichen, egalitären westlichen Weltanschauung kritisch zu dem dargestellten Frauenbild, z. B. mit Verweis auf – Menschenrechte, – Menschenwürde, – Frauenbewegung des 20. Jahrhunderts, – Veränderung der Familienstrukturen, – Veränderung in der Arbeitswelt; hinterfragt die Aktualität und Relevanz der Dramen Shakespeares und erweitert ihre/seine Argumentation um Beispiele aus anderen Dramen, z. B. je nach Schwerpunkt hinsichtlich – Geschlechterrollen, – Verhältnis der Generationen, – Lehnstreue, – Aberglaube, – etc.	5
verweist auf die sprachlichen Schwierigkeiten des vorliegenden Textes sowie anderer Dramen.	2
stellt ihren/seinen Ausführungen Argumente entgegen, die die fortwährende Aktualität und Relevanz von Shakespeares Dramen unterstreichen. Dabei bezieht sie/er sich z. B. auf – zeitlose Problematik wie Liebe, Zurückweisung, Ehrgeiz, Neid etc., – unvermindertes Interesse an Theatervorstellungen, – Erfolge von Hollywood-Produktionen, – Adaption in modernen Werken, – zeitlose Kraft und Schönheit der Sprache.	4
formuliert eine zusammenfassende, persönlich wertende Stellungnahme auf der Grundlage ihrer/seiner Argumentation.	2
	14

Themenfeld *Studying and Working in a Globalised World*

Aufgabenbeispiel Abitur Englisch Leistungskurs
Aufgabenart gemäß KLP: 1.1: Schreiben mit Leseverstehen integriert und Sprachmittlung isoliert
Thematischer Bezug gemäß KLP (Soziokulturelles Orientierungswissen): Lebensentwürfe, Studium, Ausbildung, Beruf international – Englisch als *lingua franca* *Studying and working in a globalised world*
Auszug aus einem englischsprachigen Sachtext (734 W.) (Klausurteil A, Text 1) Auszug aus einem deutschsprachigen Sachtext (492 W.) (Klausurteil B, Text 2)
Quellenangaben: Text 1: Julian Baggini, „If universities sacrifice philosophy on the altar of profit, what's next?", *The Guardian,* 21.12.2018, https://www.theguardian.com/commentisfree/2018/dec/21/universities-philosophy-profit-business-partners (Zugriff: 01.04.2022); Copyright Guardian News & Media Ltd. 2022 Text 2: Bernd Kramer, „Lohnt sich das Studium noch?", *Spiegel Online,* 19.11.2017, http://www.spiegel.de/karriere/karriere-lohnt-sich-ein-studium-noch-a-1178588.html (Zugriff: 01.04.2022)

Aufgabe

Klausurteil A: Leseverstehen/Schreiben (Text 1)

1. Point out what worries the writer considering the closure of the philosophy department at Hull University. *(Comprehension)*

2. Examine the way the writer expresses his attitude towards what is becoming of university education. In doing this, consider his choice of words and other rhetorical devices and strategies. *(Analysis)*

Choose ONE of the following tasks:

3.1. Comment on lines 106 to 110: "That's why Hull's fate is all our fates. Today, they're coming for philosophy. Tomorrow, they'll come for something else that isn't designed to turn a profit". In doing so, give your own view on profit-orientation in the globalised world. *(Evaluation: Comment)*

3.2. Imagine you are a leading member of the student union at Hull University. A large number of students demonstrate with you against the closure of the philosophy department. Give a speech at the end of the demonstration to clearly state the students' view. *(Evaluation: Recreation of text)*

Klausurteil B: Sprachmittlung (Text 2)

4. Your friend from Ireland asks you in an email what people's career chances are like when they go to university in Germany. You do some research and find this article from *Spiegel Online*. Write your answer based on this article.

Text 1 If universities sacrifice philosophy on the altar of profit, what's next? *Julian Baggini*

Hull says the subject doesn't meet the needs of 'business partners'. Try telling that to Thales of Miletus.

You might think that a university philosophy department facing closure in Hull is of as much interest to the average person as the shutting of a butcher's in Wolverhampton is to a vegetarian in Totnes. There are almost as many universities as high streets now, and for every closure here there's an opening somewhere else. But the events unfolding on Humberside are symptomatic of a deep malaise affecting not just universities but the wider culture. The crude pursuit of what is "practical", "efficient" or "useful" is threatening everything of value that isn't evidently profitable.

Philosophy has been taught at Hull ever since the University opened in 1928. The department has no problem with recruitment and has a good faculty. Because humanities courses are so cheap to teach and student fees so high, there is no conceivable way it could be losing money. In a letter to colleagues, Kathleen Lennon, emeritus professor of philosophy, insisted: "Philosophy at Hull is financially viable – providing a healthy return for the university."

So why is the university not accepting any more joint honours students and publicly entertaining the possibility "that we will not be recruiting new students" in 2019? A statement by Jeanette Strachan, the university's registrar, to the local newspaper suggests some worrying answers. Strachan said the university sought to offer students "a high-quality academic experience and ensure that their qualification holds value over time".

The word that screams out of that sentence is "value". The implication seems to be that a philosophy degree does not provide a sufficient financial return for those who "invest" in it. This impression is reinforced by Strachan's statement that the university "meets the needs of our students, research and business partners". The inclusion of that third party would baffle the thousands of people who have graduated with philosophy degrees without ever catching a sniff of a "business partner", let alone receiving any help from one.

You could easily demolish this economically reductive case on its own terms, as the British Philosophical Association has done in an open letter to the university protesting against the proposed cuts. It points out that "philosophy degrees equip students with a wide range of highly valued and sought-after skills, and there is compelling evidence that graduate employers have a high regard for philosophy degree-holders".

The BPA is surely right to plead with the university in the only language it understands, insisting there is "robust evidence of the value of philosophy". But we should not let the bean-counters who have captured too much of higher education set the terms of the debate. In a truly philosophical spirit, we should question the meaning of "value" that they are using as if it were common sense.

[...]

People who choose to study philosophy [...] could choose to study a course with a more reliable financial payoff. But their "investment" in three years of philosophy is not designed to maximise financial yields. This makes them wiser, not dumber, than those who allow money to entirely dictate their choices. Whereas money is only a means to an end, the pursuit of learning is intrinsically rewarding.

This is not special pleading for philosophy. The same argument holds for innumerable other subjects which don't have any direct economic benefit. I always cringe when people quote Socrates's line "the unexamined life is not worth living" as though it were an argument uniquely for philosophy. All the humanities, arts and social sciences have a role in helping us to live examined lives. If we cannot find spaces for them in our universities, education becomes nothing more than professional training, churning out people who can help run society efficiently but none who routinely and thoroughly ask what all that efficiency is in the service of.

The threat at Hull reflects a lamentable shift in education towards precisely this functional view of what universities are for. But it also reflects a crudely utilitarian worldview that infects much, much more. You see it manifest whenever arts funding is under threat or when the evident inability of GDP growth to capture what most matters fails to translate to concrete steps to replace it with better metrics. That's why Hull's fate is all our fates. Today, they're coming for philosophy. Tomorrow, they'll come for something else that isn't designed to turn a profit.

Annotations

Hull – Kingston upon Hull, Humberside; Northern English port and university city

Wolverhampton – industrial city in the English Midlands

Totnes – Southern English town associated with New Age spirituality, alternative lifestyles and natural health

Text 2 Lohnt sich das Studium noch? *Bernd Kramer*

Nie gab es in Deutschland mehr Studenten als heute. Viele zweifeln deshalb, ob der Abschluss von der Uni tatsächlich noch ein Garant für einen sicheren Job und ein gutes Einkommen ist.

[...]

Fest steht: In Deutschland studieren heute so viele Menschen wie noch nie zuvor, fast drei Millionen sind es. Allein zu diesem Wintersemester werden eine halbe Million Neueinschreibungen erwartet. Ein Studium galt bisher als Königsweg zu einem guten Job. Ein Uni-Abschluss war ein Versprechen auf ein gutes Einkommen, auf Status, Aufstieg – auf ein Leben in materieller Sicherheit, weitgehend zumindest.

[...]

Doch kann sich diese Hoffnung erfüllen, wenn es die Hälfte eines Altersjahrgangs in die Hörsäle und Seminarräume zieht? Verlieren die Abschlüsse dann nicht an Wert?

Diese Fragen bewegen viele Studierende in Deutschland, die Stimmung ist durchwachsen. Einerseits hat der Optimismus zugenommen. Nur eine Minderheit erwartet größere Schwierigkeiten bei der Jobsuche, das zeigt der „Studierendensurvey", für den Forscher der Uni Konstanz im Auftrag der Bundesregierung regelmäßig Studenten befragen. Andererseits ist der Wunsch nach einem stabilen Arbeitsplatz stark gestiegen. 2001 war 51 Prozent der Studierenden die Sicherheit im Job sehr wichtig, 2013 waren es bereits 67 Prozent. Deutlich mehr junge Menschen als früher richten die Entscheidung für das Studienfach nach den Arbeitsmarktchancen aus. Einfach nur drauflosstudieren, das tun heute die wenigsten – für die Forscher ein Indiz dafür, dass die „Verunsicherung der Studierenden im Hinblick auf die Zukunft" immens sein muss. Es wird schon irgendwie klappen mit dem Einstieg in den Job, aber so einfach und planbar wie früher ist es wohl nicht – so könnte man die Stimmung an den Hochschulen zusammenfassen.

Das Bundesinstitut für Berufsbildung geht sogar davon aus, dass bald mehr Akademiker einen Job suchen als in den Ruhestand gehen. Bis 2035 rechnen die Forscher mit 6,5 Millionen Hochschulabsolventen, die neu auf den Arbeitsmarkt kommen. Aber nur 3,9 Millionen Berufstätige mit Uni- oder FH-Abschluss werden im selben Zeitraum aus dem Arbeitsleben ausscheiden. Künftig suchen die Unternehmen vielleicht gar nicht mehr so dringend nach Ingenieuren, Betriebswirten und Chemikern – sondern nach Menschen mit Berufsausbildung, nach Mechatronikern oder kaufmännischen Angestellten. Pflegekräfte sind schon jetzt rar.

Ist Bildungsdeutschland manisch auf ein Studium fixiert?

Seit einigen Jahren macht daher das Wort vom Akademisierungswahn die Runde – ein Wort, das suggeriert, Bildungsdeutschland sei verrückt geworden und junge Menschen manisch auf ein Studium fixiert. In die Welt gesetzt hat es der Münchner Philosophieprofessor und ehemalige Kulturstaatsminister Julian Nida-Rümelin. Der Andrang auf die Hochschulen, so seine These, frustriere am Ende alle: die Absolventen, die nicht den Job finden, den sie sich versprochen hätten. Die Lehrlinge, die nach ihrer Ausbildung nun auch noch mit den vielen nicht untergekommenen Akademikern um Stellen konkurrieren müssten.

Und natürlich Professoren wie Nida-Rümelin selbst, die sich in den überfüllten Hörsälen voller Credit-Point-gieriger und arbeitsmarktverbissener Studenten nicht mehr so zweckfrei und leidenschaftlich wie dereinst in philosophischen Gedankenflügen verlieren könnten. Kein Wunder, dass der Beifall für die These vom Akademisierungswahn eher von der konservativen Seite kam, von Professoren, deren Selbstverständnis es ist, für eine kleine Bildungselite zuständig zu sein, nicht für den Aufstieg der Massen.

Die Frage ist: Wie berechtigt sind solche Alarmrufe? Hat das Studium wirklich an Wert verloren?

Die Antwort lautet: Es ist kompliziert.

[...]

Bewertungskriterien

Klausurteil A, Leseverstehen/Schreiben – Anforderungsbereich I (Teilaufgabe 1)

Die Schülerin / Der Schüler	max. Punkte
führt an, dass die Universität Hull ihr Philosophieinstitut mit der Begründung schließt, dass die Absolventen keine nachhaltig wertvolle Qualifizierung erlangen könnten.	4
führt aus, wie der Autor diese Schließung als Symptom einer weitreichenden Krise sieht, nämlich dass sich alles der Profitorientierung unterordnet.	4
führt aus, dass der Autor die utilitaristische Bedeutung des Wortes „value“ anprangert und vor der Gefahr der profitorientierten Weltsicht warnt.	4
	12

Anforderungsbereich II (Teilaufgabe 2)

Die Schülerin / Der Schüler	max. Punkte
benennt die tendenziöse Wortwahl des Autors, die die profitorientierte Weltsicht und ihre Vertreter/-innen scharf kritisiert (“sacrifice on the altar of profit” (Überschrift), “deep malaise” (Z. 10), “crude pursuit” (Z. 11 f.), “threatening” (Z. 13), “the only language” (Z. 61), “bean-counters” “ (Z. 64), “threat” (Z. 97), “lamentable” (Z. 97), “crudely utilitarian” (Z. 100)).	4
führt die illustrierende Bildhaftigkeit des Textes an und erläutert sie: – *comparison:* Wolverhampton/Totnes, (Z. 4 f.) – *personification:* “screams”, (Z. 37) – *metaphor* (erstarrt): “sacrifice on the altar of profit” (Überschrift)	4
benennt rhetorische Mittel, z. B. – *exaggeration:* “As many universities as high streets” (Z. 6) – *parallelism:* “Hull’s fate is all our fates”; “Today they’re coming [...], tomorrow they’ll come” (Z. 107–109);	4
benennt die Zielgruppenorientierung: – *short forms, casual tone,* trotz komplexen Satzbaus, – (rhetorische) Fragen (Titel, Z. 26–30), – Appell: “we should” (Z. 63–69), – “we” vs. “they” (Z. 63–69): Abgrenzung gegen die “bean-counters”.	4
	16

Anforderungsbereich III (Teilaufgabe 3.1)

Die Schülerin / Der Schüler	max. Punkte
knüpft an den Ausgangstext an, durch Bezug auf die Zeilen 106–110.	2

beschreibt andere Fälle der reinen Profitorientierung in Bereichen wie Forschung, medizinischer Versorgung, Kunst, frühkindlicher Bildung etc.	6
bewertet die Profitorientierung entweder im Sinne des Autors als problematisch, als hilfreich oder als ambivalent.	4
kommt zu einem dezidierten Fazit.	2
	14

Anforderungsbereich III (Teilaufgabe 3.2)

Die Schülerin / Der Schüler	**max. Punkte**
stellt einleitend die Situation an der Uni Hull dar.	4
argumentiert für den Erhalt des Faches Philosophie, z. B. mit Bezug auf – die Bedeutung der Philosophie in einer profitorientierten Welt, – die Bedeutung der Philosophie für die Tradition der Uni Hull, – das Überhandnehmen von Technokratie und Wirtschaft, – die individuellen Bedürfnisse angehender Studentinnen und Studenten, – andere besorgniserregende Beispiele von Profitorientierung, – Beispiele von Dummheit bei Entscheidungsträgern.	8
kommt zu einem dezidierten Appell.	2
	14

Klausurteil B: Mediation (Teilaufgabe 4)

Die Schülerin / Der Schüler gibt die wesentlichen Inhalte im Sinne der Aufgabenstellung sinngemäß zusammenfassend wieder:	**max. Punkte**
die Situation der Studentinnen und Studenten: – das Studium als traditioneller Königsweg zum materiellen Erfolg, – Studienwahl gezielt mit Blick auf sicheren Arbeitsplatz, – trotz Verunsicherung grundsätzlicher Optimismus für Stellensuche.	18
die Prognose der Berufschancen für Akademiker/-innen: – mehr Hochschulabsolventinnen und -absolventen als ausscheidende Akademiker/-innen, – den womöglich vermehrten Bedarf an nicht-akademischen Berufen.	
die Fixierung auf ein Studium zum Nachteil: – sowohl von Absolventinnen und -absolventen als auch von auszubildenden Personen, – der Professorinnen und Professoren, die gedrängt werden, arbeitsmarktorientiert zu arbeiten, wobei die reine Forschung und Lehre auf der Strecke bleibt.	

Original-Prüfungsaufgaben 2021

Quelle der Aufgabenstellung

Qualitäts- und UnterstützungsAgentur – Landesinstitut für Schule[1]

GK Literarischer Text mit Beispiellösung

Aufgabe 1

Klausurteil A: Leseverstehen und Schreiben integriert

AUFGABENSTELLUNG

1. Outline what you learn about the three young women's backgrounds and their current situations. *(Comprehension) (12 Punkte)*

2. Analyse how Maryam and her situation are presented. Focus on point of view and her relation to the other characters. *(Analysis) (16 Punkte)*

3. Choose **one** of the following tasks:

3.1 According to a survey conducted in 2018, 45 % of Nigerian adults say they plan to move to another country within five years, 28 % of them intending to move to the USA.[2] Comment on these figures and their implications. Refer to work done in class on Nigeria and on American myths and realities. *(Evaluation: comment) (14 Punkte)*

3.2 On her last day at the Immigration Detention Centre, Maryam writes a letter to her childhood friend Abike back in Nigeria. Write this letter, focusing on her feelings about her return to Nigeria as well as on her hopes and fears for the future. *(Evaluation: re-creation of text) (14 Punkte)*

[1] Die Lösungen sind keine amtlichen Lösungen.

[2] Phillip Connor & Ana Gonzalez-Barrera, „Many Nigerians, Tunisians and Kenyans say they plan to leave their countries in the next five years", 27.03.2019, zitiert nach: https://www.pewresearch.org/fact-tank/2019/03/27/many-nigerians-tunisians-and-kenyans-say-they-plan-to-leave-their-countries-in-the-next-five-years/ (Zugriff: 23.07.2021, verändert)

Klausurteil B: Sprachmittlung isoliert

AUFGABENSTELLUNG

4 For a school project on social mobility worldwide, your former exchange student from the USA has chosen to give a presentation on the situation in Germany and has asked you for help.
Write an email to your friend outlining what Nina Monecke's article says about the situation of young people growing up in poor families in Germany, problems they face and suggestions on how to improve their situation. *(Mediation) (18 Punkte)*

Materialgrundlage:

Klausurteil A:
Molara Wood, *The Last Bus Stop,* 2009, http://www.snreview.org/0308Wood.html (Zugriff: 23.07.2021, gekürzt)

Wortzahl: 778

Klausurteil B:
Nina Monecke, „Sarah ist mit Hartz IV aufgewachsen und wird nun als Erste in ihrer Familie studieren", *ze.tt,* 12.10.2019, https://ze.tt/sarah-ist-mit-hartz-iv-aufgewachsen-und-wird-nun-als-erste-in-ihrer-familiestudieren/ (Zugriff: 23.07.2021, verändert)

Wortzahl: 596

Zugelassene Hilfsmittel:

- Ein- und zweisprachiges Wörterbuch
- Herkunftssprachliches Wörterbuch für Schülerinnen und Schüler, deren Herkunftssprache nicht Deutsch ist
- Wörterbuch zur deutschen Rechtschreibung

Klausurteil A

The Last Bus Stop *Molara Wood*

The short story is set in London, where the three young women Sade, Ronke and Maryam became friends. Now Sade, the narrator, is about to call Ronke, who has gone to New York. She wants to tell her what happened to their friend Maryam. Before picking up the phone, she thinks back to the day when Ronke told them about her plan to leave.

[...]

"I have model friends who aren't doing badly in New York." You looked at the greying sky outside the window. "Yeah, I think that's where I'm headed. America. The Last Bus Stop."

I turned to Maryam who had sunk into the sofa, holding her mug close as though for warmth. We were thinking the same thing: we would soon be losing our friend to America. God's own country. The Last Bus Stop for many of our generation who, once they got there, never seemed to think there was anywhere left to go – or return. [...]

That was the great thing about being around you, Ronke. The confidence that the world was wide, lush and inviting and you had your place in it, a sure footing that could not slip. Back in Lagos, Maryam and I would never move in the same circles as you. We'd probably never meet your kind – rich and privileged with the world yours for the taking, able to enjoy Beethoven if you chose. But in London we were your best friends. Remember how, when irritated by those Nigerians we considered beneath us, we'd smirk, "London is a leveler"? When it came to leveling Nigerians, London was indiscriminate. It leveled either way, up or down the social ladder. Maryam and I didn't mind that London leveled us up with you, Ronke.

Looking back, I see it was all that time in your company that got Maryam thinking about becoming a model. It also fueled her dreams of escape to America, The Last Bus Stop.

Maryam was too short to be a model of course but carried herself like one. She was forced to take a break from university, unable to afford the fees. Money from home had dried up. Her widowed mother's fabric retailing business in Lagos was badly hit by a ban on imported textiles; then armed robbers swept the shop clean of expensive laces, voiles and jacquards. Maryam's student work permit ran out with her study visa, so she could not continue work as a part-time beauty consultant with her new, illegal immigrant status. She did the odd job where they were not too fussy about papers; and kept close to her beloved haunts by hanging with you. Now you are gone, and tomorrow I will not attend lectures. I must go to Maryam, you see.

I remember the day you left for New York, Ronke. We saw you off to Gatwick Airport. When it was time to go through the passengers' only gates, you wrapped us in what you liked to call "major hugs".

Maryam sobbed on the Gatwick Express back to Victoria Station and I pushed tissues into her hands, embarrassed at the sneaky glances from other passengers. I realized then that Maryam was crying more for herself than for you. She hadn't found a way to escape her predicament as you had just done. When the sniffling stopped, Maryam slipped on the Gianfranco Ferré sunglasses you gave her. She looked a bit like the model she wanted to be then, but a monologue ensued.

"I hate phoning home now, what's the use? Mum can hardly feed my brothers, let alone find the foreign exchange to support me here."

I only listened, one arm round her shoulders.

"No use calling for money ... Mum just cries and cries till my credit runs out. Last time I phoned she begged me to come back home. But, go home to what, Sade, tell me; go home to what? Go back a failure, a university drop-out. Go back with my head bowed when my contemporaries in Lagos have done better with their lives? No. I can't go back. ... I can't go back. Not just now."

[...]

Now on the lone sofa in my living room, I dial your US number. How to say it, Ronke? That Maryam was caught attempting to board a flight to America with a forged passport and is to be deported back to Nigeria? That the dodgy boyfriend took every penny she had left to facilitate her last dash for The Last Bus Stop? If Kate Moss could make it as a model without a great height, who was to say Maryam couldn't? And if she couldn't be a model in America, she could be other things, couldn't she? Ronke was there, was she not? Maryam blurted it all out to me when I saw her at the Immigration Detention Centre today. Now, I must in turn blurt it all out to you. You, Ronke, who started Maryam's dream rolling.

I hear the phone ringing from across the waters. The receiver feels moist next to my cheek as I wait for an answer. [...]

Annotations:

47 laces, voiles and jacquards – types of textiles

70 Gianfranco Ferré – an Italian fashion designer

98 Kate Moss – British supermodel that was particularly successful in the 1990s and 2000s

Beispiellösung

Aufgabe 1

Molara Wood's short story "The Last Bus Stop", published in 2009 and taken from the website snreview.org, deals with the situation of three Nigerian emigrants.
Sade, the narrator, and Maryam are university students in London, whereas their friend Ronke has left London for America in order to start a modelling career. Ronke comes from a rich and privileged family in Nigeria, her friends have a rather poor background. In Nigeria they would not have mixed, but in London they have become friends. Maryam has had to abandon her studies for financial reasons and has therefore lost her work and study visa for Great Britain. Ill-advised and deceived by her boyfriend, she tried to go to America on a false passport, was caught at the airport and is now waiting for her deportation to Nigeria at a detention centre.

Aufgabe 2

Maryam's situation is presented by Sade as a first-person narrator taking the role of an observer. Sade contemplates the circumstances mainly by means of an inner monologue addressing their absent friend Ronke immediately before she calls her on the phone.

It becomes obvious that Maryam admires Ronke and wants to be like her. The three young women are from different social backgrounds, would never have met in Nigeria but have become best friends in London. Maryam and Sade even look down on other Nigerians as they are now friends with Ronke (ll. 25 f.). Maryam wants to be a model like her although she is too short (l. 39), and when she loses her visa and her job, she still frequents the places Ronke goes to in order to remain part of this layer of society.
After Ronke has left, Maryam is devastated, but it is not so much the loss of her friend but her own situation as an underprivileged illegal immigrant that makes her unhappy (ll. 65–67). Defiantly she puts on Ronke's sunglasses (ll. 70 f.), which make her look like a model, symbolise her desire to become one and show her admiration of Ronke.
She has some support in her friend Sade, who is from a similar background (ll. 20–22), comforts her (ll. 78 f.) and goes out of her way to visit her regularly at the detention centre (ll. 55 f., 103–105). She also sides with her in what she says throughout the text. In fact, the narrator blames Ronke for Maryam's desire to become a model, addresses her as the one who has "[t]he confidence" (l. 17) and the "sure footing" (l. 19) in the world, saying the world was "yours for the taking" (ll. 23 f.) and "you had your place in it" (l. 19). In lines 34 to 38, she accuses her directly of being the cause for Maryam's hopeless dream of going to America and becoming a model.
In contrast to this, Maryam's financial situation and family background are described rather matter-of-factly, since Ronke already knows this anyway (ll. 40–53). Only in line 54, the narrator directly addresses her again, insinuating Ronke's responsibility for what has happened to Maryam and also contrasting Ronke and herself in their roles as Maryam's friends: "Now you are gone [...] I must go to Maryam" (ll. 54–56).
Maryam's determination and desperation are presented by the use of direct speech (ll. 74–89), which enables the reader to experience her state of mind more immediately. In a monologue she "blurt[s] out" (l. 103) what situation she sees herself in: no support from her family ("No use calling for money ... Mum just cries", l. 80 f.) and her shame of going back to Nigeria as "a failure, a university drop-out" (ll. 84 f.).
The consequences of this despair are related to Ronke by means of a number of rhetorical questions: "How to say it, Ronke? That Maryam was caught [...]? That the dodgy boyfriend [...]?" (ll. 92–103). She then uses substitutionary narration in reporting part of Maryam's speech that she "blurted out" to her at the detention centre, which, virtually taking Maryam's point of view, gives an insight into Maryam's belief in her success and Ronke's support (ll. 98–103).
The narrator then in turn accuses Ronke more vehemently of being responsible for Maryam's desolate situation (ll. 106 f.), repeating the expression "blurt it all out" (l. 106), which makes her appear as Maryam's mouthpiece.
All this shows how naïvely Maryam believes in a career as a model but also in the American Dream (ll. 98–102). We do not even know if Ronke has really succeeded as a model.

Aufgabe 3.1

As a 2018 survey shows, Maryam is one of almost half of all Nigerians who want to leave the country to find a better life abroad, more than half of these in the US. This reflects

the desolate state Nigerian society is in on the one hand and the unbroken attraction of the American Dream on the other hand.
Although Nigeria is the African giant, the largest economy in Africa, having the youngest population of all African countries or even the world, it does not seem to offer its citizens a lot of hope for the future.
However, it also has the largest number of people living in poverty in the world. This contrasts sharply with Nigeria housing the largest number of billionaires in Africa. With this extremely large gap between rich and poor, it is almost impossible to rise in society and succeed.
Corruption is also one of the major problems Nigeria has always been facing. The country ranks fairly high on the global corruption index. While the authorities have succeeded in curbing petty corruption – such as bribing policemen or airport officials –, grand corruption is rather increasing. Corruption within government agencies or corporations harms society and the economy immensely and is a constant danger to democracy.
Crime and every-day violence make many Nigerians suffer, as in the example of Maryam's mother in Wood's story. But also politically motivated violence, ethnic and religious terrorism, is a constant threat to Nigerians. Widely known is Boko Haram, an Islamist terror organisation, which opposes Westernisation in Nigeria and has pledged allegiance to the Islamic State.
No wonder so many Nigerians want to leave the country and no wonder it is still America that appears as the shining beacon of hope to them. Since the 19th century America has attracted immigrants from all over the world, especially those who found themselves economically deprived or those who were persecuted for political or religious reason. The American Dream has offered political and religious freedom but also – more important to most – the promise of golden opportunities.
According to what the American Dream promises, everybody can 'make it' in the US, regardless of their origin, their race, their religion and their social background. America still lures the poor with Hollywood's glamour and the shiny skyscrapers of New York. People have not understood that while it is true that anybody can make it in America, not everybody will. America's ruthless capitalism and individualism will have a lot of people fail rather than succeed. To many Africans, President Obama, whose father came from Kenya, seems to be the personification of the American Dream, yet there is so much racism in the US. The Trump years have shown the ugly face of America only too obviously. Black people are discriminated against and have to endure racism and police violence, with George Floyd being one of the most prominent tragic examples.
Emigration to America or Europe cannot be the solution for so many Nigerians (and Africans). It is a tremendous task for the African countries and the global community to make Nigeria a safe place to live and to increase prosperity for all its citizens. First and foremost, this includes education and improvement of women's rights, fighting corruption and crime, fighting poverty and human trafficking, fighting ethnic and religious prejudice and also fighting exploitation and neocolonialism. Africa is a beautiful continent with breathtaking natural wonders, ancient cultures and wonderful people. It is a shame it is being scarred the way it is.

Aufgabe 3.2

Dear Abike,

Although I'll be back in Nigeria tomorrow, I'm writing to you because I somehow have to articulate my feelings, hopes and fears before I meet you again.
First of all, I'm at this Immigration Detention Centre right now, waiting to be deported. I feel like a criminal and I actually am because I tried to take a plane to America on a forged passport. They caught me at the airport, which was the end of my dreams.
I'm not going to tell you now what forced me to abandon my studies here in London and what gave me the idea to go to America instead. Right now, I'm a lot more concerned about going back to Nigeria.
After all this time in London, it's really hard. I've experienced what it's like to be among wealthy people who live a comfortable life, who are about to get a decent education and therefore a good job. I've lived in a country where it's safe to walk at night and where a woman is respected. You can trust the police and the government and you don't have to bribe the authorities for whatever paper you need. Partly because of my family's situation, partly because of my own stupidity and naivety, I've lost everything. I've failed. I was going to be university-educated, but I had to drop out. I used to mix with university students in fancy bars and restaurants, but now I've ended up in this detention centre. I'm a failure. And this is what people will think of me back home. All of you have done better with your lives: I used to look down on you with your basic school education and your early marriages and motherhoods. But in this you didn't fail. I wanted to be something better; now look what has become of me.
I know how those that return from Europe are looked down upon back home. We have failed, we haven't made it. In Nigeria we think it's so easy, just go to England or the States and you'll have a beautiful flat and a Mercedes right away. Let me tell you it's nothing like that. But my friends and family in Nigeria won't understand. My mother is struggling with her shop – you've probably heard about it – and I don't know if she can recover from the financial loss. With me coming home there will be an extra burden. I don't think I can find a job when I'm back home. With so many people unemployed anyway, who would take a failure like me who hasn't even learned anything?
I can only hope for massive improvement in Nigeria. More democracy, more education, less corruption, less crime. There is so much potential in our country. The population is so young. We should be able to build a better society with a thriving economy, but at the moment I don't see it happening. I'm afraid of going home.

Love,
Maryam

Klausurteil B

Sarah ist mit Hartz IV aufgewachsen und wird nun als Erste in ihrer Familie studieren *Nina Monecke*

[...]

In einer gerechten Gesellschaft, in der jede*r die gleichen Chancen hat, wäre Sarah keine Ausnahme. Aber in unserer Gesellschaft ist sie es. Weil sie als Tochter einer alleinerziehenden Mutter und Hartz-IV-Empfängerin aufs Gymnasium gegangen ist, weil sie das Abitur mit der Abschlussnote 1,2 abgeschlossen hat und weil sie in diesen Tagen ihre ersten Seminare und Vorlesungen an der Uni besucht.

Für die zwei Millionen Kinder und Jugendliche, die in Deutschland in Familien mit Hartz IV aufwachsen, ist all das nicht selbstverständlich. „Statistisch bin ich nicht vorhanden", sagt Sarah. Eine Studie der Deutschen Hochschul- und Wissenschaftsforschung unterscheidet lediglich nach Bildungsgrad der Eltern: Von 100 Kindern aus Akademiker*innenfamilien studieren statistisch 79, bei Nicht-Akademiker*innenfamilien sind es 27.

Vor einem Jahr, ein Jahr vor ihrem Schulabschluss, ist Sarah mit einem Tweet bekannt geworden. Darin schrieb die heute 18-Jährige: „Hartz IV ist der größte Scheiß." Warum? Weil Kinder von Hartz-IV-Empfänger*innen nicht mehr als 100 Euro im Monat verdienen dürfen. Sie könnten, doch alles, was über diesem Betrag liegt, wird zu 80 Prozent abgezogen. Bei einem 450-Euro-Nebenjob wären Sarah am Ende 170 Euro geblieben. Sie und ihre Mutter bilden eine sogenannte Bedarfsgemeinschaft, deshalb werden die Einkünfte der Tochter mit dem Hartz-IV-Satz der Mutter verrechnet.

Was das für Sarah bedeutet? „Führerschein machen? Sicher nicht, bevor du ausgezogen bist. Du kannst ja nicht darauf sparen." Oder: „Deine Freunde fahren in den Urlaub, vielleicht sogar als Abschlussfahrt? Kannst du knicken." Sarah könnte viele weitere Beispiele nennen. Kindern, die in Armut aufwuchsen – und für die das schon schlimm genug sei – , nehme man so auch noch die Möglichkeit, sich selbst daraus zu befreien.

[...]

Im Oktober beginnt Sarah trotz allem ihr Studium an der Uni Bonn, Politikwissenschaft mit Philosophie im Nebenfach. Von der liberalen Erzählung, man könne alles schaffen, wenn man sich nur hart genug anstrengt, hält sie nichts. Dafür will sie auch nicht als gutes Beispiel herhalten. „Es geht nicht darum, dass es nicht möglich ist, es zu schaffen. Es geht darum, dass es nicht fair ist, wenn der eine durchrennt und der andere erst über drei Mauern klettern muss. Wir müssen klarmachen, wie Chancen verteilt sind, und gucken, wo wir diese Hürden abbauen können."

Sarah nennt ihre Position privilegiert, weil sie gut durch die Schule gekommen ist. [...]

Zwei zentrale Dinge müssten sich aus Sarahs Sicht ändern. Das Eine ist die Schule. Kinder nach der vierten Klasse zu sortieren, findet Sarah falsch. Es verfestige Ungerechtigkeiten nur. Wer von zu Hause nicht die Unterstützung bekomme, die er oder sie braucht, müsste diese in der Schule bekommen. Oft gehe es aber auch einfach um Geld – und damit um Teilhabe. Vieles berechne kein Hartz-IV-Satz mit ein. Zum Beispiel Geld für einen Umzug, für erste eigene Möbel, für die Kaution einer Wohnung oder eines WG-Zimmers, für Uni-Bücher. Oder auch einfach für Musikunterricht, Pizza, Kino. „Bei Chancengleichheit geht es nicht darum, dass alle Zugang zur Uni bekommen. Sondern darum, dass Kinder sich ausprobieren können und dieselben Chancen haben", sagt Sarah. „Wenn ein Kind mit Existenzängsten aufwächst, dann wird es kein glückliches Kind – und auch kein erfolgreiches."

Zuschüsse für Klassenfahrten oder Mitgliedsbeiträge im Sportverein, genau das soll das sogenannte Bildungs- und Teilhabepaket für einkommensschwache Familien fördern. Ein aktueller Bericht des Paritätischen Wohlfahrtsverbandes zeigt aber: Das Geld kommt bei vielen nicht an. Weniger als 15 Prozent der bedürftigen Schüler*innen unter 15 Jahren profitierten davon. Viele Anträge würden nicht bewilligt, die Verfahren für eben diese Anträge werden schon seit Langem als zu kompliziert kritisiert. [...]

Sarah hat sich für ein Studium der Politikwissenschaften und Philosophie entschieden, weil sie die Verhältnisse, in denen wir leben, verändern will. Verhältnisse, in denen sie die Ausnahme ist. [...]

Anmerkung:

91 f. **Bildungs- und Teilhabepaket** – staatliche Unterstützung von Kindern aus bedürftigen Familien, um diesen die Teilnahme am gesellschaftlichen und kulturellen Leben zu ermöglichen sowie ihre Bildungschancen zu verbessern

Beispiellösung

Aufgabe 4

Hello Jason,

I've found this article which gives quite a critical view of social mobility in Germany. Only 27 percent of children with parents who aren't university-educated make it to university. In fact, poor families do get support from the state. However, any extra money they earn will be partly set off against this amount. This is particularly unfair for the children because the money they earn in teenage jobs is included in the balance of the whole family. Thus, they have no chance to really save up for a driver's license, etc., and they have a hard time participating in normal teenage life like going to the cinema or going for a pizza or going on a vacation with friends.

The article suggests that although access to education is granted to everybody, chances are not fair. Selection according to children's performance at elementary school is seen as counterproductive. Children should rather get more individual support in school. Very often, having the same chances is just about money and therefore participation. Equal opportunity does not only mean access to university for everybody, it means that children have to have the chance to try out things for themselves. There are funds for school trips or member fees in sport clubs, but the money doesn't really get to the families. Many applications are rejected and the process is too complicated anyway. Thus, first generation students will remain an exception in our society. Children that are forced to fear for their livelihood won't be happy and therefore not successful.

Hope that helps. I wish you best of luck for your presentation!

Best,

XX

GK Sachtext mit Beispiellösung

Aufgabe 2

Klausurteil A: Leseverstehen und Schreiben integriert

AUFGABENSTELLUNG

1. Point out what Steven Poole says about some inventions of the past as well as the potential effects of current technological developments.
(Comprehension) (12 Punkte)

2. Analyse how the author presents his views on technological progress. Focus on communicative strategies and use of language. *(Analysis) (16 Punkte)*

3. Choose **one** of the following tasks:

3.1 "[W]e are sleepwalking towards a media dystopia" (l. 88 f.). Discuss this statement. Refer to work done in class on culture and communication in a globalised world.
(Evaluation: comment) (14 Punkte)

3.2 Your school and its partner schools in Europe have launched a joint project on *Visions for Tomorrow's High Tech World of Work*. Each participant has to hand in an online article presenting her/his personal ideas. Write your article.
(Evaluation: re-creation of text) (14 Punkte)

Klausurteil B: Sprachmittlung isoliert

AUFGABENSTELLUNG

4. An American friend of yours is studying computer science. Considering a term abroad, she/he is looking for an interesting programme. You have found the article by Annabelle Theobald and decide to write her/him an email telling her/him about the new lecture in Saarbrücken as well as its goals and content. Write this email. *(Mediation) (18 Punkte)*

Materialgrundlage:

Klausurteil A:

Steven Poole, „Wake up, humanity! A hi-tech dystopian future is not inevitable", *The Guardian,* 18.02.2019, https://www.theguardian.com/commentisfree/2019/feb/18/technological-progress-superjumbo-airbus-dystopia-future (Zugriff: 23.07.2021, gekürzt); Copyright Guardian News & Media Ltd 2021

Wortzahl: 738

Klausurteil B:

Annabelle Theobald, „Die Perle der Saar-Universität", *Saarbrücker Zeitung,* 08.04.2019, https://www.saarbruecker-zeitung.de/saarland/hochschule/auszeichnung-fuer-ethikvorlesung-fuer-informatiker-an-der-saar-uni_aid-37979021 (Zugriff: 23.07.2021, gekürzt)

Wortzahl: 596

Zugelassene Hilfsmittel:

- Ein- und zweisprachiges Wörterbuch
- Herkunftssprachliches Wörterbuch für Schülerinnen und Schüler, deren Herkunftssprache nicht Deutsch ist
- Wörterbuch zur deutschen Rechtschreibung

Klausurteil A

Wake up, humanity! A hi-tech dystopian future is not inevitable

Steven Poole

[...]

When is the future no longer the future? Only a decade ago, air travel seemed to be moving ineluctably towards giant planes, or "superjumbos". But last week Airbus announced it will cease manufacturing its A380, the world's fattest passenger jet, as current trends favour smaller and more fuel-efficient craft. Progress changed course. A more vivid reminder of lost dreams will come in a few weeks: 2 March marks the 50th anniversary of the maiden flight of Concorde. Once upon a time, all aviation was going to be supersonic. But sometimes, the future is cancelled.

What if what we think is going to be the future right now is cancelled in its turn? We are supposedly on an unstoppable path towards driverless vehicles, fully automated internet-connected "smart homes", and godlike artificial intelligence – but, then, we've been promised flying cars for half a century, and they are still (allegedly) just around the corner. We live in a time when technological change is portrayed as an inexorable, impersonal force: we'd better learn how to surf the tsunami or drown. But as a society, we always have a choice about which direction we take next. And sometimes we make the wrong decision.

[...]

For one thing, history is full of technological marvels that were abandoned for reasons that were only reassessed much later. To most people in the late 19th century, when fleets of electric taxis operated in London and Manhattan, the electric car was clearly going to win out over the filthy petrol-driven alternative. But then vast oil reserves were discovered in America, and the future went into reverse. Until, in the late 20th century, global warming and advances in battery technology made electric cars seem like a good idea again. Similarly, vinyl records have enjoyed a major resurgence in the age of the MP3: not necessarily because they are an objectively better sonic format, but because it turned out that people liked owning their culture as physical objects.

Just as we resurrect ideas from the past, we also have the power to bury ideas in the present – whether for business reasons, like Airbus, or for the wider public good. Technology isn't just something that happens to us; it's something we can decide to build and to use, or not. Should we, for example, allow anyone to make inheritable changes in the DNA of humans? One of the inventors of the modern gene-editing method Crispr, Jennifer Doudna, thinks not: she has called for a moratorium an such "germline" editing, because of the potentially disastrous consequences. Many thinkers on machine intelligence meanwhile – led by the philosopher Nick Bostrom – suggest that the supposedly sci-fi scenario of a conscious AI escaping its box and taking over the world represents such an enormous, existential threat to humanity that we ought to be taking steps right now to prevent it happening.

Not much less alarming, and far closer, is the moment when "deep fakes" – computer-generated pictures and video – become indistinguishable from the real thing. The dream is that you can make a video in which, say, Jacob Rees-Mogg breaks down in tears and admits he doesn't understand half of the long words he uses, and this would be impossible to tell from an authentic TV broadcast. Satisfying as it would be to shame some individuals in this way, the wider result would be a total corrosion of trust, not only in news media but in documentary evidence of many kinds.

So, as work continues apace on deep fakes, we are sleepwalking towards a media dystopia in which nothing at all can be trusted, and the only people to benefit will be authoritarian leaders who insist on their own fantastical realities. Therefore, it's hard not to think that researchers building deep-fake technology right now are actively working, whether they realise it or not, to destroy liberal democracy. Should we just sit back and let them, because, you know, technology will always happen anyway?

We should not, and it's time to reject the wider myth that tech is apolitical. We are so used to hearing that technological progress is smooth and inevitable these days that it just seems like common sense. But this idea may not be unrelated to the fact that the people who promote it are mainly the people with a large financial interest in the adoption of new technology. Just as our past futures need not be dead to us, our present future is not compulsory.

Annotations:

4	**ineluctably** – unavoidably
13	**Concorde** – supersonic passenger airliner retired in 2003
62	**moratorium** – a temporary stopping of an activity, especially by official agreement
62 f.	**germline editing** – process by which the genome of an individual is edited in such a way that the change is inheritable
78	**Jacob Rees-Mogg** – British Conservative politician known for his extravagant language use
87	**apace** – at a fast speed

Beispiellösung

Aufgabe 1

In his article "Wake up, humanity! A hi-tech dystopian future is not inevitable", published in "The Guardian" on 18th February 2019, Steven Poole states his opinion on some inventions of the past as well as the potential effects of current technological developments. According to Poole, several inventions of the past that were regarded as either outdated or irrelevant, are currently resurrected or adapted to present needs. In the past, air travel, for example, aimed at transporting large numbers of passengers from A to B, regardless of a plane's use of fuel. Nowadays, smaller and more fuel-efficient planes are developed and operated. Likewise, electric vehicles that were used as early as the 19th century but were abandoned when huge oil reserves were discovered in the USA, are making their comeback now – both because of global warming and improved battery technology. Lastly, sales of vinyl records that plummeted when MP3 technology was developed, are rising again as music lovers wish to own their favourite music in "solid" form instead of merely listening to the songs' digital version.

Poole therefore sees various risks for mankind if technological progress is not critically assessed but pursued at all costs. One of his examples is germline editing, which makes it possible that modifications done to an individual's genome are passed on to the next generation. He also mentions "deep fakes", which make it impossible to differentiate between computer-generated content and reality. He points out that these pose a threat to democratic values or even democracy at large as authoritarian leaders may use them to create their own version of reality to influence and manipulate public opinion. As "deep fakes" and reliable media coverage become indistinguishable from one another, people might lose trust in the media as well as in proof of any kind.

Aufgabe 2

Stephen Poole aims at raising awareness for his view that technological progress should not be pursued at all costs, but always be evaluated and assessed. With the title of his article, he already points out that he is convinced that "[a] hi-tech dystopian future is not inevitable" if mankind develops a more critical attitude towards technological progress and its possible dangers and risks. In order to make his readers question our progress-orientated lifestyle, Poole then encourages them to undertake a thought experiment: "What if what we think is going to be the future right now is cancelled in its turn?" (ll. 16 f.).

One reason why people should ask themselves the aforementioned question is that technological progress leads to various ethical issues that need to be addressed, e.g. whether it is worth "the potentially disastrous consequences" (ll. 63 f.) that follow in its wake.

Poole starts by enumerating both historical and contemporary examples which emphasise the fact that technological advancements and inventions are continually reviewed. One example he uses to highlight the fact that society "resurrect[s] ideas from the past" (l. 51) is the current increase of electric vehicles, which were originally invented and used as early as the 19th century but abandoned when "vast oil reserves were discovered in America" (ll. 39 f.). It was only in recent years that a growing awareness of the dangers of global warming and the limited availability of fossil fuels as well as technological developments regarding the necessary batteries led to a resurrection of such vehicles. Other examples from the past that Poole employs to support his opinion are the replacement of giant, fuel-inefficient planes with smaller and more fuel-efficient ones as well as the revival of vinyl records for sentimental reasons (ll. 32–50).

But not only past inventions can be revived to shape our present and build our future, but also "ideas [can be buried] in the present– whether for business reasons, like Airbus, or for the wider public good" (ll. 52–54). Poole appeals to his readers to get involved in these matters as technology "isn't just something that happens to us; it's something we can decide to build and to use, or not" (ll. 55–57).

Poole also refers to renowned experts such as geneticist Jennifer Doudna and philosopher Nick Bostrom, who – like Poole – warn society of the dangers of unmonitored technological progress (ll. 59–72).

Another communicative strategy he employs to encourage his readers to notice the risks of technological progress for mankind is to asks rhetorical questions, e.g. "Should we, for example, allow anyone to make inheritable changes in the DNA of humans?" (ll. 57–59)

or “Should we just sit back and let [authoritarian leaders destroy liberal democracy], because [...] technology will always happen anyway?” (ll. 96–99).
One can assume that most of Poole’s readers would answer such questions in the negative, but to make his opinion clear once more, he supplies the desired answer himself: “We should not, and it’s time to reject the wider myth that tech is apolitical” (ll. 100 f.).
The fact that Poole wants his article to be identified as a wake-up call becomes clear in its title, and he repeats his call to action in the course several times before he ends it with the conclusion that “[j]ust as our past futures need not to be dead to us, our present future is not compulsory” (ll. 108–110), indirectly encouraging people to take action.
Poole’s frequent use of personal pronouns like “we”, “our” and “us” (e.g. 16, 28, 51, 108) symbolises that he does not only consider himself to be on the same level as his readers but also implies that he trusts his readers to share his point of view. This is also suggested in his sentence structure, which is largely simple and relatively short (e.g. ll. 28–30). He likewise uses very short sentences to highlight individual aspects (e.g. ll. 14 f., 29 f.).
Due to Poole’s use of concrete examples and vivid language, the reader can easily follow his train of thought. His choice of words, especially of adjectives and adverbs with a negative connotation (e.g. “inexorable”, l. 26; “disastrous”, ll. 64 f.; “alarming”, l. 73), also supports his attitude towards uncontrolled technological progress.
It is noteworthy that Poole merely focuses on potential dangers of technological progress and paints a rather bleak picture of a hi-tech dystopian future while completely ignoring any of its potential advantages, e.g. curing or even preventing inheritable genetic disorders. Therefore, his article is not meant to be an objective discussion of the advantages and disadvantages of technological progress but a rather personal comment on the dangers he foresees if technological progress gets out of hands.

Aufgabe 3.1
In his article “Wake up, humanity! A hi-tech dystopian future is not inevitable”, Stephen Poole encourages people to develop a more critical attitude towards technological progress, i.e., the possible dangers that come with it.
One development he is suspicious about are deep fakes, which are often indistinguishable from reality and can be used to manipulate people so that “[w]e are sleepwalking towards a media dystopia” (ll. 88 f.). I agree with Poole that differentiating between fake news and reliable news coverage has become very difficult. It is sometimes appealing to believe everything without doing a profound background check regarding the source of such news. Social media, which are both a blessing and a curse, enable everyone to post, repost, share and comment on digital content of any kind on a whim, which results in fake news and deep fakes being spread even further. A good example for the misuse of media to manipulate the public were the attempts to influence the outcome of the 2020 presidential election in the USA. I therefore believe it is essential to raise critical awareness for our use of social media to avoid an increasing number of people falling prey to fake news and to enable everyone to confidently identify such content.
I also wholeheartedly agree with Poole when he says that “it’s time to reject the myth that tech is apolitical” (ll. 100 f.) and that “as a society, we always have a choice about which direction we take next” (ll. 28 f.).

Many areas of our lives have become linked to modern technology and the use of social media. The formerly futuristic idea of living in a "smart home", in which one can turn on the dishwasher or the lights with the help of one's smartphone while still at work or on holiday, has become a reality. However, whenever we use the internet, we leave traces behind, sometimes inadvertently, sometime deliberately, e.g., when shopping online or posting content on social networks. Security leaks that cause personal information to be revealed online, with an increased risk of it being misused by criminals, are ubiquitous. Clearly, social networking sites enable people to keep in touch with their friends and loved ones, close by or far away. Particularly during the ongoing COVID-19 pandemic, the internet was often the only means of staying in touch, as in-person contact had to be restricted. Home office and home schooling became a new reality for people all around the globe. However, some experience feelings of loneliness, sadness and alienation as they might interact with others via social media 24/7 but still lack personal face-to-face contact.

Another advantage of social media Poole entirely ignores in his article is that the world-wide connectedness also enables people to access, share and use information and knowledge stored online in an instant. When severe floods hit parts of Germany in the summer of 2021, killing many and leaving others homeless and confronted by the debris and ruins that used to be their home, social media helped organise support and shelter and raise funds for those in need. Essential information, such as where to get drinking water and food from and how to find missing friends or family members, was also published online and reached thousands of people. Without these tools, organising help would have taken much longer and would not have been as efficient.

As the examples above show, I cannot agree with Poole when he claims that "the people who promote [technological progress] are mainly people with a large financial interest in the adoption of new technology" (ll. 106–108). Modern media are far from harmless, but they can be – and are – used for a lot of good.

Aufgabe 3.2

Visions for Tomorrow's High-Tech World of Work

Let's close our eyes and imagine a world where AI jumps in whenever there are tedious chores to do like monitoring and refilling your fridge, vacuuming your apartment and mowing the lawn. Sounds too good to be true? Well, it's already a reality.

Thanks to AI, which has slowly made its way into our everyday life, all we have to do is turn our ordinary home into a "smart" one. Gadgets like automatic vacuum cleaners, lawnmowers or cookers have become a modern version of the little people we all know from fairy tales.

These changes to our everyday life seem to be rather convenient also have an impact on the world of work. On the one hand, "old" (traditional) jobs may become obsolete and disappear, e.g. cashiers in supermarkets might be replaced by self-checkouts. On the other hand, AI will also lead to the creation of new fields of work, e.g., jobs in IT.

During the ongoing pandemic, home office became the new normal, when our homes turned into offices, classrooms and meeting rooms. Online meetings enabled students and employers to keep in touch with one another and to collaborate online. But we soon

had to realise that although home office and home schooling are rather convenient (e. g. one doesn't have to commute between home and work/school), they can't replace in-person contact. In addition to that, the line between one's free time and work seemed to dissolve, as people were available 24/7 and days were less structured. This caused many to feel more stressed-out. Therefore, it's safe to say that this new connectedness has both its assets and flaws.
We live at a time when the world around us is changing at top speed, and new technology contributes to these rapid changes. I believe that new inventions and developments should always be assessed critically with regard to possible moral/ethical dilemmas they might cause. One example of this issue are "deep fake" news and media coverage that sometimes can't be identified as being fake and might be used to influence and manipulate people.
If someone asked me what I regard as one of the most pressing duties of my generation, I would answer that we must become aware of the fact that we have a responsibility for the world we live in. Of course, this applies to all aspects of life, e. g., climate change, a growing gap between rich and poor, poverty in developing countries, etc. I think it's crucial that my generation takes these challenges seriously and rises to them.

Klausurteil B

Die Perle der Saar-Universität *Annabelle Theobald*

[...] Wie geht man damit um, dass eine an sich gute Technik auch zu schlechten Zwecken missbraucht werden kann? Diese und ähnliche Fragen stellen sich Informatiker und Philosophen – allerdings selten am selben Tisch. Die Vorlesung „Ethics for Nerds“, die an der Universität des Saarlandes seit dem Sommersemester 2016 angeboten wird, hat Moralphilosophie und Informatik zusammengeführt. Der Stifterverband für die Deutsche Wissenschaft erklärte sie zur Hochschulperle. Die Auszeichnung soll innovative Projekte deutscher Universitäten sichtbarer machen.

Um das Projekt an der Saar-Universität umsetzen zu können, hat sich der Informatikprofessor Holger Hermanns an Kevin Baum gewandt, der als Erster im Saarland einen Master-Abschluss in Philosophie und Informatik gemacht hat und nun als Doktorand an der Saar-Uni beschäftigt ist. Er hält den Großteil der Vorlesung. Im Sommersemester 2015 startete das Projekt mit dem Seminar „Ethik für Nerds“, war aber schnell ausgebucht. Als klar wurde, dass das Angebot von den Studierenden gut angenommen wird, wurde daraus die Vorlesung „Ethics for Nerds“, in englischer Sprache und ergänzt durch begleitende Übungen. Im vergangenen Sommersemester nahmen an der Vorlesung etwa 120 Studenten aus Bachelor- und Masterstudiengängen teil.

Ziel der Vorlesung sei es, so Kevin Baum, Informatiker auf ihre Aufgaben vorzubereiten und sie zu motivieren, sich in den öffentlichen Diskurs einzubringen. „Die Vorlesung ist am Puls der Zeit“, sagt Holger Hermanns. Für die behandelten Themen, die sich oft im Spannungsfeld von Freiheit, Privatsphäre und Sicherheit bewegten, gebe es immer aktuelle Beispiele. Eben diese Aktualität führe dazu, dass die Studenten sich für die Vorlesung begeistern, so Baum. Der Ausgangspunkt sei dabei zunächst aber meist ein anderer: „Die Studenten gehen oft mit der Haltung rein: Das ist nicht die Verantwortung von Informatikern, sondern die der späteren Arbeitgeber“, sagt Kevin Baum. Allerdings sei das ein Fehlschluss, denn die Probleme erkennen könne letztlich nur der Informatiker und dieser trage damit auch gesellschaftliche Verantwortung.

Der Titel der Vorlesung [...] soll laut Hermanns auch öffentliche Aufmerksamkeit für das Thema schaffen. Im Duden wird ein Nerd als „sehr intelligenter, aber sozial isolierter Computerfan“ beschrieben; die Bezeichnung ist im Sprachgebrauch bisher eher abwertend gebraucht worden. „Die Wahrnehmung des Begriffes Nerds hat sich gewandelt. Mittlerweile ist der Nerd in der Mitte der Gesellschaft angekommen“, so Holger Hermanns. [...]

Die Vorlesung ist laut Baum in drei Teile gegliedert. Zunächst gebe es eine Einführung in die Moralphilosophie. Es wird darüber geredet, welche moralischen Theorien es gibt. Es geht darum zu klären, „was ist moralische Verantwortung jenseits dessen, was jeder an Vorstellungen mitbringt“, so Baum. Zudem schaue man sich die ethischen Leitlinien verschiedener Verbände an, darunter die der Gesellschaft für Informatik. Die Leitlinien erklärten zwar, worauf man achten müsse, aber für die richtige Anwendung brauche es doch mehr. Darum gehe es im zweiten Teil der Vorlesung anhand von konkreten und aktuellen Beispielen. „Da ergibt sich oft keine abschließende Antwort, sondern es werden verschiedene Argumente erarbeitet, die man danach abwägen kann“, sagt Kevin Baum. Im dritten Teil werde auf Grundlage des Gelernten beispielsweise darüber geredet, wie man autonome Fahrzeuge gestalten könnte und ob Roboter in bestimmten Bereichen Rechte haben sollten.

Einigkeit herrscht bei den beiden Forschern, dass wirkliche Herausforderungen oft die seien, die gesellschaftlich keine so große Aufmerksamkeit erfahren. „Die echten Probleme sind nicht der Terminator von morgen oder die künstliche Intelligenz, die wegläuft, sondern vielmehr, dass wir aus Versehen ein System aus Algorithmen basteln, die sich gegenseitig stützen und von denen keiner mehr weiß, wie sie wirken“, so Kevin Baum. Ein großes Thema ist daher laut Holger Hermanns die Erklärbarkeit von Systemen. Baum pflichtet bei: „Die künstliche Intelligenz muss so programmiert sein, dass deren Empfehlungen und Entscheidungen nachvollziehbar und hinterfragbar sind. Maschinen als Träger von Verantwortung sind wahnwitziger Unsinn.“

Beispiellösung

Aufgabe 4

Dear Jean,

It’s good to hear that everything is okay at your end of the world, and I think it’s a wonderful idea to spend a term abroad.

Just a few days ago I came across an article which reminded me of you as I know that you are studying computer science. This article deals with a lecture called “Ethics for Nerds”, which is offered by Saar University in Saarbrücken and is open to both bachelor and master students. Its rather provocative title was chosen to catch the attention of a wider audience.

It’s an interdisciplinary lecture designed by the Philosophy and the Computer Science department and offers an insight into moral issues that arise when new technology is developed and put into use. What is unique about this lecture is that these issues are not merely looked at from either a philosophical or scientific angle alone and that it is aimed at enabling students to establish awareness of the responsibility scientists have for the outcome of their research and its impact on society.

The lecture consists of three individual parts: discussing ethical questions in general, analyzing various official ethical guidelines and applying the skills and knowledge acquired in the first two parts of the lecture to current issues. The course deals less with end-of-the-world scenarios but rather with questions such as how algorithms should be designed to be understandable by everyone and whether robots should receive rights in certain areas.

As there is a growing interest in this lecture, it is now also offered in English.

What do you think about this kind of lecture? Could this be something for you?

Hope to hear from you soon.

Best,

XX

LK Literarischer Text mit Beispiellösung

Aufgabe 1

Klausurteil A: Leseverstehen und Schreiben integriert

AUFGABENSTELLUNG

1. Outline the speaker's views of Africa. *(Comprehension) (12 Punkte)*

2. Analyse how the speaker's views are presented. Focus on structure, use of language and poetic devices. *(Analysis) (16 Punkte)*

3. Choose **one** of the following tasks:

3.1 Assess to what extent Igbinedion's poem can be seen as a comment on social and political realities in Nigeria today. *(Evaluation: comment) (14 Punkte)*

3.2 For the project course "Africa rising – Africa's role in a globalised world" you have been asked to write an article for the course's website. You decided to take a quote by the African Kumi Naidoo, the former Secretary General of Amnesty International and Executive Director of Greenpeace International, as a starting point: "Economic growth is not sustainable without social and environmental justice."[1] Write the article, taking into account economic, ecological and political issues of globalisation. *(Evaluation: re-creation of text) (14 Punkte))*

1 Africa Renewal Online, „We need a sustainable path for our future", https://www.un.org/africarenewal/web-features/%E2%80%98we-need-sustainable-path-our-future%E2%80%99 (Zugriff: 23.07.2021)

Klausurteil B: Sprachmittlung isoliert

AUFGABENSTELLUNG

4. Your friend from the UK is doing a school project on the importance of poetry in the 21st century. She/He has asked you for information on current trends and their perception in Germany.
   Write an email to your friend, outlining the different views on instapoetry presented in Eileen Breuer's article. *(Mediation) (18 Punkte)*

Materialgrundlage:

Klausurteil A:

Osayande Igbinedion, „Africa", in: GMT Emezue (Hrsg.), *New Voices. A Collection of Recent Nigerian Poetry,* Oxford: Handel 2008, S. 135–137

Wortzahl: 273

Klausurteil B:

SPIEGEL.de (ehemals bento), Eileen Breuer 30.08.2019. https://www.spiegel.de/panorama/instapoetry-warum-auf-instagram-jetzt-gedichte-ganz-gross-sind-a-570d093c-4f8f-48f6-b356-5ccab2d44969 (Zugriff: 23.07.2021, gekürzt)

Wortzahl: 601

Zugelassene Hilfsmittel:

- Ein- und zweisprachiges Wörterbuch
- Herkunftssprachliches Wörterbuch für Schülerinnen und Schüler, deren Herkunftssprache nicht Deutsch ist
- Wörterbuch zur deutschen Rechtschreibung

Klausurteil A

Africa *Osayande Igbinedion*

Osayande Igbinedion is a male poet from Nigeria.

Africa, my Africa,
Africa my motherland,
Africa the land of the black race,
Torn in a conflict
Africa of high and low lands,
Africa of thick forest and shrubs,
Africa in which abound many rivers,
And natural wealth
Bountiful and splendid
Africa, my Africa,
A race struggling within
For a place in the sky;
Wither do you go now?

When the white race
Had lunged upon you
A cloud overshadowed you,
In a wave of cultures
Like the mighty roars of the Atlantic
Across the beaches of Lagos.
You were torn apart,
Body and soul,
In bits of disgusting rags ...

When believers and ministers of imported religions
Go back to their African roots
You are an edifice of tattered cloths
When teachers and students of white knowledge
Go up and down in the mystery of the same
You are an effigy of the past.
When the series of the western trials
Have failed us as we have failed them.
You are in chaos.
When orthodox medicine swallowed tradomedics
Struggling to re-emerge.
You strangulate between them.

When laws are turned upside down
And jungle justice and witchcraft reign.
You too are turned to rags
Metaphysical science still
Has a place in our wars.

When tradition goes on
In the presence of a foreign marriage.
You are in a great confusion.

Africa, my Africa,
Africa, my fatherland,
Africa of past proud warriors,
Africa then and now,
Africa of the black race,
Torn in conflict
Knowing not how to mend the rags.

And now, arise, Africa!
Wake up from your slumber, Africa!
You either be up or down the ladder
The present midway takes your breath.

Annotations:

32 tradomedics – traditional medicine

Beispiellösung

Aufgabe 1

Osayande Igbinedion's poem "Africa", taken from GMT Emezue's anthology "New Voices. A Collection of Recent Nigerian Poetry", published in 2008, deals with the African continent torn between modernism and traditionalism and suffering from its colonial past. The poem refers to Africa's natural beauty, its topography and its natural diversity and abundance. Its people, however, struggle to find their place and lack perspective.
This is mainly depicted as the result of Africa's colonial past. The Europeans brought their culture, their religion, their world views and their science to Africa, which collided vehemently with the ethnic and religious diversity which was already in place. The resulting mix of traditionalism and modernism, Western and traditional thinking has led to chaos and unrest. The speaker points out that adopting Western values may be as harmful as going back to traditional views and rituals. The poem thus articulates the urgent need for African people to take a clear stance and position themselves as self-confident and self-determined nations.

Aufgabe 2

The central idea of a continent and a people torn apart is repeated several times (ll. 4, 20, 48), but it is also illustrated and emphasised by a number of poetic devices, by the use of language and by the structure of the poem.

At first sight it becomes obvious that the poem does not follow any poetic rule or strict form. There are no rhymes, no metre and lines are of different lengths, as are the stanzas. Punctuation seems arbitrary. This irregular structure reflects the view of chaotic disorder that the speaker holds of Africa.

The speaker's thoughts, however, follow a clear structure: The first four lines utter the main idea of this poem: Africa is "torn in a conflict" (l. 4). At the same time, he expresses his deep emotional affinity to the continent by stressing "my Africa" (l. 1) and "my motherland" (l. 2). These lines are varied in lines 43 to 49, thus serving as a frame for the main part of the poem. The speaker's deep feelings for this continent are stressed by the word "motherland" (l. 2), with "mother" suggesting a feeling of protection, home, belonging and love, whereas the word "fatherland" in line 44 may rather suggest patriotism and pride, which is exactly what this penultimate stanza is about.

The speaker goes on to praise the beauty of his beloved continent by enumerating aspects of its natural diversity (ll. 5–9), which he emphasises by anaphora ("Africa of high and low lands", l. 5) and parallelism ("Africa of [...] / Africa of [...]", ll. 5 f.). He then comes back to the people, who are "struggling within / For a place in the sky" (ll. 11 f.), suggesting not only rising from the ground where they are trodden down but also finding a place where they are seen and not hidden.

With the question, "Wither do you go now?" (l. 13), the speaker personifies Africa, which again underlines his close affinity to and identification with the continent, especially as he uses the personal pronoun "you" throughout the poem from thereon.

The social and political realities which are both cause and result of the prevailing conflict are presented by means of an anaphorical "when" (ll. 14, 23, 26, 29, 32, 35, 40), which introduces each problem the speaker refers to. As well as a particular choice of words denoting disruption, violence and chaos ("struggling", ll. 11, 33; "lunged", l. 15; "chaos", l. 31; "strangulate", l. 34; "upside down", l. 35; "jungle justice", l. 36; "witchcraft", l. 36; "wars", l. 39; "confusion", l. 42), Igbinedion makes use of imagery in order to illustrate the conflicting forces the African people are exposed to.

Colonialism appears as a "cloud" which "overshadowed" the Africans (l. 16), suggesting darkness and cold as the traditional image of evil and misery. The alien cultures come in a "wave [...] / Like the mighty roars of the Atlantic" (ll. 17 f.), with the speaker drawing on the destructive power of water as much as the deafening sound of breaking waves, which eliminates all other sounds and voices.

Modern medicine is personified in the word "swallowed" (l. 32). There may be some irony in the fact that the word "swallow" even belongs to the semantic field of medicine. Swallowing equals destruction here, elimination, as in the case of a wild animal or a greedy person.

The main image, however, when the speaker seeks to illustrate the inner conflict of the African people, is the metaphor of clothing. Africa's body and soul are torn into "bits of disgusting rags" (l. 22). This not only evokes the image of disruption but also suggests

poverty, illness, misery, especially as the noun "rags" is supported by the strongly negative adjective "disgusting" (l. 22). The textile metaphor is used again in line 25 ("tattered cloths"), where it suggests fragility and instability, as well as weakness in line 37 ("turned to rags") and line 49 ("Knowing not how to mend the rags").
This last image is followed by the speaker's appeal. Torn in conflict, the speaker berates his fellow countrywomen and -men for being lethargic. Therefore, using imperatives and exclamation marks, the speaker urgently appeals to Africa to "arise" and "[w]ake up" (ll. 50 f.) and at least decide on a direction ("either up or down", l. 52). The present situation is seen as a "midway" (l. 53), which is exhausting and unhealthy.

Aufgabe 3.1

It is arguable if the present political and social situation in Africa can indeed be seen as a "midway" situation that could be changed or improved by just deciding on a certain direction, but the poem definitely hints at a number of deplorable facts that are true for most African nations, in particular for Africa's biggest nation, Nigeria.
Colonialism has overshadowed the country since the 17th century when the slave trade to America began and more and more slave ports were established on the Nigerian coast. British missionaries spread Christianity, Western culture and education as well as the English language by building schools. This led to cultural clashes in a country already marked by ethnic diversity. In particular, a strong divide between the North and the South resulted from British dominance in the south and Muslim dominance in the north, with totally different ideas of law and justice. With Western influence on the educational system and therefore rapid modernisation of the southern economy, this divide became wider. Even today, it still manifests itself in the gruesome terrorism of the Islamist group Boko Haram, fighting against Western education and culture, which they see as evil.
After gaining independence, the ethnic and religious differences in Nigeria could not be reconciled. The tension between the ethnic groups led to the foundation of the Republic of Biafra and consequently to the Biafran War, in which hundreds of thousands of people were killed. After reintegration, the country did not find peace. Military regimes alternated with civilian governments, and even now, with a democracy in place, Nigeria is suffering from corruption, violence, mismanagement, crime and poverty, poor education and poor infrastructure. Especially the large gap between rich and poor is appalling. In addition, foreign companies exploit Nigeria's oil resources, which again leads to controversy and violence as various groups demand more control over the resources in the Niger Delta.
As a result, many people try to leave the country. They do not see a chance of social mobility or material success. America or Europe are the places where they want to try their luck. Many fall victims to traffickers and women end up as prostitutes, especially in Italy and Germany.
Meanwhile, music, cinema and literature have become a means of self-realisation in Nigeria. But even here, individualism and identity are not free from Western influences. Nollywood, the Nigerian film industry, which is the second largest in the world, has even got its name from Hollywood. It is certainly no coincidence that the worldwide hit by the rapper Falz is a copy of an American rap video, and as far as literature is concerned, it

is striking that the most successful and most famous Nigerian writers are expatriates, at least for a considerable period of their lives.
As said above, Osayande Igbinedion's poem sees a solution to these various conflicts in a clear decision of Africans to position themselves. Apart from the fact that the speaker of the poem does not give a concrete idea of what "up" or "down" means with regard to the economy, politics or culture, I doubt that this one path to a self-determined future can exist. Africa's colonial past and its influence cannot be undone, nor can the ethnic, religious and cultural diversity of the continent be easily reconciled. If there is a solution to the chaos that prevails in Africa, it should lie in reason, education, justice and human rights – not just in Africa but also worldwide.

Aufgabe 3.2
"Economic growth is not sustainable without social and environmental justice."
This quotation by Kumi Naidoo, the former Secretary General of Amnesty International and Executive Director of Greenpeace International, should be the guideline of this project course. When we are dealing with Africa's economy and its role in this globalised world, sustainability and justice are key terms. Therefore, this article will take Kumi Naidoo's statement as its starting point.
Justice must be understood on a national scale, within a society, within a national economy, but justice must also be understood on a global scale, with all the people on our planet having the chance of getting a fair share.
Looking at rising African economies, it becomes quite obvious that wealth is unevenly distributed. The gap between rich and poor is wider than anywhere else in the world. For example, half of the people in Nigeria live in extreme poverty, while on the other side there are more billionaires and millionaires than in any other African country. In spite of the country's increasing prosperity, a majority has no access to proper drinking water nor to decent sanitation facilities. Even electricity is not available to most of the population. The standard of education is likewise very poor, with a literacy rate of below 60 %.
Internationally, it is especially the global corporations that profit from Africa's resources. Usually, workers are excluded from the profits. A well-known example are the coffee and cocoa production, in which the local farmers only get a fraction of the profits they generate. It is hard to accept that the average cocoa farmer may never have had a piece of chocolate.
It is also the environment that suffers from economic and social injustice. To people who are struggling to stay alive, caring for the environment is a luxury. In addition, those without education are often unaware of the impact of pollution. With Africa's ecological footprint being a lot smaller than that of the North, i. e. with Africans producing a lot less CO_2, they still have to bear the brunt of climate change. They have to pay for the North's overconsumption with climate catastrophes like droughts, fires, tempests and flooding. Given Africa's dependence on agriculture, it is particularly hard for these nations to adjust to the climate crisis. Moreover, global companies exploit natural resources and cause environmental damage, drilling for oil and mining for all kinds of minerals to sustain Western wealth and luxury.

Furthermore, the lack of democratic structures leads to political injustice. Ethnic and religious minorities are oppressed or at least disadvantaged. This causes violence and migration as well as the detriment of these countries' economies. National prosperity can never thrive in political unrest, and millions of young people in particular leaving a nation is a loss of human resources that cannot benefit an economy.
In order to secure a sustainable development, it is high time for African governments but also for those that globally pull the strings, namely Western governments, global corporations and institutions, to take responsibility and seek to improve the above-mentioned deficits. Justice has to be secured for people and countries. This means strengthening young democracies and fighting dictatorships. This means putting up programmes that help the people and not the international world of finance. Fair trade programs have to be encouraged, NGOs that work globally or locally have to be supported. Conflicts have to be overcome, not fuelled.
A central issue is education. People have to have access to better jobs, but in particular they have to be able to be aware of global issues, the importance of human rights, the importance of women's rights, the importance of environmental protection and the importance of sustainability in general.
Therefore, in this project, let us learn and work together for peace and justice, for sustainability, for steady improvement of international relations. Let us spread the idea of climate protection and human rights, of fair trade and – above all – enlightenment: for a better future of the African continent in a better world.

Klausurteil B

Wie der junge Goethe: Warum gerade ausgerechnet auf Instagram Gedichte ganz groß sind *Eileen Breuer*

[...] Poeten haben Instagram für sich entdeckt und teilen ihre Werke mit tausenden Followern.

Unter dem Hashtag Instapoetry finden sich dort fast drei Millionen Beiträge, tippt man die deutsche Entsprechung Instalyrik ins Suchfeld ein, werden einem mehr als 6000 Treffer angezeigt. [... D]och warum sind die Gedichte auf Instagram so erfolgreich?

Eine der bekanntesten deutschsprachigen Poetinnen auf Instagram ist Clara Louise, 26 Jahre alt. Ihr folgen dort mehr als 166.000 Menschen.

Sie hat mit etwa 13 Jahren begonnen, Gedichte zu verfassen: „Ich habe einfach alles niedergeschrieben, was mich belastet hat oder was in meinem Kopf vorgegangen ist“, erzählt sie bento. Die Poetin schreibt meistens über Liebe – die zu anderen und die zu sich selbst. „Die Gedichte haben mir dabei geholfen, mich selbst zu verstehen.“

Clara wollte die Gedanken nicht mehr nur für ihre heimische Schublade aufschreiben, also fing sie an, Ausschnitte auf Instagram zu veröffentlichen. Manchmal in Retrooptik auf der Schreibmaschine getippt, manchmal in verschnörkelter Handschrift. Es sollte ein Testlauf für einen Gedichtband sein. Die Likes und steigenden Followerzahlen gaben ihr recht: Als Clara anfing, lag sie bei gut tausend Followern, heute zählt sie 160-mal so viele.

Obwohl sie ihre Ideen lieber ins Handy tippt als zum Notizblock zu greifen und Verse in den sozialen Medien postet, will Clara nicht als Insta-Poetin bezeichnet werden. „Ich verstehe nicht, was es für einen Unterschied macht, ob man etwas auf Instagram veröffentlicht oder nicht. Es ist nur ein Medium, wo man sich und das, was man macht, präsentieren kann. Es ist aber keine andere Form von Lyrik“, sagt Clara Louise.

Literaturwissenschaftler Niels Penke ist anderer Meinung. Er arbeitet am Germanistischen Seminar der Universität Siegen und setzt sich unter anderem mit Popkultur auseinander. Seiner Ansicht nach zeichnen sich die Gedichte auf Instagram durch andere Charakteristika aus als konventionelle Lyrik. Während Gedichte der zeitgenössischen Lyrik oft irritieren und Fragen aufwerfen, könne dies auf Instagram nicht funktionieren, sagt Penke: „Hier geht es darum, nicht zu irritieren, sondern ohne große Voraussetzungen verständlich zu sein. Nicht formal komplex, sondern formal einfach.“

Die Art des Mediums habe Auswirkungen darauf, was dort veröffentlicht wird, so der Wissenschaftler: „Der Erfolg der Instapoetry liegt vor allem darin, dass die Affordanzen des Mediums befolgt werden.“ Affordanzen sind Spielregeln und Funktionsweisen, die ein Medium mit sich bringt.

„Das Formbewusstsein, ob man nun ein Sonett oder eine Ballade schreibt, spielt hier gar keine Rolle. Auf Instagram gilt es, sich möglichst kurz zu halten – es muss auf dem kleinen Bildschirm gut lesbar sein – und den Effekt zu provozieren, geliked, geteilt und kommentiert zu werden.“

Außerdem prägen sentenzenhafte Verse die Instalyrik, sagt Penke. Damit werden kurze und prägnante Zeilen beschrieben, die sich dem Leser ins Gedächtnis einbrennen. „Die Lyriker veröffentlichen auf

Instagram Sätze, die man sich auch als Kalenderspruch vorstellen, auf ein T-Shirt drucken oder auf den Unterarm tätowieren lassen kann", sagt Penke.

Tatsächlich hat Clara schon oft Bilder von Tattoos ihrer Gedichte zugeschickt bekommen. Sie denkt, dass die Menschen sich aus einem Grund wieder mehr nach Poesie sehnen: „Dieses Bewusstsein dafür, dass Dinge sich verändern, dass wir an einem Maximum angekommen sind und es irgendwann nicht mehr weiter nach oben geht, ist vielleicht ein Grund dafür, warum die Leute sich wieder mehr mit sich selbst befassen anstatt mit allem, was um sie herum passiert."

Niels Penke sieht dabei eine Ähnlichkeit zum jungen Goethe des Sturm und Drang. Dessen Erlebnislyrik handele ebenfalls von Erlebnissen und Empfindungen, die authentisch und glaubwürdig wirken sollten. „Von besonderen Erfahrungen authentisch zu schreiben, das hat immer schon in bestimmten lyrischen Traditionen eine Rolle gespielt", sagt Penke. Die jungen Lyriker heute würden in ihren Gedichten oft Stimmungslagen ihrer Generation aufgreifen – damit könnten sich die Nutzer identifizieren. [...]

Anmerkungen:

19 bento – Magazin des Spiegel für junge Menschen von 18 bis 30

Beispiellösung

Aufgabe 4

Hi Oliver,

Concerning your school project, I've found an interesting article on instapoetry, which is quite trendy in Germany right now. Two opposing views on instapoetry are presented. On the one hand, there's Clara Louise, who is an Instagram poet with 160,000 followers. She started writing poetry at 13 and began publishing on Instagram when she became tired of writing just for herself. She doesn't see a difference between traditional poetry and instapoetry. To her, Instagram is just another medium. She believes that the success of instapoetry lies in people's awareness that things are changing, that we've reached a maximum (whatever that's supposed to mean) and that people want to reflect on their lives rather than on what is around them. Niels Penke, a literary scholar, holds the opposite view. To him, instapoetry is marked by different characteristics than traditional poetry. Modern poetry often tries to be confusing or disturbing and raises questions. This does not work on Instagram. Instapoetry must be immediately comprehensible and formally simple. The requirements of Instagram determine the poetry. On Instagram, your texts have to be short and easily legible on a small display for the sake of being liked, shared and commented on. Penke does, however, see a parallel to Goethe's early poetry. Just like instapoetry, it deals with authentic experiences and sentiments. The young poets of today reflect the mood of their generation in their poetry, making users identify with it.

Hope I could help you. Good luck with your project!

Best wishes,

XX

Die sprachliche Leistung im Abitur

Der Stellenwert der sprachlichen Leistung

Bei der Bewertung der Abiturprüfung können 150 Punkte vergeben werden. Davon fallen 90 Punkte für die sprachliche und 60 Punkte für die inhaltliche Leistung an. Über das Fachwissen zu den lehrplanrelevanten Inhalten hinaus ist also die sprachliche Leistung im Englischen für ein gutes Ergebnis in der Abiturprüfung von grundlegender Bedeutung. Natürlich bedingen sich die beiden Teilbereiche gegenseitig: Ohne stichhaltigen Inhalt kann nicht die volle Punktzahl im Bereich Sprache erreicht werden und umgekehrt.
Die Entwicklung der englischen Sprachkompetenz ist ein komplexer Prozess, der sich über viele Jahre hinweg bis zum Abitur hin entfaltet. Es ist an dieser Stelle nicht möglich, eine umfassende Revision der sprachlichen Grundlagen anzubieten, aber Sie finden hier Hinweise auf die wichtigsten Aspekte, die Sie zum Zeitpunkt des Abiturs beherrschen sollten. Bei Bedarf können Sie dann das eine oder andere Kapitel mit Hilfe eines grammatikorientieren Buches wiederholen.

TIPP zur individuellen Wiederholung der Grammatik

Wenn Sie das Gefühl haben, in wichtigen Bereichen der Grammatik noch Defizite zu haben, analysieren Sie gezielt Ihre persönlichen Schwachpunkte aus den Klausuren und wiederholen Sie selbstständig die entsprechenden Kapitel anhand einer Grammatik oder eines Übungsbuches auf Sprachniveau B2 des Gemeinsamen Europäischen Referenzrahmens.
Klassische Fehlerquellen sind zum Beispiel if-Sätze, Passivkonstruktionen, die Wahl der richtigen Zeitform oder Präpositionen nach bestimmten Verben.

Die Leistungskriterien

Eigene Fehlerschwerpunkte erkennen

Um eigene Fehlerschwerpunkte zu erkennen, ist es empfehlenswert, die Darstellungsleistung in eigenen Klausuren genau zu analysieren.

- Lesen Sie Ihre eigenen Klausuren inklusive der Randbemerkungen und Kommentare Ihrer Englischlehrkraft erneut durch und halten Sie auf einem separaten Blatt fest, welche Teilbereiche besonders „fehleranfällig“ sind.
- Wenn Ihre Klausuren mittels eines Korrekturrasters bewertet worden sind, studieren Sie dieses im Hinblick auf die Darstellungsleistung genau: In welchen Teilbereichen haben Sie besonders wenige Punkte erhalten? Lesen Sie nun Ihre Klausuren im Hinblick auf diese Teilbereiche erneut durch. Halten Sie schriftlich fest, wo Ihre individuellen Fehlerschwerpunkte liegen.

Wenn Sie die eigenen Fehlerschwerpunkte identifiziert haben, sollten Sie diese beim Anfertigen – und anschließenden Korrekturlesen – schriftlicher Hausaufgaben und Klausuren besonders im Blick haben.
Defizite im Bereich der Grundgrammatik können Sie mit entsprechenden Übungsbüchern aufarbeiten. Auch hier gilt: Üben Sie konsequent über einen längeren Zeitraum hinweg und trainieren Sie immer wieder das Verfassen schriftlicher Texte, indem Sie z. B. im Unterricht angefertigte Stichpunkte ausformulieren.
In den meisten Wörterbüchern finden Sie Zusammenstellungen der unregelmäßigen Verben und der wichtigsten ***phrasal verbs.*** Es empfiehlt sich, diese vor Klausuren zu wiederholen.

Die Vorgehensweise in Klausuren und in der schriftlichen Abiturprüfung

Um in Klausuren und in der schriftlichen Abiturprüfung ein möglichst gutes Ergebnis zu erzielen, ist es unerlässlich, eine sinnvolle und gut strukturierte Vorarbeit zu leisten. Lassen Sie sich nicht von Mitschülerinnen und Mitschülern aus der Ruhe bringen, die nach kürzester Bearbeitungszeit und ohne Notizen sofort anfangen zu schreiben!
Je intensiver Sie sich mit der Aufgabenstellung und dem Ausgangstext auseinandersetzen und entsprechende Notizen anfertigen, desto einfacher wird es Ihnen fallen, die Aufgabenstellungen in zusammenhängenden Texten zu bearbeiten.

Die Bearbeitung in folgenden Schritten hat sich bewährt:

1. Lesen Sie zunächst die Aufgabenstellung und den Ausgangstext ein erstes Mal durch. Achten Sie hierbei auch auf eventuelle Erläuterungen, die dem Ausgangstext vorangestellt sind. Diese sind meist kursiv gedruckt und enthalten wichtige Zusatzinformationen, die Ihnen die Bearbeitung der Aufgaben erleichtern. Beim ersten Lesen sollten Sie auch Wörter unterstreichen, deren Bedeutung Sie nicht kennen und auch nicht aus dem Kontext erschließen können.

2. Schlagen Sie nun die Wörter nach, die Sie beim ersten Lesen nicht verstehen bzw. erschließen konnten, und die für das Textverständnis von Bedeutung sind. Oft lassen sich unbekannte Wörter aus dem Zusammenhang bzw. mit Rückgriff auf andere Sprachen erschließen.

3. Bevor Sie den Text nun erneut lesen, sollten Sie die Aufgabenstellungen einer genauen Betrachtung unterziehen. Achten Sie auf die verwendeten Operatoren – diese „verraten" Ihnen, was genau Ihre Aufgabe ist bzw. welche Aspekte sie untersuchen sollen. Auch im Abitur werden Sie die Dreiteilung in „Comprehension", „Analysis" und „Evaluation: Comment / Recreation of text" vorfinden. Beachten Sie: Bei der Bearbeitung der „Comprehension"-Aufgabe sollen – im Gegensatz zur „Analysis"-Aufgabe – keine Zitate und Textverweise verwendet werden!

4. Lesen Sie nun den Ausgangstext erneut und nehmen Sie zunächst (farbige) Markierungen und Randbemerkungen für die Bearbeitung der ersten Aufgabe vor. Auf einem separaten Blatt sollten Sie darüber hinaus Stichpunkte anfertigen, die Ihnen die anschließende Bearbeitung der jeweiligen Aufgabenstellung erleichtern. Bevor Sie die Stichpunkte ausformulieren, empfiehlt es sich, diese in eine sinnvolle Reihenfolge zu bringen, etwa durch Nummerierung. Denken Sie daran, Ihre Ausführungen zur ersten Aufgabe mit einem entsprechenden Einleitungssatz (Nennung von Autor/-in, Titel, Textsorte, Erscheinungsdatum, Quelle und Thema) zu beginnen. Anschließend wenden Sie diese Verfahrensweise auf die Aufgaben 2 und 3 an. Hier ist es nicht notwendig, den Einleitungssatz der ersten Aufgabe zu wiederholen – Ihre Leserinnen und Leser wissen ja nun, welcher Ausgangstext Ihren Ausführungen zugrunde liegt! Es ist allerdings notwendig, kurz darzulegen, welche Aspekte nachfolgend untersucht bzw. bearbeitet werden.

5. Nachdem Sie alle Aufgaben bearbeitet haben, sollten Sie ausreichend Zeit (ca. 20 Minuten) einplanen, um Ihre Klausur Korrektur zu lesen. Achten Sie dabei auf Ihre individuellen Fehlerschwerpunkte!

In der schriftlichen Abiturprüfung haben Sie im Fach Englisch im Grund- und im Leistungskurs die Auswahl zwischen jeweils zwei Klausurvorschlägen.
Hierbei handelt es sich stets um einen literarischen Text und einen Sach- oder Gebrauchstext – möglicherweise in Kombination mit einem Cartoon, einer Grafik oder einer Statistik.

Sie haben 30 Minuten Zeit, sich mit beiden Themenvorschlägen zu befassen und einen der beiden zur Bearbeitung auswählen. Der nicht gewählte Vorschlag verbleibt bei Ihnen. Theoretisch könnten Sie sich nach zwei Stunden noch umentscheiden. TUN SIE DIES JA NICHT! Wenn Sie sich entschieden haben, legen Sie den Vorschlag weit weg, am besten auf den Boden, um Verwechslungen zu vermeiden!
Anschließend dürfen Sie sofort mit der Bearbeitung des von Ihnen gewählten Vorschlags beginnen, d.h. Sie müssen nicht das Ende der dreißigminütigen Auswahlzeit abwarten.

Nur ein- und zweisprachige Wörterbücher und der Duden (für die Sprachmittlung) sind in der Klausur als Hilfsmittel zugelassen.
Bislang bezieht sich dies jedoch ausschließlich auf Wörterbücher in Printform. Elektronische Wörterbücher sind also im Abitur nicht erlaubt.

Kommunikative Textgestaltung

Aufgabenbezug, Textformate, Textaufbau, Ökonomie, Belegtechnik

Aufgabenbezug

Hier wird bewertet, ob der von Ihnen verfasste Text konsequent an der jeweiligen Aufgabenstellung ausgerichtet ist.
Dies hört sich recht banal an, doch aufgrund des im Unterricht erworbenen Vorwissens zu einem bestimmten Themenbereich ist in Klausuren die Versuchung oft groß, eben dieses Wissen in seiner Gesamtheit abzubilden und sich damit in Details zu verlieren. Achten Sie also genau darauf, was von Ihnen verlangt wird. Auch hier hilft Ihnen das Anfertigen von Stichpunkten zu den verschiedenen Aufgaben dabei, Ihre Gedanken zu bündeln und nicht den Überblick zu verlieren.
Die im Abitur gestellten Aufgaben enthalten stets die vom Schulministerium aufgelisteten Operatoren, die Sie auch auf S. 13–15 in diesem Buch finden.
Den verschiedenen Anforderungsbereichen („Comprehension“, „Analysis“ und „Evaluation“) sind dabei unterschiedliche Operatoren zugeordnet, deren Bedeutung klar definiert ist.
Vor Bearbeitung der konkreten Aufgaben empfiehlt es sich, die Aufgabenstellung genau in den Blick zu nehmen. Es ist hilfreich, wenn Sie die verwendeten Operatoren farbig markieren und dann für sich die folgenden Fragen beantworten:

- Welche Operatoren werden verwendet?
- Was wird konkret von mir erwartet?
- In Hinblick auf welche inhaltlichen Schwerpunkte soll ich bei der Aufgabe „Comprehension“ den Text wiedergeben? Welche Gestaltungsmerkmale / stilistischen Mittel innerhalb des Textes soll ich bei Bearbeitung der Aufgabe zur „Analysis“ näher untersuchen?
- Welches Zieltextformat wird bei der Aufgabe „Evaluation: Recreation of text“ verlangt?

Textformate

TIPP zum Punktesammeln

Beim Verfassen der Zieltexte sollten Sie stets darauf achten, welche Textsorte Sie produzieren sollen. Eine Übersicht über die verschiedenen Zieltextformate, die in Klausuren von Ihnen verlangt werden können, finden Sie ab Seite 103 in diesem Buch.
Denken Sie daran, bei den oben genannten Teilaufgaben keine ***short forms*** wie *don't, isn't* oder Ähnliches zu verwenden. Davon ausgenommen sind nur informelle Texte wie persönliche Briefe/E-Mails in Aufgabe 3.

Nachfolgend finden Sie eine allgemeine **Übersicht** über die Konventionen der verschiedenen Zieltextformate innerhalb der Schreibaufgabe:

Comprehension:

Beginnen Sie Ihre Ausführungen mit einem **Einleitungssatz** (Autor/-in, Titel, Textsorte, Publikation, Ort und Jahr der Erscheinung). Sollte es sich bei dem Ihnen vorliegenden Text um einen Textauszug handeln oder sollte der Text an eine ganz bestimmte Zielgruppe gerichtet sein, dann merken Sie dies ebenfalls im Einleitungssatz an.
Zitate und Textverweise sind bei Teilaufgabe 1 **nicht angebracht.**

Analysis:

Während bei Aufgabe 1 eine erste inhaltliche Annäherung an den Text erfolgen soll, wird bei der zweiten Aufgabe **eine detaillierte Analyse des Ausgangstextes** unter Beachtung der in der Aufgabenstellung genannten Gesichtspunkte und **mit Rückgriff auf Zitate** beziehungsweise **Textverweise** verlangt.
Die Bearbeitung der zweiten Teilaufgabe sollte in einem **sachlich-neutralen Stil** erfolgen. Eine Darstellung der eigenen Meinung oder eine Wertung erfolgen also nicht.
Zu den verschiedenen Herangehensweisen an die Analyse von literarischen Texten sowie von Sach- und Gebrauchstexten sei auf das entsprechende Kapitel in diesem Buch verwiesen (S. 78–102).

Evaluation:

Bei der dritten Aufgabe („evaluation") haben Sie die Wahl zwischen zwei unterschiedlichen Aufgabentypen: der Kommentierung eines entsprechenden Sachverhalts („comment") oder einer kreativen Schreibaufgabe („recreation of text").

Comment:

Hier sind Sie aufgefordert, Ihre **eigene Meinung** zu einem beziehungsweise **Ihre subjektive Sicht auf einen bestimmten Sachverhalt** zu erörtern und begründen.
Achten Sie darauf, Ihre Argumentation **logisch** zu entwickeln und die einzelnen Argumente sinnvoll aneinander anzuschließen.
Ihre Ausführungen sollten mit einem **abschließenden Fazit** enden.

Recreation of text:

Sollte es bei der kreativen Aufgabe durch die Vorgabe der anzufertigenden Textsorte (z. B. Dialog, Blogeintrag, E-Mail, innerer Monolog) nicht zwangsläufig gefordert sein, sollten Sie beim Verfassen Ihres Zieltextes auch bei Aufgabe 3.2 (bzw. 4.2) auf die Verwendung umgangssprachlicher Formulierungen, Slang und Kurzformen *(can't, wouldn't, doesn't* usw.) unbedingt verzichten.
Achten Sie auch stets darauf, an wen Ihr Zieltext gerichtet sein soll. Bei Verfassen eines *speech script* ist es zum Beispiel mit Blick auf das Vorwissen und den Erfahrungsschatz der Zielgruppe ein großer Unterschied, ob Sie sich an High-School-Absolventinnen und -Absolventen oder eine Versammlung von Führungskräften richten. Dies sollten Sie durch die Verwendung passender sprachlicher Mittel kennzeichnen.

Textaufbau

Der von Ihnen verfasste Text soll leicht lesbar sein – und das nicht nur mit Hinblick auf das Schriftbild und die formale Gestaltung.
Mit „Textaufbau" ist vielmehr gemeint, dass ein für die Leserinnen und Leser leicht erkennbarer „roter Faden" durch Ihren Text führt und der von Ihnen verfasste Text klar und sachgerecht strukturiert ist.
Damit ist gemeint, dass Sie Ihren Text in klar erkennbare Abschnitte gliedern, die auch inhaltliche Sinneinheiten ergeben. Leiten Sie neue Gedanken durch die Verwendung von ***signal words*** (etwa *First ..., Second ..., Third, ...)* ein. Diese ermöglichen Ihnen die sinnvolle Gliederung Ihres Textes und strukturieren diesen auch für die Lesenden in klare Einheiten.
Denken Sie daran, Ihre Argumentation logisch aufzubauen und vermeiden Sie Gedankensprünge, die den Leserinnen und Lesern das Textverständnis erschweren.
Durch Verwendung geeigneter Konnektoren gelingt es Ihnen, Ihre Argumente und Beobachtungen sinnvoll zu verknüpfen, sodass Ihre Leserinnen und Leser Ihren Ausführungen leicht folgen können.

Nachfolgend eine Übersicht über die wichtigsten Konnektoren:

Reihung von Argumenten

and	und
first(ly) ... second(ly) ... third(ly) ...	erstens ... zweitens ... drittens ...
furthermore	außerdem / darüber hinaus
in addition to	zusätzlich zu
moreover	ferner/überdies
not only ... but also	nicht nur ... sondern auch
as well as	sowie
finally	schließlich

Gegensatz

but	aber/sondern
although	obwohl
however	jedoch
despite the fact that	trotz der Tatsache, dass
in spite of	trotz
nevertheless/nonetheless	nichtsdestoweniger
even so	selbst dann
on the contrary	im Gegensatz dazu
on the one hand ... on the other hand	einerseits ... andererseits

unlike	anders als
whereas	während/wogegen/indessen
while/whilst	während (dagegen)
yet	dennoch

Bedingung

if	falls/wenn
unless	wenn nicht
otherwise	ansonsten

Folge

because	weil
since	da
so	daher
consequently	folglich
as a result	demzufolge
therefore	daher/deshalb
due to	infolge
accordingly	daher
that is why	deshalb

Vergleich

like	wie
in comparison with	im Vergleich zu
similarly	ähnlich
equally	gleichermaßen

Intention der Autorin bzw. des Autors

An mehreren Stellen in Ihrer Abiturklausur werden Sie Ihre eigenen Aussagen in Relation zur Meinung der/des Verfassenden setzen müssen. Dafür empfiehlt es sich, eine Reihe von sprachlichen Ausdrücken parat zu haben, z. B.:

He/She points out / argues that ...	Er/Sie weist darauf hin / argumentiert, dass ...
He/She implies/claims/states that ...	Er/Sie behauptet, dass ...
He/She believes/suggests ...	Er/Sie glaubt / schlägt vor ...

He/She emphasises ...	Er/Sie legt sein/ihr Hauptaugenmerk auf ...
His/Her idea was to ...	Er/Sie wollte ...
He/She writes with the intention of *(+ gerund)* ...	Er/Sie schreibt mit der Absicht ...
His/Her aim is to ...	Sein/Ihr Ziel ist es ...
His/Her attitude towards ...	Seine/Ihre Einstellung gegenüber ...
When he/she says/writes ... he/she means that ...	Wenn er/sie sagt/schreibt ..., meint er/sie ...
According to the author ...	Dem Autor / Der Autorin zufolge ...

Ökonomie

TIPP zum Punktesammeln

Vorweg: Der Umfang des von Ihnen verfassten Zieltextes ist nicht zwangsläufig ausschlaggebend für die Qualität Ihrer Klausur. Bearbeiten Sie die Ihnen gestellten Aufgaben zielgerichtet und hinreichend ausführlich, aber vermeiden Sie inhaltliche Doppelungen. Anstatt einen Sachverhalt zu wiederholen, sollten Sie auf bereits erfolgte Erläuterungen zurückverweisen.
Verwenden Sie konkrete Beispiele, um komplexe Sachverhalte zu illustrieren.

Belegtechnik

Um Ihre Aussagen zu belegen, fügen Sie geeignete Zitate aus dem Originaltext in Ihre Antworten ein. Setzen Sie diese in englische Anführungszeichen – diese beginnen oben und enden oben. Da es sich in der Abiturklausur um einen relativ kurzen Ausgangstext handelt, genügt als Quellenangabe die Angabe der Zeilennummer in Klammern direkt hinter dem Zitat.

<u>Beispiel zu Shakespeare, Romeo and Juliet:</u>
In his speech Prince Escalus speaks about the Montagues and the Capulets as "enemies to peace" (l. 1) and finishes by even threatening them with "pain of death" (l. 23).
Verwenden Sie nicht das ganze Zitat, können Sie die ausgelassenen Passagen mit Punkten in eckigen Klammern kennzeichnen. Genauso können Sie ein Bezugswort in eckigen Klammern einfügen, wenn dies aufgrund der Satzkonstruktion notwendig ist.
Die wörtliche Übernahme von Formulierungen aus dem Ausgangstext beziehungsweise einem anderen Text ohne entsprechende Kennzeichnung ist nicht zulässig und wird negativ bewertet.
Da mit Zitaten Aussagen belegt oder gefestigt werden, stehen sie normalerweise nach der entsprechenden Behauptung. Diese sollten Sie zunächst mit eigenen Worten paraphrasieren. Synonyme hierfür finden Sie in Ihrem einsprachigen Wörterbuch.

Ausdrucksvermögen / Verfügbarkeit sprachlicher Mittel

Eigenständigkeit, allgemeiner und thematischer Wortschatz, Textbesprechungs- und Textproduktionswortschatz, Satzbau

Eigenständigkeit

Es wird in Klausuren von Ihnen erwartet, dass Sie einen eigenständigen Text formulieren und sich vom Ausgangstext lösen. Sie sollen also nicht Formulierungen aus dem Ausgangstext in Ihren Text übernehmen, ohne diese kenntlich zu machen.
Selbstverständlich können und sollen Sie aus dem Ausgangstext zitieren, um eigene Gedanken zu stützen. Allerdings müssen Sie Zitate auch immer als solche kennzeichnen, damit die Eigenständigkeit Ihrer Leistung zu erkennen ist.
Dennoch ist natürlich stellenweise ein kreativ verarbeitendes Vorgehen mit dem Sprachmaterial des Ausgangstextes durchaus notwendig und erwünscht. Dies ist insbesondere beim Aufgabentyp 3.2 (bzw. 4.2) der Fall.

Allgemeiner und thematischer Wortschatz

Es wird erwartet, dass Sie sich sachlich und stilistisch angemessen ausdrücken. (Beachten Sie das jeweilige Zieltextformat!) In diesem Buch finden Sie eine Vielzahl von Wortlisten, die Ihnen dabei helfen können, Ihren thematischen Wortschatz zu den einzelnen Unterrichtsinhalten zu festigen und zu erweitern.
Auch Wortwiederholungen sollten Sie vermeiden. Nachfolgend finden Sie eine Übersicht über Synonyme für häufig verwendete Wörter und Begriffe. Diese ermöglichen Ihnen, sich variantenreich auszudrücken und einen abwechslungsreich formulierten Text zu verfassen.

to say **(im Sinne von „sagen"/„ausdrücken")**

state, remark, announce, affirm, assert, maintain, declare, express, put into words, tell, phrase, communicate, make known, convey, reveal, disclose, indicate, suggest

to see **(im Sinne von „erkennen"/„verstehen")**

grasp, get, comprehend, follow, take in, know, realise, discover, learn

to think **(im Sinne von „denken"/„meinen")**

believe, suppose, expect, imagine, surmise, conjecture, guess, consider

to understand

comprehend, apprehend, grasp, see, take in, recognise, think, believe, conclude

because / because of

because:
since, as, in view of the fact that, owing to the fact that, seeing that
because of:
on account of, as a result of, owing to, by reason of, as a consequence of, thanks to, by virtue of

many

numerous, a large/great number of, great quantities, multiple, various, several, frequent

a few

not many, a small number, one or two, a handful

in addition to

additionally, besides, as well (as)

furthermore

moreover, further, additionally, on top of that, also, as well

Vermeiden Sie auch sogenannte ***false friends.*** Als *false friends* werden Wörter und Begriffe bezeichnet, von denen man annimmt, dass sie in Mutter- und Fremdsprache die gleiche Bedeutung haben, weil sie sich im Schriftbild oder in der Aussprache ähneln beziehungsweise identisch sind. Ein bekanntes Beispiel ist das im Deutschen für Mobiltelefone verwendete Wort „handy", welches im Englischen zwar existiert, aber dort unter anderem „geschickt" und „praktisch" bedeutet.

Hier finden Sie eine Übersicht über häufig miteinander verwechselte *false friends:*

deutsch	**englisch**	***false friend***
bekommen	to get	nicht: „become"
die Kritik	criticism	nicht: „critic" – der Kritiker
die Politik	politics	nicht: „policy" – persönliche Strategie, außer in Begriffen wie „foreign policy" – Außenpolitik
sensibel	sensitive	nicht: „sensible" – vernünftig
meinen/ glauben	to think	nicht: „mean" – bedeuten (oder Adj. = gemein)

aktuell	current	nicht: „actually" – in der Tat
also	so	nicht: „also" – auch
brav	honest, good	nicht: „brave" – mutig, tapfer
Chef	boss	nicht: „chef" – der Küchenchef
engagiert	committed	nicht: „engaged" – verlobt; besetzt
eventuell	possibly	nicht: „eventually" – schließlich
Handy	mobile phone (AE: cell phone)	nicht: „handy" – handlich, praktisch
Konfession	denomination	nicht: „confession" – die Beichte
Konkurrenz	competition	nicht: „concurrence" – Zusammentreffen
konsequent	consistent	nicht: „consequently" – folglich
Lager	warehouse	nicht: „department store" – Warenhaus
mobben	to bully	nicht: „mob" – das gemeine Volk
Mörder	murderer	nicht: „murder" – der Mord
prägnant	concise	nicht: „pregnant" – schwanger
prinzipiell	fundamentally, basically, in/on principle	nicht: „principally" – hauptsächlich
Prospekt	brochure, leaflet	nicht: „prospects" – die Zukunftsaussichten
Protokoll	minutes	nicht: „protocol" – die Etikette (außer bei EDV)
Publikum	audience	nicht: „public" – die Öffentlichkeit
rentabel	profitable	nicht: „rentable" – zu mieten
Rückseite	back	nicht: „backside" – Hinterteil
spenden	to donate	nicht: „to spend" – ausgeben

Textbesprechungs- und Textproduktionswortschatz

Selbstverständlich ist es von großer Bedeutung, dass Sie nicht nur die geforderten Zieltextformate erstellen, sondern dass Sie dabei auch die entsprechenden sprachlichen Mittel verwenden.
Nachfolgend erhalten Sie einen ersten Überblick darüber, welche Art von Vokabular bei den Teilaufgaben 1, 2 und 3 des Klausurenteils A von Ihnen erwartet wird.

Teilaufgabe 1: Um diese Aufgabe erfolgreich bearbeiten zu können, sollten Sie über Vokabular zur Wiedergabe und Zusammenfassung von Inhalten verfügen.

Teilaufgabe 2: Grundsätzlich ist die Analyse eines Ausgangstextes – dies können auch Filmausschnitte, Karikaturen, Grafiken usw. sein – Gegenstand der zweiten Teilaufgabe. Vokabellisten, die Ihnen die Analyse von Texten erleichtern können, finden Sie im Kapitel „Methoden der Textarbeit“ (S. 78–102) in diesem Buch.

Teilaufgabe 3.1: Zur Bearbeitung dieser Teilaufgabe ist vor allen Dingen Vokabelmaterial zur eigenen Meinungsäußerung und Bewertung von Sachverhalten erforderlich. Wichtige Redewendungen sind in der nachfolgenden Übersicht enthalten.

Teilaufgabe 3.2: Bei dieser Teilaufgabe müssen Sie darauf achten, welches Zieltextformat von Ihnen verlangt wird, und das von Ihnen verwendete Vokabular entsprechend anpassen. Die verschiedenen Zieltextformate werden Ihnen auf den Seiten 103–112 genauer vorgestellt.

Eine sichere Behauptung oder Fakten ausdrücken

The fact is that ...	Es ist eine Tatsache, dass ...
It cannot be denied that ...	Man kann nicht leugnen, dass ...
It goes without saying that ...	Selbstredend ...
Undoubtedly, ...	Zweifellos ...
I am convinced that ...	Ich bin überzeugt davon, dass ...
It is indisputable/obvious that ... / There is no doubt that ...	Es ist unbestreitbar / offensichtlich / ohne Zweifel, dass ...
It is inevitable that ...	Es ist unvermeidbar, dass ...

Eine Vermutung ausdrücken

Apparently, ...	Anscheinend (am Satzanfang) ...
They will probably ...	Sie werden wahrscheinlich ...
It seems highly likely that ...	Es scheint äußerst wahrscheinlich, dass ...
It may be the case that ...	Es kann sein, dass ...

Einen Zweifel ausdrücken

It is doubtful whether ...	Es ist zweifelhaft, ob ...
I wonder if ...	Ich frage mich, ob ...
There is no proof/evidence that ...	Es gibt keine Beweise, dass ...

Einen Sachverhalt betonen

In order to stress that ...	Um hervorzuheben, dass ...
to emphasise	betonen
I would like to make it clear that ...	Ich möchte klarstellen, dass ...

Eine Meinung ausdrücken

In my opinion ... / To my mind ... / From my point of view ...	Meiner Meinung nach ...
My thoughts on the subject are ...	Meine Meinung zu diesem Thema ist ...
Personally, I think ... / My personal view is that ...	Ich persönlich denke, dass ...
As far as I am concerned ...	Was mich angeht ...
From my point of view	Aus meiner Sicht
I assume ...	Ich vermute, dass ...
I am (not) convinced that ...	Ich bin (nicht) überzeugt davon, dass ...
I cannot help thinking that ...	Ich kann nicht umhin zu denken, dass ...
I get the impression that ...	Ich habe den Eindruck, dass ...
I am afraid that ...	Ich fürchte, dass ... (abschwächend)
Honestly ... / To be honest ...	Ehrlich gesagt ...
I cannot judge ...	Ich kann ... nicht beurteilen.
I am in no position to say ...	Es steht mir nicht zu, mich zu ... zu äußern.

Einen Widerspruch einräumen

in contrast to	im Gegensatz zu
on the contrary	ganz im Gegenteil
whereas ...	während ... hingegen ...
I strongly object to ...	Ich spreche mich deutlich gegen ... aus.
One could argue that ... but ...	Man könnte argumentieren, dass ... , aber ...
Although it is true that ..., it would be wrong to claim that ...	Obwohl es wahr ist, dass ..., wäre es falsch zu behaupten, dass ...

Zustimmung ausdrücken

Fortunately, ...	Glücklicherweise ...

I entirely agree with ... / I share the opinion that ...	Ich stimme vollkommen mit ... überein.
I support his view.	Ich unterstütze seine Meinung.
I share her views.	Ich teile ihre Meinung.
I am of the same opinion (as) ...	Ich bin der gleichen Meinung (wie) ...
I approve of his/her opinion.	Ich bin mit seiner/ihrer Meinung einverstanden.
I take your point about ...	Ich akzeptiere Ihre Meinung über ...
I am in favour of ...	Ich bin für ...
He rightly mentions that ...	Zu Recht betont er, dass ...
I will not object to ...	Ich widerspreche ... nicht.
It cannot be justified that ...	Es gibt keine Rechtfertigung für ...
Nobody would disagree with that statement.	Niemand würde dieser Behauptung widersprechen.
This statement is very convincing.	Diese Aussage ist sehr überzeugend.
I have to admit that the author ...	Ich muss zugeben, dass der Autor / die Autorin ...

Ablehnung ausdrücken

It is only partly true that ...	Es entspricht nur teilweise der Wahrheit, dass ...
I disagree completely with ...	Ich muss ... vehement widersprechen.
I see things differently.	Ich sehe den Sachverhalt anders.
I have to disagree on this matter.	Ich bin in dieser Angelegenheit anderer Meinung.
One cannot possibly accept that ...	Man kann unmöglich akzeptieren, dass ...
I must object to ...	Ich muss ... widersprechen.
I have to criticise strongly that ...	Ich muss scharf kritisieren, dass ...
I doubt whether ...	Ich bezweifle, dass ...
however	jedoch
It is not as simple as it seems.	Es ist nicht so einfach wie es scheint.
Unlike the author, I think ...	Abweichend vom Autor / von der Autorin glaube ich ...
I cannot share the author's view on ...	Ich kann die Meinung des Autors / der Autorin über ... nicht teilen.
This statement entirely contradicts ...	Diese Behauptung widerspricht ganz und gar ...

Einen Grund angeben

As/Since ...	Da/Weil ...
In view of the fact that ...	Angesichts der Tatsache, dass ...
The reason for this development lies in ...	Der Grund für diese Entwicklung liegt bei ...
This causes confusion.	Das sorgt für Verwirrung.
That is why ...	Aus diesem Grund ...
Given that ...	In Anbetracht der Tatsache, dass ...
therefore	deshalb
This was caused by ...	Das wurde verursacht durch ...
for this reason/purpose	aus diesem Grund

Eine Folge darstellen

Consequently, ... / As a consequence, ...	Folglich ...
In view of this statement ...	In Anbetracht dieser Behauptung ...
in order to	um zu
as a result of	als Folge von

Vergleiche anstellen

to be comparable	vergleichbar sein
compared to / in comparison with	im Vergleich zu
to be different from	sich unterscheiden von
differentiate between (A and B)	(A von B) unterscheiden
to be considerably better than	wesentlich besser sein als
get more and more difficult	immer schwieriger werden
Nowadays, it is less and less common that ...	Heutzutage ist es immer weniger üblich, dass ...
superior/inferior to	überlegen/unterlegen
the former ... the latter ...	der erstere ... der letztere ...
They have little in common.	Sie haben wenig gemeinsam.
They are equal in price.	Sie haben den gleichen Preis.

Beispiele anführen

for example/instance	zum Beispiel
Let me give you an example.	Lassen Sie mich ein Beispiel anführen.
such as	wie (zum Beispiel)
Look at ...	Sehen wir uns einmal ... an.

Conclusion

To sum up, ...	Zusammenfassend kann man sagen, dass ...
I come to the conclusion that ...	Ich komme zu der Schlussfolgerung, dass ...
In short, ...	Kurz gesagt: ...
(to put it) in a nutshell	um es auf den Punkt zu bringen
I can support the author's view on ...	Ich kann die Ansicht des Autors / der Autorin über ... unterstützen.
To summarise, ...	Um das zusammenzufassen ...
All in all, I believe that ...	Insgesamt glaube ich, dass ...

Satzbau

Ein abwechslungsreicher und klarer Satzbau erhöht die Lesbarkeit Ihres Textes.

TIPP zum Punktesammeln

Versuchen Sie nicht krampfhaft, mehrere Gedanken in einen Satz zu packen.
Bedenken Sie: Überlange Sätze sind fehleranfälliger als mehrere kurze, prägnante und sinnvoll miteinander verbundene Sätze.

Machen Sie sich gegebenenfalls noch einmal mit den grammatischen Eigenschaften von z. B. Aktiv- und Passivkonstruktionen sowie Gerundial-, Partizipial- und Infinitivkonstruktionen vertraut.

Sprachliche Richtigkeit

Wortschatz und Grammatik

Zu den Bereichen Wortschatz und Grammatik ist an anderer Stelle in diesem Buch schon einiges gesagt worden. Der Übersicht des Ministeriums auf der nächsten Seite können Sie entnehmen, wie die für diese Kriterien maximal erreichbaren Punkte aufgeteilt sind.

Orthografie

Beim Verfassen eines Klausurtextes passiert es schnell, dass sich Rechtschreibfehler einschleichen.
Daher ist es wichtig, dass Sie zum Korrekturlesen Ihres Textes genug Zeit einplanen.
Achten Sie insbesondere auf Wörter, deren Aussprache oder Schreibweise zwar ähnlich oder sogar identisch ist, deren Bedeutung aber eine vollkommen andere ist, beispielsweise„sale" (Verkauf) und „sail" (das Segel, segeln).

Orientierungsangaben des Ministeriums für den Bereich Sprachrichtigkeit

Punkte	Wortschatz	Grammatik	Orthografie
volle Punktzahl keine Punkte	– Der Wortgebrauch (Struktur – und Inhaltswörter) ist fast über den gesamten Text hinweg korrekt. – Vereinzelt ist eine falsche Wortwahl feststellbar. Abschnitte bzw. Textpassagen sind weitgehend frei von lexikalischen Verstößen. – Einzelne Sätze sind frei von lexikalischen Verstößen. Fehler beim Wortgebrauch beeinträchtigen z. T. das Lesen und Verstehen. – In nahezu jedem Satz sind Schwächen im korrekten Gebrauch der Wörter feststellbar. Die Mängel im Wortgebrauch erschweren das Lesen und Textverständnis erheblich und verursachen Missverständnisse.	– Der Text ist weitgehend frei von Verstößen gegen Regeln der Grammatik. Wenn Grammatikfehler auftreten, betreffen sie den komplexen Satz und sind ein Zeichen dafür, dass die Schülerin / der Schüler Risiken beim Verfassen des Textes eingeht, um sich dem Leser differenziert mitzuteilen. – Es sind vereinzelt Verstöße gegen die Regeln der Grammatik feststellbar. Jedoch sind Abschnitte bzw. Textpassagen weitgehend frei von Grammatikfehlern. Das Lesen des Textes wird durch die auftretenden Grammatikfehler nicht erschwert. – Einzelne Sätze sind frei von Verstößen gegen grundlegende Regeln der Grammatik. Grammatikfehler beeinträchtigen z. T. das Lesen und Verstehen. – In nahezu jedem Satz ist wenigstens ein Verstoß gegen die grundlegenden Regeln der Grammatik feststellbar. Diese erschweren das Lesen erheblich und verursachen Missverständnisse.	– Der Text ist weitgehend frei von Verstößen gegen orthografische Normen. Wenn vereinzelt Orthografiefehler auftreten, haben sie den Charakter von Flüchtigkeitsfehlern, d. h. sie deuten nicht auf Unkenntnis von Regeln hin. – Es sind zwar durchaus Orthografiefehler feststellbar, jedoch sind Abschnitte bzw. Textpassagen weitgehend ohne Verstoß gegen orthografische Normen. Das Lesen des Textes wird durch die auftretenden Orthografiefehler nicht wesentlich beeinträchtigt. – Einzelne Sätze sind frei von Verstößen gegen orthografische Normen, Orthografiefehler beeinträchtigen z. T. das Lesen und Verstehen. – In nahezu jedem Satz ist wenigstens ein Verstoß gegen die Regeln der Orthografie feststellbar. Die Orthografiefehler erschweren das Lesen erheblich und verursachen Missverständnisse.

Quelle: https://www.standardsicherung.schulministerium.nrw.de/cms/zentralabitur-gost/faecher/getfile.php?file=4307 (Zugriff: 01.04.2022)

Stichwortverzeichnis